THE
LATE-NIGHT
WITCHES

TITLES BY AURALEE WALLACE

EVENFALL WITCHES B&B MYSTERIES

In the Company of Witches
When the Crow's Away

The Late-Night Witches

THE LATE-NIGHT WITCHES

AURALEE WALLACE

ACE
NEW YORK

ACE
Published by Berkley
An imprint of Penguin Random House LLC
1745 Broadway, New York, NY 10019
penguinrandomhouse.com

Copyright © 2025 by Auralee Wallace
Excerpt from *In the Company of Witches* copyright © 2021 by Auralee Wallace
Penguin Random House values and supports copyright. Copyright fuels creativity, encourages diverse voices, promotes free speech, and creates a vibrant culture. Thank you for buying an authorized edition of this book and for complying with copyright laws by not reproducing, scanning, or distributing any part of it in any form without permission. You are supporting writers and allowing Penguin Random House to continue to publish books for every reader. Please note that no part of this book may be used or reproduced in any manner for the purpose of training artificial intelligence technologies or systems.

ACE is a registered trademark and the A colophon is a trademark of
Penguin Random House LLC.

Illustrations by Vikki Chu

Library of Congress Cataloging-in-Publication Data

Names: Wallace, Auralee, author.
Title: The late-night witches / Auralee Wallace.
Description: First edition. | New York: Ace, 2025.
Identifiers: LCCN 2024052183 (print) | LCCN 2024052184 (ebook) |
ISBN 9780593818558 (trade paperback) | ISBN 9780593818565 (ebook)
Subjects: LCSH: Witches—Fiction. | Vampires—Fiction. | Halloween—Fiction. |
LCGFT: Witch fiction. | Vampire fiction. | Fantasy fiction. | Novels.
Classification: LCC PR9199.4.W3423 L38 2025 (print) |
LCC PR9199.4.W3423 (ebook) | DDC 813/.6—dc23/eng/20241129
LC record available at https://lccn.loc.gov/2024052183
LC ebook record available at https://lccn.loc.gov/2024052184

First Edition: August 2025

Printed in the United States of America
1st Printing

The authorized representative in the EU for product safety and compliance is
Penguin Random House Ireland, Morrison Chambers, 32 Nassau Street,
Dublin D02 YH68, Ireland, https://eu-contact.penguin.ie.

More than anything, this is a love story. A story of love lost and love found. A story of the love between sisters. And a story of a mother's love for her children. Most important, though, it is a story about loving oneself.

It's also a story about witches slaying vampires.

Don't worry. Most of the vamps suck.

THE LATE-NIGHT WITCHES

CHAPTER 1

A man staggered down the sidewalk, his feet swallowed by a swirling blanket of sea fog. At times he veered dangerously toward the curb, but just before he would teeter over its edge, he'd lurch back to shamble over the damp grass of his neighbors' lawns. Each plodding step seemed destined to be his last, but he lumbered on, his unfocused eyes and sickly pale cheeks gleaming under the streetlamps, his jaw hanging loosely like a corpse's.

Cassie Beckett put down the yellow highlighter she had been using to mark up the family calendar as he approached. She tilted her chin to the black cat seated primly on the top edge of her wicker chair. "He doesn't look so good, does he?"

The cat didn't reply.

"Hey, Gary," she called out from the porch. "How's the training going?"

The man stopped his forward momentum but continued to step on the spot. He pulled up the pants of his gray sweatsuit and took a sip from his water bottle. "Made it two K yesterday."

Cassie smiled. "Nice."

"Is it okay if I leave this here?" He shook his bottle. "It's empty and I don't want it weighing me down."

"Be my guest."

Gary was training for a half-marathon. He claimed he ran at night because of work, but that didn't make much sense given that he was an accountant. Cassie suspected he was embarrassed about the shape he was in, but he didn't have to be. Not with her. She admired him for trying something new.

"Thanks." He plunked the plastic container on her mailbox as an infant's cry pealed out from an open window down the street.

Cassie smiled and looked over to the house with the cranberry door, its brass knocker winking in the dark. Every neighborhood had its secret nightlife, and hers was no exception. As though on cue, a man with a baby strapped to his chest emerged from the house. The piercing cries faded away as he walked down his driveway with careful, bouncing steps. When he reached the street, he turned around and walked back toward the house, making sure to keep a steady rhythm.

"Poor guy." Gary pushed up the Rocky-inspired headband that had slipped down his forehead. "Rumor has it the baby is his sister's. She wasn't ready to be a mother, so he stepped up."

Not much stayed secret in the Burrow. The neighborhood wasn't much more than a street in an old suburb of Charlottetown, Prince Edward Island, and nobody could remember how it had gotten its name, but it was quaint with its old homes and tall trees, and Cassie couldn't imagine calling any other place home.

Their newest neighbor had only moved in a month or so ago, and Cassie hadn't had the chance to introduce herself. Granted, she hadn't gone out of her way to either. He was intimidatingly handsome. He had the glasses and bashful air of an English teacher or librarian, but the build of a quarterback. His hair was honey brown and always messy—that was probably because of the baby—but she hadn't seen his eyes up close. If she had to guess, they were hazel. She thought he might have a dimple too, but—all this was ridiculous because Cassie was technically married, even if it didn't feel too much like it these days.

Gary must have caught her look because he chuckled and said, "Yeah, he's a good-looking guy. You'd have to be dead not to notice."

Cassie smiled, hoping the darkness hid the burn coming to her cheeks. "What's his name again?"

"Ben. He's a history professor. Some sort of expert on island lore."

A history professor. She knew she'd been on the right track.

Gary cleared his throat and hiked his pants again. "Anyway, got to get back at it. The longer I stop, the harder it is to get going again."

That observation rang true for Cassie on many levels. "Good luck. And don't forget to take breaks."

He waved and pushed on.

Cassie scratched her cat's chin. "He'll be fine, right?"

She purred.

Janet was right. Gary was an adult. He could take care of himself. Besides, she had enough on her plate. Cassie looked down at the calendar on the old cast-iron coffee table. *Crap.* All of October was yellow. Every square had something. Doctor appointments. Dentist appointments. Hockey games. Basketball tryouts. It was never-ending. She scanned the to-do list running down the column at the side. She was also volunteering for two field trips, which meant she needed to trade shifts at work, and she had to get her daughter skates before her class started its weekly trip to the rink. *Oh God*, and the twins needed Halloween costumes! If only she could cut holes in sheets like moms used to do in the old days. Those women knew how to live.

The jack-o'-lantern sitting on the top step of the porch drew Cassie's eye. At least that was done, and she hadn't had to lift a finger. It had been the strangest thing. The pumpkin had shown up that morning, its carved face peering into her front door. Someone had obviously spent time on it. Its triangle eyes—peaks pointed in—had been cut to a devilish angle, and its mouth with its two long fangs looked ready to tear through steel. There had obviously been some sort of mistake, but she had no clue what to do about it.

Cassie stared into the dark hollows of the jack-o'-lantern's eyes. While its sudden appearance was somewhat convenient, it was too creepy for her liking. It almost felt like it was challenging her.

"You want to go, Creepy?" she muttered, then looked back at her packed calendar. Who was she kidding? She didn't have time to duel with jack-o'-lanterns. Not with this schedule.

Cassie leaned back in her chair. Being out on the porch of her century-old home always brought her peace. The wood planks were wobbly, and the sage-green paint was peeling, but she had fixed it up with hanging plants, rugs, blankets, and lanterns, and over time it had become her favorite part of the house. It was the perfect spot to watch the moon rise and soak in the night air. Not that she'd have a whole lot of time for that this month. She put her feet on the table, pushing the calendar an inch or two away with the toe of her boot. It was fine. She could do this. As long as she didn't get sick or require more than six hours of sleep—something she didn't seem capable of anyway—it was fine.

Janet nuzzled Cassie's ear as she pulled her mug of herbal tea close to her chest, inhaling its sweet grassy scent. She'd been having some insomnia lately. Stress, probably. She did her best to keep everyone on track, but ever since her husband, Matt, had left for his second tour with Doctors Without Borders—leaving her with their fifteen-year-old daughter and eight-year-old twin boys—it always felt like she wasn't doing enough. Or doing it right. Or doing it the way everyone expected her to. Other moms made it look so easy. At least the ones on social media did.

But ongoing stress aside, something more was going on with her. She'd had this strange, tense feeling lately that there was something she was supposed to be doing. Something aside from all the other things she was supposed to be doing. It was like there was an undercurrent of electricity constantly pricking at her skin, prodding her to do . . . *something*.

It was probably the change in weather. Those first gusts of cold wind always made her restless.

Cassie shifted her tea to her other hand and dug her fingers into her jean pocket as she watched the heavy fog swirl. She slipped out her coin, a relic from childhood, and flipped it mindlessly between her fingers, feeling the familiar grooves of the engraved sun and moon on either side.

The day had been brilliant and pleasantly cool. The kind of fall day that made a person want to walk around under a canopy of red and gold leaves, wearing a scarf and drinking pumpkin-spiced coffee. Not that Cassie had done any of that. She had spent the day at work discussing circular saws with chainsaw attachments and the intricate workings of septic bed treatments. But it was still nice getting in and out of the van. As soon as the sun had set, though, tendrils of cold mist reached in from the harbor, flooding the neighborhood in a gloomy haze. It had a strange murkiness to it. At times, instead of reflecting the light from the streetlamps, it swallowed it, darkening all it touched.

And it moved in peculiar ways too. One minute she could see all the way down the street, but the next, the world beyond her front steps disappeared. For all she knew, someone could be in that cold mist right now staring at her. The thought sent an icy shiver up the skin on the back of her neck, even though she knew there was nothing in the fog. Janet would know if there were.

A low growl rumbled by her ear. Cassie jolted, spilling her tea. "What the heck, cat?" She said it quietly though. Janet did sometimes growl at absolutely nothing—or ghosts, she couldn't be sure—but there were other times when her feline friend picked up on real creatures going bump in the night. Cassie held her breath to listen and heard a grunt come from up the street. Her shoulders dropped. She knew that grunt. And she should have seen this coming.

It was Thursday. Karaoke night.

Cassie slipped her coin back into her pocket and swatted at the drops of tea on her cable-knit sweater, but her hand fell away when the willowy silhouette of a woman emerged from the fog. She was swaying, not unlike Gary, but that wasn't what had Cassie concerned. She was also dragging something. Its metal tip scraped noisily along the pavement.

A baseball bat.

Janet jumped down from the chair and up onto the porch railing in a fluid motion. She gathered herself up into a tight perched position. Cassie considered throwing her granny square afghan over her head, but it was too late. The woman had already spotted her. "Hey you!" she shouted as though it wasn't the middle of the night. "Just the person I wanted to see!"

Eliza, Cassie's sister and in most ways her first child, was stunning. Her hair was long, black, and straight—as opposed to Cassie's sandy waves that lived in a messy bun—and her eyes were large and dramatically dark. That being said, she looked a little rough tonight. The black tank dress wasn't too bad—it showed off her sister's slender arms and the bangles clustered at her wrists—but the work boots on her feet and the flannel shirt tied around her waist looked wrong. So did the scraped knee glaring angrily through her torn black tights.

"Go away," Cassie said tiredly. "I don't want what you're selling."

"Is that any way to welcome your sister home?"

Cassie pointed down the street. "You live that way."

Eliza ambled halfway up the lawn before suddenly pitching forward in giant, awkward steps. When she caught herself, she frowned at the football lying innocently in the grass, then kicked it over to the property next door. One of her oversized boots tumbled after it.

"No. Go get that. Mrs. MacDonald is going to flip out." Cassie didn't talk to her neighbor all that much, but when they did speak, it was almost always about property lines. Mrs. MacDonald was big on property lines. She probably didn't want the chaos of Cassie's life spilling into hers.

"No time for that," Eliza said. "You're going to want to hear about what I've been up to. I promise it has a happy ending."

Cassie did want to hear about what her sister had been up to—in the way she wanted to know about an outbreak of lice in the boys' classroom—but she also didn't want to encourage whatever this was. Besides, she didn't need to ask Eliza where she had been. She knew the answer to that. And she didn't have to ask her who she was with. Cassie knew that too. She certainly wasn't going to ask her sister how much she'd had to drink. She didn't want to know the answer to that. And she definitely wasn't going to ask her—

"Why do you have a bat?" *Frick*.

"Great question. Wait. Why are you out here at—" Eliza looked at her wrist, making her bracelets jangle. She didn't wear a watch. "Why are you out here?"

"Couldn't sleep." Cassie looked pointedly at the bat. "Now you."

Her sister groaned. "It's a long story."

"One you seemed eager to tell me a moment ago."

"Yeah." Eliza sighed. "But now that I've had time to think it over, I've realized I don't come out particularly well in it." She trailed off, distracted by the cat pinning her with a judgmental gaze. "You know what, Janet?" She challenged the cat with a glare, but couldn't finish the thought.

"Eliza. Focus."

"It was self-defense."

"Against?"

"A two-thousand and nine Ford F-150."

Cassie pressed her fingers against her eyelids. "No. Absolutely not. I want no part of this." Destruction of property was not on her calendar. "Wait, was it parked or moving?" What was wrong with her? Why was she still asking questions?

"Parked. Definitely parked. But..." Eliza trailed off again, her eyes tracking a late moth fluttering up to the streetlamp.

Cassie snapped her fingers in the air. "Okay, start from the beginning." She suspected she already knew the end.

"You want me to start from the beginning? I can tell you the whole story with one word." She struggled to untie the flannel shirt fixed around her waist, then threw it to the ground. "It was Tommy. The asshat."

"Hey!" Cassie shot a look up in the direction of her boys' window.

"Oh shit." Eliza slapped her hand over her mouth. "Sorry."

THE LATE-NIGHT WITCHES

"You know what? Don't start from the beginning. Just tell me one thing. Tell me you did not commit a Carrie Underwood on his truck."

Eliza opened her mouth then shut it again before squinting and chewing her thumbnail. Cassie imagined she was mulling her strategy. A moment passed and Eliza flung her hand away. "Of course I committed a Carrie Underwood on his truck! Well, half an Underwood. Have you ever tried to beat up a truck? It's harder than it looks. I may have dislocated my shoulder."

Thoughts of damage, insurance, and possible legal action swirled through Cassie's mind.

"Do not give me that look," Eliza snapped. "You would have done the same thing."

That was incredibly doubtful.

"He cheated." She threw her hands wide. "Tommy cheated. Now you know." Eliza stamped on the flannel shirt on the wet grass, then kicked her remaining boot off into the hedge. It was clear who those belonged to.

Even though Cassie had known where the story was headed, it was still a shock. Or maybe just a disappointment. Tommy seemed like a nice guy. The best out of all the men Eliza had dated. Then again, they had only known each other for three and a half weeks. "Who was he with?"

"I don't know. She snuck out the back of the bar. Besides, does it really matter? I wasn't dating the rando chick. I was dating the lying, cheating ass—" She cut herself off and smiled. "Close one." She looked up at the boys' room and mimed turning a key over her lips. "Anyway, he was acting all confused like he didn't know what happened, so I left, and that's when I saw the bat just lying there in his truck bed. I mean . . ." She scoffed and held her hands out.

Cassie pinched her lips together and nodded. *What else could she have done?*

"Hey, you have a pumpkin," Eliza said, her voice instantly changing tone. "It's too early for a pumpkin. You're going to have a pumpkin puddle." She stumbled up to the jack-o'-lantern and grabbed the ropy stem, tossing the top off to the side. She reached in for the candle. "And have you met my nephews?" She climbed the steps and dropped the candle, wick down, into Cassie's tea. "You're welcome." She blinked. "So, where was I?"

Cassie's mouth opened, but all she could do was shake her head.

"Oh yeah, so after the truck, I may have taken a short forest nap behind the bar, and I think Tommy came out." She winked and slumped against the porch railing. "See? Happy ending. Just like I told you."

"How is that a happy ending?"

"Because he didn't kill me! He couldn't have missed what I did to his truck."

Cassie rubbed her forehead.

"I know what you're thinking—*Eliza screwed up again*—but I was really starting to like him, Cass." Her voice cracked in a way that made Cassie's own throat tighten. "He may not be the brightest bulb in the book, but he was super sweet and made me laugh, and sometimes he could be surprisingly deep, almost poetic."

Brightest bulb in the book?

Cassie pushed herself to her feet. She knew she should send Eliza home. She had to stop cleaning up her messes, but tonight didn't seem like the night. "Come on." She held out an arm draped in the blanket. "Let's go inside and get some sleep before the cops come looking for you."

Eliza pushed herself off the railing. "Tommy wouldn't call the cops." Suddenly her eyes grew wide. "You don't think he'd call the cops?" She ducked underneath Cassie's outstretched arm.

"We'll figure everything out tomorrow. You're sleeping on the couch though."

"The couch," Eliza whined. "Your bed is much more comfortable. I promise I won't steal the covers."

She couldn't promise that. She always stole the covers. But Cassie was too tired to fight. Besides, it did remind her of when they were young, and Eliza would climb into her bed after a bad dream. They only had each other back in those days.

Cassie ushered Eliza to the door, calling out, "Come on, Janet." She tossed a look over her shoulder. Janet had risen to all fours on the railing. Her back was arched, and a ridge of fur had risen along her spine. A high-pitched yelp tore through the night. Janet jumped a foot into the air, landed on the porch, and tore past Cassie, claws scrabbling against the wood planks.

What the . . . ?

Cassie suddenly noticed her hands were tingling. It was a peculiar sensation, almost like a warning somehow. "Eliza," she whispered, "did you hear that?"

Her sister leaned against the doorframe and closed her eyes.

That was probably a no. Cassie shook her shoulder. "You go ahead. Wait for me at the bottom of the stairs. I'm right behind you."

Cassie shuffled back out to the edge of the porch. She peered in the direction the sound had come from, but the fog made it impossible to see more than a few feet. She waited. It must have been a fox. Or a raccoon. Or a fox fighting a raccoon. Whatever it had been, it sounded like some poor creature had met its end. As Cassie stared into the swirling mist, the thought of being watched by someone or something hidden in the fog returned. She retreated in slow steps, catching sight of the jack-o'-lantern still staring at her. "What are you looking at, Creepy?"

The jack-o'-lantern held its fanged smile.

Cassie slowly reached back for the door to push it open wider. It was ridiculous, but suddenly she didn't want to turn her back to the grinning pumpkin.

Stupid gourd. He should have been a pie.

"Watch yourself," she said, tossing it one last look. "Or I'm going to light you up." As she turned and stepped inside, a hot gust of air whooshed behind her, and a fiery glow reflected off the outer wall of the house. She whipped back around. The jack-o'-lantern eyes were still black pits, and the candle was still in the mug.

"I'm losing it." Cassie pressed her perfectly normal, non-tingling hand to her forehead. "I'm absolutely losing it."

CHAPTER 2

"Coffee?"

Eliza groaned from the kitchen table where she sat slumped over, head resting on her forearms.

"What about eggs? Toast? Therapy, maybe?"

Her sister managed a muffled laugh, which was in fact funny because Cassie hadn't been kidding.

The kitchen glowed bright orange in the morning sun beaming through the window above the sink. Cassie had fallen in love with her two-story century-old home on sight, but it did need work. The only reason she and Matt could afford the down payment back when he was in school was because it was a fixer-upper. The house had remained largely untouched since it had been built—which was great in some ways. It had large bay windows, plaster cornicing, and beautiful warm paneling by the stairs. The bathrooms hadn't been updated since the fifties, though, and the kitchen—well, the kitchen was all seventies. The floor was a linoleum sheet of brown-and-orange squares, and the wallpaper had a harvest design with columns of overflowing cornucopias. As the pièce de résistance, the light fixture above the table was made from brown glass panels in a tiered loop, a little like an upside-down wedding cake. It was a lot. But on the bright side, the room was in season once a year, and, truthfully, there was something soothing about its retro vibe. It made life seem simpler. The kitchen was also the hub of their family life. The house had two staircases and, of course, a front door, but it was the steps leading up from the kitchen that everyone used, and the side door that everyone came in and out of.

Cassie leaned against the counter and reached for her coffee, listening to Eliza's light snores. She had managed to stay awake a whole twelve minutes.

What am I going to do with you?

She had been asking herself that question almost since the day Eliza had been born twenty-five years ago, and at thirty-three Cassie still didn't know the answer. She had been eight—the same age as her boys—when she and Eliza were placed in foster care, and her sister hadn't been much more than a newborn. The couple who had taken them in had done their best. They were good-hearted people, and Cassie would be forever grateful to them for not separating her and Eliza, but it had never been a good fit. They were conservative and saw the world in black-and-white. They had a hard time understanding a free-spirited child like Eliza, let alone knowing how to parent her. Every time she brought home a stray or got into a fight at school, they despaired. And then there was the *incident*. It wasn't something Cassie liked to think about. The point was she had picked up the parenting mantle early on. She wouldn't have had it any other way. She wanted to help her sister feel like she belonged in the world despite not having a permanent home, but being a kid herself she hadn't known how to do that, and Eliza had been floating through life ever since.

Not that Cassie was in any position to preach about living one's best life. She was barely hanging on to hers.

The thought faded at the sound of light footfalls creaking down the stairs. She knew which of her children was coming before she appeared. Each kid sounded different.

Cassie's fifteen-year-old daughter, Sadie, came into the room, took one look at Eliza, and said, "Whoa. You look rough."

Sadie's resemblance to her aunt was undeniable. She had Cassie's gray-green eyes, but everything else was Eliza. They were both tall and lean and had the same long black hair. Even their features—the elegant slope of the nose, the high cheekbones—were nearly identical. It was only the slightest bit annoying. And great. Of course, great. But also, a tiny bit annoying. Cassie and Eliza had a complicated mother-daughter-sister relationship.

Eliza dragged her head upright, then dropped her temple on the heel of her palm. Her head slipped, but she caught herself in time. "I must have drifted off for a minute there." She squinted at her niece. "You learn from this. Alcohol is no one's friend."

"Thanks for the tip. Looks like you had fun though."

"No. No." She brought her fist to her mouth and belched softly. "Bad choices were made."

Cassie grabbed a box of cereal from the cupboard, closing the door with an intentional bang. She passed it to her daughter. This was an issue that had been simmering for a while now. Sadie looked up to her cool, fun aunt. She didn't need to see her like this.

"Sadie, given your aunt's state, I was hoping you could do me a favor." Cassie did her best to keep her voice strong and authoritative, but she could hear the underlying fear. There had been a time when her daughter always wanted to help her. She wanted to help her cook, do her nails, even change diapers. But those days were long gone.

Sadie slid her gaze over.

Don't show fear. Teenage girls rule by fear. "Could you make sure the boys get to school? On time?"

Her daughter's jaw dropped at the outrageousness of the request.

"Or not on time," Cassie added quickly. "Just getting them there is a win."

"They are not babies anymore. They can walk themselves."

A chuckle came from the table. "Not without committing a felony."

Sadie smiled. Actually smiled. Cassie couldn't remember the last time she had made her daughter smile, but they sure came free and easy when her sister was involved. But this was just a stage. The terrible fifteens. It wouldn't last.

"Sadie, please. I need to talk to your aunt before work."

"I have plans." She pulled a handful of cereal from the box and dropped some flakes into her mouth.

Eliza rolled her eyes. "You have plans before school?"

"Maybe?" she mumbled.

"You don't have plans," Eliza scoffed, making her niece smile again.

Breathe, Cassie. "Look, I know I have been asking a lot of you lately, but ever since your dad left—"

"Dad is a hero for what he's doing."

Cassie did her best not to react. The past year had been hard on everyone, but Sadie was having the most difficult time with it. Not that she'd talk about it. At least not to her.

And if anyone knew that Matt's actions were heroic, it was Cassie. It was incredibly meaningful work, and Matt had always needed to feel like he was doing something big and meaningful. It was one of the things that first attracted her to him. He was a dreamer chasing his life's purpose, and she had always supported him in that. Sure, it was hard being the one doing the day-to-day—largely unrecognized—work of parenting, but she was glad he was fulfilled. Hopefully he'd end up being so fulfilled, he'd stay home after this tour ended.

"Of course, your dad is a hero."

"Besides it's not like you're doing anything with your—"

"Hey!" Eliza flung her head up. "You'd better think hard about how you're going to finish that sentence, young lady. I'm the only one who can be a—banana to your mom." She gave Cassie a thumbs-up and nauseous smile.

Sadie's cheeks flushed the way they always did when she was about to cry. Cassie wanted to hug her, but she knew that would be the wrong thing. She might lose both arms.

"Sorry," Sadie mumbled. The apology was directed to Eliza. Not to her. To Eliza.

It was *fine*.

Rapid-fire thumps came from the stairs, and the boys exploded into the room. Sly and Eddie. Not the most common names for eight-year-olds. Matt had a great-grandfather named Sylvester with—surprise, surprise—an identical twin named Edwin. He thought it would be fun to carry on the tradition. Eliza was horrified, but Cassie had been so worn down by nine months of twin pregnancy, she could barely think, let alone argue with anyone. And as with all names, first impressions gave way to the colorings of love.

"Sly. Ed," Eliza said with a pained smile. Cassie suspected the cacophony of thumps had been painful. "Where's the fire?"

"School!" They swarmed Eliza on either side. She pulled her

arms in close to her chest and shielded her face with her hands. The boys kissed her anyway. "Love you too. That's enough now."

"Let's get going, everyone." Cassie opened the fridge to grab the boys' lunches. Except she hadn't made the boys' lunches. *Frick.* "Okay, get your shoes on. I just have to . . ." She grabbed two yogurts from the fridge, then slammed it shut. Bananas! Bananas were good. They came in their own packaging. Cassie frantically looked around, then darted for the pantry cabinet. A box of crackers and two tins of pineapple chunks. Why not? The cans had pull tabs. She just hoped no one lost a finger with the lid. She then rinsed two dirty spoons under the faucet because she had forgotten to start the dishwasher too, then passed the collection over to the boys in a single plastic bag. They'd figure it out. "I don't know where your little freezer packs are, so eat the yogurt during your first break." She couldn't tell if they were listening to her. "I'm serious. If you don't eat it first, it will rot, and you will both die horrible deaths."

"You know, they can get food at the office," Sadie said, her tone the equivalent of an eye roll. "They always have extra lunches."

"Yes, but that would make me look like a terrible mother." And right now, she was clearly killing it.

"Whatever. Can I have money for lunch, so I don't die a horrible death?"

Cassie grabbed her wallet off the counter and flipped it open. She always kept cash for emergencies. "Here," she said, passing her daughter a ten. "On the condition you walk them the whole way there."

"Fine." Sadie took the bill. "But I'm not promising both will make it alive."

THE LATE-NIGHT WITCHES

"I wouldn't respect your judgment if you did. Now get going."

The boys raced by, shouting identical *I love you, Mom*s. Eddie grabbed half a bag of chips off the counter on his way out, but Sadie snatched it from him and put it back, giving Cassie a pointed look.

The door slammed. Cassie pulled back the frilly curtain to watch her kids trek down the driveway. Huh, Gary's water bottle was still on the mailbox. He must have given up on the last lap.

"What's up with Sadie?" Eliza drawled. "I love the girl to death, but I wouldn't have given her any money. She might hire a hitman."

Cassie dropped the curtain. She loved it when her sister gave her parenting advice. *Crap!* She hadn't fed the boys breakfast!

"And I'm sorry," Eliza continued, "but hero?"

"Some people do consider Doctors Without Borders heroic. And raising a teenage daughter is not easy." It was a little like training an alligator to give kisses. Hard and dangerous. "Besides, I owe her. She has been doing a lot to help with the boys."

"If you say so."

Instead of dropping back onto the table, Eliza slumped in her chair. Cassie took that as an opening. "So, what's the plan with Tommy?"

Her sister wrapped her arms over her stomach. "I'll talk to him. Offer to pay for the truck. You know, Ms. Underwood really should have covered the legal ramifications of her actions in that song."

Cassie sipped her coffee. It tasted more bitter than it had a moment ago. "And how exactly are you going to pay for the truck? You have no money."

"Well," Eliza said, picking at a dried bit of tomato sauce cemented to the table, "you could loan me the money."

"*I* have no money."

Eliza grimaced. "There's always Matt's car."

☾

That third cup of coffee had been a mistake. The acidic brew sloshed around in Cassie's stomach as she slipped a plastic-encased lightbulb onto a utility hook jutting out from the wall. At least she was on stocking duty. She didn't think she could handle talking to customers today. It was hard to discuss paint colors and humidifiers on four and a half hours of sleep. It was also hard to think about selling her husband's car.

Cassie hadn't promised Eliza anything. She certainly hadn't said yes, but she had said *maybe*, and that had propelled her sister to throw her arms around her. They both knew Cassie had a hard time saying no when Eliza needed her. Besides, she *could* sell Matt's car. The ownership was in her name. She could probably sell it for enough money to fix Tommy's truck and have plenty left over for a new clothes dryer—her current one was beating itself to death—and maybe some extra Christmas presents.

Money had been tight for a while now.

Cassie and Matt had gotten together in their first year of university. They met in September and were pregnant by April. It had been a shock, but not a tragedy. Cassie was head over heels in love. Matt was smart, charismatic, and ready to take on the world. He was thrilled about the baby and confident they could make everything work. More than work. They were going to build a spectacular life together. So, Cassie dropped out, and they got married. The plan was that she would go back to school once Sadie started kindergarten, but when the time came, Matt was starting his residency, and it didn't seem like the right time. A few years later the boys came along, and Cassie's plans were pushed off again. She loved being with her kids when they were little, but it was hard. Rewarding . . . but hard. Then plans changed again about two years ago when another surgeon at the hospital, Dr. Miranda Sharp, suggested Matt join her on a tour with Doctors Without Borders. Cassie had tried her best to like Miranda, but it wasn't easy, especially when she asked Cassie every time they met if she was a stay-at-home mom and replied *That's so nice!* when Cassie confirmed she was. But Matt loved the idea of making a difference . . . even though it meant him being a world away from his family. How could she deny him that? Besides, the first tour was only six months, and she was used to being the main parental figure for the kids. Granted, it was harder when he signed up for the second tour, but he promised that would be it. That's when Cassie took the job at the hardware store to help make ends meet. Matt's income had dropped, and they hadn't paid off his student loans or made much of a dent in their mortgage. They would be fine in the long run, but in the meantime, managing the budget was tricky.

Cassie still thought about going back to school even though she didn't relish the idea of being the oldest student in the class, but there was a problem. She didn't know what she wanted to study. She could rattle off her children's favorite video games, movies, clothing brands, snacks, but she was at a total loss when it came to knowing what she liked.

So, maybe selling Matt's car wasn't a terrible idea.

He wouldn't argue. Matt never argued. *Do whatever you need to do, Cassie. I fully support you.* That was his answer to every problem. He would probably be relieved that he could help back home while he was being *heroic* overseas. The idea bothered her though. Something about it felt final.

"You all right, hon?"

Cassie jolted, fumbling the lightbulb she had been holding. Once she had it firmly pinned against her chest, she smiled at her coworker, Patty, who had her own hands out in case the package made another break for it. Patty was incredibly sweet. So sweet, in fact, that if Cassie had to choose another life, she would want to be one of Patty's grandchildren—in no small part because she always smelled like cookies. Cassie frowned. These seemed like weird thoughts to be having. She really needed to get more sleep.

"Cassie?"

"Yeah, sorry. I'm here."

"No, I'm sorry," Patty said, straightening the cardigan she always wore under her blue work vest. "I didn't mean to startle you. I know you must have had a late night."

And there it was. It hadn't taken long for reports of her sister's misadventures to spread. "I'm guessing everyone has heard?"

"I would think the entire island by now." Patty nodded sympathetically. "Eliza did a number on Tommy's truck."

"Where are people landing on it?"

"Fifty percent feel it was justified. The other fifty percent own trucks."

Fifty percent wasn't terrible.

"I wouldn't worry. Tommy is such a sweetheart." She frowned. "At least I thought he was. I hope there isn't another explanation." Patty's frown turned grim in a way Cassie didn't understand. "While we're on the topic, there's something else I wanted to talk to you about."

Cassie waited as the sweet older woman fidgeted, straightening the row of plugs on the wall. Suddenly she snapped her fingers. "But first, Sean is going to ask you to cover for him on your lunch break while he takes his grandfather to the optometrist. Say no."

"Say no? I mean, I can do it if he needs me to."

"Cassie, one of his grandfathers died before he was born. The other three years ago when his tractor rolled over on him. You were at the funeral."

She did remember that, but she had only gone to the visitation. The boys had ear infections.

Patty shook her head. "He has a new girlfriend that he wants to make out with in the parking lot."

"That's sweet." Cassie remembered the making-out-in-parking-lot days. They hadn't been *that* long ago.

"No! You are too nice. And too thin. You need to eat on your lunch break. Keep your strength up."

Cassie smiled. "Understood. Now the other thing you wanted to talk to me about?" It had occurred to her that Patty was stalling. She couldn't imagine what it could possibly be that had her so nervous. To be honest, they both led quiet lives.

Patty chewed her lip, then said, "I'm not sure if you've heard, but Gary Nesbitt is missing."

Gary? Her Gary? Well, not her Gary. But Gary?

"He went for a run last night and never came home. His wife is fuming." Patty whispered the last part even though there was no one around. "She thinks he did a runner. Not that I'd blame him if he did. She's a piece of work that one."

That didn't sound like something he would do. Yes, Gary's wife was kind of mean, especially to him, but he wasn't the type to simply get up and leave. "Are the police looking for him? It was so foggy last night. A car could have hit him, or he could have had a heart attack, fallen in a ditch."

"It's too soon to report him missing." Patty's brow creased with worry. "But given that it happened last night, I thought you should know."

"I'm not following. Why does it matter that it happened last night?"

"Well, they think it was after midnight, so . . . October first?"

Cassie shrugged.

Patty studied her face. "You know what? Never mind. I don't know what I'm saying. But maybe you should talk to your aunt Dorcas."

Dorcas?

Out of all the things Cassie might have guessed Patty would say, that was not one of them. "Patty, you know I don't talk to Dorcas."

She shrugged lightly. "Now might be a good time to start. Anyway, I only wanted to make sure you knew." She spun around and called out to a customer, "Let me help you, dear!"

Cassie slid the lightbulb package onto the hook as Patty hurried away. That was definitely the strangest conversation she had ever had with her coworker. What did the date have to do with anything? And why would she want Cassie to talk to Dorcas? And . . . Gary couldn't be missing. There had to be some sort of mistake, some miscommunication between him and his wife. Cassie tried to reassure herself with the thought, but the yelp she'd heard last night echoed in her mind. It had been a fox. She was sure it had been a fox.

Except she wasn't.

Instead of eating her lunch, Cassie stayed on hold with the police during her break. When she finally got through and told the officer all about the fox and the water bottle, he thanked her and hung up. She would have talked to Patty again, but she had gone home with a headache.

At five sharp, Cassie said goodbye to her coworkers, pulled on her peacoat and gloves, and stepped out into the gathering twilight. She had walked to work that morning hoping it might help her stay awake, but given how tired she was now, she wished she had taken the van. She tried to focus on the earthy scent of the leaves covering the ground, but she couldn't get her mind off Gary.

The Burrow was not the kind of place where people randomly went missing. Everybody knew everybody in the neighborhood, and people left their doors unlocked. Cassie had always let the boys roam the streets before dark without ever worrying about their safety. And aside from an abandoned house exploding a few years back—some random gas leak—nothing much ever happened. But now that she was thinking about it, things *had* felt off lately, like something new had come into her neighborhood. Something wrong. Cassie shoved her hands deep into her pockets and kicked a rock down the sidewalk. If she wasn't careful, she'd turn into Dorcas with those kinds of thoughts.

The sky was crimson by the time Cassie made it to her street. The days were getting noticeably shorter. Hopefully the boys were home already. She pulled her collar close to her throat. It was getting colder and . . . the fog was back.

Fingers of gray mist reached toward Cassie's ankles. She

hadn't noticed it roll in, but the thin blanket of mist was everywhere now, twisting around trees and lampposts. Cassie hurried for her house, but her steps faltered when she noticed Gary's water bottle was gone. Anyone could have taken it, including his wife, but it still felt ominous. Then she saw something even more disturbing: her neighbor, Mrs. MacDonald, standing in her driveway.

CHAPTER 3

Cassie forced her steps in the direction of her house, resisting the urge to run back down the street.

Mrs. MacDonald had always intimidated her. She had to be in her seventies, but her posture was ramrod straight and she always looked good with her perfectly coifed white hair. She was from the oldest, most distinguished family on the island, and she knew everything about everyone. Her house was perfectly maintained, her flower beds were always weeded, and her hedges were always trimmed. From what Cassie had heard, she had raised seven children on her own after her husband drowned trying to pull up a lobster trap, and she had built a small fortune in investments. For all Cassie knew she had single-handedly developed the polio vaccine in her free time.

"Hi, Mrs. MacDonald. If this is about the football on your lawn, I apologize. It won't happen again." Heading her off at the pass seemed like the best approach.

"This is not about the football."

Well, crap. She could only imagine this was about something else the boys had done. They had probably played tag in her yard or dropped their homework in her bushes.

"Your boys, while sword fighting with hot dog skewers, impaled the inflatable pool in your backyard. The fetid water drained into my new shrubbery."

Huh. Didn't see that one coming. Cassie closed her eyes. She knew she should have taken the pool down, but she didn't know how to drain the water without it going into Mrs. MacDonald's yard. *Funny.* "I am so sorry."

"I don't want you to be sorry."

Cassie opened her eyes just in time to see Mrs. MacDonald cross her arms over her chest. "Cassandra, how do you think it is my family has survived so long on the island?"

Cassie had no clue where this was headed now. Maybe they avoided germs from small children?

"It's October. Have you prepared at all?"

"I have a pumpkin," Cassie stammered, glancing over at her porch.

Mrs. MacDonald arched an eyebrow. "It's time to get yourself together. Past time. You are not the first woman to have her husband leave her."

Cassie's jaw dropped. *She did not just say that.*

"You have responsibilities. People counting on you. It's also time to talk to Dorcas if you haven't already. You're running out of time." With that, she strode away, headed back for her house.

Oh no, no, no. That woman could not simply walk away after saying something like that. "You are . . . that was . . . my husband didn't . . ."

Mrs. MacDonald slammed her door shut.

☾

Get yourself together. You get yourself together.

The warm glow of the kitchen welcomed Cassie as she

dropped her bag to the floor and collapsed into a chair. Her brain was buzzing. *What a freaking day!* Why was everybody being so weird? And mean?

Cassie pulled her phone out of her pocket and placed it on the table. Matt hadn't texted, but he probably would soon. They did message each other regularly, but their communications were mainly focused on the business of keeping the family running. She had asked him about the car earlier but hadn't heard anything back yet. It was fine though. All she wanted to do now was make sure everyone was fed, put the boys to bed—she could save the destruction-of-property speech for tomorrow—have a bath, then go to sleep. Once upon a time, she and Sadie would have made popcorn and watched TV together, but that wasn't a thought she wanted to dwell on. It would happen again. She needed to be patient. And grateful for the fact that her house was quiet.

Wait. Why was her house quiet?

Actually, it wasn't completely quiet. The dishwasher was humming. Cassie looked over at the appliance as though it was the first time they had met. Had it learned how to start itself? No, that was impossible. Maybe someone had come into her house and turned it on? It didn't seem probable, and yet more likely than the alternative. Something else was weird. There was an odor. A food odor. Cassie looked around the room until she spotted the cooked frozen lasagna sitting on top of the stove. How had that happened? Oh God, and she couldn't hear the boys! No thumping. No screaming. Someone had broken into her home, washed her dishes, made her dinner, and kidnapped her children. It was the only explanation. She should probably be more upset.

Cassie spun in her chair to face the person coming down the stairs. "Did you do all this?"

Sadie shrugged. "It wasn't a big deal."

Given that it had never happened in the history of their family, Cassie disagreed. She studied her daughter. Sadie looked tired, and it wasn't because she was already in her flannel pajamas with her hair up in a scrunchie. The tiredness was in her eyes . . . and her shoulders were slumped. She looked almost somber or defeated, maybe? Cassie tried to think about what was going on at school. Had volleyball tryouts been this week? Were there any big tests? She couldn't remember. Maybe it was a boy? She had noticed that Sadie hadn't been going out with her friends as much. Maybe something was going on there. "Where are your brothers?" she asked lightly.

"I sent them to their room after Mrs. MacDonald stopped by. I said you'd talk to them when you got home."

"And they listened to you? They went to their room?"

"I hid their electronics and told them they'd never see them again if they didn't behave."

"Sadie," Cassie said with a gasp, "you could have died."

She shrugged. "Then they definitely wouldn't see them again. Just don't forget about them up there like you did the last time."

Cassie scoffed. "I didn't forget about them." She hadn't. She had fallen asleep. "I wanted to give them time to think about what they had done."

Sadie laughed. "Right." It had been a weak laugh, but it was still a laugh.

Silence flooded the kitchen. Things were rapidly becoming awkward, and adolescents had a low tolerance for awkward. Cassie had to say something, but what if Sadie wanted to say something first? After a few agonizing seconds, her daughter broke the stalemate, taking shuffling steps to the kitchen table and pulling out a chair. "Mom, can I talk to you about something?"

Cassie's heart banged against her ribs. She had been dreaming of this moment, but she had to be cool. "Uh-huh."

Sadie sat down and crossed her arms over her chest, pinning her hands, but she didn't say anything.

"Is there something going on at school?"

Her daughter rolled her eyes.

"Okay," Cassie said evenly, measured, like she wasn't massively anxious to peek behind the curtain of her daughter's life. "Is it about all I've been asking you to do lately?"

"No."

Cassie's phone buzzed on the table. They both looked at the screen. Eliza. Why would Eliza be calling instead of texting? Didn't matter. Cassie ended the call. "It's fine. Is this about your dad?"

"No! Oh my God. Why do you blame everything—"

"Sorry! Sorry!" She held her hands up. "Why don't I shut up, and you tell me what's going on?"

The anger drained from her daughter's face. She was about to speak when the phone binged. There was the text Cassie had been expecting in the first place. The preview had a lot of words. Sadie leaned over to get a better look. Cassie grabbed her phone and flipped it over.

"You can read it if you want," Sadie said with a shrug. "It's not a big deal."

Cassie disagreed. Again, it was a big deal. Sadie hadn't asked to talk to her in over a year. "No, I am one hundred percent focused on you right now."

The phone binged again. This time Sadie grabbed it before Cassie could snatch it away and read the screen. She flipped it back around. "Nine-one-one."

"It's fine."

"Mom, nine-one-one does not mean fine. Call her."

Cassie took Sadie's hand, and for once her daughter didn't pull away. "Whatever you have to say is more important than anything your aunt has going on right now."

"What if she's been arrested?"

Cassie released her grip and squeezed her eyes shut. "You heard all that this morning?"

"Last night. My window was open."

The phone binged again. Then again. Sadie held it out to her.

"Fine." Cassie took her phone but pointed it across the table. "Don't move."

The call had barely connected before Eliza answered. "Cassie! Why weren't you—"

"I can't talk right now."

"You have to! Something really bad has happened."

Cassie smiled at Sadie, then pulled the phone away from her ear to give it a look. It was vibrating. Not like a notification, but like a weak electrical current was running through it. It looked fine, so she put it back to her ear. "Did you beat up another truck?"

"No, I did not beat up another truck! It's Tommy."

Cassie tensed. Tommy had never seemed like the kind of guy to get aggressive, but Eliza hadn't known him long.

"Something's wrong with him, and it's my fault."

It sounded like Eliza was somewhere outside. Cassie glanced over at the window. Pitch dark. If only she could buy a sister-sized box that she could keep Eliza in when she couldn't supervise her. Again, weird thoughts. "What are you talking about? What's wrong with him? And how is it your fault?"

"I didn't remember until today, but last night, I was upset, and I did something stupid."

"Something other than the truck?"

"Yes, something other than the truck! Why are you so hung up on the truck?"

"Stop yelling at me! I don't know!" Cassie smiled at Sadie again. She was up on her elbows leaning forward on the table, her eyebrows peaked with concern. This was ridiculous. Cassie needed to calm down before she got them both upset over what was likely nothing. "What did you do?"

Eliza moaned. She was probably chewing the side of her thumbnail and bouncing up and down. She always did that when she was afraid to say something. "You're not going to believe me," she cried. "I don't even know why I called you."

"Okay, bye."

"Cassie!"

"What?" she snapped, turning her back to Sadie as though that would help. "What are you trying to tell me?"

"When Tommy came out of the bar last night, I was upset. Like really, really upset."

"Of course you were," Cassie said through her teeth. "Anyone would be. So what?"

"I did something I shouldn't have."

"For the love of God, Eliza. Just tell me. I'm in the middle of—"

"I told him a story."

CHAPTER 4

"I'm hanging up now."

"No! Don't hang up!"

Cassie knew—*she knew!*—her sister working at that shop was a bad idea. Eliza had let all this story stuff go when they were kids, but then she started working at the Grubbling.

The Grubbling was a curio shop in one of the oldest stone buildings in town. Apparently the word *grubbling* meant to rummage through pockets and drawers, and the shop was an eclectic assortment of knickknacks, jewelry, and antiques. It also had a *vibe*. Every time Cassie walked through the old stone building, navigating the mazes of wooden shelves, she worried she might stumble across some cursed monkey's paw, or something preserved in a jar that really should have been buried long ago. There were beautiful objects too: romantic paintings, leatherbound books that smelled of the past, and antique rings with semiprecious stones that sparkled in the dim lighting. But even with those, Cassie could never shake the sense that every object had a secret. It was great for tourists, but not so much for Eliza.

But a job was a job, and Eliza was only supposed to ring up purchases at the counter. As an added bonus, it gave her a place to live. The owner, Carl, closed shop every year to head for Florida as soon as the tourists left, and he had offered Eliza the apartment upstairs if she kept an eye on the place. Which was great, practical, but then before Cassie could blink, Eliza was telling fortunes.

To say that the idea of soothsaying made Cassie uncomfortable was an understatement. Accepting money from vulnerable people to tell them what they wanted to hear was shady at best. Eliza swore up and down she only charged people looking for fun, but that didn't mean she couldn't do real harm. As per usual, though, nothing Cassie said mattered. She tried to convince herself it was fine. Eliza was an adult. She could make her own choices.

But then it got worse.

After a couple of coincidences, her sister had come to believe that she *was* seeing into the future. Like truly, genuinely believing it. Cassie had tried to reason with her. After all, if you tell a young woman who is looking for love that a man will be coming into her life, there is a good chance it will happen. She just had to swipe right. Or left. Cassie had never online dated. And sometimes scratch-off tickets did result in a windfall. But her reasoning with Eliza didn't work.

And then it got even worse. Eliza wanted to talk about the *stories*.

When they were little, every night Cassie read her sister fairy tales from the only book she had been able to keep when they were placed in foster care. It was a giant tome of fairy tales, with an elaborately cut leather cover. Eliza had loved its stories. Ogres. Sprites. Princesses. Witches. She couldn't get enough. She spent hours daydreaming about them, dressing up in costumes she'd put together herself, acting out plays. Eventually she started to make up her own stories, and she'd be the one to entertain

Cassie before they went to sleep. Her tales were great. Amazing even. Eliza had a wild imagination, and her creations had just the right mix of magic, danger, and romance.

But then things got weird.

Her little sister started to make up stories about people she knew. Nothing crazy, just made-up tales about things she'd like to see happen. They'd be lying in bed at night, and Eliza might say, *Once upon a time, there was a boy named Ryan Myers who fell madly in love with a princess named Eliza, and he bought her chocolates for Valentine's Day. The End.* It was cute. Funny. But they never came true.

Until some of them did.

Like the time Eliza saw a classmate crying, stressed about a big test, and she told her, *Once upon a time, there was a girl named Missy who got the highest grade in the class on her math test. The End.* And sure enough, Missy got her first A+. Once again Cassie had explanations at the ready. Sometimes people needed a boost to do their best. To see themselves as the hero of their own story. But Eliza—she started to believe.

And then it all went wrong.

The *incident*.

The thought of that day still made Cassie sick. Eliza and their foster mother were always butting heads. Her sister's daydreams about slaying dragons and casting spells didn't sit well with Mrs. Wheeler's beliefs. Cassie couldn't remember what Eliza had done that day to make their foster mother so upset, but she did remember Mrs. Wheeler sitting her down at the kitchen table to give her a talking to.

We have rules in this household, Eliza, and we expect you to follow them. Why can't you be more like your sister? She knows how to behave.

Cassie hated it when Mrs. Wheeler said things like that. It wasn't fair. She was eight years older. But there was a part of Cassie that wished Eliza *would* follow the rules. Her sister didn't understand how lucky they were to still be in the same house together. But Eliza didn't like rules. The fight went on until Mrs. Wheeler had had enough and decided to punish her sister by taking their book of fairy tales away.

Cassie had never seen Eliza so angry as Mrs. Wheeler stomped off to their bedroom. Her little cheeks had flamed bright red, and her eyes almost glowed with fury.

If you take that book, you'll be sorry.

Something in the air changed when her sister said those words, like an electrical charge had filled the house. The look on Mrs. Wheeler's face when she turned around to see Eliza standing in the threshold of the bedroom chilled Cassie to the core. Her lips were pinched, tight with anger, but all the blood had drained from her face.

I'm warning you.

Mrs. Wheeler laughed at that, but the uncertainty showed in her eyes. She picked the book up off the nightstand and clasped it to her chest.

Once upon a time, there was a mean old woman who tried to take a book that wasn't hers. She dropped it on her foot. All the little bones broke to pieces. The End.

Mrs. Wheeler's jaw dropped and so did the book. Her foot broke in three places.

Eliza had been horrified with what she had done. Cassie tried to convince her that it wasn't her fault. That it was a horrible coincidence. She had told lots of stories. Some of them came true but others didn't. Ryan Myers never once bought her chocolates. But it didn't matter. Eliza was convinced. She begged Mrs. Wheeler for forgiveness and promised she would never tell a story again. Their foster mother did forgive her—at least she said she did—but things were never the same.

Cassie had really believed that Eliza had given up on her storytelling in the years that followed. It was a huge relief. Not only because of their living situation, but because she never wanted her to end up like Dorcas. Cassie knew she should tell Eliza more about their aunt and her beliefs, but it was a painful topic for them both. Their mom had died from an infection after Eliza was born, and Dorcas instantly gave up custody. It wasn't a period of their lives they liked to talk about.

"Are you still there?"

"Eliza, be serious for a second. You must know that you can't"—Cassie fumbled for the right words—"control fate. Tell me you know that." A tiny spark from the phone snapped by her ear.

"You don't understand. Tommy is—I don't know what he is! And the things I said to him last night? They were awful."

"What did you say?"

"I told him he would die a dried husk of a man." Eliza moaned. "I don't even know where that came from."

Cassie dropped her forehead into her hand and squeezed her temples. "You are not the first woman to say nasty things to her cheating boyfriend."

"And I knew something was wrong. Even before I went to find him today. I knew it. My hands were tingling like crazy."

Cassie whipped her head up. Her sister's hands were tingling too?

"Then I went to his house and there was blood! Blood, Cassie! Blood on his truck and on the ground. I banged on his door, but there was no answer. I didn't know what to do, so I left—"

Oh thank God.

"—but then I went back."

Cassie whimpered. She switched her phone to her other hand. Her fingers were thrumming with the current her phone was giving off. She held it an inch away from her face and smiled at Sadie. Why had she told her to stay?

"That's when I spotted him weaving around the road on his bike. He was in a total daze. He wouldn't even talk to me. But he was super pale, his eyes were bloodshot, and he had this bloody bandage on his neck. That's when it hit me. He was going to see his new girlfriend! She's probably got him hooked on some crazy new drug!"

Cassie blinked. *Drug? What?*

"Finally, he stopped at the stone bridge. You know the one at the old Anne of Green Gables sign? He looked like he was waiting for someone. Something's wrong, Cassie. Something more than drugs."

"You are making absolutely no sense. Wrong how?"

"Like really wrong." She moaned again. "You're going to think I'm crazy—you always do—but it all adds up."

Cassie braced herself. She didn't know where this was headed, but she had to be prepared for anything.

"The story I told him? The confusion? No, trance. It was a fricking trance! The wound on his neck?"

Oh no. Cassie could see where this was going now.

"I think he may have been attacked by a—"

Don't say it, Eliza. Don't say it.

"Zombie."

What?! "Your cheating boyfriend was attacked by a drug-dealing zombie?" She caught herself too late. She rolled her eyes over to Sadie and batted her hand, mouthing the words *It's fine.*

"Not like a *zombie* zombie. But maybe a zombie virus. What if he wasn't cheating at all? What if she was feeding on him?"

"Where are you now?" Cassie needed to know this so she could pick her up and have her committed.

"I told you! I'm at the bridge! Well, hiding behind the sign at the bridge."

"You're still there?!"

"I can't leave him! He's bad, Cassie. And it's my fault."

"It is not your fault!" *Why?!* Why couldn't this day just end? "I'm coming. Don't move. I'm—" Cassie yelped as her phone zapped her again, this time letting out a shower of sparks. She dropped it on the table and a spiral of smoke rose from its dead body.

"I have to go." Cassie rose to her feet. "I am so sorry."

"Is she okay?" Sadie asked, eyes wide with worry.

"I think so." That was a lie. She *hoped so* would have been more accurate. Cassie pulled on her coat. "I am so sorry."

"It's fine. Go."

Cassie rushed for the door but stopped when she grabbed the knob. She looked back. "Promise me we'll talk later."

Sadie nodded.

Her daughter was never going to talk to her again.

☾

Cassie's van bounced over the dirt road. It had been in much better shape ten, twenty years ago. Back then it had been one of the main routes to get to Green Gables—which wasn't really Anne's house, just a house Lucy Maud Montgomery had visited, but people could believe whatever they wanted, including her sister, who apparently believed she could curse people with stories. But whatever.

THE LATE-NIGHT WITCHES

The van's headlights struggled through the thick fog.

This was it. This had to be it. She couldn't keep doing this. Eliza was never going to make better decisions unless Cassie stopped running to the rescue every time she got herself in trouble. What if Tommy *was* on drugs? What if he *was* meeting his dealer? There were a million reasons why it was not a good idea for her sister to follow him, but Eliza wasn't thinking of any of them. That was Cassie's job. It had always been Cassie's job.

Suddenly the front right tire of the van dropped into a pothole with a thud. It popped back up again, and for one brief, beautiful second, Cassie thought everything was fine, but then the van shuddered. At first it was just a wobble, but it didn't take long for it to turn into violent shaking.

Cassie pulled over to the side of the road. *Please don't be a flat.* She clutched her hands to her chest and took small steps through the swirling mist around the front engine. When she saw the tire, her hands dropped. Flat.

No! Come on! Cassie hopped in a circle. This was all wrong. Why couldn't she be at home hiding in the bath instead of being stranded out here in the middle of nowhere drowning in fog?

Cassie shook her shoulders and flapped her hands out. Having a temper tantrum would not change the situation. It probably wouldn't make her feel any better either. Tackling her sister and throwing her in the trunk of her own car, though, that might help turn this night around. Unfortunately, she had to find her first.

Trees crowded in from either side as Cassie walked the dirt road in the direction of the bridge. Every now and then the fog would part, revealing a bright full moon, but it would be gone a second later. It was also eerily quiet, making Cassie's crunching footsteps sound incredibly loud in the noiseless dark. Maybe it was too late in the season for toads and grasshoppers, but the vacuum of noise felt... unnatural.

A minute or two later she spotted a faint rectangle of blue light. Eliza's phone! The glow lit up the outline of the billboard behind her. The sign was maybe six feet by ten feet, and low to the ground. It had been there for as long as Cassie could remember, and it looked like it. The wood was rotting in several places, and the edge farthest from the road was dipping down toward the ditch. Both sides of the board featured a waving Anne with her straw hat, braids, and white apron. She got you both coming and going. And while most of her had faded over the years, her teeth were still gleaming white. The stone bridge was maybe a hundred meters beyond that, but Cassie didn't care about finding Tommy. She stayed focused on her sister's silhouette.

Just before she was about to call out, Cassie's boot caught something. She stumbled and landed on the handle of a long paint roller. She squinted at the ground and was able to make out a couple of dented paint cans and a tipped-over stack of plywood. It looked as though someone had thought about fixing up the sign, but then gave up, about a decade ago.

She picked her way over the abandoned supplies and hurried for her sister. Eliza spun at her approach. "Oh my God, you scared the shit out of me."

"Super sorry about that." Cassie linked her arm through hers. "Let's go."

Eliza untangled herself from her grip. "I can't go."

"Yes, you can. Walk with me. I'll show you how."

"Tommy needs help."

"Not from you! Maybe from someone he hasn't cheated on."

"There were clearly extenuating circumstances." Eliza gave Cassie an incredulous look. She who was wearing a faux leather moto jacket. Not even zipped up. That must be the problem! Eliza had hypothermia. Hypothermia caused confusion, didn't it? Cassie pulled off her gloves. "Put these on."

Eliza accepted them without a thank-you. "I have to see who he's meeting."

"You mean the woman with the zombie virus?"

"I didn't mean she was a literal undead zombie. Tommy is definitely sick though."

"Eliza," Cassie snapped in a whisper, "I appreciate the amount of thought you have put into this, but a simpler explanation might be that he cheated and is now trying to ghost you."

"You haven't seen him."

Cassie bounced on her toes. "Come on. It's freezing and my van has a flat. You need to drive me home. We can make popcorn. Watch a movie. I'll trim your hair!" Cassie pinched a black lock between her freezing fingers and flipped up the ends. "You need a trim."

"I do not want a trim." Eliza batted her hand away. "You know what? The only way you're going to believe me is if I show you." She stepped out from behind the sign. Cassie hurried after her, but as she picked up speed, Eliza picked up her own. They were in a speed-walking race. Because this night wasn't ridiculous enough.

"Eliza?" Tommy called out pitifully. "What's happening?"

"You know me. You're back!" Eliza sprinted with her arms outstretched, but Tommy backed away, waving his hands out. "Don't come near me." He took a step toward her. "You smell so good." He backed up again. "But stay away."

Coming to her sister's side, Cassie got her first good look at Tommy. Eliza hadn't been exaggerating. His face had a pearlescent glow in the moonlight, but there were dark stains in the hollows of his cheeks, around his mouth, and beneath his eyes. His once-tousled dark hair was matted and grimy, and his eyes looked painfully bloodshot.

And then there was the stained bandage clinging to his neck.

"Stay back. Please. I don't know what I'll do."

Cassie's mom instincts kicked in. She had dealt with this sort of thing before. Maybe not exactly this kind of thing, but when the kids were sick and barfed all over their beds, did she want to be the one to clean it up? No, she did not, but someone had to take charge, be the adult. And unfortunately, if it were a contest between the three of them, Cassie was hands down the adult. "We need to go to the hospital."

Tommy moaned. "I can't leave."

What was with these two? "Yes, you can. Eliza, you take the left. I'll take the right. We'll get you in the car."

Eliza stepped toward him again.

"Get back!"

All right, that was it. Cassie was cold, and tired, and disappointed with everyone's decision-making skills. Her nose was also running, and she did not have one of those little packets of tissues other mothers always seemed to have. "Tommy, I don't want to scare you, but . . ."

He raised his eyebrows much like a golden retriever would. A zombie golden retriever.

"You're dying. Like right now, you're dying."

Eliza elbowed her in the side. "What the hell, Cass? That's pretty scary."

"You guys should be scared! We are in the midst of a medical emergency! I'm calling nine-one-one. Give me your phone."

Tommy jumped toward Eliza and batted it from her hand, much quicker than Cassie would have thought he was capable of given his current state. "Don't bring more people. It's too dangerous. You have to go." Tommy looked over his shoulder at the bridge. "She's coming. Hide. Hide. Hide." He waved his arms violently at them.

"What's happening?" Cassie reached for her sister.

"Don't let her see you!"

Eliza cocked her head. "I'm sorry. Don't let *her* see *me*?"

"Please," Tommy begged. "Just go. I love you."

Cassie yanked her sister's arm, dragging her back.

"Wait, what?" Eliza looked at Cassie. "Did he just say he loved me?"

"Yup, absolutely. Let's go talk about what this means. Behind the sign." Cassie dragged her sister in stumbling steps back to their hiding spot, just as a car's headlights tilted over the bridge.

CHAPTER 5

"Did he seriously say he loved me?"

"Uh-huh." Cassie peered around the sign.

"None of the guys I've dated have ever told me that."

Cassie pulled back. Now was so not the time, but what did Eliza just say? She knew her sister could be intimidating, but not one had said *I love you*? She was going to have to follow up on this later. Right now Cassie needed to focus on the black Mustang creeping over the gravel. Hey, she knew that beat-up Mustang! It made a ninety-degree turn in front of Tommy, pinning him in its headlights. The door opened with a clunk, then a grind, and a woman stepped out into the night.

Eliza made a surprised noise. "Is that . . . ?"

"Joanne." Cassie's hairdresser. It took a second to recognize her, but the ultra-blonde hair shining in the car's headlights was unmistakable. This was good. Joanne was okay. She yanked a bit hard with the hairbrush sometimes, but she was normal. Certainly not a drug dealer. Probably. Besides, Joanne was five foot two and approaching fifty. They could take her in a fight. Not that there would be a fight! Jesus, what was wrong with her?

Cassie shook her hands out before consciously realizing they were tingling again.

"I'm going to have a word with her." Eliza pushed up her jacket's sleeves, which immediately fell right back down.

"Let's wait and see what this is first."

Joanne stroked Tommy's cheek. Eliza flinched and Cassie grabbed her arm to hold her back. Staying hidden was the only way they'd really see what was going on here. Cassie squinted at the pair in the distance. It was hard to be sure, but Tommy didn't look scared anymore. Or miserable. He looked like he was in a *trance*. That's what Eliza had said. There wasn't a better word for it. They were far back, but his face was blank, his arms hung limply at his sides, and he was swaying gently on his feet . . . like some undead creature from a B movie.

A cold, watery sensation churned in Cassie's gut, draining down into her knees. This was wrong. The mist twisted around their feet almost purposefully, and somehow it was even quieter. Strange shadows darted over the road, but the fog parted, allowing a moonbeam to light up Joanne and Tommy as though it wanted them to see. A primal sensation crept up Cassie's spine.

We have to get out of here.

She pulled on Eliza's arm, but her sister wasn't budging.

Joanne trailed her fingertips over Tommy's face once more, this time reaching around the back of his head. She pulled him down, his neck moving toward her mouth. Eliza jumped forward and, without thinking, Cassie jutted her foot out between her sister's legs, hooking her boot around her left shin. Eliza dropped to her knees and Cassie threw herself on her back, forcing them both to the ground.

"What are you doing?" Eliza squirmed, planting her hands

in the dirt, trying to flip Cassie off. "She's attacking my boyfriend!"

"I don't know what's happening, but you can't go out there. Something is wrong."

"*Now* you think something is wrong?"

It wasn't only the physical sensations. Cassie didn't realize it at first, but Joanne didn't seem like Joanne anymore. For one thing, she had walked over to Tommy with the grace of a ballerina. Joanne had sciatica. They had talked about it at length at her last appointment. And her posture—it was completely straight now. That wasn't right either. Joanne's shoulders were permanently rolled forward from years of brushing and drying hair. And speaking of hair, the glow coming from hers was beyond anything that came from a bottle. No, this Joanne was very different. Her transformation was as dramatic as Tommy's, just in the opposite direction.

An invisible roller of nails pricked up Cassie's arms from her fingertips to her shoulders, electrifying her down to the bone. The sensation grew until it hummed throughout her body. Something was happening to her. She couldn't catch her breath, tension crackled in her muscles, and her gaze had sharpened to a startling degree.

She also had to pee.

Eliza suddenly lurched beneath her and rolled to the side. Cassie's back hit the dirt. She made a grab for her sister's ankle as Eliza jumped to her feet, but her fingers slipped over her jeans. Eliza strode purposefully toward the pair. "Hey!"

Joanne turned and Tommy dropped to the ground.

Cassie raced after Eliza, smacking into her shoulder when her sister skidded to a stop. "What?" She followed Eliza's gaze back to Joanne. Except Joanne *really* wasn't Joanne anymore. Her eyes were now neon yellow, and her lips and chin were covered with blood. Cassie couldn't look away as the corners of her hairdresser's mouth pulled toward her ears. She knew what would be revealed underneath.

Long, sharp, gleaming-white fangs.

Cassie clutched her sister's arm and stumbled backward, muttering, "Not a zombie. Not a zombie."

The transformed hairdresser took a step toward them.

"Hey, Jo," Eliza called out. "You doing okay? Cassie was going to call an ambulance for Tommy. Should she make it two?"

Joanne rolled her head like a snake and hissed. "He's awake."

"So that's a no to the ambulance?"

"The Maker of Shadows, the Begetter of Demons, the Deliverer of Fear, Sorrow, and Death is finally awake."

That didn't sound good at all.

"The Thirteenth Witch will die."

"Cassie," Eliza whispered, "I know you don't think I can do this, but I'm going to tell her a story."

"Now is not the time to tell a story!" Cassie yanked Eliza back behind her. "We're going to run for your car."

"Are you sure that's a good idea? She looks like she might be fast."

"It's our best bet." They had a good lead, and Joanne's legs were still little. "Go!" Cassie slapped her sister on the shoulder, and they whipped around as a whoosh sounded overhead. Joanne landed on the hood of the car with an earsplitting bang, leaving a crater in the metal. When she looked up, her ferocious, hungry gaze landed on Eliza.

Cassie dropped down to pick up a long shovel abandoned on

the ground and lifted its scoop out in front of them. "Don't even think about it."

"Not you." The hairdresser leaped from the hood of the car onto the dirt. "He said not you."

"I don't care what *he* said." Cassie's hands ached with pressure. "Back off."

"I'm so thirsty."

For a crazed second Cassie thought about the juice boxes she had back in the van, but somehow, she knew they wouldn't help. She jabbed the shovel out in warning. "Stay away from my sister."

Joanne laughed. The sound filled Cassie's eardrums like an acidic cloud. Then, in a horrifying flash, her hairdresser lunged, clawed hands reaching for her.

Eliza screamed as Cassie squeezed her eyes shut and swung the shovel. The shaft jerked in her hands as the flat bottom of the blade smacked against what had to be the side of Joanne's head.

"Oh shit," Eliza whispered.

Cassie peeked her eyes open and dropped her weapon. It was hard to understand what she was seeing. Joanne's head was not where it should be. In fact, it looked like it was gone. Cassie leaned to the side to get a different angle. Joanne's head was still attached, but the back of her skull was lolling gently against her shoulder blade.

Eliza shook her arm frantically. "How did you do that?"

Cassie didn't know. She didn't think she was strong enough to knock someone's head off their shoulders. "I think I killed her."

"You think?!"

"So why is she still standing?" The weight of Joanne's head was making her list to the side, but she was still on her feet.

Eliza picked the shovel up off the ground.

"What are you doing? Don't hit her again!"

"It's freaking me out the way she's just standing there. I'm going to give her a poke."

Cassie wasn't sure if it was a good idea or not, but Joanne was freaking her out too. She grabbed the wooden shaft with both hands, above her sister's grip. They jabbed the edge of the scoop into Joanne's belly. She didn't move. She wasn't even swaying anymore.

The tip of the shovel dropped to the ground. They instinctively backed away as Joanne's hands reached for her head, gripping it at the sides, then tilting it back up until her glowing eyes landed on them. She lowered her head onto her spine and with a sharp twist locked it back in place.

They were going to die. Her hairdresser was going to eat them. Of all the ways Cassie had imagined dying, this was not one of the possibilities.

She didn't know what to do, but then something burned in her pocket against her thigh. Her coin? Buried childhood memories pressed against her consciousness.

"I know you don't believe me," Eliza whispered, "but—"

"Tell a story!" Cassie yelled. "Do it now!"

Joanne crunched toward them. Her jaw juddered as she swayed her head, showcasing her fangs.

"Once upon a time there was a hideous vampire," Eliza rattled off. "She got what was coming to her. The End."

Joanne stopped, frowning at her, then broke out into a run. She was going to leap into the air, knock them down, and tear them apart. Cassie's body burned and hummed, set to explode. She had to do something now!

Flip the coin!

Cassie reached into her pocket, but when she touched the metal, she was flooded with dread. Before she could decide what to do, Joanne's foot landed on a steel pipe. It rolled beneath her, sending her staggering back. Her arms pinwheeled as she stumbled out from behind the sign. For the strangest second, her body lit up.

Then a Volvo sedan plowed right into her.

CHAPTER 6

The force of the hit should have been enough to send Joanne flying down the road, and it would have, if it hadn't been for the tree branch that impaled her through the chest.

"What did you do to me?" Joanne screamed. Her arms and legs flailed like she was a pinned bug, but then she slumped forward, her limbs dangling loosely in the air.

Cassie shook her head in small jerky motions. The sound of a car door reached her ears, but she couldn't look away from Joanne. Drops of blood dripped to the ground, making a soft *pat, pat, pat* sound as they hit the dirt.

A man ran into view. "She came out of nowhere!"

Cassie blinked. Was that her new neighbor? Ben? Small world. Dark laughter bubbled up her throat. Maybe she would finally get a chance to introduce herself.

Ben clutched his head as he stumbled in a circle beneath Joanne, and then he jerked to a stop. "Olive!" He ran back out of view.

"Don't worry," Eliza called after him. "It's not what you think."

Cassie tried to say something too, but she was already mumbling. She didn't know what she was mumbling, but she was definitely mumbling. Maybe it was about the fog? The fog was gone, and the grasshoppers were chirping. They weren't all dead after all. Not like Joanne. She was hanging dead from a tree.

"We have to do something," Ben shouted behind her. Another door opened. Cassie thought she heard him say something about never leaving babies unattended in a car, but she couldn't understand what he meant. She couldn't understand anything, but . . . something wasn't right. Vampires weren't right. Impaled vampires hanging from tree branches weren't right either. But it was something else. Right on the tip of her tongue. If only she could hear what she was saying.

Ben came back into view, with a baby pressed to his chest. "Don't look, Olive. You can't see this. Look at Anne. Oh God! No! Don't look at Anne!" Anne must have gotten some vampire blood on her. The thought made the corner of Cassie's mouth twitch, which was bad. She was going to go to Green Gables hell.

Ben backed up to where Eliza was standing under the tree. "Is she alive?"

"No," she answered flatly. "I don't think so."

"We have to call nine-one-one." Ben patted himself over with one hand as Olive tilted sideways in the crook of his other arm. He grabbed to right her.

"It's okay," Eliza said. "You don't have to call anyone."

Cassie was mumbling louder now. She could almost hear what she was trying to say.

"It's okay?! How is any of this okay?"

"She's not what you think," Eliza said. "She's . . . a vampire."

Vampire.

That one word transported them to a whole new reality.

"*Was* a vampire. Cassie smacked her with a shovel, I cursed her, and then you hit her with your dad car. Group effort."

Ben's jaw dropped.

"Why is she not disintegrating?" Cassie asked in a whisper. That was it! That's what all the mumbling was about. If Joanne was a vampire, she should be disintegrating. At least that's what happened in the movies.

"Cassie? Are you okay?" Eliza asked before shouting, "Oh my God! Tommy! I forgot about Tommy." Her sister's footsteps smacked against the dirt as she ran away.

Cassie looked at Ben. "Why isn't she disintegrating?" He was a professor. He knew things. He would know this.

"I don't understand." His palm was over Olive's eyes. She wrapped her tiny hand around his baby finger, trying to pull it down.

That's adorable. A manic snort of laughter finally broke free, but Cassie cut it off. "I have three children. I can't hide a vampire body."

Ben shook his head, his gaze darting back and forth between Cassie and the hanging vampire.

But was she a vampire? Maybe they had made a mistake. Everything was suddenly very confusing. "She's not disintegrating."

"You're in shock. Give me your phone. I can't find mine."

Cassie chuckled again. Her phone was dead too. She stared at Joanne's drooped body. She didn't look like a vampire anymore. Her face was a normal hairdresser face. They had made a mistake. Maybe they were drugged? Or sick? Zombie drug–virus sick. This could not be happening. They had killed someone.

Ben touched her arm. "Maybe you should look away."

She shook him off, refusing to take her eyes from Joanne.

The drips of blood had all but stopped.

Please.

Suddenly a violent gust of sand and grit—and God only knew what else—blasted Cassie's face. She reflexively squeezed her eyes shut and held her hands up to ward off the burst of scalding air. When she was finally able to open her eyes, Joanne was gone.

She let out a jubilant cry...

...then threw up.

Eliza's boots came into view. "That's right. Get it all out." Her sister pulled her hair back. "Take your time." She said the words sweetly, but Cassie could hear her gagging. When she was done, she rose back up to standing, hoping she'd be able to stay upright. Every part of her body trembled. She wiped her mouth with the corner of her coat sleeve. "Sorry about that."

Ben attempted a smile, but he looked sick too. Baby Olive, though—she was clapping her hands happily, her chin shining with drool.

"Let's get you home." Eliza wrapped her arm around Cassie's waist. "Tommy! We're going!" He staggered toward them. Cassie never would have believed he could look any worse than when she first saw him, but he was proving her wrong. Then again, she hadn't believed a lot of things were possible that now were.

They shuffled toward Eliza's car but stopped when they saw the caved-in hood. Eliza leaned in close and whispered, "What's the new guy's name?"

"Ben."

"Hey, Ben," she called out.

He hadn't moved from his spot, but he did blink at them.

"Could you give us a ride?"

"I..."

"Great!" She shot him a thumbs-up. "Tommy, get in the trunk."

THE LATE-NIGHT WITCHES

☾

Snacks.

They needed snacks.

That's what you did when you had guests over. You offered them snacks.

Cassie rose from the table and walked over to her kitchen sink. She opened the cabinet underneath and pulled out the garbage pail. She reached for the box hidden behind. Halloween treats. Her kids hadn't discovered this hiding spot yet. They had an instinctual fear of garbage pails. Even looking at one made them vulnerable to being asked to take it outside.

She put the box of chips on the counter. They had been on sale. A good deal. She wondered if she'd be able to get them at the same price. Cassie pried underneath the lip of the cardboard on one side and gave it a pull. The tape running down the middle stretched but held on. She pulled harder. The cardboard ripped at the corner but didn't give way.

Huh. This was frustrating.

She balled her fingers into a fist then pounded the top with the side of her hand.

"Cassie?" Eliza asked. "You good?"

She couldn't answer any questions right now, not when she had the box on the ropes. Cassie hit the cardboard top a good five or six more times until the tape finally gave out. A smile came to her lips as her shoulders dropped. *There.* Hopefully she hadn't woken the kids. She walked back over and dumped the contents onto the table. The box tumbled to the floor as she dropped into her seat.

"I'm not sure I can eat," Ben said as he reached around the

bulk of the baby hidden in the leopard print carrier strapped to his chest. Cassie was guessing his sister had picked it out. He opened a bag without looking at it and put a chip in his mouth. His eyes went blank as crumbs fell onto baby Olive's head.

"Hey, guys?"

Cassie jolted then flicked her gaze over to Tommy. His pale, discolored face was pressed up against the screen of the window over the sink. They had agreed it best he wait outside.

"I don't want to make problems, but I'm really thirsty."

Cassie got up again. She opened the fridge and pulled out a carton of milk. She held it up to the window. Tommy frowned. She grabbed the orange juice next. He shook his head and then pointed to a package of ground beef with reddish liquid sloshing around the edges. Cassie had put it on the counter to defrost for a chili she had intended to make sometime in her previous life. She picked it up, walked over to the door, and threw it outside. Tommy was gone in a flash, and Cassie sat back down.

"So, I'm just going to say it," Ben mumbled, brushing the crumbs off Olive's head. "Vampires are real."

"Looks that way," Eliza answered.

"And your friend out there is a . . . ?"

"Vampire," Cassie said, her voice barely audible. This was a dream. That would explain everything. Drugs. Zombies. Vampires. She scoffed in her head. Ridiculous. But a dream. That made total sense.

Ben dipped his head to catch her gaze. His eyes *were* hazel! And pretty. "Hey, are you all right?"

Cassie nodded, unable to look away from his pretty, pretty eyes.

Eliza looked back and forth between the two of them. "Um, she's fine. And we don't know for sure Tommy's a vampire."

"I think I am."

All three jumped this time. Tommy was back at the screen licking his lips. "Sorry."

Eliza cleared her throat. "I didn't want to get into this in front of everyone, but what happened at the bar? How did you hook up with Joanne?"

"I don't know." He closed his eyes. "One minute everything was fine. I was talking to the boys, waiting for you. Then she came to the door, and everything faded to black, except her. She didn't say anything, but I could feel her reaching into my mind." Tommy's eyes pooled with fear. "She made me want dark things. Even when she was feeding off me," he said, touching the bandage on his neck, "I didn't want her to stop. I wanted to drown in her oblivion." He shuddered then chuckled. "Pretty messed up, eh?"

"Mm, okay." Eliza rolled her eyes.

Cassie had never heard Tommy say more than a single sentence at one time. But it was okay. Because this was a dream.

Ben leaned toward the table, pressing the sides of the baby carrier over Olive's ears. "We don't have to kill him, right? Because I don't think I can kill anyone else right now."

"No!" Eliza snapped in a whisper. "We don't know if he is fully a vampire yet. I think he has to kill someone first."

She got that from a movie. Cassie was sure of it.

Eliza peeked over at Tommy. "You haven't killed anyone, right?"

His blood-filled eyes looked hurt. "How could you ask that? You know me."

"Just confirming for these guys." She jerked her thumbs to either side before lowering her voice again. "We have to save him. This is my fault."

Cassie almost argued out of habit, but she had seen it with

her own eyes. Eliza had told a story, and Joanne got what was coming to her. She had the vampire dust in her hair to prove it.

"Wait," Ben said. "How is this your fault?"

Eliza slumped back in her chair. "It's a long story. Or a really short one." She snorted and winked at Cassie.

"Okay," Ben said slowly. "Let's circle back around to that later, but for right now, we need to tell people about this. There might be more vampires on the loose. Aside from Tommy." He said the last part quietly, then smiled over at the vampire in the window. "We need to call the police."

"No police," Eliza said. "They'll never believe us."

"We have to do something. People could be in danger. We don't know anything. Like how many vampires are out there, or why they're here all of a sudden. We need more information. We—"

"He's awake." Cassie's voice sounded weird. Did she normally sound like that?

Ben frowned. "I'm sorry?"

"Joanne, the vampire, said he's awake and the Thirteenth Witch will die." She pushed her chair back. "Do we need more snacks?"

"We're good." Eliza patted her hand. "You stay."

"The Thirteenth Witch?" Ben leaned forward until the baby carrier bumped against the table. "You're sure that's what she said?"

Cassie nodded.

He pushed his glasses up his nose. "I've heard of her before. I wrote a chapter about the Ghost Ship of Northumberland Strait for a book on island legends. It's a fascinating ghost story about a schooner that erupts in flames to warn of coming storms. You two probably know all about it."

Eliza nodded. "No."

"Doesn't matter. There was another chapter in the book about the Thirteenth Witch. I never got around to reading it." Ben's voice had risen, making Olive grumble. He bounced in his seat, tapping her back through the carrier. "I've still got the book somewhere."

"That is so great," Eliza said with a big smile. "It's almost like we were meant to run into you. Or for you to run into Joanne." Her smile turned to a grimace. "So, why don't you start researching? Let us know what you find out, and in the meantime, Cassie, you should probably stay indoors with the kids. I'll take care of Tommy. Find him some more blood and get him underground before the sun—"

"What?" The shock that had Cassie in its grip suddenly let go.

Eliza frowned. "What, what?"

"You're not leaving. There are vampires out there. Your ex-boyfriend is one of them."

"Ex?" Tommy shouted. "Are we breaking up?"

"No. We're good." Eliza gave Cassie a pointed look then whipped around to face Tommy. "Eat the rest of your meat. Or drink it." She turned back and whispered, "I mean, we might be breaking up. I'm not sure how I feel about this development. It's a whole lot less romantic than *Twilight*."

"Eliza, you are not leaving this house."

"Somebody has to take care of Tommy."

"Not you. And how would you even take care of him?"

"I'll put him in the basement at the Grub," she answered with a shrug. "It's all stone with a big wooden door. It's almost like it had been made for vampires... which is also kind of weird." She shrugged. "Anyway, I'll lock him in for the day. Okay, Tommy?" she called over. "It's cold and dark and quiet."

Like a tomb, Cassie thought. What was happening to her life?

"I'll figure out the blood situation later," Eliza finished.

Cassie couldn't believe what she was hearing. Her sister was acting like they were making arrangements for dog sitting, not housing a literal monster. "No, that is unacceptable. We—" Cassie said, patting her chest, "you, me, and the kids—are not leaving this house until we know it's safe." Cassie could feel Ben's discomfort at witnessing their domestic dispute, but given all that had happened, she could stand a little more mortification.

Eliza planted her hands on the table and met Cassie's gaze with challenge. "I agree that you and the kids should stay indoors. I'll pick up some supplies for you. But I'm going to help Tommy." She leaned back. "I'll be careful. I'll follow all the vampire rules. I won't run around after dark. I won't invite anyone in. I definitely won't look anyone in the eye. And I'll see about picking up some garlic."

"Oh, okay, Buffy." Cassie grunted with frustration. "I mean, we don't know if any of that will work, but why not?"

"It's the best we've got. We can't stay inside and starve to death."

Eliza had a point, but this was all too much. And it was happening all too quickly! Cassie had to do something. She couldn't let her baby sister leave with a vampire. She needed to pull rank. "Eliza, if you walk out that door right now, you are not welcome back."

"Really?" Her sister dropped her chin and looked up at her with an arched eyebrow.

"No! Of course not really!" Cassie snapped. "But this is crazy! And dangerous. And—"

"Let's go, Tommy." Eliza pushed her chair back. "Get in the car." She jerked to a stop. "Except I don't have a car. Ben?"

He blinked then gathered up his baby bag. "Yeah, sure."

"Thanks for the drink," Tommy called out.

Cassie got to her feet, grabbing her sister's arm as she walked by. "Why are you so calm?"

Eliza shrugged. "I don't know. It sounds weird, but it almost feels like I was expecting something like this to happen." She gave Cassie a quick hug. "Just keep yourself and the kids safe. Text me if you need anything."

"Get out of my house," Cassie said, letting her sister go before making another grab for her. "Or don't. Please stay."

"I'll be careful." Eliza smiled. "Love you. Try not to worry."

She left. Ben and Olive too. Cassie sat back down. *Try not to worry. Right. No problem.* Her sister did have a point about one thing though. She had to focus on her kids. Nothing was more important than keeping them safe. She could do that. It wasn't like it was something new. The moment they had come into this world, they had been her number one focus.

Soft footfalls came down the stairs.

Cassie's boys appeared, rubbing their eyes, still wearing their clothes.

"Mom?" Sly asked in a sleepy voice.

"Yeah, baby?"

"Are we still in time-out?" Eddie finished.

Cassie dumped her face into her hands. "Who wants chips?"

CHAPTER 7

V*ampire!*
Cassie groaned and blinked her eyes open. Her brain was still half asleep. Some of the shock from the night before had worn off, but there was still a good deal of shock remaining. For the first time in history, the boys didn't want chips. They were too tired. Cassie got them back to bed, apologizing the entire time, then went to bed herself. Unfortunately, by the time she actually fell asleep, she only managed to get—she peeked at the clock on her bedside table with the cat seated beside it—four and a half hours of sleep. *Again.*

"Janet, what do you know about vampires?" Cassie mumbled.

The cat let out a gentle *reow*.

"Okay, we'll talk after you've eaten." She grabbed the glass of water she kept on the nightstand and placed the bottom of it on her forehead. It wasn't so much her head but her brain that was hot. She switched hands, then grabbed for her phone. Somehow it was working again. It was crazy given all the sparking and smoke, but Cassie wasn't about to question small mercies. She held it up and squinted at the screen. A text from Matt. She tapped it with her thumb.

> Sorry I missed your call. Swamped. Hope you have a good day!

She had tried calling him before she went to sleep but hadn't been surprised when she didn't get an answer. When Matt was passionate about something, he was all in. At one time, his passion had been her, but that was a long time ago. They hadn't actually video-chatted or spoken on the phone one-on-one in over five months. She didn't share that information with anyone, especially not Eliza. It was embarrassing. There were only so many times she could explain that he was doing such meaningful work while telling herself that her marriage was fine. How could their marriage be fine when they led such separate lives? Last night was the perfect example. She had no clue how much she planned to tell him. It seemed like a lot to start back up with. But she wanted to tell him something. She wanted reassurance, understanding. She wanted him to say, *Don't worry. I'm coming home. We'll face this together.* But she knew that wasn't about to happen.

It was probably for the best that he hadn't answered. If she told him everything, he would justifiably think she was insane. He might even send some of his doctor friends to come get her, and she couldn't have that. She was going out today.

Despite everyone agreeing last night that it was best she stay in the house, Cassie knew she couldn't. Not yet at least. She had to talk to someone, and given that it was the weekend, she knew exactly where to find her.

Cassie pulled on some jeans and a sweatshirt, wanting to go before she changed her mind. Dust motes spun in the low light of the hallway as she tiptoed past the boys' room. She knocked softly on her daughter's door before opening it a crack. "Sadie?"

The lump under the comforter didn't move. She could only see the top half of her daughter's face. Her dark eyelashes lay softly on her cheeks, and her eyelids still had that soft sheen all kids possessed. Her heart ached with love.

"Mom, stop." Sadie rolled over to face the wall. "You're being creepy."

Well, it had been nice while it lasted. "Sorry. I have to go out. The boys are still in bed."

"Fine. Shut the door."

"There's one other thing." Cassie tensed in anticipation of the coming onslaught. "I need you and the boys to stay inside the house."

Sadie flung up to a seated position. "What? Why would you ask me to do that? They'll go crazy. No."

"I'm sorry. But I need you to do this."

"Why?"

"Your aunt," Cassie said, infusing her voice with concern, "she's been exposed to a virus, and she may have exposed us to the virus." She had come up with this explanation right before she had fallen asleep. It wasn't entirely a lie. Vampirism could be a virus. "We need to quarantine."

"So, *we* have to quarantine, but *you're* going out?"

Frick. This was the problem with making plans in the wee hours of the morning. "I spoke to public health. I'm allowed to get us some food, outdoors, at the farmer's market. But that's all. If we don't obey the order, I'll get fined. Maybe even go to jail." *Crap.* That was probably too far. Sadie was never going to buy that.

And she didn't. It was written all over her face, but she flung herself back onto her mattress and pulled the comforter over her head.

"Thanks. Love you." Cassie moved to shut the door when she remembered their conversation from the night before—before the entire world had flipped on its head. "I do have to go, but if you wanted to tell me whatever was on your mind last night, I could always—"

"Oh my God, get out."

Didn't think so.

☾

Cassie hadn't been lying about the farmer's market. It was the one place she knew she could find her aunt without going to her house. Dorcas had one of the most popular booths at the market. Everyone loved her vegetables, soaps, and other concoctions. Or so she had heard. Cassie had made it a point to stay away from the park on weekends.

Yellow leaves damp with morning dew stuck to Cassie's boots as she walked the path that led to the market. The crisp sea air was tinged with the tart smell of overripe apples, and as she neared the park, she caught the scent of spiced coffee and popcorn. Now that autumn was here, the square wooden archway at the market's entrance was decorated with scarecrows and sunflowers welcoming visitors inside.

As Cassie walked through the throngs of couples and families strolling through the stands, drinking cider and carrying bags of the season's last offerings, she was struck with surreal horror. These people had no idea of the danger they were in. Suddenly she wanted to jump on a hay bale, wave her hands in the air, and shout *Vampires are real!* but she resisted. She bought a maple syrup lollipop instead. It was the only thing standing between her and madness.

Cassie's heart thumped as she walked the length of the dirt

corridor. She'd asked around. Dorcas's stall was the last on the left.

This was a bad idea. Terrible.

The last time she had seen Dorcas up close had been the day her mother died. Up until that point, Cassie had been raised by both her and Dorcas. She couldn't remember much at all about that life, but she had a sense she was happy . . . and then it was over. The social worker had explained at the time that her aunt wasn't well, that she held strange—no, delusional—beliefs, but that didn't ease Cassie's pain at being abandoned.

Not that Dorcas had abandoned them completely. She had tried in her own way to keep in touch most of Cassie's life. When she was school-age, Cassie often caught her aunt watching her at recess, which was creepy, and not unlike what she had done to Sadie that morning. But there were also the notes.

Mrs. Wheeler, Cassie's foster mother, had spoken several times to the social worker about keeping Dorcas away. She thought her presence would be disruptive. But Cassie's aunt had still found ways to get notes to her. Sometimes they'd be tucked in the spokes of her bike. Sometimes in the crook between the branches of her favorite climbing tree. Other times she'd find them tucked beneath her pillow, which should have been concerning, but never seemed to worry Cassie the way it probably should have. And then when she went off to university, she'd find envelopes pinned between her window and the frame, even though she was on the third floor. Cassie couldn't understand how Dorcas did it or why her aunt didn't just speak to her in person, but those were questions she had given up on getting the answers to.

More recently Cassie found messages tucked beneath her welcome mat.

THE LATE-NIGHT WITCHES

The notes always left Cassie feeling sad, mainly because they were invariably strange.

> Don't forget low tide is at 3:20 p.m. this Thursday. The moon is waning crescent. Say hi to Eliza.

What was she supposed to do with that?

> Bernadette has dropped her litter. Three calicos. You know what that means. Ha! Ha! Delightful. Say hi to Eliza.

Cassie did not know what that meant. In fact, the only thing the notes communicated to her was that all the other adults in her life were right. Dorcas wasn't well.

Two years ago, the notes had stopped altogether. The last one read,

> He's dead! Thank the stars! Come to Sea House when you're ready. I will wait as long as it takes. Bring Eliza.

Cassie had searched the obituaries, but she couldn't find anyone dead that would make Dorcas happy. But then again, she didn't know her aunt well enough to guess.

Eliza wasn't aware of any of this. Cassie had meant to tell her but kept putting it off. She felt pretty guilty about it. She also felt guilty about the fact that they were Dorcas's only living relatives, and their aging aunt was living alone in a broken-down house by the sea. But Cassie couldn't bring herself to reach out. While she had almost no memories of her early childhood, she did have one that stood out vividly. A warning from her mother. *You can't trust Dorcas. Don't believe a word that comes out of her mouth.*

But last night they had met a vampire, and suddenly everything she knew was being called into question.

Cassie inhaled deeply. She had to do this. Rip the bandage off. She walked with determination toward the last booth on the left, putting one foot in front of the other, despite wanting to run away screaming.

There she was. Cassie would recognize her anywhere.

Dorcas was laughing and talking to a customer like she didn't have a care in the world. And she didn't exactly look like a helpless old woman living by the sea. Yes, her hair was gray, silver actually, but it was long, thick, and wavy. Despite the cool temperatures, she was wearing a thin army-green T-shirt, revealing lean, muscled arms, and a pair of fitted leather pants that looked kind of . . . hot. That was weird. Maybe even disturbing. Sadie would probably have the same reaction if she were wearing them. But, overall, she looked great. Unique. Cool.

Cassie was wearing jeans and a hoodie.

Dorcas held a cream-colored candle out to a girl holding her mother's hand. The child inhaled and smiled. The gesture felt familiar. How many times had her aunt held an offering out to her? A gut punch of emotion hit Cassie.

This really was a bad idea. She had no reason to believe Dorcas could help. She should go. Cassie was about to turn on her heel when a strange noise swelled from her aunt's booth, a hum growing in volume and pitch. Cassie's eyes widened as the vibration morphed into an out-and-out scream. Several people turned to stare as Dorcas leaped over her counter and rushed through the crowd with her arms outstretched, headed directly for Cassie.

Cassie punched her hand out, still gripping the lollipop, to stop her aunt's charge.

Dorcas skidded to a stop, smiling joyously. Then she dropped her gaze to the sucker grasped in Cassie's fist. She leaned forward and put her mouth over the hard candy, trapping it with her teeth. When she leaned back, she took the lollipop with her, its white stick jutting out from her grinning lips . . .

. . . and with that maple syrup lollipop went the last bit of Cassie's sanity.

CHAPTER 8

"Polliwog, this is delicious, and so very considerate of you," Dorcas mumbled. "Wait." She turned to an unsuspecting man walking by and took the coffee he held in his grip. "Thank you, sweet market-dweller." His eyes widened but his concerned wife pulled him away before he could say anything.

"For you." Dorcas held the coffee out, curtsying with her head bowed.

Polliwog?

This was too much, worse than she had expected. Why? Why had she thought this was a good idea?

"Um, no thank you."

Dorcas didn't surrender her lock on Cassie's gaze but threw the cup to a trash can a good ten feet away. It landed dead center amidst the other cups and wrappers.

"Look at you," Dorcas said softly, clutching her hands to her chest, sucker still sticking out the side of her mouth. "It's been so long. I always hoped you'd reach out. I wanted to but couldn't. And when I could, I couldn't, not sure that you would want it. But I hoped you would." She threw her hands in the air. "Round and round and round we go!"

THE LATE-NIGHT WITCHES

Cassie curled her fingers into fists. Her hands were tingling again.

"You're so beautiful!" she went on. "I have so many questions about Sadie, Sylvester, and Edwin. And, of course, Eliza. I've wanted to meet her for so long, but I wasn't sure if she wanted to meet me. And you! I want to know all about you."

Cassie scratched her temple. "I didn't come here to catch up. Sorry. I . . . came to ask for your help."

"I know why you're here." Dorcas nodded solemnly. "The anniversary. But I promise that you have nothing to worry about. You got my note?"

"I did." Cassie's mouth went dry. A balloon clutched in a toddler's hand bonked her on the side of the face. She couldn't do this. She could not talk vampires with her estranged aunt at a farmer's market. "I need to go. I'm really sorry."

Dorcas grabbed her arm as she turned to leave. Her grip was ridiculously strong. "What is wrong with your hands?" In an instant, her aunt changed, her posture, her voice, her energy, all darkened.

"It's nothing." Cassie slipped her arm away despite finding Dorcas's touch warm, almost comforting. "Just some tingling."

Dorcas grabbed her hands and pulled her in. She closed her eyes and frowned. "How long has this been going on?"

"Not long. A day or two. But—"

"Is this the first time you've tingled?"

Suddenly this felt like an uncomfortable line of questioning. "In my hands? Yes."

"No," Dorcas said firmly. "No. No. What else?"

"Nothing." That wasn't entirely true. There was her coin and its burning, but something deep within warned her not to tell Dorcas about any of that. "Well, Eliza is tingling too."

Her aunt paled as her hands dropped to her sides. "It can't be." A cloud moved over the sun, instantly cooling the air. "It must be a mistake. Or a stray! That's all." She gripped Cassie's arm again and widened her eyes to a disturbing degree. "But what if it's not?" Suddenly a strong gust of wind blew through the corridor between the stalls. Vendors grabbed at their wares and shoppers crouched down low, holding their hats to their heads. Loose hay and dirt swirled through the air as garbage cans overturned, sending food wrappers flying.

Dorcas blinked. "Oh dear. My bad." The wind suddenly dropped. She stepped away from Cassie and shouted, "Sorry, everyone! Sorry." She laughed cheerily at all the confused people staring at her. "I must have lost myself for a moment. But can you blame me? My niece is here! Isn't she beautiful?"

Cassie smiled weakly and raised a hand to smooth down her messy bun, which was a lot messier after the sudden windstorm.

"I know. I know. You want to meet her, but she's all mine." Dorcas turned back to Cassie and whispered, "Well, that was exciting. Where were we?"

"I . . . have no idea."

"Oh yes, the stray." Dorcas looked deadly serious again. "I'm telling you there is no possible way. Unless there is. Either way you must be careful."

On some level, Cassie knew kind of what Dorcas was getting at, but she didn't want to know. Yes, she had been the one to seek her out, but as the hours passed, Cassie found her mind desperately trying to slip away from the reality of vampires. "Again, I should go."

"Yes, go." Dorcas scanned the crowd then stared oddly at the ground before grabbing Cassie by the shoulders and turning her around. "Go now." She pushed her on the back. "You shouldn't be outside. Even during the day." She leaned toward her ear and whispered, "Minions."

Cassie's feet dug in the dirt, and she forced her way back around. It was one thing when she *wanted* to go, but she wasn't about to let Dorcas push her away again. "What is going on? Should I be worried?"

"Of course not. I will take care of it. I'm sure your hands are confused. Now go home. Stay in the house. Eliza too."

"But—"

"Precautionary. That's all!" Dorcas laughed in an awkward trill. "I'll come see you when I know what's happening." The corners of her eyes creased. "If you'll allow it?"

☾

Against her better judgment, Cassie had said yes. She didn't know what else to do.

She went home without anything from the market, but if Sadie noticed, she wasn't letting on. The hours passed peacefully enough. She gave the boys unlimited screen time, which meant that aside from the occasional scream of *Let's go!* she didn't hear from them. And Sadie, she only came out of her room to get snacks and use the bathroom. Cassie wanted to talk to her, but aside from the frosty vibe holding her back, she wasn't sure what she would say. Sadie knew she had lied to her that morning—and the night before—but it wasn't like Cassie could tell her the truth. She didn't want her kids to live in a world where there were vampires, and maybe other things.

Other things like Dorcas.

Cassie texted Eliza throughout the day, begging her to stay inside, but her sister's replies were elusive. On the bright side, Eliza had found a butcher willing to hook her up with some blood, which Cassie supposed was a win. She didn't know anymore. And Eliza had offered to bring food over—Cassie's credit card was on her phone—but she declined. They were good for a day or two.

Ben texted them both a few times. He couldn't find the book with the chapter on the Thirteenth Witch but promised he'd do a thorough search of the attic once Olive was asleep. If she slept.

Cassie meant to keep on texting Eliza throughout the night to make sure her vampire boyfriend was behaving himself, but after the boys went to bed, she fell asleep on the couch, and the day ended with a whimper.

The next morning, however, began with a bang.

Cassie awoke to the sound of cupboards slamming and boys shouting. She dragged herself up and into the kitchen. Sly and Eddie were standing on the kitchen table playing tug-of-war with a cereal box. She made a grab for it, but it slipped from their hands, sending flakes of cereal raining down to the floor. The boys watched her silently as she crunched over to the fridge. If she had had the energy, she would have told them to get the broom. But she did not have the energy to fight. So, she made smoothies instead.

The day did not improve from there.

She kept the twins inside again, so they were restless and bored, which meant property damage, and Sadie was still ghosting her. Cassie had called her mechanic, and he was going to drop off the van later that day with a new tire, but she knew they shouldn't go anywhere. How long could they keep this up? She should have demanded more specific answers from Dorcas. Being stuck inside with nothing to do but chores was going to make her crazy. Cassie couldn't keep folding laundry and picking apart the fabric of reality. She would go insane. So, when Ben texted both her and Eliza asking to come over, she was thrilled. It was much more fun to pick reality apart with other people.

Five minutes after Ben was supposed to arrive, Cassie heard the back door open. She put her laundry basket on the coffee table and got up off the couch. "Hello?" She walked into the kitchen.

"I can't do this anymore." Eliza peeled her jacket off and dumped it on the table.

Cassie peeked out the kitchen window. Eliza's car—crater and all—was parked outside. "You drove that here?"

"It's fine. But I'm going crazy in that basement. The dark. The smell." Eliza gripped the back of a kitchen chair and shook her head. "I hope Professor Ben has found something useful."

"The smell?" Cassie asked. "Like mold?"

Her sister's lip curled. "No, not mold. Tommy's starting to smell like rotten meat." Eliza caught Cassie's look of horror. "I know. It's bad. I fixed him up with plenty of pig's blood, but I don't think it's what his body is aching for."

"Where is he now?"

"In the trunk." Eliza jerked her chin in the direction of the driveway. "He can't sleep, and he didn't want to stay alone at the shop." She seemed nonplussed, so Cassie guessed it was fine. "How are the kids?"

"Bored. Frustrated. Mad. The boys are playing video games, again, but Sadie is in her room. Probably hating me."

Eliza nodded. "She texted."

Cassie felt her nonexistent quills go up. "She texted you? What did she tell you? What did you tell her?"

Eliza winced in sympathy. Possibly patronizing sympathy. "She asked me not to tell you anything."

Could there be times when violence *was* the answer among siblings?

"But I told her she should talk to you. I think the real problem, though, is that you need to talk to her. Like really talk to her."

"Are you suggesting I tell my fifteen-year-old that we killed our vampire hairdresser the other night?"

Eliza rolled her eyes. "I knew you'd say that. No, I don't think you should tell her that. At least not like that. But she knows something's up."

"Now is not the time!"

Her sister lifted her hands in surrender. "Okay, okay." She then leaned to look out the window. "Man with a baby coming in hot."

Cassie opened the door while Ben struggled to secure the brake on the stroller. "I'm so sorry I'm late." He yanked a bag free from the compartment underneath the chair. "I forgot to pack the baby stuff, then Olive had a blowout. Something I did not know existed until today. And then we had a wrestling match getting dressed." He straightened and Cassie smiled. His hair was disheveled, his eyes red, and he had skipped a button on his shirt. He was adorably rumpled. Or just rumpled. Adorable was not a word she should be using. "The point is, I'm sorry. I didn't mean to come this close to dusk."

"Maybe we should have had this meeting online?"

Ben's face dropped. "I did not think of that." He shook his head. "No, this is too important. I have to tell you what I found out in person." He nodded then kept on nodding.

Cassie peered at him sideways. "So, you read the chapter?"

"No, I couldn't get up to the attic to find the book I was telling you about." He blinked. "Every time I put Olive in the crib, the second her back touches the mattress, her eyes pop open. Is there a hack for that?" Cassie was about to reply when he put his hand up. "Don't answer. I don't want to be that guy who only talks about his baby. Or his sister's baby. But I called the author of the chapter. Couldn't get her. Then I talked to a few historian friends who led me to some primary documents. Then the author called me back. And then I went to some dark places on the web, which I do not recommend. But I had to be sure. Or as sure as I could be when nothing makes sense." He laughed then pressed his lips together, still nodding.

"That's so great," Eliza said. "So, you found something out."

"I did. But it's not great."

"What is it? Did—" Cassie sniffed the air. "What's that smell?" She sniffed her way over to Olive, who immediately grabbed for her hair. Cassie peeled her blankets back. Not only did she reek, but she was also wearing her undershirt over her sleeper. Cassie peeked up at Ben.

"I dipped her onesies in garlic. Garlic oil, actually. Made it myself. Then I realized it could burn her skin off, at least according to the internet, so I put it on the outside."

"Smart," she said lightly.

Olive didn't seem too bothered by the smell. In fact, she found Cassie leaning in to be quite amusing now that she had a good chunk of her hair wrapped around her fist.

"Ben, are you okay?" Eliza asked.

He shuddered. "Why do you ask?"

"You've been nodding for at least three minutes now."

He didn't stop. "I've had a lot of coffee. Good thing I'm not breastfeeding." He laughed, then cringed. "You know, now that you mention it, I'm not sure I am okay. I have never raised a baby before or fought vampires. I'm pretty sure I can do one or the other, but I can't do both."

Cassie freed herself from Olive's grip and straightened. She wanted to tell him that she thought he was doing an amazing job, but he wasn't done.

"Sorry. Sorry. I don't know what's wrong with me." His gaze went blank. "Aside from the vampires, getting three hours' sleep, and not showering in a really long time. I mean, what do you do?" His gaze snapped back into focus with renewed intensity. "I can't hear the baby monitor over the water. Do I put her in a bouncy chair in the bathroom? It's all so confusing." He planted his free hand on his hip and looked down at Olive. "Where is your hat? You had a hat."

Cassie picked up the pink knitted beanie from the porch.

"And how do you keep hats on babies?"

"You don't," Cassie stammered. "Hats and socks. It's impossible."

Eliza touched Ben's elbow. "You should come inside. We'll take care of the baby. You can shower, and then we'll talk."

"I couldn't. It wouldn't be fair to you guys or Olive. She is very complex. She has favorite blankets and teething toys, and did you know she can't eat most foods yet?"

"I did not," Eliza answered. "But Cassie probably did. She has kept three of these things alive."

Cassie nodded.

Ben looked down at Olive again. She held up her teething ring to him and all his frantic energy drained away. "Thanks," he said, smiling at her. "But you keep it."

Eliza tugged on his arm. "Come on, big guy. You'll feel better after you get cleaned up."

"I don't remember what it's like to be clean. I think there's baby formula crusted on my back."

She nodded sympathetically. "It happens. Let's go."

Olive smiled as Cassie dug her hands in around her. "Your uncle is losing it. Yes, he is. Yes, he is." She lifted her to her chest. "And he's not the only one."

Olive laid a wet hand on her cheek. For the first time in days, Cassie felt normal. Good, even. Her heart squeezed remembering what it was like when her kids were in diapers. God, it had been hard, but also wonderful. They had needs, and she could meet those needs—most of the time—and that made them happy, which had made her happy. Her kids were so much more complicated these days.

Cassie smiled down at Olive. "Who smells like spaghetti? Do you smell like spaghetti? I'm going to eat you right up." As she dug her mouth into Olive's neck, she saw Eliza looking at her from inside the house. "Coming."

CHAPTER 9

Cassie's living room was not about to win any awards for design, but it was cozy despite the mess, or maybe because of the mess. They only had couches and armchairs that could be spilled on without punishment of death, and they were comfy. The coffee table was beat up too, with its dents and water rings, but it was also the table her babies had hung on to when they were learning to pull themselves up. There were so many memories in this house.

Cassie had sent the kids upstairs after she introduced them to Ben, and they got a look at the baby. She lied again. She told them a public health nurse was coming by to give them information. It landed as pathetically as it felt.

The windows rattled with the wind as Cassie searched for candles. A storm was brewing. Her power often went out, and it was near dusk, so she wanted to be prepared. She then peeked into the twins' old bassinet where Olive was sleeping. When she first brought her into the living room, Cassie had spread out her blanket on the floor as per Ben's instructions and set her down on her front. She had missed her tummy time, and he had read all about the dangers of baby flat head, but after about a minute

THE LATE-NIGHT WITCHES

of pushing herself up, Olive collapsed and closed her eyes. Cassie was tempted to join her, and she would have if she weren't waiting on important vampire information. Once she had carefully transitioned Olive to the bassinet, she dropped down onto the couch. Eliza had gone outside to keep Tommy company before dusk and to bring Ben's sedan over so that he could go from her garage back to his own when they were through. They didn't know if vampires had to be invited into a dwelling or not, but it seemed like a good precautionary measure. Hopefully garages counted. Of course, it would be fine if he and Olive stayed the night. These were insane circumstances, but Cassie was having difficulty managing the thought of him being in her shower—as in difficulty not thinking about it.

"Hey," Eliza said, letting in a gush of cold wind. She had come in the front door this time, making Cassie jump. She smiled slyly. "What were you thinking about?"

"Nothing."

"You're thinking about the professor, aren't you?"

"No."

"It's okay. There is a hot, naked professor in your bathroom. You'd have to be dead not to think about it."

Cassie nodded. She'd heard something like that before.

"Oh crap!" Suddenly Eliza ran over to the window and pushed up the heavy pane. Tommy was on the other side. "Sorry, you probably heard that dead joke."

He shrugged, making his earlobe jiggle in a way that looked loose to Cassie. "You don't think I'm dead, do you?"

"No," she said. "But you've, uh, got something right there." She pointed to the side of his head that had Cassie concerned. When he scratched, the entire ear jiggled as though it might come off. Eliza jerked. "You got it! Stop now. You're good."

"I don't know what I'd do without you." Tommy smiled miserably.

She nodded, giving him sad eyes. "Why don't you go check out the backyard? See if you can find any squirrels."

"Good idea." He leaned toward her with his lips pursed, but when he reached the threshold of the window, his face bounced off an invisible barrier. So, vampires did have to be invited in. Good to know. Tommy sighed and settled for, "You are the best, baby."

"Yeah, you too." She watched him trot off, then collapsed onto the couch.

"Eliza, I don't want him eating my squirrels. I like my squirrels."

"Don't worry. He'll never catch any. Not in his state."

"It's not just the smell?"

Eliza stared blankly into the room. "Three of his toenails came off today. He asked me to glue them back on."

"Did you?"

"How do you say no to that?" She swallowed hard then trembled all over. "Where were we? Oh right, the naked guy upstairs. The one who only has eyes for you." She looked over to the baby asleep in the bassinet. "And you." Olive gently sucked her lower lip in her sleep. "I bet he has all of his toenails."

"You know I'm married, right?"

Eliza squinted. "Are you though?"

"I am not doing this with you. I am well aware of your feelings when it comes to Matt. Not that you ever gave him much of a chance."

"That's because he has always been a selfish toad."

Cassie gave her a warning look.

Eliza sighed dramatically. "Who sired three spectacular children. Who will never ever hear me say a disparaging word about the man who gave them life."

"Good. Now shut up." Cassie swatted her sister on the arm. "Ben's coming."

Solid footsteps came down the stairs. A second later, Ben walked into the room, smoothing down his damp hair. "I can't thank you both enough." He immediately went to the bassinet. "And you got her to sleep." He looked at Cassie. "You have the magic touch."

"She does," Eliza agreed. "In all the ways."

Cassie jumped to her feet. "Let's go to the kitchen, shall we?"

Ben rolled the bassinet from the living room at a turtle's pace, successfully moving Olive without waking her. He then took some folders out from his baby bag. Cassie made them all a cup of tea, and the three sat once more at the kitchen table.

"So," Cassie said, "what did you find out?"

Ben looked at her, too soberly for her liking. While the shower had clearly done him a world of good—all his frenzied energy had been washed away—he seemed deeply serious, even considering the circumstances. He was giving off a strong funeral director vibe. "Well, after talking to my colleagues and reading as much as I could get my hands on, I compared the legend of the Thirteenth Witch with stories about the Deliverer and pulled together the commonalities. Together they form a somewhat coherent story."

Eliza rubbed her hands together excitedly. "I love stories." Low thunder rumbled in the distance. "Tell it."

Ben nodded. "Well, there was—"

"*Once upon a time*, please," Eliza said. "Trust me, stories always have more power when they begin with *once upon a time*."

Ben gave Eliza some serious side-eye before taking a gulp of his tea like it was a shot of whiskey. "Once upon a time there was an incredibly powerful witch."

"Love it already."

Cassie swatted her sister. "Stop interrupting."

Ben straightened the papers lying on the table. "She was a sea witch—I should have mentioned that. Apparently, witches who have a full connection with the sea are quite rare and very powerful. Anyway, she lived in Scotland with her family, helping sailors and fishermen safely navigate temperamental seas. It was said she could steer ships away from hidden rocks and calm stormy waters. It was also said, if angered, she could call the winds and conjure hurricanes."

"Nice," Eliza whispered as the kitchen lights flickered.

"This witch was perfectly content living her life and using her magic to help others until a plea for help came from overseas. A vampire was decimating a tiny island, and no one knew how to stop him."

"The tiny island was PEI, am I right?" Eliza asked.

"You are correct," Ben answered. "It was believed the monster had been sired by the original vampire, but this new monster was even stronger than his maker. In fact, before he had even fully turned—before he even had fangs—it is said he killed his vampire father and drank all his undead blood. This vampire came to be known as the Deliverer of Fear, Sorrow, and Death."

"Knew it," Eliza said, slapping the table. "And gross."

Cassie closed her eyes. "Please stop."

A blast of wind hit the window. The storm was getting closer.

"Anyway, throughout Europe, there were many who had fought the original dad-vampire, including the witch, and while she had not been able to kill him, she was the only one to survive the encounter. Because of this, she felt duty bound to fight this new creature. She had honed her skills since her fight with his sire and knew she might very well be the island's only hope."

Suddenly Ben smiled gently, and his eyes grew distant. "There are lovely accounts of her voyage. Sailors on the boat claimed that while she was aboard the ship, the wind was strong and true, yet the water remained calm, and at night, silver sea creatures followed the boat, glittering in the dark sea." He blinked. "When she arrived on the island's shore, it was assumed she would immediately fight the vampire, but she knew that would be foolhardy. If she truly was the only being powerful enough to face him, she couldn't risk death. She had to be sure of her victory.

"The witch wanted to concoct a spell that could end him, kill him outright, but the fates—the powers that be—whatever you want to call them, wouldn't allow it. She asked for too much. Whenever she tried to infuse her potions with the intent to kill, she found herself unable to channel the necessary power. The fates did not approve of her simply ending his life—they seem to have a bizarre sense of fairness—so she tried another curse. The witch hoped she could put the vampire to sleep forever, but again, it didn't work. The potion wouldn't ignite."

Cassie frowned. "Ignite?"

Ben adjusted his glasses. "If I'm correct, most potions are made up of basic or non-magical ingredients. The witch must infuse the brew with intent and power in order for it to work. If she is successful, the potion glows. That tells her the fates have granted her wishes."

"Cool," Eliza whispered.

"Yes." Ben smiled weakly. "So, the witch persisted in her efforts to devise a potion that could curse the Deliverer. There was a period of trial and error that lasted weeks, and with every day that passed, more lives were taken. She added caveat after caveat until finally she was able to come up with a spelled potion that satisfied the fates, and the terms of her curse were accepted. The Deliverer would sleep for a quarter century but then wake for one month."

Cassie scratched her temple. "Was that month October?"

Ben nodded. "It was. After that month, he would return to his cursed sleep."

"Why a month?" Eliza asked. "So he can feed?"

"No, the month was a necessary condition for the potion to ignite. The fates wanted the Deliverer to have a chance to break the curse. That's where the Thirteenth Witch comes in."

More thunder rumbled and the kitchen light flickered once more.

"I almost forgot about her," Cassie said.

Ben chuckled morosely. "You're probably going to wish you had." He tapped the table with his finger. "First, the moniker—the Thirteenth Witch—is misleading. There is no one witch destined to be the thirteenth . . . at least not until she dies. You see, during one of her many trials, the original witch used her own blood magic to make a potion that would sacrifice her life in order to take the vampire's, but the powers that be denied her will. They demanded a greater offering. The witch realized she couldn't trade her mortal life for an undead and potentially everlasting one, but if she cursed her entire bloodline, the fates might be satisfied. She thought she had found a loophole. Her parents were beyond their childbearing years, and while she'd once had a child, it had died at birth, and she never intended to have another. It meant her family magic would die, as it only passed through their direct line, but the Deliverer had to be stopped. So she tried the spell again with this added element. The curse dictated that the Deliverer could free himself from the imprisonment if every twenty-five years he killed a specific descendant from the original witch's bloodline on Halloween night between sunset and sunrise. The descendant was always the oldest daughter, and she was called the witch of her generation. If he managed to kill thirteen of these descendants, he would be free."

Cassie's heart beat painfully in her chest. "Why thirteen?"

"The number thirteen is associated with tragedy in Norse and Christian traditions, but the important thing is the number has taken on power because so many people believe it is unlucky. Belief is like fuel." Ben shook his head in bewilderment. "Anyway, the witch thought she had found the perfect solution. If there were no more witches in her direct bloodline, she could trap the Deliverer forever. He would still be free for a month every quarter century, but that was a problem for another time. Unfortunately, things didn't turn out as she planned."

"Her baby didn't die," Cassie whispered.

"No, she did not." A loud blast of thunder boomed, rattling the windowpanes. "The details are hazy, but apparently the witch had gone into labor unexpectedly in a forest but was lucky enough to make it to an old crone's—pardon the archaic language—cottage. During the birth, the witch fainted, and when she woke, the crone convinced her the baby was dead. In actuality, she had already whisked the infant off to the church to be saved from her mother's wickedness."

"So, the Deliverer had his chance," Cassie said.

Ben shook his head. "The fates wouldn't have it any other way."

"These witches of their generations," Eliza said, "are they the only ones who can kill the Deliverer?"

"I think anyone theoretically can, but by all accounts, only an extremely powerful witch has a shot."

Cassie swallowed hard. "Ben, these descendants—"

A knock at the front door of the house made them all jump... and Cassie may have screamed just a little. Fortunately, Olive slept on.

"Are you guys expecting someone?" Ben asked quietly, resting a hand on the bassinet.

"No," Cassie whispered.

"Oh shit." Eliza pushed her chair back. "I forgot I ordered dinner."

Cassie gripped her sister's wrist. "You invited someone to my house?"

"I'm not going to invite them in." Eliza pulled away and got to her feet. "We need to eat! But wait until I get back to finish the story." She smiled. "Maybe use the time to get to know each other." She walked away, saying, "I'm going to use your credit card, okay?"

Cassie threw her hands up, then turned back to Ben. "These descendants... I'm afraid to ask."

Ben gripped his pencil. "Maybe we should wait until Eliza gets back."

"Please, just tell me. I think I already know."

He nodded. "Well, from what I could find—"

Cassie held up a finger. She could hear her sister saying, "You can leave it on the porch." Silence followed. "Then just toss me the machine." Eliza sounded frustrated. She was obviously having trouble paying without breaking the barrier of the door. If she so much as thought about inviting the delivery guy in...

"I am not throwing you the machine," a man said loudly. "It's expensive. You're going to get me fired."

"Well, I don't have cash."

"There's money in my wallet!" Cassie shouted. "It's in my coat pocket. Just throw some out." She thought she heard the carrier mutter something about all the weirdos being hungry tonight. "Sorry." Cassie turned back to Ben as lightning flashed outside. "You were about to say?"

The funeral director vibe was back. "Are you sure you don't want to wait?"

"Please, you're really freaking me out. Just say it."

"I can't find your wallet!" Eliza shouted.

"The black peacoat!"

Ben reached out his hand, looking like he might take hers, but then curled his fingers into a fist. "The witch who started the curse was your many-times-over great-grandmother." Cassie's fingernails scraped against the table as though she were holding on for dear life.

"Cassie, can you come here a sec?" Eliza shouted.

"Oh my God! It's there!" Why could no one find anything in this house but her? "Look again!" Cassie's throat tightened as thunder rolled out in a sheet over the house. "How many witch descendants has he killed so far?"

"I know at least one of your ancestors survived his awakening." He didn't meet her eye. "But that meant the curse—or the title of 'witch of her generation'—was simply passed on to the next generation."

"Ben..."

He winced. "I can't be a hundred percent certain, but I think he's killed twelve."

Dorcas. Is that why she had been so freaked out at the farmer's market? She had been in such a hurry to get her to leave. She was the eldest sister in her generation. The vampire must be coming for her, and she didn't want Cassie to be in the line of fire. Or fang. Plus, she had said she'd take care of it. So, did that really mean Dorcas was a . . . ? "My aunt . . ."

He nodded. "I can see why you'd think she'd be the one." He dropped his eyes to the table and grabbed his pencil again, almost like it was a stake. "But—"

"Um, Cass? You need to come here. He wants to talk to you," Eliza called out.

Cassie rose to her feet, still looking at Ben. She shuffled back toward the living room. "Hang on, okay?"

Eliza stood to the side of the open door, her back pressed against the wall. Standing on the porch was a delivery man wearing a red cap with a matching striped vest. Cassie recognized the uniform. They were having sushi tonight. "What's going on?"

Her sister's eyes bulged. "He says he has a message for you."

A deafening clap of thunder shook the house and the lights snapped out. Cassie's hands suddenly burned as she peered through the darkness. She could only see the silhouette of the man until lightning cracked in a series of flashes. In each burst of light, the man's mouth stretched, opening wider, to reveal gleaming white fangs. "The Deliverer of Fear, Sorrow, and Death has a message for you."

Cassie shook her head in shock. But it wasn't just at the vampire. Someone else was creeping up the stairs of her porch. The vampire smiled, completely unaware of the dark figure rising from the shadows behind him.

"The end of the curse is nigh. The Thirteenth Witch will—"

A curved blade sliced into the vampire's neck, releasing an explosive cloud of sticky dust before emerging on the other side. For a horrifying second, time froze, then the head tipped over and dropped to the porch with a thump. It rolled side to side before settling, the eyes landing on Cassie. She opened her mouth to scream, but only a small whine escaped.

The body dropped a second later, revealing the hooded figure with the scythe looming in the darkness.

"What the . . . ?" Eliza whispered.

"Oh my God." Ben came to Cassie's side. "What is going on?"

"Eliza!" she snapped. "Go check on the kids!" Her sister reacted without question, sprinting for the stairs.

The dark figure pulled back her hood.

"It's you," Cassie whispered. "You're the witch of her generation. You're the one the Deliverer wants to be his Thirteenth Witch."

Her aunt's eyes softened with heartbreak. "Oh Polliwog, twenty-five years ago, yes, but my time has passed."

Ben's hand touched her shoulder. She looked up to meet his gaze.

"It's you, Cassie. You're the one the Deliverer wants dead."

CHAPTER 10

Cassie couldn't see or hear anything. She was floating in an abyss. A nice, warm abyss. She liked it. In fact, she wanted to stay forever. Or maybe she had always been there. It was hard to tell. Nothing ever happened in the abyss. She could just float, float, float . . .

A high-pitched ringing swelled in her ears, breaking through her solitude, and a tunnel came into view, her sister standing at the other end. *No.No.No.* She tried to swim in the other direction, but Eliza grabbed her shoulders and pulled her through. "Cassie!" she snapped, shaking her. "Say something!"

"Do I have vampire on me?"

Her sister's hands dropped from her shoulders, and the world stopped shaking. "Phew. I thought we lost you there for a second." The lights flickered back on as a heavy sheet of rain pounded the house.

"The kids?"

"They're fine."

Cassie raised a shaky hand to her cheek.

"Let me do that." Eliza licked her thumb. She smeared it across Cassie's cheek, then her chin, then her forehead. She almost licked her thumb again but thought better of it, opting instead to smooth down Cassie's hair. "There. You're perfect. So pretty." She smiled. "But you might want to wash your hair later."

Cassie nodded absently as Ben picked up the food bags from the porch, keeping a careful eye on Dorcas. And the head. Suddenly a cacophony of footfalls tumbled down the stairs.

Eliza's eyes widened. "Kids!"

Cassie stiffened as all three of her children, pushing against one another, broke into the room.

"Food!" Sly shouted.

"I tried to stop them," Sadie said.

Eliza stepped forward, blocking their field of vision. "I told you to wait." She chuckled awkwardly. "But yes, the food is here. Yay!" She shook her fists in the air with unnatural enthusiasm, like a children's performer on public access television. Cassie almost laughed. Her sister would be a terrible children's performer. She'd teach them all the bad words. Eliza glanced over to Dorcas. "But I maybe didn't order enough."

Eddie hit her with a hug. "Order more!"

She patted him on the head. "I think deliveries are done for the night."

The boys grabbed the bags from Ben, but Sadie snatched them away. "The food is for everyone." She looked at Cassie, concern creased in her brow. "Mom? Are you okay?"

"Uh-huh." She wanted to smile, but she must have left her smile back in the abyss.

"Who's that?"

Cassie was confused. Who was who? Reality slammed back into her head. *Dorcas!* Dorcas was on the porch with a scythe! And a dead vampire! She whirled around. The vampire's body was gone. The head too. It took everything in her not to vomit with relief. Because that was a thing in her life now. And Dorcas was no longer holding any weapons, which was good, but she did have her hands clutched to her chest and there were happy tears in her eyes. She stepped forward. "Oh Sadie! I've waited so—"

Cassie blocked her path, and Dorcas's face dropped in defeat. "She's the public health nurse I was telling you about, so can you guys go back upstairs? Take all the food if you want."

"What?" Eliza snapped while the boys hissed a *yes* in unison. Sadie tightened her grip on the bags, searching her mom's face.

"Everything is fine. I'll explain later."

The boys took off. Sadie reluctantly followed, looking back at them until she was out of the room.

"Did you have to let them take all the food?" Eliza asked.

"How are you still hungry, after . . . ?" Cassie flapped a hand at the door.

"Don't judge me. Everyone reacts to stress differently." She then peeked around the door. "Should we invite the vampire slayer in?"

"She's not a vampire slayer," Cassie said weakly. "She's—"

"I'm your aunt!" Dorcas shouted. Cassie couldn't hold her back this time. She strode inside and wrapped Eliza up in her arms. "I can't tell you how I've longed for this day."

"I, um, okay," Eliza replied, patting her back. "I think I may have seen you around town before."

"Oh yes, I like to watch you."

Cassie shuffled to the door and pushed it closed. Dorcas was in her house. Hugging her sister. The sister she had spent most of her life trying to protect from her worst impulses, all of which were embodied in Dorcas. But now it seemed like all their impulses came from a good place, or at least a real one. It was Cassie who was wrong about everything, like vampires.

And now she was the witch of her generation?

"Look at you! You're so beautiful! Just like your mother." Dorcas pushed Eliza back by the shoulders to get a better look. "And all of your hair is in the right spots!"

"I have always thought so," Eliza said seriously. "Thank you for noticing."

They were two peas in a pod. Eliza was going to kill her. Absolutely kill her when Cassie told her all the things she never believed were true.

"And who is this handsome man?" Dorcas asked, stepping around Eliza, headed for Ben. "Cassie, did you finally get rid of that absentee husband of yours?"

"What? No, this is Ben. He's a professor."

"I'm a friend." A blush crept up his neck. "And neighbor."

"And is this your baby?" She glided into the kitchen to peek in the bassinet.

"She's my niece."

Dorcas straightened and smiled back at him. "Perfection is what she is. You might want to give her a bath though. Vampires love babies, and she smells deliciously appetizing."

The blush along with all the rest of the blood drained from Ben's face. "I thought garlic repelled vampires."

She walked up to him and touched the side of his face. "My dear man, this is why we don't let humans fight the vampires." She tapped his cheek then walked on.

"Humans?" Eliza cleared her throat. "Someone is going to have to catch me—" She screamed as a bang came from the window behind her. "Tommy!" She clutched her chest then muttered, "I have to put a bell on him."

"Eliza, I need your help."

Cassie cringed. He looked even worse wet. His dark hair was plastered to his skull in uneven chunks and his skin was waxy.

"What's wrong?"

He turned his head. "I think my ear is falling off. I need you to glue it back on."

Cassie swallowed hard. He wasn't wrong. It was dangling precariously now.

Dorcas came up to Eliza and whispered, "Who is this vampire?"

"He's my . . . it's complicated."

Tommy's eyes widened. "Complicated? Is it because of the ear?"

Eliza shrugged lightly. "I mean, it's not not because of the ear."

"Would you like me to kill him?" Dorcas asked.

Tommy yipped and dropped from view. Cassie could feel the pull of the void once again.

"Wait!" Eliza rushed over to the window. "Come back. It's fine. We're fine. We'll figure it out." She sighed and sat on the windowsill.

"Cassie," Ben said gently, "are you okay? I mean, I know you're not okay, but do you want to talk about what we were talking about before the food arrived?"

"We must discuss everything," Dorcas said. "There isn't a moment to lose."

Cassie welcomed the buzzing noise once again humming in her ears. It needed to be louder though. She could still hear them.

"Did you guys keep going after I left?" Eliza asked.

"I . . ." Suddenly Cassie's mind felt like it was filled with bubbles and the world was tilting. She slid a foot to the side to steady herself. Everyone rushed toward her at once. "No!" she shouted. "I need a minute."

They all froze in some weird pantomime of concern.

THE LATE-NIGHT WITCHES

"Actually, I need everyone to leave."

Nobody said anything, but nobody moved either. That was a problem. Because if they didn't all leave, now, she would start screaming. And she couldn't do that. Her kids were upstairs eating California rolls.

"Cassie?"

Eliza's brows tilted together, making her eyes appear even larger. She looked like a little girl again. A scared little girl. It wasn't a side her sister revealed often, but when she did, it went right for Cassie's heart. "It's fine. You didn't miss anything." She noted Ben and Dorcas exchanging looks. "It's just the decapitation getting to me. You know I'm slow when it comes to accepting... decapitations."

Eliza's shoulders dropped.

"Let's postpone this meeting, okay? We'll talk about everything later."

"Cassandra," Dorcas said, sounding way too motherly. "Later when?"

A panicked scream tore through the open window. "My pinky finger! Where's my pinky?"

Eliza closed her eyes.

"You go," Cassie said, pulling her sister in for a hug, "before he loses another body part. I'm fine. Everything's fine."

"Are you sure?"

"One hundred percent. We'll talk later."

"I'll text you." Eliza hurried to the kitchen to get her jacket. "I'll text you too, Ben! We need answers."

As she left, Dorcas stepped forward. "I should go with her. There may be more vampires lurking." She snapped her fingers at Ben. "Tall man, you and your delicious baby should come with us. The vampires will smell her from miles away."

"Oh my . . . thanks." He patted himself over. It didn't look like he knew what he was trying to find. Babies did come with a lot of accessories though. He then looked up at Cassie. "I'm sorry about the curse. I didn't want to tell you this way."

"Why is it me? How can you be sure?"

"You're the oldest daughter of your generation. It's always the oldest of the current generation until the Deliverer returns to his sleep. Then the curse moves to the next generation," Dorcas said. "But fear not, you will never become the thirteenth Beckett witch to die. I won't allow it." Her voice had darkened to a dangerous degree and her eyes seemed to glint with orange light. "I will kill the Deliverer. This All Hallows' Eve will be his last." She smiled at Ben. "Shall we?"

Ben stared wide-eyed at Dorcas before dragging his gaze back to Cassie. "Um, call me anytime," he said, shuffling toward the kitchen. "If you want more information, I mean."

Dorcas opened the door and collected her scythe. "You and the children should come with us. We need to discuss what has happened, and what will happen. You'll be safer at Sea House."

Sea House.

The name pulled at her heart . . . but *now* her aunt wanted her there? Cassie laughed in disbelief.

"I know I have a lot to explain."

"Not now you don't." Cassie folded her arms over her chest. "Please leave."

Dorcas nodded. "Think about what I have said. Come to me when you're ready." She paused, weighing her words. "He won't let you hide from this. Not when he's so close." She walked past Cassie, the hem of her cloak brushing her leg. "Stay inside sunset to sunrise. Trust no one."

Cassie followed them out the kitchen door. Dorcas walked to a beat-up Jeep parked on the road while Ben navigated the covered walkway to the garage. The rain had eased to a soft patter. She walked around the porch to the front as they drove caravan-style down the street to Ben's house, Eliza in tow. As soon as all three vehicles arrived, her sister's car jerked in reverse and whined back down the street. She stopped halfway and put down her window.

"Tommy! Did you find your finger?"

A dark figure, one hand pressed to the side of his head, pulled free of the shadows. "False alarm. It was there the whole time! And I found my boots! They were in the hedge. So weird." He loped over to the passenger side and dove in. The car jerked forward again.

Cassie hugged herself against the cold. Even though everyone was gone, she could still hear voices.

It's you, Cassie . . .

He won't let you hide from this.

The Thirteenth Witch will die.

This could not be her life. She was not a witch. She was a mom who worked part-time at a home improvement store. She did things like coach kids' soccer teams, sew costumes for school plays, volunteer to take scouts on camping trips. Actually, she did none of those things. She felt really guilty about it though. But the point was, it was what she should be doing. Not fighting off legendary vampires who wanted her dead.

As the thoughts tumbled through her mind like clothes in her half-dead dryer, Cassie's gaze landed on the jack-o'-lantern glowing darkly on her porch. Someone had turned it so that it was facing the house again. She couldn't take it anymore. She was getting rid of it. She bent to lift it, gripping its cool sides, but then stopped, inhaling deeply. Pumpkin. Of course the jack-o'-lantern smelled like pumpkin, but this one smelled ...

Burned.

Cassie peered inside the pumpkin's head.

Black. Every fibrous inch was charred black. Not a candle in sight.

I'm going to light you up.

Cassie backed into the house. She slammed the door and collapsed against it. A second later her phone binged, nearly dropping her to her knees.

She pulled it out, her hand shaking. Matt.

Sorry I missed you again! Hope you had a great day!

CHAPTER 11

The next morning Cassie called the kids' schools to report them absent and went to work.

Not to actually work, but to shop. She didn't like leaving the kids alone or having to tell Sadie to keep the boys inside again, but it was a necessary evil, among all the new evils in Cassie's life.

In the bright light of day, all Ben's and Dorcas's talk about her being some generationally cursed witch seemed . . . well, it seemed ridiculous. There had to be some kind of mistake. She would know if she were a witch. And there were reasonable explanations for everything, even the pumpkin. Teenagers probably did that. Instead of smashing pumpkins, they were burning people's jack-o'-lanterns for sport. Made sense. And even if, in the unlikeliest of scenarios, she was a descendant of some supposed über-powerful witch, that didn't mean she had to fight vampires. She'd abdicate, if that was the right word, and hide in her house until she and her children were safe. That's why she needed to shop. She didn't have any money to go shopping, but she could put it on the card, and instead of the new pair of jeans Sadie wanted for Christmas, hopefully she'd be okay with a flamethrower. The store didn't have any in stock, but she could order one.

Towers of building supplies loomed over Cassie as she rolled down the aisle, pushing one cart in front, dragging another behind. She grabbed everything she thought might be useful. Hunting knives. A fire extinguisher to go with the flamethrower. Sunlamps! Most of them were too big and bulky to be useful, but maybe she could put them on the porch. Or strap one onto a backpack? It was worth a shot. And what about hedge clippers? Could they come in handy? It was hard to say, but she was leaving with all of it.

Cassie was mulling the pros and cons of a circular saw blade when a hand landed on her shoulder. The spiked metal disk clattered to the floor an inch away from her toe.

"Sorry!" Patty said. "I did it again."

"No, it's my fault. Another late night." Cassie dropped to retrieve the blade, looking up to meet Patty's gaze. "It's nice to see you . . . not avoiding me."

Her coworker clutched her hands together, her fingers fumbling over one another. Cassie's righteousness crumbled. "Don't worry. I get it." And she did. She wanted to stay as far away from this situation as possible, and she was the witch of her generation. *Maybe.*

"It looks like you talked to Dorcas," Patty said sheepishly. "I'm so sorry. I thought you already knew everything."

"How do *you* know?"

"Well, I don't. Not usually. Everything starts to come back right around the time *he* wakes up, but only for people from the older families."

"How does that work?"

"Nobody knows. It's like some collective amnesia falls over the island."

Must be one of those caveats to the curse demanded by the fates.

"But I didn't think it applied to you."

Cassie frowned. "So, you remember the last time the Deliverer woke up and Dorcas fought him?"

"I do," Patty said with a nod. "But not the details. I never saw him. And I'm not sure how much more I should say. I have my grandbabies to think about. *He* has his ways of targeting people who don't stay out of his business, but . . ." She shook her head. "I was born on this island, so were my parents, grandparents, great-grandparents, and beyond. I may not be able to"—she looked side to side, then whispered—"fight. But if you want weapons, I know the person you need to see."

Cassie looked over her carts. She hadn't thought of any of her selections as weapons per se—more like tools for self-defense—but that's what they were. And when she thought of them that way, she couldn't help but wonder if there were better options out there. Images of Joanne and the delivery guy—and their fangs—chomped through her mind. Yes, she needed weapons. Serious weapons.

"I'll tell you how to get there. If you still want all this stuff afterward, it will be here waiting for you." She squeezed her arm. "You can do this, Cassie. You were born to do this." Patty led her over to an unused checkout station. She grabbed a notepad and scribbled out directions. "Now, this is important." She pointed the tip of her pen. "When you turn in the drive, you'll be surrounded by trees. Just before you get to the clearing, honk the horn a couple of times. Hank is not the type of guy you want to sneak up on. Tell him who you are and that I sent you."

"Okay," Cassie said weakly. "Thank you."

"No, thank you. This island owes you and your family

so much." Patty wrapped her up in a big hug. She smelled like cookies.

☾

The wind snatched at the directions in Cassie's grip as she stepped out of the store. She shoved the paper deep in her pocket and pulled her jacket tight to her throat. The skies were turbulent from the storm the day before. Brilliant patches of sunlight shifted in and out with shadows from fast-moving clouds, and her hair whipped wildly around her. Which was probably why she didn't see her sister sitting in the passenger seat when she climbed into the van.

"Good morning."

Cassie screamed. "Are you trying to kill me?"

"No, I think the vampires have got that covered." Eliza chuckled.

"What are you doing in my van?"

"Drinking coffee. Waiting for you."

Cassie slumped against her seat. How nice. Once again, her sister seemed to be handling recent horrifying events much better than she was. Cassie slid her eyes over to Eliza's Tim Hortons cup. "Did you get one for me?"

Eliza wrinkled her nose. "I thought you would have had yours already."

Cassie slid her gaze back out the windshield.

"And maybe I would have thought of it if you'd answered any of my texts."

She had her there. Cassie had been avoiding all contact with her sister. Not purposefully exactly. She needed time to process this whole Thirteenth Witch business. She had many emotions that were threatening to erupt, and if Eliza knew what was going on, her emotions would erupt too. All over the place. She wasn't ready for that. "I'm sorry. I passed out after everyone left. It must have been the adrenaline."

"I get it," Eliza said. "And this morning?"

"I came to the store to pick up a flamethrower, but we're out of stock."

"Seriously?"

"I don't know." Cassie covered her face with her hands.

"Ben is not answering my texts either. I don't suppose you know anything about that?"

"He's probably busy," Cassie suggested with what she hoped was a nonchalant shrug. "He's got a baby."

Eliza inhaled deeply. "Right. So, we should probably talk about our aunt Dorcas, the vampire slayer."

Vampire slayer among other things.

"But I'm guessing you don't want to do that right now."

"Nope." Or was it *yup*?

"Okay, then." Eliza took a sip of her coffee. It smelled really good. "Are you headed home?"

She wished. "Patty gave me a tip on where I could get some real weapons to protect us against . . . the Deliverer." Some of the manic laughter she had been holding back escaped.

Eliza pulled on her seat belt. "What are we waiting for? Let's go."

Cassie was about to argue, but, truthfully, she didn't want to go alone. She turned the key in the ignition.

"And I've been thinking we should call the Deliverer something else. How do you feel about Del? It takes some of the power away, don't you think?"

Why not?

☾

The winds rocked the van, forcing Cassie to keep a tight grip on the steering wheel.

The directions weren't exactly straightforward, and the house, if that's what they were headed for, did not turn up on any GPS. There were many dirt roads, and shortcuts, a couple *turn right*s at the purple house—even though there was no longer any purple house—but, thankfully, having grown up on the island, she was able to follow along. Mostly. After a couple missed turns, they found their way to the drive Patty had described. It was hard to miss given the six *No Trespassing* signs nailed to the trees on either side.

The winding dirt drive, tunneling through dense brush on either side, forced Cassie to slow the van to a walking pace. Thin branches scraped the sides, releasing eerie high-pitched shrieks. Eventually she caught a glimpse of a faded red barn through the dense forest. "I think the opening is up ahead."

Eliza wrapped her arms around her knees, forming a tight ball. "Good, because there could be a hundred vampires hidden in these woods looking at us right now."

"What is wrong with you? Why would you say that?!" The van broke through the clearing. "Besides, it's daytime." The words had barely left Cassie's mouth when movement caught her eye. In the first half second of awareness she thought it was a bird, but it was traveling way too fast.

It wasn't until it struck the tree outside Cassie's window that she realized what it was. She gawped at the thick black arrow reverberating in the bark, then whipped her gaze back to her sister. "I was supposed to honk the horn."

Eliza blinked. "Beep. Beep."

CHAPTER 12

The property consisted of two buildings. One, the faded red barn Cassie had seen through the trees, and the other, a makeshift shed with a pencil chimney sticking out the top. A man stood in the doorway.

Cassie lowered the driver's side window, sinking down in the seat. "Um, hi? My name is Cassie Beckett. This is my sister, Eliza. Patty sent us."

The man had a scruffy gray beard that reached his collarbone, and he wore a steel-colored jumpsuit with a John Deere cap. Both had seen better days. He wasn't bad-looking. He might even be considered handsome by some in a rugged, older guy kind of way—but the arrow he had shot at Cassie had taken some of the shine off. He stomped toward them in heavy rubber boots before waving them down the drive. It was much colder in the forest, and the frosty air coming through the window bit at Cassie's cheeks. She edged the van forward a few feet before shutting the engine off.

"I was wondering when you girls would show." The man's words puffed out his mouth in icy clouds. "Where's Dorcas?"

Eliza raised her brow as she got out of the van. "At home, maybe?"

"Still mad, huh?" He tipped his chin up and scratched his hairy neck. "Name's Hank. Follow me." He clomped away, his boots splashing through mud puddles the size of small ponds.

"Are we sure about this?" Eliza whispered. "I think that might be a murder barn."

Cassie jabbed her elbow into her sister's ribs even though it totally did look like a murder barn.

A cloud blocked the sun as they entered the worn outbuilding, darkening its interior. Cassie squinted to make out the dim shapes. The wood beam structure was two stories with a loft running along the far end. It reeked of old dust and hay mixed with oil and varnish. It wasn't the appearance or smell that was remarkable though. It was the tables. Four rows of them ran the length of the barn, every inch covered with weapons. Or mostly weapons. Cassie couldn't tell what some of the contraptions were.

"Isn't she beautiful?" Hank threw his arms wide. "It has taken me forty years to build this collection. This side is for sale." He stuck out his arm toward the middle aisle, then swung it to the left. "The other is for show."

Eliza shuffled toward the first of the for-sale tables. "Is this a mace?" she asked, running her fingers down a wood handle attached to a chain with a ball covered in spikes at its end.

Hank considered the question. "*Flail* might be more accurate."

She lifted it off the table. It immediately smashed to the floor, its spikes piercing the wooden planks. Her fingertips shot to her mouth. "Sorry."

"Heavy, isn't it?" He chuckled. "Gets everybody the first time."

Eliza wandered over to the next aisle while Cassie picked up the flail and put it back on the table. It *was* heavy.

"And is that a guillotine?"

"Stay away from that one," Hank called out. "She's touchy."

Eliza's eyes widened with ghoulish pleasure.

Cassie walked by her sister, surveying the collection. There were lots of swords, and battle-axes, clubs, and hammers, all appearing as heavy as the flail. "Where did you get all of these? And more importantly who do you sell them to?"

Hank shrugged. "I know a few artisans, and the bulk of my clientele is made up mainly of fantasy types. Gamers. LARPs. You know the kind. Never seen a battle that wasn't in their mama's basement, but real active imaginations."

Eliza, looking delighted, mouthed, *Mainly?*

Cassie frowned sternly. This situation was not delightful. Not even a little bit delightful. "These are"—she struggled to find the right word—"delightful." *Frick.* "But they seem heavy."

"Do you have a woman's section?" Eliza inquired.

Before Hank could answer, Cassie grabbed her sister's arm and pulled her farther back into the barn. "Can you give us a moment?"

Hank raised a hand. "Take your time."

"I don't think there's anything here we can really use, do you?" Cassie searched her sister's face for agreement. "On the one hand I want to be safe. On the other, these weapons seem better fit to storm a castle." She looked down at a battle-ax with an intricate design etched into the blade. "I mean, are we really going to be able to decapitate a master vampire?"

"We won't know until we try."

"No! That does not apply here. All these weapons are for

close-contact fighting. I have no intention of getting up close. And you shouldn't either."

"I hear you. I don't want to hear you, but I do." Eliza jerked her chin back at Hank. "But we've come all this way, and I feel rude not buying anything."

Cassie did too. It felt like they had been tricked into attending some Tupperware-candle-lingerie-medieval-warfare party where you didn't technically have to buy anything, but actually you kind of did.

"How's it going, ladies?" Hank called out.

"These are beautiful, really." Cassie looked down at a giant scimitar. "But I'm not sure either of us can learn the necessary skills required for these weapons in time." She hadn't meant to say *in time*. It had just come out. "For our big hunting expedition."

Eliza punched Cassie on the arm. "Big-time Bambi killer, right here."

"Hunting expedition, huh?" Hank chuckled ominously. "I guess that's one way of looking at it. Let's stop pussyfooting around. I don't forget the way the rest of the islanders do, thanks to your aunt." He walked past them into the gloom at the back of the barn. Eliza shot Cassie a confused look, but she walked away pretending not to notice. When Hank reached the last table running against the back wall, he held out a hand. "What about these?"

"Whoa," Eliza whispered.

Crossbows.

"This here is what you need," Hank said, picking one up. "The prod and tiller design means you don't have to be full of muscles to get force. And because of the locking mechanism," he said, sliding something back, "you can handle stronger draw weight and hold it for longer. More time to aim. Overall, this beauty will give you great precision with no training required. It's a point-and-shoot." He walked over to some stacked pyramids of what looked like modified arrows. "Here you have your bolts. They come in different sizes and can be heavier than arrows. You can also fit them with different heads. Living on the island, I've modified some into . . ." He reached behind the stack, grabbing something. When it came into view, Cassie spoke before the thought reached her consciousness.

"Stakes."

He smiled and loaded it into the crossbow.

"Hank," Eliza said, planting her hands on her hips. "I didn't understand about eighty percent of what you said, but it sounded beautiful." She reached for the weapon. "Let me hold that."

Hank's brow creased as he passed it to her. "Now you be careful. It's loaded."

"Nice and light," she said, bouncing it in the air. Hank reached to take it back, but she turned away. She tossed her hair over her shoulder and lifted the weapon to her sight line, digging the butt into the crevice by her collarbone. "This could definitely work." Suddenly the crossbow snapped, shooting the stake toward the wall of the barn. In less than a second, it shattered the wood planks, leaving a hole five times the size of the stake.

"I told you to be careful, girl!"

Eliza looked over her shoulder. "We'll take it."

☾

The clouds vanished as they left Hank's place. Eliza was jubilant when they first headed out, but her mood shifted to something more contemplative the longer they drove. Eventually she said, "So, you ready to talk?"

Cassie sighed.

"Look. I get it. I can see why you wanted to keep Dorcas at a distance. Hey, I did too, and that was before I actually met her. I mean, she is . . . wow. But now that we've established that she is more than just eccentric, I think we could use her help. She might know a way I can save Tommy."

Cassie kept her eyes on the road.

"I know you want to stay out of this, but a vampire came to your house."

"You don't think I know that?"

Eliza grumbled with frustration. "What is going on? Why are you acting so weird? What did Ben tell you last night before things went all vampire-y?"

"Nothing. It was confusing. The legend says that the Deliv— Del can be free of his twenty-five-year curse if he kills some witch. She would be the Thirteenth Witch we've been hearing so much about, because Ben seems to think he's already killed twelve others." Cassie was starting to hate herself for continually lying to her sister, but she also couldn't seem to stop.

"Yeah, I was there for most of that," Eliza said before jolting up in her seat. "Wait . . . is it Dorcas? Does that mean . . . ?"

Wow, Eliza got there quick and with less information than she had. "I asked the same thing, but no, she's not." Not entirely a lie.

"Cass, I get that you are having a difficult time accepting all that has happened, and that's fine." Eliza looked out the window. "I also appreciate that Tommy is not your problem."

Except he was her problem because he was Eliza's problem. And Eliza's problems were her problems.

"But I need answers," she said. "So, tomorrow morning, first thing, I am going to Sea House."

Cassie shot up in her seat, gripping the steering wheel. "No, you are not."

"Look, I love you. I respect you. I appreciate the occasional use of your credit card. But you can't stop me. I am an adult. I can make my own decisions."

Cassie huffed a laugh. "Yeah, you've made some great ones lately." Regret came as soon as the words left her mouth. "I'm sorry. I—"

"No, no," Eliza said with forced calm. "Don't tell me you didn't mean it when we both know that you did."

This day. And yesterday. And the day before that. Cassie was really tired of all these days. "What do you want from me, Eliza?"

"I want you to stop treating me like a child and snap out of this denial that you're in. I also want you to come with me to Sea House."

Tension gripped the muscles in Cassie's neck. "Listen. All I do is try to think about how to keep everyone safe, including you. But going back to Sea House, bringing everyone closer to whatever this is, is not the answer. I don't trust Dorcas. I can't. So, we are going to stay in my house, with the kids, and our crossbow, and wait until Halloween is over. Maybe Tommy will be fine when Del is in vampire dreamland." She didn't want to imagine what that was like.

"Cassie . . ."

"I am not going back to that house. Neither are you." And Cassie wasn't in *complete* denial. The whole time she had been telling herself she couldn't be the witch of her generation, another part of her consciousness had been working on what to do if she was. Worse yet, she had this horrible feeling that she was forgetting something. And it wasn't something like figuring out ways to defend her family from, say, being smoked out of the house by exploding gas lines or grenades thrown by vampires. Those scenarios had been constantly running through her head. It was something else. She needed more time! Why was everything coming at her so fast? She couldn't process any of it, let alone make good decisions.

"Well, I am going to Sea House, and you can't stop me."

"You know what?" Cassie sniffed sharply. "Fine."

"Fine?"

"Yup.

"Well, I guess that settles it." Eliza crossed her arms over her chest. "I'll tell you what I find out."

☾

Cassie dropped Eliza off at the Grub, then headed home. She could tell her sister was confused that she wasn't more upset, but what Eliza didn't know was that there was no way she was going to make it to Sea House, and Cassie didn't have to do a thing. Regardless, it was hard when children grew up, even if the child was your sister. For a long time after Eliza had moved out, Cassie found it difficult to relax when she didn't know where she was. And now she had three other children. It was easier when Matt was around. She knew he loved the kids.

Maybe just not her.

Whoa. Where had that come from? She pushed the thought away. It was the vampires. And witches. She had much better control of her thoughts when she lived in a world without vampires and witches. Plus, seeing Dorcas had stirred up feelings that Cassie preferred to keep at the bottom of her psyche's ocean. And maybe memories too.

Cassie pulled the van into the drive and took the key from

the ignition. She sat with her hand on the wheel, watching a red leaf float down to her windshield. Cassie didn't have any real memories of Sea House, and yet she had dreamed a lot about it over the years. They were incredible dreams but also impossible, made-up ones. Or so she had thought. There was one in particular that had been gnawing at her. Not because it was bad, but because it was wonderful. Cassie closed her eyes.

In it, she was on the beach, and it was a brilliant day. The sun was high, the sea sparkled, and she had been sitting in her mother's lap on a blanket laid over the brick-colored sand. She couldn't have been more than four or five.

Cassie could still hear her mother's voice. *Hold out your hand.* Her mother pinched some of the red grit between her fingers and dropped it in Cassie's palm. The warmth sent shivers up her arms. Her mother placed her palm underneath hers, keeping it steady. *Do you remember the merry-go-round we went on at the fair? Look at that sand and remember the merry-go-round. Remember everything about the fair.*

Cassie remembered the smell of caramel apples and popcorn and the look of the beautiful white horse she had ridden. She remembered the cool, smooth feeling of the pole gripped in her hands and the gentle rise and fall as the carousel picked up speed.

That's it, Cassie.

She didn't know what she was doing, but she could feel her mother's excitement building.

Round and round and round we go. Say it with me. Round and round and round we go.

Suddenly her palm tickled, and the sand twirled in a tight circle. Her entire being filled with wonder watching that ring of sand spin around her palm. And the pride she felt when her mother said, *Well done, my girl. Well done* . . . it had been everything.

Cassie eyed Eliza's used coffee cup in the holder of the console. She lifted it and found crumbs underneath, just as she knew there would be. Mostly from fishy crackers if she had to guess. She pinched a solid amount and dropped it in her palm. She held her hand out in front of her, then took a slow, deep breath. "Round and round and round we go." Nothing happened. She closed her eyes, trying to remember the merry-go-round, and said the words again in her mind. She peeked an eye open. Still nothing. Maybe it wasn't the merry-go-round she needed to remember. Maybe it was that day on the beach. She closed her eyes again. She could hear waves, and the caw of seagulls. She could feel the warmth of her mother's arms. "Round and round and round we go."

A sharp smack hit the window.

Cassie screamed and threw the crumbs in the air.

Eddie had his hands pressed against the glass. His mouth strained open as he sucked in a big gulp of air.

"Don't you do it!"

He blew a giant blowfish on her window.

Cassie stared at the grimy mark he left behind. "You little stinker!" She jumped out of the van. "And why are you outside?" She tackled him into a pile of leaves, knowing that blowfish mark would probably be on the van window until spring.

Hopefully she'd be alive to see it.

CHAPTER 13

Evening fell.

The rest of the day had gone as expected. Sadie stayed in her room while Cassie and the boys made popcorn, watched movies, and played Monopoly, which, of course, ended with the board being flipped. Trying to be present for the kids while her brain was overflowing with terrifying thoughts was one of the hardest things Cassie had ever done. She didn't think the boys noticed, but Sadie, she was always watching—when she actually came out of her room—always in deep thought behind those big sea-green eyes.

When Cassie got into bed, she knew she wouldn't be able to sleep. She needed to talk to someone who wasn't her sister. She tried to video-chat with Matt but couldn't get a connection. She gave up and tried a good old-fashioned phone call. After some strange buzzing noises, she heard a click. "Matt? Are you there?"

Static filled her ear, but there was background noise too. Someone was shouting orders. "Matt?"

"Yeah. Sorry. I'm here. Are . . . kids all right?"

"They're fine." She didn't know if that was true. They'd all most likely need therapy by November first. "But something is going on. The other night—"

"I'm headed into surgery." Despite the static, she heard that invigorated tone she knew so well. "Can we . . . later? I'm . . ."

The line went dead.

Cassie pressed the top edge of her phone to her forehead. Great talk. Just what she needed. She got up and shuffled over to the window. Janet was perched on the sill, as elegant as a sphinx, her gaze focused on the dark. The fog wasn't as bad tonight, but sinister wisps still snaked around the trees and over the lawns. From the second floor, Cassie could see Ben's house. Yellow light poured out from almost every window.

He did say she could call anytime.

But she shouldn't. It wasn't appropriate, considering the shower thoughts she'd had about him. But those thoughts were innocent enough. And she needed a friend. As long as she thought of him that way, it was fine. She pressed the call button.

He answered on the first ring. "Cassie? Is everything okay?"

"Yeah, fine. Sorry for calling so late."

"No worries. We keep strange hours in this house."

She laughed, but now that she had him on the phone, she had no idea what to say.

"How are you holding up?" he asked.

An uncertain whine passed her lips as she paced her bedroom floor.

"That's better than I'd be doing. I don't know how you're keeping it all together." His voice was warm and empathetic, like a mug of hot cocoa. What was wrong with her? Friend thoughts only. Ben the friend. "Everything that's happened?" he went on. "It's too much. And it's coming so fast."

Cassie came to a dead stop. "Exactly!" That had come out with more enthusiasm than she had intended.

"Have you told Eliza about"—he paused, lowering his voice to a whisper—"being the witch of your, or I guess her, generation?" It was cute. She didn't think Eliza could hear them from the Grub.

"Not yet. I'm going to." Cassie squeezed her forehead. "I just..."

"Need more time to process."

She dropped down on the edge of her bed. "You get it."

"I do, but..."

"The longer I wait the worse it's going to be when she finds out the truth?"

"Pretty much."

Cassie flopped back onto the mattress. "Ben, I'm not even sure I believe any of this witch stuff."

The line went silent, making her heart thump. Finally he said, "This may be too personal, but do you think you have ever done any magic?"

The ceiling fan stared down at Cassie. "I have some childhood memories that may or may not be real. My hands tingle around vampires and maybe at farmer's markets, but that could be due to a lack of oxygen. I forget to breathe a lot these days." She wasn't going to get into the coin. "And I may have lit a pumpkin on fire the other night with my mind, but that also could have been teenage hoodlums."

"Teenage hoodlums?"

"The town's full of them." Cassie dropped her hand on her forehead. When she said it out loud, it sounded ridiculous. But more ridiculous than her being a witch? "You must think I'm crazy. Or in denial. Or both."

"No, not at all. I've had those thoughts about me. But not you."

There was something in the way he said that last part that warmed Cassie all over. It almost sounded like it was inconceivable that he could ever see her in a negative light.

"I know it's not my place," Ben said hesitantly, "and feel free to tell me it's none of my business, but I think you should go to Sea House and talk to Dorcas. I'll keep researching. I want to help. But she's the expert on this."

Cassie pulled herself up to sitting. "There's a lot of history there. I'm not sure I'm strong enough to face it right now. It might be the straw that breaks the witch's back."

He chuckled. Thank God. Because that was a terrible joke. "I know I've only known you a short time, but didn't you knock a vampire's head off her shoulders?"

Cassie scoffed. "Not all the way off." Another moment of silence passed before she said, "Thank you, Ben. I really appreciate the advice. I may not be able to follow through on it, but thank you."

"Anytime. Killing that vampire together was a real bonding experience." She could hear the smile in his voice. "Cassie, can I ask you one more thing before I let you go?"

"Of course."

"It's kind of embarrassing," Ben began, "but I went to this Mommy and Me group, and it turns out all the other babies Olive's age are sleeping through the night. Some of the moms were looking at me like I had no idea what I was doing, which is fine, but . . . I've tried everything. I track her eating to make sure she's getting enough. We have a bedtime routine. The doctor says she's healthy. I know there's sleep training, but I don't think I can let her cry it out. What am I doing wrong?"

"Absolutely nothing," Cassie said. "All babies are different. My kids didn't sleep through the night until their last teeth came in."

"When does that happen?"

Three. Three years old. "You know, I don't remember," Cassie said. "The important thing is every adult who has ever taken care of a baby has wondered if they're doing it right. By asking the question it usually means you are."

Ben exhaled heavily. "Thanks." Just then a wail sounded in the distance. "Speaking of Olive . . ."

"You'd better go. I hope you get some sleep tonight."

"You too. Thanks for calling."

The line went dead. Cassie clutched the phone to her chest. *Thanks for calling.* She was the one who was supposed to be thanking him, but it sounded like he meant it.

☾

The first dreams Cassie had that night were among the sweetest she had ever known.

There was no coherent storyline, just gently tumbling images and sensations of Sea House, her mother, and Dorcas. It began with the feeling of soft rain on her cheeks. She was running over wet sand, looking over her shoulder at the trail of dry footprints she had left behind. Then the sun filled the sky, and her hands were clasped with her mother's and her aunt's. *Hold tight!* They swung her up to the endless blue sky. When she came back down, she was sitting in her mother's lap on the porch at night, her hands outstretched, fireflies dancing just above her fingertips. She looked back into a window and she was in the kitchen with Dorcas, who was stirring something in a bubbling copper pot shooting steam. She felt herself being lifted and placed on her aunt's hip, dancing, swaying, then—*Cassie, watch!*—a spin, a fling of the hand, and an eruption of flames ignited in the kitchen hearth. *You two better not being doing what I think you're doing!* Then they were crawling under the table, giggling, as her mother's legs came into view. *How many times do I have to say it? No fire.* The vignettes came faster. She tasted red currants and vanilla ice cream on a hot summer's day, then ginger cookies and peppermint at Christmas. She was blowing bubbles across the shimmering red sand, then making mud pies in the garden. It all came in a rush before settling down into a single moment. Her mother was tucking her into an old feather bed, covering her with quilts, protecting her from the bitter cold pressing against the frosted windowpanes. She sat on the edge of the bed, wearing a white nightgown fringed with lace. *Here come the butterfly kisses.* Cassie clutched her sheets to her neck, smiling as a cloud of tiny glowing butterflies appeared, swooping down to tickle her face before drifting away into sparkling dust. Her mother then stroked her forehead and sang the lullaby about the moon man fishing the sea.

Cassie fought against her heavy eyelids as her mother reached for the candle on the bedside table.

No! It was too soon. She wanted to stay. She wanted . . .

Sweet dreams, love.

Her mother blew the flame out.

Cassie wasn't in her bed anymore. She was an adult again, lying on the beach, cold sand pressing against her back. Near-silent waves rippled on the shore, afraid to make too loud a noise, and the sky above was black and empty, the stars gobbled up by some hidden monster. The ocean should have been in front of her, but when she pushed herself up to stand, there was only dark red sand reaching as far as she could see. She looked behind. More sand. Sand in every direction. Cassie spun in a circle.

Round and round and round we go, where we stop—

The world blinked, and the sea was all around her. She stood on a quickly shrinking island. Beyond, a towering leviathan of fog, rolling at an incredible speed, was closing in from every direction.

She couldn't let it touch her. If it touched her, she'd be lost.

Nowhere to run, she dropped low and hugged her knees to her chest. The mist's bone-chilling breath rolled over her, blanketing her senses. The sound of the waves disappeared. All she could see was the gray swirl of fog.

The fear of being lost swallowed her whole, but she wasn't the one who was lost anymore. It was her children! Her children were lost. Lost in the fog.

She opened her mouth to scream, but seawater rushed into her lungs.

Suddenly a voice rippled around her in a low, mocking whisper.

Cassandra...

Somewhere beyond this world, wakeful realization called to her. This was a nightmare. That's all this was. She was going to wake up now.

Cassandra, I've waited so long.

She was not doing this. *Wake up!* If she could move, run, strike out, she knew she could break the nightmare's hold, but she was frozen, paralyzed, wrapped up in a shroud of fog, trapped.

Cassandra, look outside. Laughter rippled around her. *I have a present for you.*

Cassie jerked awake. Her heart was pounding, and she was

bathed in sweat. She reached her hands to either side, fighting to place herself in the dark. This was her bed. The blue light that suffused her room was from her clock. And that noise coming from the window? That was her cat growling.

Her cat was growling.

Cassie turned her head, afraid of what she might see.

Janet vented a hiss before returning to her low grumble, dancing angry steps on the windowsill.

She would not look outside. She didn't have to. Dream vampires couldn't tell her what to do. And she doubted vampire presents were ever good.

Janet's growl rose to a scream.

Cassie threw her legs over the side of the bed. She didn't want to do this. Really, really didn't want to do this. But she had no other choice. She was the mom. A whimper trembled over her lips. Why did she always have to be the mom?

Dim light reached through the window. The sun was coming up. Cassie forced herself to peek over Janet's head.

Oh no . . .

The sight forced her back in stumbling steps before she spun on her heel and ran out of her room to the stairs. Cassie gripped the banister every few steps to keep herself from falling, then lunged for the door.

Gary, still in his jogging suit, now stained with blood, stood on her front walkway. His headband sat crooked on his forehead, and his skin shone a sickly hue under the streetlamp. She had never seen anyone look so confused, miserable, sick, or bloody. Even Tommy looked better than poor Gary.

"Cassie, I don't feel well. I think I ran too far."

She tried to smile, but she felt closer to tears.

THE LATE-NIGHT WITCHES

"I've been in my shed. Maybe for a couple of days now?" He shook his head. "I don't think I should be around people. I was going to stay there, but a voice called me. He said I had to deliver a message to you."

Cassie truly didn't want any messages, but she didn't want to upset Gary any more than he already was.

"The voice said, *Tell her she can't run. She can't hide. The Thirteenth Witch will die.* Does that make sense to you?"

She nodded.

"I'm so thirsty. Can I come in? I think everything will be all right if I get something to drink."

"You know what?" Her voice quavered. "I have a better idea. Why don't we—"

"Mom?"

Cassie whipped around. Sadie was standing on the stairs in plaid pajama bottoms and a T-shirt. "Is everything okay?"

Suddenly Cassie knew what she had been forgetting.

She had forgotten about Sadie. How could she have forgotten about Sadie? Her only daughter . . . which also made her the oldest daughter.

"Everything's okay, baby. We're going on a road trip." She forced another smile.

"What?" Sadie dropped down a step. "What about school? Your work?"

Cassie shot her hand up to stop her daughter from coming any closer. "We're playing hooky. Now, go back upstairs and pack a bag. Get your brothers to pack one too. I have to run out for a second."

"What's happening?"

"I'll explain everything on the way. Go."

Cassie waited until her daughter had disappeared up the stairs before turning back to the newly turned vampire outside. "Gary, I'm going to take you to a place where you can get a drink. Does that sound good?"

He nodded miserably.

One more vampire for the basement . . .

CHAPTER 14

Eliza, *where are you?*

Cassie took Gary to the Grub in the trunk of Matt's car. Even though she had the tire fixed on the van, she wasn't sure if she could trust Gary's self-control just yet, and it didn't have any secure compartments. Unfortunately, when they arrived, her sister wasn't there. Tommy was though, and he seemed excited about the idea of having a roommate. As for Gary, he was excited to see the plastic tubs of blood in the fridge. Tommy showed him how to warm it up to the right temperature in the microwave, and they became fast friends. Eliza had managed to really trick the place out. Even though the basement was basically a large square room made from heavy stone, alongside the fridge and microwave, there was a sofa and a full gaming system set up with a wide-screen TV and speakers. Sure, it smelled like mildew and death, but given it was a basement that housed vampires, that seemed fair.

Eliza also wasn't answering her phone. Tommy said she was out running errands and wouldn't be back until nightfall, but he didn't know where she had gone. The obvious answer was Sea

House, but there was a problem with that theory. There was no way Eliza was going to find it on her own.

Sea House was completely off the grid. Locals knew it existed. They could see it beyond the rocky cove from the water, but finding it by land was nearly impossible. In high school, Cassie tried looking it up, along with its address, in the island's historical records, but all she could find was that the house had been built in 1860 in a Scottish Gothic style right on the beach, near Thunder Cove. So, one day shortly after she had gotten her license, she decided on impulse to drive out there. She drove purely on instinct, taking turn after turn until she thought she'd never find her way home, but finally she ended up deep in a forest after turning onto a pebbled drive hidden behind a giant oak. Cassie knew if she traveled to the end of that rocky path, it would take her back to Sea House, but she couldn't do it.

In hindsight, it was all a little weird, but she wasn't ready to call it *magical*. She had lived there until age eight. Eliza, though, had only been a baby, so she was probably lost. Lost forever in the woods because Cassie had withheld information from her. Again. And now what was she supposed to do? Take the kids to Sea House without her? Thankfully Cassie didn't have to make that decision because Eliza was waiting for her in the driveway when she got home.

She didn't look happy.

Cassie climbed out of the car with an expression of what she hoped looked like sisterly concern. "What are you doing here? I thought you'd be at Sea House by now."

"I thought so too." She leaned against the van. "But it turns out nobody knows how to freaking get there."

"Oh no!"

"I've been driving all morning following all sorts of crackpot suggestions, but I don't think I even got close." Eliza folded her arms, covered once again in faux leather, over her chest. She was seriously going to freeze to death this winter if she didn't get herself a warmer coat. Which she wouldn't. Cassie added *Take Eliza shopping for secondhand winter coat* to her mental to-do list.

"That must have been so frustrating," Cassie said. "I didn't even think about giving you directions."

"Oh my God, shut up. You knew I wouldn't be able to find it. That's why you were so okay with me going."

Cassie dropped her unnatural look of concern. "Maybe, but guess what? Turns out I'm taking the kids to Sea House today. You can come along."

Eliza pushed herself up off the van. "Sorry, what?"

Cassie told her sister all about Gary and taking him to the shop. She didn't tell her anything beyond that yet. It would make for an awkward drive. There was plenty of time for recriminations later. "So, let's get going. I'm going to grab the bags. You put Janet in her crate."

Eliza laughed. "If it's a choice between death by vampire or death by Janet, then I choose vampire."

"She's not that bad."

"Then you put her in her crate."

"Okay, no. Get a can of tuna and put it in the van," Cassie said, hurrying away. She stopped dead on the porch steps and whirled around. "But no talking about anything on the way. Not with the kids."

Eliza put two fingers to her forehead and saluted.

☾

Even though this month had been a stunner so far, driving to Sea House reminded Cassie of why Anne of Green Gables was so grateful to live in a world where there were Octobers. They drove through small town after small town, decorated with cornstalks and scarecrows, past fields with pumpkins and golden hay bales, and into shining forests with trees wearing cloaks of red, yellow, and orange. Sea House was less than an hour away, but Cassie felt like they were traveling back in time to another world, another life.

All she told the kids was that they were going to meet a family acquaintance who lived by the sea. The boys were thrilled. Any escape from school was a gift. But Sadie said nothing, which was somehow worse than arguing.

Once again, Cassie was able to find her way fairly easily. Eliza slept the entire drive, her temple pressed against the passenger side window. She had to be tired from being awake night and day. As the dirt road dwindled to its end, the towering oak from Cassie's memory appeared, its branches quivering with golden leaves. She eased the van around it onto the camouflaged dirt track, praying the van's suspension would hold up. Fortunately, the trail was in better shape than she remembered. Dorcas's Jeep must have beaten it down over the years. The van still rocked, though, waking Eliza and encouraging the kids to put down their devices to look outside. As they pulled free of the forest, the sea rose into view.

Sunlight bathed the russet sand, but granite-colored storm clouds loomed on the horizon. The sea heaved weighty breaths as seagulls circled above, ready to scavenge for what might be churned up from the ocean's depths.

Home. The word came to mind before any conscious thought. It wasn't the past, the house, or her aunt stirring the feelings though. It was the sea. It always made her feel like she belonged to something bigger. And yet, it had been a long time since she had made an effort to take it in. Kind of funny given she lived on an island.

Cassie parked the van at the tree line by Dorcas's Jeep. "Now, kids," she said, breaking the spell, "the woman who lives here is a bit eccentric."

"What does *eccentric* mean?" Sly asked.

"It means she's weird," Sadie replied.

"I wouldn't go so far as *weird*," Cassie said, though she totally would. "But she does have unique ideas, and she jokes a lot. She sometimes says things that aren't true for laughs. You know what I mean?"

"No," Eddie said, gripping the sides of her seat.

Cassie patted his hand.

A wooden pole buried in the sand with an arrow-shaped plank at its top pointed them in the direction of the Sea House. Cassie wasn't sure who the sign was for given the secrecy of the house's location, but something about it felt good, welcoming. "Looks like we're walking, guys." As soon as she turned off the engine, the boys were gone, running for the sea.

"Wait!" Cassie shouted. "Stay away from the water!" The wind snatched the words from her mouth.

Janet jumped out next, headed in the direction of the house, almost as though she knew the way.

Cassie and Eliza exited the van and trailed over to the lowest dip between the coppery red dunes sprouting with marram grass. Sadie followed behind, clearly not in the mood to share whatever it was she was thinking. They climbed a small slope, and when they reached the top, the house materialized. It stood back from the water on a hill of more solid ground. It should have been swept away by sea wind decades ago, but it stood proud, beautiful, and just a little bit crooked.

Sea House.

It was such a simple name, but even turning the words over in her mind made Cassie's heart swell. Hazy memories, like roots from a tree she thought dead, reached for her present mind. The porch wrapped all the way around the two-story structure, giving the house spectacular views of both the sea and the forest. The decorative trim on the eaves looked almost untouched by the elements, and all the handblown glass windows were still intact. The shingled outer walls, though, had faded to gray, but it didn't take away from the stunning mansard roof with its copper crest resting on top of it all like a crown.

"This is amazing." Eliza picked up her pace, forcing Cassie to do the same. As they neared the house and the veranda came into better view, she found herself scanning the porch.

"Is it just me," her sister said, grabbing her elbow, "or are there about a dozen cats up there?"

There were. Every spot on the veranda with a flat surface—windowsills, seats, backs of chairs, every step leading up to the door—had a lounging cat. There were large and small ones, long- and short-haired, in all different colors. And three chimera calicos.

Eliza smiled a truly joyful smile. Cassie didn't know it was possible, but it made her even more beautiful. Or maybe *beautiful* was the wrong word. She looked peaceful, content, at home. *Oh God.* Was this really happening?

"It almost looks like they were expecting us." Eliza ran to the steps, then picked her way around the cats, headed for the door, when Cassie called her back. There was a large raised vegetable garden behind the house overflowing with late harvest vegetables. A thick wooden pole stood in the center with a burlap dummy. A scarecrow with fangs. Dorcas was also in the garden.

She had bundles of branches and was waving them in the air as she swayed with the wind.

"What is she doing?" Eliza asked.

"No idea."

Suddenly Dorcas threw the branches in the air, crying out with joy.

Uh-oh. Cassie braced herself, suddenly wishing she had brought a lollipop.

CHAPTER 15

Dorcas ran toward them, arms flying, as she slipped over the sparse grass and loose sand. Her long silver hair flew around her, the wind-whipped curls tossed in all directions. Despite the cold, she was wearing filthy denim overalls with a once-white tank top underneath. Her bare arms pumped with her jog, showcasing her sculpted muscles. Cassie tensed when she approached, but she needn't have bothered. Dorcas ran right by.

Sadie's eyes widened as her great-aunt descended upon her. Cassie rushed to intervene, but Dorcas got the better of her this time.

"Finally!" she shouted, pulling Cassie's daughter to her chest. The two struggled to stay upright with the force of the hit.

"You were at our house," Sadie stammered over Dorcas's shoulder that was digging into her throat. "You're the public health nurse."

"Yes! No! I'm your aunt! Great-aunt! Isn't it wonderful?" She picked up locks of Sadie's hair and held them out to the sides. "You're wonderful. I watch you all the time. And the boys!"

Concern touched Sadie's eyes.

"That must have sounded strange," Dorcas said, smiling, not offering an explanation. "Now you can call me Great-Aunt Dorcas. Or Dorcas. Or Auntie. Or Dorrie. Or—"

"Okay," Cassie said, extricating her daughter's hair from her aunt's fingers. "Sadie, could you go check on your brothers?"

She didn't groan, sigh, or roll her eyes. Cassie thought she must be processing all that was Dorcas.

"I can't wait to talk to you later," Dorcas called after her, blowing a kiss and jumping in the air. "Have fun!" She hopped back around to face Cassie and Eliza with her hands clasped to her chest. "They told me you were coming today."

Eliza leaned toward Cassie and whispered, "By *them*, does she mean the cats?"

Before she could answer, Dorcas threw her hands in the air. "I do. I do mean the cats."

"Just wanted to be sure," Eliza said.

"Come! Let's go to the house, so we can talk. The wind is turning wild. Don't you love the change of seasons?! The tug-of-war. The best of the sun and the worst of the clouds!"

"Maybe I should call the children," Cassie said.

"There's time. They've never seen a squall roll in over the sea here. You can't deny them the pleasure."

Cassie pondered whether denying pleasure was part of a mother's job description, but she already had enough on her mind. Eliza hurried on ahead as Dorcas came up beside her. "I'm so relieved you came." Her gaze softened. "I suspected you would arrive sooner than later. You were in shock the other night, but I knew it would hit you before long."

Cassie looked down at her boots, now dusty with ruddy sand. She took a breath, then met her aunt's eye. "Dorcas, I'm going to be honest. I don't trust you, but I have nowhere else to turn. I'm asking you to help me. Begging. This has to end with me. I won't pass this curse on to my daughter."

"You don't have to ask." She reached out, but Cassie stepped back.

Taking no offense, Dorcas spun in a pirouette. "Let's go inside. There's not a moment to lose."

☾

Stepping into Sea House was a little like being flayed alive. Not so much in the sense that it hurt physically—although somehow it did—but more in the sense that all Cassie's vulnerable bits felt like they were being exposed, and she still couldn't remember the reasons why.

"Go sit," Dorcas said, waving them toward the parlor. She stayed by the door, holding it open for an orderly line of cats—Janet in the middle—trailing in. "Come on now. Hurry up." Once she had closed the door, she skipped to the kitchen. "I'll wash up then bring out the refreshments."

Eerie gold sunbeams filtered through the many windows, warm rays battling the first reach of storm clouds. Even without her memories, Cassie somehow knew the house had always been one of light and shadow. The dark hand-hewn beams with square head nails seemed to absorb the light, but the grand stone fireplace crackled with welcome fire. Soft glints from the flames bounced off the many metal trinkets and colored bottles placed on shelves around the room, while velvet divans and plush, satiny chairs with richly colored cushions sat beckoning all to their embrace.

The stone floors and beams carried on from the parlor into the kitchen, which had a cast-iron stove and copper pots hanging from the rack over the island along with bundles of dried herbs. As Dorcas busied about, her movements sent fragrant ripples of pumpkin and spices—nutmeg, cinnamon, cloves, and ginger—swirling through the air.

Eliza moved to a shelf of books beside the fireplace. She trailed her fingertips over the spines, stopping when she reached an empty space. Cassie knew without knowing that most of Sea House's books were kept in the library, but this was where Eliza's collection of fairy tales once sat. The one she had read to her sister when she was little.

Eliza turned toward her, but she stepped away before their eyes could meet. Cassie walked back past the central staircase, toward the dining room on the other side of the house. The sliding doors were closed and there was a chain and padlock keeping them shut tight. *Okay.* That wasn't at all concerning.

"Just another moment," Dorcas called out.

Cassie wandered back to the parlor as her aunt came in, wearing a faded black apron and holding a tarnished silver tray loaded with sliced pumpkin bread, figs, nuts, honey, and tea. Cassie remembered the scent of that tea. For a second, she was back with her aunt and her mother sitting in this room laughing and drinking it as the wind howled outside, but then it was gone, leaving her to wonder if it was real.

Once Dorcas had placed the tray on the low, square table in the middle of the room, they sat. Eliza chose the deep purple armchair with its back to the window and Dorcas the leather ottoman by the fire. Cassie opted to pull up an antique straight-backed chair from the corner. She placed it close to the entranceway in case she needed to make a quick getaway.

"I can't tell you girls how wonderful it is to have you both back at Sea House," Dorcas began. "I wish it were under different circumstances." Her gaze drifted to the fire, and her face contracted with unspoken pain. "I was so sure it was all over. But we're here now, and we will persevere." She slapped her thighs and then poured a cup of tea. "I hardly know where to begin." She passed the first cup to Eliza, then set to pouring another. "We didn't have much of a chance to talk at the farmer's market the other day—"

Cassie resisted the instantaneous pull of her sister's glare. They were only getting started.

"—but what have you learned on your own, Polliwog?"

"Polliwog?" Eliza's voice had taken on a scary edge. One that Dorcas didn't seem to notice.

"When Cassie was little, I used to read to her from a book with a baby frog on the cover. She was so adorable. And powerful. Your sister, not the frog." She wagged a finger in the air. "Although you'd be surprised by the things frogs are capable of."

Eliza raised an eyebrow. Cassie knew a part of her sensed where this was going, but she wasn't sure yet. And that's why Cassie still lived.

"Oh, but the things your sister could do." Dorcas rocked back, clutching her knee. "Without even being taught. It all came so naturally." She then passed Cassie her own cup and saucer.

Eliza narrowed her eyes, making Cassie wonder if she should run now. The cats seemed to feel the shift in energy too. Several of them stopped their grooming to look at her sister, one with its pink tongue hanging out.

"Just to clarify," Eliza said, resting her forearm on her crossed legs. "What kind of powers are we talking about? Exactly."

Dorcas frowned, then looked back and forth between the two of them. "What do you mean?"

"What do you mean by *power*? Do you mean muscular

strength? Mental acuity? Or are you referring to something else?"

Dorcas shot Cassie a questioning look. "Polliwog? Don't tell me you didn't tell her?"

"Tell me what?" Eliza demanded.

"I didn't know anything," Cassie sputtered. "Not until the other night."

"But how could you not know?" Dorcas asked.

"I don't have any real memories of living at Sea House," Cassie said. "I mean I had heard some things over the years about you thinking you might be . . . and your notes were . . . *wow*. But then you and the other night happened and everything just kind of came together." Cassie looked down to her hands folded in her lap.

"No," Dorcas murmured. "That's not possible. The lullaby was only supposed to . . . are you sure? No memories at all?"

"What is going on?" Eliza shouted.

Dorcas shook her head, her eyes wide with disbelief. "My dear girl, this may come as a shock, but we're witches."

CHAPTER 16

An unnerving hush settled over the room. It wasn't completely silent though. The fire crackled on with its gentle snaps and pops, the grandfather clock continued ticking away, and the wind kept up with its rattling assault on the windows. All were proof that time had not, in fact, stopped. It just really, really felt that way.

"I knew it!"

Cassie gripped the sides of her chair as her sister jumped to her feet.

"I've always known it." Eliza gasped loudly, whirling on Cassie. "I asked you if Dorcas was a witch and you said she wasn't!"

"No, you asked—"

Eliza's hand jerked out in a vicious point. "Stop talking. You don't talk right now." Her eyes snapped back to her aunt. "Prove it."

"I'm sorry?" Dorcas laughed. "Prove that I'm a witch? Right now? I haven't even had my tea."

"If you're a witch, then prove it."

Dorcas brought her hand to her chest. "I'm not some show monkey you can command to perform. And it's such a spur-of-the-moment request. I have nothing prepared." She lifted her hand and reached for the black cat, Janet's doppelganger, seated on the armrest of her chair. "Besides, I'm sure you've already experienced magic without realizing it. It is, as they say, everywhere." Dorcas touched the cat's nose with the tip of her finger, tracing a line from its head, all the way down its spine, to the tip of its tail. A wave of snowy fur followed in its wake, leaving the cat pure white.

All the world dropped away from Cassie as her sister whispered, "Holy shit."

Dorcas clapped her hands. "I've always liked that one too." She looked over to Cassie. "That's Janet's grandmother, by the way."

Janet, who was stretched out by the fire, diligently licking a paw, looked up.

"No. No." Cassie's head shuddered. Janet wasn't part of this. Janet was a normal cat, a stray. She didn't come from this magical fur hoard.

"I sent her your way," Dorcas said proudly. "She has wonderful instincts."

Pinpricks of light darted across Cassie's vision. What . . . was happening?

"We're forming a coven!" Dorcas shouted.

A surprised yelp spurted out of Cassie's mouth. Had her aunt just read her mind?

"Yes! Isn't it wonderful?"

"No." Cassie put down the teacup that was rattling in its saucer. This . . . was too much. Everything was getting away from her. If she had any sense she would walk out of this crazy, crooked house right now, drive away with her kids, and never come back.

Except there were vampires out there, weren't there? Vampires who wanted her dead.

The pure white cat arched its back in a long stretch, and its fur rippled back to black. It then dropped down from the chair to touch noses with Janet.

"Teach me," Eliza said, taking a step toward Dorcas. "Teach me how to do that."

"Teach you that?" Dorcas scoffed. "I plan to teach you much more than basic glamour. Follow me and I will lead you down the path to real power. I will show you what it means to be a Beckett witch." Her voice dropped. "I will teach you how to fight!"

Eliza laughed crazily, like she could not believe her luck.

"But first, I need you both to know that I never wanted us to come together this way. I was certain I had killed him." Dorcas grabbed the woolen throw at her side and squeezed the fabric in her fist. "A few years ago, I discovered where he slept, so I staked him, then I blew up the house." She released her hold on the blanket and sighed. "Originally, I was hoping to preserve his head to keep on the mantel as a remembrance." All three of them looked at the mantel. Dorcas with contemplation, Eliza with excitement, and Cassie with horror, which was clearly the only appropriate reaction. "But that's the sort of thing that earns a witch a bad reputation, and I didn't want the cats nibbling at it."

She was kidding. She had to be kidding.

"You . . ." Cassie cleared her throat. She didn't sound like herself. She sounded like someone being strangled. "You blew up a house? The house on the street next to mine? That was you?"

Dorcas sniffed with revulsion. "He has some sort of attachment to the area. That's where the battle always takes place. Can you imagine him asleep all those years right by the children?"

No. She could not. She would not! Cassie's mouth went dry.

She reached for her tea, then decided against it. She might end up with white fur.

"By *him*, do you mean Del?" Eliza asked. "I mean, the Deliverer of Fear, Sorrow, and Death?"

Dorcas beamed. "So, you do know some things!"

"Cassie's boyfriend told us."

"He's not . . . we're not . . ." Cassie pressed her fingertips into her temples. She didn't know who or what anyone or anything was anymore.

"Ah yes, the large, handsome man with the garlic baby." Dorcas delicately pinched the handle of her teacup between her thumb and forefinger. "Well done, Cassie." She took a sip, then returned the cup to its saucer. "The point is, while I don't understand how it is we got here, here we are!"

Eliza raised her eyebrows. "And where is *here* exactly?"

"The here and now where we prepare. Well, I prepare. I need to teach you two how to stay safe, though, before I end that demon once and for all. There is so much to learn in a short period of time." Dorcas focused back on Cassie. "He will be relentless now that he is so close."

Eliza looked at Cassie too, struggling to pull all the pieces together, a shifting tangle of fear and anger playing out on her face. "That witch Ben told us about, the one Del wants to kill . . . ?"

Cassie closed her eyes. There was no point trying to hide it anymore. Maybe there never had been. "I'm the witch of her generation." The words felt very strange coming out of her mouth, but she suspected the next ones would feel even more so. "And the Deliverer wants me dead."

CHAPTER 17

"Mom! Mom! Mom!" The front door banged open, letting in a powerful gust of wind. Sly raced into the parlor with sparkling eyes and red cheeks. "We found a starfish!"

Cassie tried to smile, but it was really hard given the furious side-eye her sister was giving her.

"You made it all the way to the tide pool?" Dorcas exclaimed. "Bravo, Sylvester!"

Sly gave her two sideways looks in rapid succession before turning back to Cassie. "Eddie wanted to pick it up, but Sadie told him not to because if it gets stressed it will die! He thought she was lying, so he was going to do it anyway, but she tackled him and sent me for help. She said you'd give me five bucks if I told you."

Despite the threat to starfish life, relief washed over Cassie. She needed a moment of normalcy, and her children fighting was well within her comfort zone. She scooted forward on her chair to stand, but Dorcas beat her to the punch.

"I'll go. You two should talk." She walked over to Sylvester and placed a hand on his shoulder. "Did you know if a starfish has one of its legs bitten off, it will grow back?"

Sly peeked up at her with big eyes.

"Look at you!" She laughed, cupping his cheek. "Are you afraid I will eat the starfish's legs?"

He nodded.

"Good boy." She tousled his chestnut curls. "It's wise not to trust old women who live alone by the sea." She guided him outside. "No matter how much fun we may be."

And then there were two.

Cassie pinned her hands between her knees. She was not at all comfortable with the reversal of roles that had suddenly taken place between her and her sister. She was the one who normally did the questioning and chastising. While she had never relished the role, it was much more comfortable than this one.

Centuries passed before Eliza asked, "How much did you know?"

"Almost nothing," Cassie pleaded. "Like I said before, I don't have any real memories of my life here."

"No *real* memories?" Her sister arched an eyebrow.

"I have tiny snapshots of moments, and sometimes I have dreams that feel kind of real, but nothing concrete."

"And you never found that strange?"

"Not really." Cassie shrugged helplessly. "I was eight when Dorcas gave us up, and our mother had just died. I figured I repressed it all."

Eliza nodded, looking at the floor. "You suspected something was different about Dorcas though." Her gaze snapped back up. "For a while now. Maybe our entire lives?" A few cats slunk out of the room.

"It wasn't like that. When we were taken from here, everybody told me Dorcas wasn't well. That she had strange beliefs. I trusted them. Why wouldn't I?"

"Of course. I get it," Eliza said evenly. "After all, her notes were so strange."

Craaaaap. "Yes, every now and then, Dorcas would send notes. Weird, incomprehensible notes." Cassie's shoulders dropped with sudden weariness. "She says hi by the way."

Eliza threw a cushion at her. "Seriously?!"

"I know it sounds stupid given all this." Cassie gestured around the room. "But I was trying to protect you."

"You didn't trust me to handle it is what you really mean."

"No!" Well, it was possible that was a tiny bit true, but she was in enough trouble.

Eliza cocked her head, regarding Cassie closely. "So, when did you change your mind? I mean you went to the farmer's market to talk to Dorcas. Was it after Joanne that you started to think something more might be going on? Something—*I don't know*—witchy?"

"There was no single moment," Cassie said. "Things started piling up, like burned pumpkins, and vampires, and vampire nightmares, and . . ."

"Burned pumpkins? Vampire nightmares?" Eliza muttered. "And?"

Cassie squinted. "Remember how you called that night when you were following Tommy and my phone cut off? In hindsight, I think I temporarily blew it up." She squinted harder. "Or you did."

"What?!" The fire surged as the words left Eliza's mouth.

Okay, that was new. Cassie kept her face very still. "Maybe we should save talking about those things for another time. My brain feels like it's going to explode."

"Fine," Eliza said evenly. "Let's talk about something else, like maybe how you're the witch of her generation or Thirteenth Witch, or whoever it is that Del wants to kill!"

Cassie threw her head back and groaned.

"You didn't think I'd want to know about that?"

This line of questioning felt judgmental. It wasn't like there was a manual on how to tell your family you're the linchpin in a centuries-old curse. "I didn't know what was real and what wasn't! I needed time to get my head on straight." Suddenly Cassie found herself jabbing her finger repeatedly at her sister. "But I brought you here. So that's proof I wasn't hiding it from you."

Eliza held her gaze, then dropped her face into her hands. "Ten minutes ago I was experiencing the greatest moment of my life, and then you had to go and ruin it with your impending death."

"I am very sorry about that," Cassie answered. "And my death is not *impending*! You heard Dorcas. She is going to kill Del. We are going to stay safe."

Eliza whipped her head up, then smoothed her hair down. "Swear to me, right now, that you didn't know Dorcas was a witch, and that you really don't have any memories of your life at Sea House."

Cassie shook her head in a big side-to-side motion. "I swear."

Eliza's shoulders dropped, but she was still giving her an intensely disappointed look. "You should have told me about the notes."

"You're right." Cassie released her clutch on the pillow she was using as a shield. "I'm sorry."

"I don't forgive you," her sister grumbled, "and you really need to start having more faith in me!"

The memory of her sister stumbling down the street dragging a baseball bat sprang to mind, but Cassie nodded.

"At the end of the day," Eliza said, planting her hands on her thighs, "all I really care about is keeping everyone safe."

"Me too."

"And saving Tommy."

Cassie rubbed her temple. "Sure."

"And becoming the most powerful witch on the Eastern Seaboard."

Okay, then. They fell back into silence, but it wasn't long before Cassie noticed her sister's index finger reaching for Janet's nose. *Oh, for the love of . . .*

"Eliza," she said tiredly. "Do not touch my cat."

Her sister curled her finger back in. "What? I wasn't going to do anything."

"Don't touch my cat."

☾

The rest of the day passed in relative peace after the morning's fireworks. The monstrous clouds threatened throughout the afternoon but didn't break, so the kids were able to spend the entire day on the beach. The boys ran, climbed, and explored, while Sadie sat on a sand dune contemplating the sea and listening to music on her phone.

As for the adults, Eliza and Dorcas sat together in the kitchen drinking tea and getting to know each other while Cassie explored the house. It was the strangest experience. She knew things like what room she was about to enter before she opened the door, but specific, concrete memories were still out of reach.

The emotions weren't though. Like when Cassie saw the rocking chair in the library, her heart swelled to an almost unbearable degree. She could feel warm arms around her, and she could hear the turn of a heavy page, but all the rest was lost. She also somehow knew there was a fire that burned many of the books in the library to ash a long time ago, but she couldn't pinpoint how she knew.

With the heavy cloud cover, dusk fell quickly, and the children came in as the rain began to fall. They sat at the kitchen island with the copper pots glowing overhead in the candlelight, and Dorcas served them lobster chowder with homemade bread for dinner and a warm berry pie for dessert. Everything was delicious, but there was also something that felt homey about the food. Cozy. Safe.

During the meal, Dorcas peppered the kids with questions. The boys chattered endlessly as though nothing were strange about having a new family member, but Sadie clearly knew something was up. She answered all her great-aunt's questions politely enough, but her curious gaze never left Dorcas's face. When they were through, Cassie took the children upstairs. Dorcas had made up all the rooms in expectation of their arrival. Cassie wanted Sadie to have her old one. Not only did she think it would be too overwhelming to sleep in it herself, but it had a window seat that looked out to the sea, which she knew her daughter would love. The boys got a room with twin beds. As they snuggled under the sheets, several cats trailed in. They jumped on the beds and picked their way over the quilts to find warm nooks and crannies inside the boys' elbows and behind their knees.

Once they were settled, Cassie headed back down the stairs. When she reached the halfway mark, she paused. She could hear her aunt and her sister speaking in hushed tones. Her name stood out among the mumbles. She gripped the banister. Though it was annoying, it wasn't like she didn't know what they were saying. It was probably stuff like *Can you believe Cassie kept us apart all these years? She never even told me about your notes! And what about the children? They love it here. It's horrible they've had to miss out.* Or *There's no way Cassie can be the witch of her generation. She can't do magic. She can barely remember to make the boys' lunches. She's totally going to die.* It was possible she was getting carried away, but she doubted it.

Cassie resumed her step, making sure the last footfalls hit with loud thumps. The low voices of her aunt and sister abruptly cut off as she leaned against the wide entryway of the kitchen. "Am I interrupting?"

Dorcas turned from the sink with a magnificent smile. "Not at all. We were just finishing the dishes."

Uh-huh.

"But now that we're all here," Dorcas said pulling off her apron, "we should get started."

Cassie was afraid of this. She knew in some surreal way that she needed to begin *witch* training. God only knew what that entailed. Collecting toadstools, maybe? Breaking a seal on Satan? Throwing babies into sacks, then fleeing in a hut with chicken legs? It didn't matter. The truth was, tonight, she didn't have the strength to stake a pillow let alone a vampire.

"I know you're exhausted, Cassie," Dorcas said, once again reading her mind, which—despite the growing evidence—was hopefully not something she could actually do. "So, there will be no magic lessons tonight."

"What?" Eliza threw her tea towel on the counter. "No. I'm not tired."

"I suspect you rarely are. But what I have to show you will be enough for one evening." She waved a beckoning hand. "Come." Dorcas picked up a candle by the brass finger grip of its holder, guiding them to the chained dining room doors. She passed the candle to Eliza, then pulled a key out from the pocket of her overalls. She clicked the lock open and removed the chains, showing them to Cassie. "These are for humans." She then muttered something beneath her breath. Cassie's teeth vibrated with a strange, electric energy. A moment later, Dorcas snapped her fingers and the doors slid back.

"Oh my God, yes," Eliza whispered.

"That's for the vampires." She looked back at them with a raised eyebrow. "Follow me."

Darkness swallowed their aunt as she stepped into the dining room. Cassie moved to the side, allowing her sister and a few cats to go next.

While only a fraction of the size of Hank's weapons barn, the dining room was just as impressive. There was so much to take in. Tall glass-paned cabinets covered the walls on either side, and while it was hard to be sure in the dim candlelight, they appeared to be crammed full of corked jewel-toned bottles of various shapes and sizes. The long dining room table was weighed down with enough stakes to kill a hundred vampires, and in three of the room's shadowed corners leaned battle axes, spears, and scythes. In the fourth corner stood a rack overflowing with what looked to be leather garments.

Neither Cassie nor Eliza could speak.

"There's more out back. I'm almost embarrassed by my stockpile." Dorcas took the candle from Eliza and lit another. "But while *he* slept, I prepared." She ran a finger along the table, then studied the tip. "Sorry for the dust. After I thought I killed *him* with the explosion, there was no need to come in. A month or so ago, I nearly donated the entire collection." She laughed. "Good thing I didn't."

Cassie agreed. For many reasons.

"This table is hundreds of years old." Dorcas lifted a fluffy gray kitten from the surface. "How did you get up there?" She lowered it gently to the floor. "It was made from the wood of the ship that brought your grandmother—many times over—across the sea. It smashed on the rocks as they were about to make shore."

Cassie made a mental note to tell Ben that. It seemed like something he might be interested in.

"Our witch grandmother didn't cause the wreck, did she?" Eliza asked.

Dorcas's eyelids flittered. "I have never considered that." She shrugged. "Cassie, I wanted to show you what this room held so that you might feel some reassurance." Dorcas regarded the collection. "The contents represent generations of knowledge. While each of your ancestors' deaths has brought the Deliverer closer to freedom, with every battle, more was learned of his weaknesses. Those who were left behind made new potions for the next witch to use, like passed-down recipes. As a result, each witch was better prepared for the next fight. You are well defended."

"You know what I don't get?" Eliza asked. "Why didn't the witches hide? Or not have babies? Or fight as a team?"

"I doubt the powers that guide the universe would allow that," Dorcas mused. "And maybe some did fight as a coven, but the Deliverer is powerful. Each witch of her generation wouldn't have wanted to put her loved ones in danger. Besides, living in fear is against a witch's nature."

That settled it. Cassie couldn't be a witch because living in fear currently seemed like her default way of being.

"Our gifts are meant to be used and shared, not just to protect the beauty of life, but to create it. Every witch who has faced the Deliverer and lost her life because of it made sure to live fully before the call to battle, and that included having children, or delighting in her sister's children, as the case may be." A shadow crossed Dorcas's face.

"Is that allowed?" Cassie asked. Maybe she had found a loophole. "What constitutes a direct line? You're the oldest, so it should have been your daughter. Maybe I'm not—"

"But I didn't have a daughter, so it's direct enough. The fates don't put up with those kinds of tricks. You most certainly are the witch of her generation. I know it, and the Deliverer knows it too."

Too bad Cassie didn't know it.

"The point is every witch who fought the Deliverer appreciated what it might mean, and I believe each had hope they would prevail while still being consoled with the knowledge that if she were to die, she would be helping the next witch."

All three fell into contemplative silence as the rain tapped gently at the windows.

Suddenly Dorcas clapped her hands. "But things will be different this time around. While the Deliverer won't let you hide, Cassie, I will not leave your side." Dorcas's expression turned thunderous. "I will kill that vampire once and for all, and I will enjoy doing it. After I tear apart every cell of his wretched existence, I will dance in the dust of his unnatural flesh." Her face brightened. "But you can help. It will be so much fun!"

"Let me think about it," Cassie murmured.

"Can I fight the Deliverer too?" Eliza asked. "I think I'd be good at it."

"Certainly, we—"

"No," Cassie snapped. "Eliza, you just found out you were a witch, and you've never done any magic."

"Not unlike you," Eliza drawled. "And yes, I have too done magic! My stories? I told Dorcas all about them. And they are totally a thing."

"Totally," Dorcas said, nodding with big eyes.

"And Tommy will be saved when she kills the Deliverer, so there." Cassie wouldn't have been surprised if her sister had finished by sticking her tongue out.

"Only if he doesn't feed on a human," Dorcas added. "And while I appreciate your bloodlust, Eliza, I'm afraid I must side with Cassie. By all means, you can and should train with us—you both need to learn how to defend yourselves against vampires—but if your sister is concerned about your safety during the final battle on All Hallows' Eve, that might be a distraction. And if Del succeeds and she becomes the thirteenth witch to die, the curse will be broken, and the island—maybe the entire world—will be doomed."

Wow. Cassie had never felt so important, useless, or terrified.

"So," her aunt continued, spinning in a circle, "the good news is we have all of this at our disposal."

"What's the bad news?" Cassie asked.

"These are simply tools. There are only three ways to kill a vampire." Dorcas held them both in a level gaze. "Fire. Staking. Decapitation. Everything else is—"

"No," Eliza moaned.

Dorcas's eyes widened, serious offense taking shape in the lines of her face. "I'm sorry?"

"This is fantastic. Really," Eliza said. "And I am seriously looking forward to trying this stuff out." She sighed with frustration. "But anyone can do those things."

That was not a statement Cassie necessarily agreed with.

"I want to learn magic. I mean, you want to learn magic, right, Cass?"

Cassie jerked to attention. With all that had happened, she'd never considered whether she *wanted* to learn magic. She *had* to learn magic, and fast. But if there was a choice between learning magic and not being in this situation at all, the answer was pretty clear.

"Eliza," Dorcas interjected, "it's not as easy as you think. There is no such thing as an all-powerful witch who can destroy her enemies with inherent power. Think of witchcraft as a sport," Dorcas said. "Every witch—or player—is born with talent, some a little, some a lot, but if you don't practice and build your endurance, you will never achieve greatness. Even a witch at the top of her game," she said, laying her fingertips on her chest, "does not have unlimited power. We can only channel so much energy before we are drained. We need potions, curses, fighting techniques, and weapons. We will explore your gifts at some point, but given how little time is left, we must focus on the basics." Dorcas snapped her hand out. "Fire." Bright orange flames erupted from her outstretched palm. "Staking." A stake flipped up from the table into the same hand extinguishing the flames. "Decapitation." Cassie ducked as a battle-ax flew across the room into her aunt's other hand, making the flames of the candles shudder.

Eliza collapsed against the wall with a thud. "Forget the vampires. I'm already dead."

"Thank you." Dorcas inhaled stiffly, then directed her focus to Cassie. "All that being said, I am curious about your gifts, Polliwog."

"Sorry?" Cassie's voice cracked. "My gifts?"

"Your special talents, like how your sister can nudge fate with her stories. Or how I can call the wind and clouds, infuse my cooking with emotion—"

Cassie knew that dinner had been tainted with... *loveliness.*

"—talk with the dead and play siren songs on my fiddle. There are many more, but I don't want to brag. Oh! Levitation?! Can you float objects?"

Cassie blinked. "I've never tried, but I'm going to say no?"

"Invisibility?"

Invisibility? Seriously? Cassie stared bug-eyed at her aunt. "Is that a thing? Can you do that?"

Dorcas smiled slyly. "Wouldn't you like to know." Suddenly she startled. "Fire! That's a ubiquitous skill."

Cassie squinted. "I mean, maybe? There's this burned jack-o'-lantern I may have been responsible for."

"Good," Dorcas said, clearly not meaning it. "I suppose I was hoping for fireballs or streams of flames, but that's certainly a place to start. What else?"

Sweat prickled on Cassie's brow. "Phones don't always work around me."

Dorcas nodded. "Well, no need to be alarmed. Sometimes a witch's gifts come out quite suddenly. That's how the fire started in the library all those years ago. A great-great-aunt of yours was startled by a cat and, in a flash, fire was everywhere!" Dorcas smiled. "Anyway, I'm sure your powers will emerge during the graveyard test." She lifted an orange cat off the table, but this time cuddled it to her chest.

"Wait. There's a test? At a graveyard?"

"Didn't I mention it?"

Cassie was one hundred percent certain she would have remembered being told about a graveyard test.

"As the witch of her generation, you must perform the graveyard test. It is a rite of passage. An initiation of sorts. Even though you won't be fighting, it will be a good learning experience. All the firstborn Beckett witches do it." Dorcas held up the cat to look it in the eye. "Isn't that right?" She glanced back at Cassie. "We go tomorrow night."

Tomorrow night?! Cassie bit her lip so she wouldn't scream, even though screaming seemed appropriate.

"We don't have time to waste." Dorcas lowered the cat to the floor. "In order to keep you alive, we must determine where your talents lie."

Cassie nodded then shook her head. "But what am I being tested on?"

"Your ability to kill a vampire, of course. To use some delightfully human turns of phrase, this is sink or swim, Polliwog. The training wheels are off."

But they had never been on! She hadn't grown up with all this.

"I'd go on to say this is trial by fire, but there's some history there." Dorcas walked over and gripped Cassie by the arms. "I know you're afraid, but I've seen your power with my own eyes. As a toddler you were terrifying."

"All toddlers are terrifying!" Cassie cried. "And that was a long time ago."

"Nonsense." Dorcas patted her on the shoulders, then turned away. "You'll see." She wagged a finger in the air, walking to the other side of the room. "This hunting trip is the very thing to prove it to you." Suddenly she whirled around, eyes sparkling.

"When you see that flash of fang coming straight for your neck—that exhilarating glimpse of death—it will force the magic right out of you!"

Nothing about that sounded good.

"Now," Dorcas continued, pausing to blow out one of the candles, "let's get some sleep." She linked arms with Eliza, and they left the room once again speaking in hushed tones. Cassie shuffled after them. As she passed the buffet, she couldn't help but trail her eyes over the bottles, absentmindedly scanning the labels, until she came to one that read *Head Preservation*.

So, Dorcas hadn't been kidding. Good to know.

CHAPTER 18

Fresh sea breeze caressed Cassie's cheeks as she blinked her eyes against the sunlight pouring into her room at Sea House. The sensation was wonderful, deliciously cool, the kind of breeze that lulled early risers back to sleep, but . . .

Hadn't she closed all the windows last night? Yes, she definitely had. She'd been a little freaked out when she went to bed at the thought of vampires floating around outside and peering in at her. So, either Dorcas had snuck in and closed them, or . . .

Sea House knows what you need.

Cassie's eyes snapped all the way open. Was that another memory? Or was she hearing voices? She stared at the beamed ceiling and shook her head. It didn't matter. This was her life now. Hearing voices was to be expected. Self-opening windows too. And really, the breeze was nice. The entire night had been pretty great, actually. When Cassie had finally closed her eyes, she thought there was no way she would sleep, but being tucked underneath the quilts on the plush bed made her feel safe in a way she hadn't expected, and the sound of the waves stilled her mind. In fact, she couldn't remember having a better sleep.

Suddenly the muscles in her neck spasmed. Okay, maybe not

everything had been perfect. The pillow she had used was a good inch or two thicker than the one she used at home. She should have known the danger because she was in fact that old. She groaned and rolled out of bed. Time to save humanity.

Cassie pulled on her jeans from the day before and felt for her coin in the pocket. She had been thinking about it a lot lately, like there was something she needed to remember. Something important. Somehow, she knew her mother had given it to her before she died, but she couldn't remember how and why. Not knowing was putting her on edge. It wasn't as though she wanted to get rid of the coin, but for some reason, she felt like she needed to be careful.

Cassie finished getting dressed and tightened her messy bun. She had some household management issues to attend to before her graveyard test. First order of business was calling the schools. Again. She planned to tell them the kids would be out for at least a week, using the same virus excuse she had come up with before. But to do that she needed a phone that could actually make a call. Service on this side of the island was spotty. Sadie had found a sand dune that got her a few bars, but other than that they were out of luck. Speaking of Sadie, her phone had to be dead. In her rush to get them out of the house, Cassie had forgotten to bring chargers. Not that chargers would have helped. As far as she could tell, Sea House didn't have electricity, and somehow, she doubted Dorcas had a phone. She probably videochatted through the steam of her cauldron.

The old wide-planked floors creaked as Cassie tiptoed to Sadie's room. She mentally prepared herself to wake her daughter for the second time in one week on a day she didn't have to go to school. Hopefully she'd be able to state her purpose before she got hit with another pillow. Cassie knocked gently and turned the brass engraved knob. "Sadie?" She peeked her head in. "You awake?"

The bed was empty and made. A thousand needles stabbed Cassie's heart, but then she saw her daughter on the window seat with a light blanket wrapped around her shoulders. She was reading.

"Hi," Cassie said carefully. "I didn't expect to find you up."

"I went to bed early. My phone's dead." Sadie didn't look over at her, but she didn't sound upset either.

"I figured." Here came the tricky part. "So, I'm going into town. I thought I might take your phone with me and charge it."

Cassie waited for her daughter to demand she take her along, or at least give her a straight answer about what was going on, but all she said was "Sure," without moving her eyes from the book resting against her thighs. "Thanks."

Cassie cocked her head. She had no idea how to interpret that. Was her daughter grateful? Did she truly not care? Was this passive-aggression? Not out-and-out anger, but maybe in-and-in anger? "Are you good?"

Sadie shrugged. "When Dorcas said good night, she offered to teach me how to bake the pumpkin bread we had yesterday."

Okay. That rankled a bit. Cassie wanted to bake with her daughter . . . if there was ever a time when they weren't busy, annoyed with one another, or exhausted. She thought about the October calendar she had so carefully organized. It felt like a lifetime ago when, in reality, it hadn't even been a week.

"I like it here. And don't worry. We'll watch the boys."

We'll. Dorcas got a *we'll* and they had only known each other for a day. "That's great." Cassie walked over to the nightstand by the wrought iron bed and picked up the phone. She backed up to the door, eyes on her daughter, wondering if she would give her any contact at all, but Sadie merely turned a page in her book. "Okay, bye."

Cassie closed the door. That had gone much better than she had expected. Pretty good even. But even though it had gone well, the whole thing left her feeling kind of bad.

Or maybe the badness was coming from the throbbing in her neck. Cassie dug her knuckles into the muscles at the base of her skull, then tilted her head side to side. She was in no physical condition to fight vampires. She couldn't remember the last time she worked out. This was going to be a disaster, and if tonight was a disaster . . .

Cassie reached for her phone and cleared her throat. "Set a reminder on Halloween to take an anti-inflammatory before battle."

"Done," her phone chirped happily.

Done.

☾

After some debate, Cassie convinced the others that she would drive herself into town. Once she realized Dorcas was serious about not giving her any preparation for the graveyard, she decided she needed some alone time in her own house where she could relax. Theoretically. Dorcas would meet her there later, so they could go to the cemetery together. Eliza was staying at Sea House with the kids. Their friendly vamps in the basement had enough provisions for a couple of days at least, but that didn't make Eliza any happier about the situation. She loved the idea of hunting non-friendly vampires in a graveyard. *Weirdo.*

It was another lovely sunny day. Painted leaves reflected the brilliant sun, and the sky was a vibrant blue, but Cassie had trouble registering any of it. She drove in a daze and went into her house on autopilot. She mechanically started some laundry and washed the few dishes that had been left in the sink. Then she called the schools and packed some more clothes for the kids. Finally, she plugged in everyone's devices. When she was through, she flopped on the couch with a box of crackers, not feeling much like the witch of her generation.

But Cassie wasn't going to think about that anymore. She was done with thinking. TV was better. Watching turtles in the Galapagos float was much easier than contemplating vampires, at least until the baby turtles hatched and had to run with their little flippers for the ocean while under attack by seagulls. At that point she switched to a baking challenge. Buttercream icing was soothing. There was a bright, hot needle of fear being dragged through her veins the entire time, but she was ignoring it. If she followed that needle back to the source, she'd be a mess, and really, it wasn't like she would die tonight. This was an exercise. She knew deep down if—how had Dorcas put it?—a *flash of fang came straight for her neck*, her aunt would take that vamp's head off. Probably.

As the day stretched on, Cassie's eyelids grew heavy. She glanced at the clock. Just after five. If she fell asleep right now, she could get at least an hour's sleep. The moment she closed her eyes, though, a knock sounded at the door.

She could ignore it. Nobody knew she was home except Ben. They had been texting a bit here and there about diaper rash, mashed carrots, and vampire curses, but she knew it wasn't him. They had agreed to keep Olive far away from any vampire business. And that knock had been a jaunty rap, probably from a door-to-door salesperson. There was no reason to get up. They would go away. Strangely, though, Cassie found herself holding her breath.

The knock came again, followed by "Hello in there! You should resume your taking of breaths. I wouldn't want you to faint."

Cassie looked side to side, but there was no one around to confirm that she had just heard the most politely terrifying voice ever, belonging to someone who could apparently hear her not breathing. She got to her feet and tiptoed over to the fireplace to grab the poker. When she got to the door, she leaned to the side and pulled back the sheer covering the long, thin window.

A smiling man also tilted, mirroring her posture. "There you are!"

Granted, Cassie was new to all this, but the man on her porch looked like a tall, thin vampire. Maybe it was the outfit. He wore a black suit with a black tie and his shoes shone like a Magic 8 Ball. He was also wearing a wide-brim black hat and was holding a black umbrella.

"Don't worry. I'm not here to hurt you. The master would be displeased. And he already has me on a diet. He does love his punishments." He laughed in dusty breaths. "I'm here to extend an invitation."

"Who are you?" It came out as a whisper, but he heard her just fine.

"Who I am is not important." He smiled, a touch bitterly, revealing his teeth. His long, yellowed teeth. "You may consider me a butler of sorts."

"You're not supposed to be out there. The sun hasn't set."

"Ah yes, due to an unfortunate twist of fate and an unwise deal on my part with a rather shady figure, I am more ghoul than vampire. My transformation has made me quite powerful in some ways. The sun is a mere annoyance. But unfortunately, it has also stolen my beauty."

"Right. I don't want any invitations. Thank you." Cassie almost released her grip on the curtain, but the man held up a knobby finger.

"I'm afraid your preferences will not be taken into consideration." Suddenly his gaze flicked to the pot of mini chrysanthemums by Cassie's door. "Pardon me." His long stick legs bent to right angles as he lowered to the planter. He snatched up something hidden in the flowers, stood, then held it out to Cassie. "May I?"

She frowned. A toad?

In a flash the ghoul popped it in his mouth and chewed with heavy bites. At one point some webbed toes slipped out, but he tucked them back in with his finger.

Cassie pulled away, silently screaming.

"Hello?"

She forced herself back and peered out.

"My apologies. My current dietary restrictions have me peckish. As I was saying, you will meet the master on the thirteenth of October, at Salty's." Judging by his delivery of the word, he was unimpressed with the sophistication level of the bar. The *toad eater* was unimpressed. "I would recommend arriving shortly before midnight or—"

"No." She had intended for it to come out as a bold declaration, but it sounded more like a question.

The ghoul sighed. "Indentured servitude. I do not recommend it. If you would allow me to continue? For every five minutes you are late, the Deliverer of Fear, Sorrow, and Death will kill one of your neighbors."

Cracker bile crept up Cassie's throat.

"You understand? Say yes."

"Yes."

"Lovely. Until then the master will be watching."

The man spun on his heel and walked down the path to the sidewalk, where he turned sharply and walked away in odd giant steps.

Cassie opened the door, her poker still clutched in her hand. She tiptoed onto the porch and down the steps. He was gone—completely, impossibly gone. Nobody walked that fast. Her shoulders slumped. Maybe he had turned into a bat.

The sun had nearly set, its last crimson streaks fading away. Cassie turned to head back inside when the sensation of being watched made her pause. She looked up to the second floor of Mrs. MacDonald's house. Sure enough her neighbor had the curtain pulled back and was looking down at her. She probably didn't approve of Cassie's visitor. Well, that was fine because Cassie didn't approve of the toad-eating freak either. She hopped up the steps. Hopefully if she was a little late to the bar, Del would start next door.

Bad thoughts, Cassie. Bad.

☾

Loud seconds ticked by on the kitchen clock. Dark had fallen over the Burrow hours ago, and her aunt still hadn't arrived. With night, Cassie realized more had changed on her street in the past days. The neighborhood had an odd hush to it. It was as though every living creature on their tiny bit of land was uneasy, tense, afraid of the sound of its own heartbeat.

Where are you, Dorcas?

They had agreed that she would arrive after sunset but never settled on a time. Cassie knew going later was wise, given there wouldn't be people around. She definitely didn't want an audience or another half-vampire on her conscience. But she was hoping Dorcas would come a little early. Maybe give her a pep talk. Go over a few moves she might try. She texted Eliza, repeatedly, to see if Dorcas had at least left Sea House, but none of her attempts made it through.

Cassie wrapped her arms around her waist and paced the living room floor. To be honest, she didn't want to be alone. It was funny because sometimes it felt like that's all she'd wanted since the kids had been born. A half an hour to take a bath in peace. Maybe an afternoon to read a book. But now that the sun had gone down, her house felt odd, disconcerting, cold. Her ears searched for the thumps on the stairs. Or the sound of water rushing through the pipes from one of Sadie's forty-five-minute showers. Or Janet's soft meow! Even though her cat had turned out to be a sleeper agent, Cassie still wanted her.

It was midnight before headlights swept the room. Cassie ran to the window and spotted Dorcas's Jeep pulling up to the curb. *Thank God.* She hurried over to the door and swung it open. She almost stepped outside but thought better of it. There could be vampires everywhere.

Dorcas's dark cloak brushed the ground as she walked toward the house empty-handed. *Huh.* Cassie had expected her to be carrying some sort of sack or satchel—like the size of one of the boys' hockey bags—for all the axes, stakes, and potions. Must be in the Jeep.

"Tonight's the night," Dorcas called out when she spotted Cassie. "Are you excited?" *Excited* was not the right word. It didn't matter though; her aunt wasn't expecting an answer. "Shall we? I'll drive."

Cassie peeked her head out, then looked side to side before craning her neck to peer up above the threshold. She then took a cautious step outside. Dorcas gave her a funny look but didn't say anything. Once they were driving, Cassie said, "I had a visitor today."

"What kind of visitor?"

"Del's butler." Cassie filled her aunt in on all that had transpired, including the toad—that was not something she could carry alone. When she was through, Dorcas made a contemplative sound.

"What are you thinking?"

Her aunt tapped the steering wheel. "I'm curious about why he wants to meet you, but I'm also wondering if this could be an opportunity."

Cassie's face prickled. "Please tell me this opportunity you're considering is a way to get us out of battling Del on Halloween?"

"Maybe. The Deliverer must kill you on All Hallows' Eve, but I've never heard of a rule that says we can't end him sooner. But it does mean you'll have to be *bait* for this meeting at Salty's."

Well, frick.

"Let me give it some thought," Dorcas finished.

Minutes later, the Jeep turned onto the drive of the cemetery, lighting up the iron gates on either side. Pale tombstones rose from the shadows, and a cold, sculpted angel looked down on them, weeping—which somehow felt personal. But from an objective standpoint, the location was a good choice for the test. It was large, far back from the road, and it had an old-school graveyard atmosphere. Cassie wasn't sure that sort of thing mattered to vampires but suspected it might.

The Jeep crept forward, gravel crunching noisily beneath its wheels. Cassie squeezed her hands together. "Before we get there, I need some clarification. We're not planning on killing any vampires like Tommy, right? You told Eliza we could save him, but you also offered to kill him, so I'm confused."

"*We* won't be killing any vampires. *You* will be killing vampires. And I offered my services to Tommy as a mercy," Dorcas answered. "You've seen what is happening to that poor boy. It will only get worse as time passes unless he drinks from a human. Donated blood helps, but in a perverse caveat the universe has put forth, for him to feel well, he needs to kill. As the days pass, the pain and horror of what is happening to him will grow. He will almost certainly cave to his bloody desires and become a full vampire."

Cassie's stomach fell. "I guess that means you don't think you can actually kill Del and save him?"

Dorcas's gaze jumped to her. "Of course I will kill the Deliverer. That's not what I meant at all. No, Tommy is putting on a brave, albeit decaying, face. The inner strength he must possess to endure the constant torture is remarkable." She eased the Jeep carefully around a crumbling mausoleum. "Some people who are bitten give up their humanity right away. It's as though they had been waiting for it to happen, to be freed from their moral chains. Others last only days, less commonly weeks. Tommy is doing well, all considered." She sighed. "But everyone has their limit. We must keep an eye on him."

The thought made Cassie sad, not only for Tommy, but Gary too, and all the other people she didn't know about who might have been turned since Del's awakening. "I don't think I'm ready for mercy killings."

"No, of course not," Dorcas said. "Not unless they ask."

"Still not ready. And I don't want to kill anyone by accident. Not when they have a chance of turning back. How will I know for sure? And how do you even know there will be a vampire here?"

"You'll know a fully turned vampire when you see it," Dorcas said, parking the Jeep beside the gnarled branches of an old oak tree. "Aside from the fact that they won't be rotting, you'll feel the evil, and don't forget the tingling in your hands. That is an excellent warning sign. They must have burned when that vampire showed up at your house."

Huh. Cassie couldn't remember any tingling or burning in her hands. Certainly not like the sensations she had experienced before.

"They did tingle, yes?"

"No."

"Not at all?"

"Nope."

"Oh dear."

"He did say he was more ghoul than vampire."

"That must be it." A slight grimace passed over her aunt's features. "As for how I know there will be a vampire here: there are always vampires here. They are predictable creatures." Dorcas hopped out into the night.

Cassie didn't move from her seat. She chewed her lip instead. Dorcas hadn't looked convinced by the ghoul thing. What did it mean that her hands weren't tingling? Was she somehow losing the few powers she might actually possess? Dorcas had all but guaranteed her magic would come when she needed it most, but if her hands weren't even tingling . . .

This didn't seem like the best night for a test. She needed to investigate this further. Maybe be examined by a doctor. A witch doctor. Not that kind of witch—

Dorcas rapped on her window. Cassie screamed.

Why did people keep doing that to her?

Her aunt opened the door. Cassie reluctantly stepped out and straightened her jacket over her jeans. She had opted for the peacoat because it had the thickest material of all her jackets, and she had chosen her jeans for the same reason. She doubted either were fang-proof, but they might help. She also went with a black fisherman's cap for stealth purposes, even though vamps probably had good night vision. It might have been nice if her aunt had offered her a leather garment, but nope, that hadn't happened. Oh God! Why hadn't she worn a turtleneck! It was so obvious! She didn't even have a scarf to protect her arteries!

She was losing it. Hysteria was setting in.

It's okay, Cassie. You're still learning.

Learning how to die!

Dorcas waved her toward a gravel path. They walked in silence, which gave Cassie time to settle her breathing. She could do this. She was the witch of her generation. She needed to be positive and manifest dead vampires. That didn't sound quite right, but it's not like there was time to make a witch-of-her-generation vision board. They headed toward the older section of the cemetery. After a few minutes, she asked, "So do we just wander around until someone starts biting?"

"Oh no," Dorcas said. "That would be a waste of time. I know where they are." She pointed to the top of a hill rising in the distance. "Up there."

Cassie spied a small, dark building at its peak. "What is that?"

A slow, terrifying smile spread across her aunt's face. "That, Polliwog, is the dead house."

CHAPTER 19

The octagonal building floated on a sea of mist at the top of the hill. Its pyramid top pointed up through the fog, and a half-moon hovered at its shoulder.

The dead house.

Sounded appropriate. Not terrifying at all.

Even though it was a small building, Cassie couldn't help but think you could fit at least twenty vampires in there if you packed them in.

"They always seem to gravitate here when they're first turned," Dorcas mused. "Maybe it's some instinct to make friends or form a hive."

They formed hives?! Cassie already had enough going on in her head without imagining what a vampire hive might look like. "Wait. We have to go back to the Jeep. We forgot the weapons."

"Oh, I didn't bring any weapons."

"You didn't bring any weapons?" Cassie asked in a panicked whisper. "Why wouldn't you bring any weapons? Are you working for him? Do you want me dead? Why do we not have weapons?"

Dorcas took slow steps toward her with her hands up. "Calm.

You are okay." Once she was close enough, she cupped Cassie's cheeks. "Rely on yourself. Trust your magic. Twelve Beckett witches—thirteen, if you count me—have faced this trial before you. All of them survived."

"And then they died!" Cassie suddenly frowned. "Except you. I'd really like to hear more about your encounter with Del. It might help. We could go to a coffee shop right now and—"

"That is a conversation for another time. Now breathe." Dorcas inhaled and exhaled noisily a few times. "You were born to do this. Everything you need is inside of you. You are magic."

Cassie didn't know about that. "I should've at least been allowed to bring my crossbow. Or a potion!"

Dorcas nodded. "I might have allowed it. It is important to be prepared." Then she laughed far too loudly. "The look on your face. Bring that to the fight. And keep in mind there are weapons everywhere."

A small animal scurried into a bush near Cassie's feet. She hopped to the side and grabbed her aunt's arm. "Just so we're clear. You will step in if things get dicey, right?"

Dorcas hummed with uncertainty.

"No, I need you to promise me right now that if fangs are about to pierce my neck, you will intervene."

"I don't know. Without the real threat of death, you may not experience the necessary fear required to discover what you are capable of."

Cassie chortled. "Believe me. Fear is not an issue. I have all the fear. Fear is all I am now. So promise me, or we're calling this off."

Dorcas rolled her eyes. "Cassie, you should enjoy this more. It's not every day that a witch gets to kill her first vampire."

That sounded like something Eliza would say. Lucky, lucky Eliza who was probably playing cards with the kids right now by lantern light, eating pumpkin bread and drinking tea.

"No more stalling. Your nerves will get the better of you."

Cassie's thoughts swirled, searching for a way out of this, but she had already thought all the thoughts to be had. The time had come.

The dead house looked down at Cassie as she climbed the path. She scanned the pine needles covering the ground looking for a weapon. A rock, maybe? A broken beer bottle from a graveyard party? That might be hard to find. Oh! A stick! Cassie stooped to pick one up. It wasn't particularly thick, but it could work. It had to work.

"That looks thin," Dorcas called out helpfully.

Cassie glared back at her, whispering, "You are a horrible, horrible person. And keep your voice down."

Her aunt tittered with glee.

"And here I thought we had trust issues before," Cassie grumbled, climbing the slope. It wasn't all that steep, but she struggled to keep her breath even. As she neared the top, she spotted a plaque beside the old, planked door.

The Octagonal Dead House 1886

Historical details followed, covering the significance of dead houses, names from the cemetery committee that had commissioned its construction, and then...

> **Inside are shelves on which caskets were stored during the winter when graves could not be dug.**

Cassie did not know that was a thing. It made sense given that digging frozen ground was near impossible. It was practical. Not at all ghoulish. Now, if only she could stop herself from imagining shelves of caskets holding bodies with blue skin, bulging eyeballs, and mouths twisted in frozen screams.

She leaned her ear to the door. It was awfully quiet. There definitely couldn't be twenty vampires inside. She doubted there were any. Some of the pure terror she had been feeling dribbled away. It wasn't her fault if Dorcas had been wrong about this being the vampire hot spot. As far as she could tell, it was time to call it a night. Cassie skipped back down the path. "Guess you were wrong." She shrugged. "Nobody's home." She headed for the Jeep, but Dorcas blocked her path. "Let's be sure."

Cassie wanted to argue, but, again, this was what she had come to do. For Sadie. And humanity. That still sounded funny. She climbed back up the hill until she stood before the door. Should she just go in? She didn't like the idea of getting pulled into a brick hut with nowhere to run. Maybe she could knock? Why not? If the doorknob turned, she would get a head start. Wait, she wasn't running. She was fighting. Killing. Slaying. If the doorknob turned, she'd plunge her stick into the monster's heart! Kill it dead!

She raised her fist to knock while clutching her one weapon at her hip. Well, her one weapon aside from her hidden volcano of power waiting to erupt.

"Overhand, dear!" Dorcas shouted.

Cassie jolted. All the vampires in town would know she was here if her aunt didn't keep her voice down. Cassie reversed her grip, raised the stick into the air, then knocked.

Nothing. No sound at all. No movement. Nothing. The relief

almost dropped her to her knees. And she didn't fail! With that knock, she had walked into the sleeping dragon's cave with her wooden sword. Maybe it wasn't much, but—

Cassie shrieked as a black figure descended from the roof. The stick cracked in her grip as she jumped back, sending her rolling down the hill. When she stopped, she was flat on her belly, hands planted by her sides. She tilted her chin to look back up the hill. A gigantic bald vampire with a nose ring piercing his septum stood at the top. He had to be at least six five, probably six six. That was not fair. Why couldn't she start with, say, a child vampire? Oh God, no! How could she even think that? Aside from the horrific tragedy, that would be creepy, especially if it had braids . . . or bangs. Maybe a small ballerina vampire? No, also terrifying. A normal-sized human vampire! Why couldn't she start with that?

The figure stalked down the hill in big steps. Cassie could swear the earth was trembling. "What do I do?" she shouted.

"Well, first, I would get up," Dorcas called out helpfully, "and then summon your powers." Her aunt said it as though it were the simplest thing in the world. "They are there. Invite them to play. See what they do."

Cassie pushed herself to her feet and searched her body. It felt empty of power but still chock-full of fear. The vamp descended slowly. She deeply appreciated the fact that all the vamps she had met thus far seemed to enjoy stalking their prey. Although she could also see the benefit of a swift death.

Focus, Cassie. It was time to try.

Okay, magic. Time to come out and play. She jutted her hands out and squinted as though bracing against a hurricane-force wind.

The vampire stopped and cocked his head.

Cassie didn't feel any magic, but maybe she needed to look within. She closed her eyes. She couldn't see anything. Just darkness. The soothing darkness of the abyss . . . which she did not have time for! No, she was the witch of her generation. It was time to just let it rip. "Fire!"

Cassie had expected to hear flames whooshing through the air or maybe giant vampire screams, but all she got was silence.

She peeked an eye open and looked at her hands. No fire. Just regular fleshy palms.

Laughter ricocheted through the graveyard.

It wasn't coming from the bald, muscular vampire or Dorcas though. Cassie scanned the cemetery until she found him.

Standing on top of the dead house, his dark silhouette outlined by the light of the moon, was Del. It was him. She knew in her core it was him. The monster who was responsible for the wretched state of Tommy and Gary and God only knew how many others. The monster who was threatening her life. Who was threatening her family members' lives. It was him. Then again, a minute ago, she had been pretty sure she could throw fire, so . . .

"Make sure you leave her alive," he called out, his words piercing the air like shards of ice. "But feel free to enjoy yourself."

Then he was gone. One second he was there. The next he was gone. Cassie was so stunned she didn't see the giant vampire lunging for her hand until it was too late. He grabbed her wrist and tossed her into the air like a rag doll.

She hit the ground hard, making her ribs howl with pain. On the one hand she was glad the master had instructed the big guy not to kill her. On the other, *Enjoy yourself* felt broad. And painful. And her aunt hadn't intervened! "Thanks for the help!" she gasped, struggling to get up.

"I have every faith in you." Dorcas must have followed her

flight path because she was leaning against a nearby tree, arms crossed over her chest.

That was it. Cassie was either going to end this vampire without magic, or he would leave her a bloody pulp. Except . . . was that her coin burning? Cassie thought maybe it was, but once again she didn't want to reach for it. Instead, she pulled her jacket down with a determined yank. She needed a weapon, and her stick was long gone, but Dorcas had said there were weapons everywhere.

She glanced around. To her right, farther down the hill, there was a tombstone, at its side a short, wrought iron pole for hanging flowerpots. If she could get there before he pounced, she could pull it from the ground and thrust it through his chest. It was the best option. The only option she could see. "Dorcas! Will an iron stake work?"

The vampire frowned in confusion, then looked over to Dorcas, also awaiting her answer.

"Excellent question. I don't know. I've always used wood. But I can't wait to see!"

Yeah, me neither. Cassie huffed three quick breaths. *Go!*

She lurched around and broke into a run, pumping her arms and legs. At first she felt good, fast, faster than she had ever been, but then she was reminded there was such a thing as too fast. Gravity pulled at her, yanking her down the hill. Her arms flailed as her feet pounded the earth at wrong angles, jarring her knees. She could not let herself fall, not with the vampire grunts so close behind.

She was almost there.

The slope of the hill was easing, but she couldn't slow down. She wasn't going to be able to stop. She would have to run right by the gravestone. But she needed that pole! Maybe she could grab it, then veer instantly to the side. It was the only way she could think of. He was breathing down her neck.

Cassie put her hands out in front of her, using every bit of the strength in her legs to stay upright. She grabbed the rod with both hands and yanked. Horror hit as the ground held the stake a half second too long before releasing its grip, sending Cassie careening toward the gravestone. As her hip smashed against the granite block, sending her toppling backward, she whipped the pole up, and the vampire ran right into it.

The giant bloodsucker followed her over the top, throwing his hands out to land on either side of her head with heavy thuds. Cassie cringed, peeking out the slit of her right eye. *Please explode into dust. Please explode into dust. Please . . .*

"Ow."

Cassie opened her eyes all the way. She had missed. The pole had gone into his shoulder. "Oh my God, I am so sorry."

"Don't apologize to him!" Dorcas shouted. "He kills people!"

"You are going to pay for that." The vamp's voice was so deep and raspy, Cassie's bones quivered. He pulled the rod out of his arm and tossed it to the side. He then raised his fist and drove it toward Cassie's head. She twisted to the side and his knuckles smashed into a flat concrete marker. He grunted in surprise. His hand was stuck in the cracked stone. Cassie strained to the side, reaching her fingers out, searching for any weapon. She chanced a look over. The pole hadn't gone that far. She could almost reach it. Dorcas stood on the other side, watching with interest.

"Help. Me," Cassie grunted.

"Call it to you. Use your magic." Cassie's brain vibrated with anger. How was she supposed to call it to her? Especially after her fire summoning had gone so well. She stretched her fingers out farther as the vampire grunted beside her.

"Dorcas, please!"

"You almost have it."

Cassie looked at the pole lying in the wet grass. Was it shaking? It was too dark to tell.

The vampire snorted and huffed with frustration.

"Oh dear," Dorcas said, eyes wide with concern. "I would hurry."

"I'm trying!"

Suddenly a spray of rock and dirt hit Cassie in the face. He was free! "Dorcas!"

"You've made a good start!" She flipped the pole up with the toe of her boot. Cassie fumbled it then steadied her grip before turning and driving it once again into the vampire. Well, into the vampire's other shoulder. He roared.

"So close," Dorcas said. "Pull it out. Try again."

Cassie was surprised she had time to pull it out. The vampire's other arm must have been damaged with her first strike. She yanked on the rod, and it released with a sucking noise. He reared up and she drove it into him again. The side of his stomach this time.

"One more time," Dorcas said.

Cassie yanked it free and rose to her feet, her legs trembling with spent adrenaline. She raised the pole up as the vampire kicked her shin. She fell forward, driving the makeshift stake into his thigh. He gripped her hair and dragged her across the earth as he pulled the rod out and tossed it away again. "You are really bad at this," he growled before lifting her to her feet.

"Help!"

Dorcas stood frozen, paralyzed with indecision.

Cassie pushed against the vampire's chest as his fangs headed for her neck.

"Just a taste." He yanked her head to the side, exposing her turtleneck-free throat.

"I see fangs! I see fangs!" But then Cassie didn't see fangs because his mouth was closing in. Deathly cold breath radiated over her as two sharp points grazed her skin. A wad of sticky fluid then slapped against her neck.

"You know what, little witch?"

She whined.

"I'm bored." He threw her again.

This time, when Cassie stopped rolling, she was lying on her back. She gazed up at the stars, then brought her shaking fingertips up to her neck to swipe the slippery goo the vampire had left behind. It looked like a bluish-green slime-saliva mix. Vampirism did not do good things to the body. Her hand flopped back by her side.

Dorcas's face appeared above her, blocking the night sky. "Polliwog?"

Cassie jerked. "Where is he?!"

"He left. Are you all right?"

Cassie blinked. Angrily. Hopefully it came through.

"I know you probably don't want to hear this right now, but overall, I think that went well."

Cassie kicked her foot out to hit Dorcas's ankle, but she easily stepped away, making the night somehow feel complete.

CHAPTER 20

"He laughed at you? What a dick!"

Eliza stood beside the stone fireplace in the parlor, her eyes flashing brighter than the flames.

Cassie agreed with her sister's assessment, but it hurt to talk. It hurt to breathe. It hurt to blink. And it hurt to think about any of these things. She sat on the divan ever so carefully, planting her palms on the satiny surface to scoot her butt back before lifting her feet.

Dorcas came into the room holding a steaming ceramic mug. "Let's focus on the positive. We may not have unearthed Cassie's magical gifts, but our Polliwog fought a vampire tonight."

Cassie glared at her but did accept the mug. She sniffed the steam. Chai, maybe, with honey and red pepper, and something else she couldn't identify. Hopefully opium. Her aunt had also brought out a plate of cookies and some sort of gooey black currant square. They looked delicious, but every time Cassie thought about eating, she remembered the vampire slime on her neck. As soon as she could stand upright, she was taking a shower. If Dorcas even had a shower.

"That's something," Eliza said cheerfully. "And you didn't die either. Total win."

THE LATE-NIGHT WITCHES

Janet jumped up on the divan and began kneading Cassie's belly. She grimaced. Those paws could not be good for her internal damage.

"On a happier note," Eliza chirped, "I have something to show you guys."

Dorcas scooted to the edge of her seat and pyramided her fingers beneath her chin. Cassie did nothing. Cassie hurt.

"After the kids went up, I tried something." She smiled mischievously. "I didn't think I could do it at first, but . . ." Eliza rubbed her hands together and placed them on her knees. She then took a deep breath and stared at the low table between them. It was hard to tell what she was doing at first, but suddenly her mug rattled, then rose an inch into the air, wobbling side to side.

Dorcas gasped. "Eliza!"

Her sister focused even more intently, and the mug soared at least three feet higher.

Cassie's face flushed. "Wow. That's great."

"Wait for it," Eliza said. Dorcas's mug rattled next, then joined its floating cousin. "Cassie, put your mug down."

She curled it into her chest. "I'm still drinking. I don't want you to spill it."

"Don't worry. I've been doing this all night."

"All night?" Dorcas gushed. "It's your first time. You must be exhausted."

"Not even a little. Cassie, do it. Put down your cup."

Cassie leaned through excruciating pain—which nobody seemed to notice—to put her mug on the coffee table, and sure enough it rose to greet the others. Then they began to turn in some porcelain ring-around-the-rosy.

"Marvelous! You're a natural levitator! This with your storytelling abilities? Well, you are just full of talent!" Dorcas jumped to her feet and danced around the mugs in the opposite direction. "Astounding! Such control."

"Very . . . Mary Poppins," Cassie muttered.

"Thank you." Eliza guided the mugs back down with her gaze. They landed perfectly. "You see, Cass? Once I figured out how to move the cup a little, everything fell into place. It's so easy." She snapped her fingers and a cookie flipped up from the tray into her mouth.

Dorcas squealed with delight.

"It will happen for you in no time," Eliza mumbled.

That. Was. It.

"I'm sure you're right," Cassie muttered through her teeth gritted in pain. "I'm going to bed."

Dorcas moved to help her up, but Cassie held her back with a look.

"I know you're tired, Polliwog, but we should start planning for the upcoming meeting with the Deliverer."

Cassie waddled around the low couch. "You two go ahead and brainstorm. Catch me up later."

"Well, if you're sure . . ." Dorcas said. "But bring this with you. It will help." She handed her the mug. "And don't forget. We start training first thing in the morning."

"Looking forward to it." Cassie dragged herself up the stairs. "Good night. I hate you both."

"What's that, dear?"

"Nothing."

☾

"Try again."

Much to Cassie's surprise, the following morning's training

was not magical in nature. Dorcas took them for a run on the beach. Cassie couldn't remember the last time she'd run, and given the way she had been tossed around the graveyard the night before, well, it was hideous.

After the run, Dorcas put them through an equally hideous strength-training circuit of pull-ups, push-ups, and sit-ups—all the *ups*. Apparently Del's awakening was supposed to trigger physiological changes that would help Cassie build strength and speed, but she had yet to see any of that materialize.

After the physical training in the morning, the three spent the afternoon practicing magic. Dorcas used a glamour spell to keep their activities veiled from the kids, and Cassie tried every area of witchcraft her aunt could think of—divination, enchantment, animal summoning, compulsion, to name just a few—but her magic was still in hiding. Eliza, of course, was there too, watching Cassie's every failed attempt while she levitated random objects in the background.

Once that was through, they turned to weapons.

"One last try," Dorcas prodded. "I have a good feeling."

Cassie raised the crossbow they had purchased from Hank and anchored the butt into her shoulder. She squinted against the sun at the vampire dummy staked into the sand maybe fifty feet away. It turned out Dorcas had a bunch of monster scarecrows stored in a shed. Where she found the time to do everything was anyone's guess. Cassie hadn't managed to hit the straw monster at all in her first attempts. It was extremely annoying. Not just because she'd like to believe she could kill a vampire if need be, but because the stake covered a lot of ground and Dorcas made her use the same one over and over even though there was an endless supply. Retrieving the stake turned out to be worse than the morning run.

"Focus on the heart this time," Dorcas instructed.

Cassie rolled her eyes. What did her aunt think she had been doing all this time? If this experience taught her anything, it was that she was going to have to rethink all the *helpful* comments she gave the boys before their hockey games. Besides, she was making some progress. It seemed she had a real knack for hitting vampires in the thigh.

"And try aiming a little higher."

Dorcas was reading her mind. She knew it.

Despite the cool autumn breeze, the sun, high in the sky, caused sweat to roll down the back of Cassie's neck. She could do this. Point and shoot right at the straw heart. She squeezed her finger against the trigger and—

Thunk!

Right in the belly button.

"Okay," Dorcas said with faint enthusiasm. "You're getting closer."

Cassie dropped her weapon to the sand and walked toward the house.

"Don't worry!" Dorcas called after her. "I'll make a potion to help it fire true."

Cassie waved a hand without turning. *Super.* Why they couldn't have started with that, though, was beyond her.

☾

They followed the same routine for the next few days, and while Cassie continued to struggle with *everything*, the kids were thriving at Sea House. The boys spent their days exploring dunes and collecting sand dollars, chasing each other on the beach and climbing rust-colored rock formations. Cassie didn't love that one. It was bad for the sandstone. Sadie seemed content too. She spent most days reading in her room in the top corner of the house. Cassie couldn't blame her for loving it, with its slanted ceilings and view of the sea. She was making her way through the books in the library, huddled under a quilt of blue squares stitched with tiny stars surrounding a crescent moon. Dorcas brought her an endless supply of soups, warm bread, black currant squares, and spiced apple tea, and in return, Sadie helped her cook in the evenings.

Every day Dorcas bonded more with the kids, and every day, Cassie's guilt grew for keeping them apart. But there was so much history between them, history they were both tiptoeing around. It wasn't that Cassie didn't have questions. She had so many questions. Why hadn't Dorcas raised them? Why did Cassie have memories of fearing her aunt? She thought it might have something to do with her coin, but what? And why had her mother told her, with her last breath, not to trust Dorcas? Cassie stopped herself from pushing for answers though. She knew if she wanted to survive Halloween—which she really, really did—she needed her aunt. She couldn't risk blowing everything up.

At night Cassie and the kids spent time together in ways they never had before. They played games—cards, charades, backgammon—by the fire. And then before bed, Dorcas would tell them stories about witches standing on cliffs, summoning sea monsters from the ocean depths to play under the moon. On one stormy night, Dorcas had even pulled out her fiddle and sung mesmerizing lullabies about sailors and mermaids, lulling them with her siren magic.

Sea House seemed to take them out of time—a week felt like a year—and somehow it also felt like nothing bad could touch them. Part of Cassie wished it could last forever, but the days died away like all the witches who had come before her.

There was not much to do about it, though, other than stay calm and carry on. Cassie was having difficulty with the first of those, but she had no choice when it came to the second.

Given how much the boys liked playing on the sand and given the unpredictable fall weather, footwear had become an issue. Cassie needed to get them rubber boots and Eliza needed fresh blood, so they went into town together.

"So," Eliza said, propping her feet up on the van's dash, "how are you feeling about everything?"

"Fine," Cassie said, swatting her feet back down.

"Come on. I know you must be worried that your magic hasn't starting flowing."

"I'm managing. Besides, Dorcas is the one who is going to fight Del, and she might not even have to if our plan works when I meet him at the bar." Cassie kept her eyes on the road. They had indeed come up with a plan of sorts. Thankfully, even though she was the bait, there wasn't much else she had to do.

Eliza looked out the window at the cornfields rushing by. "Are you scared?"

Cassie had a hard time believing her sister would even ask that question, but then again, Eliza hadn't been at the graveyard, and Cassie was doing her best to act normally around the kids. "I'm trying not to think about it."

"I wish you would talk to me. Like really talk to me," she said. "I can handle it, you know."

No good would come out of that. Eliza would be upset if she knew how scared Cassie was, and that was not something she could deal with on top of everything else. "Aren't we talking right now?"

Eliza huffed a laugh.

After stopping off at the butcher's, Cassie took Eliza and her bucket of blood to the Grub and went shopping for boots. The trip was uneventful, and she was able to get a buy-one, get-one deal, but when it came time to pick up Eliza and head back to Sea House, a funny impulse hit her. She wasn't too far from home, but that wasn't where she wanted to go. Instead, she headed for the street that ran parallel to her own. It was identical in style. It had the same old homes, the same wide yards, and the same antique-looking streetlamps. In fact, it would be hard for someone unfamiliar with the neighborhood to tell the two streets apart if it weren't for the deserted lot, standing out like a missing tooth. Or fang.

It had been nearly two years since the house had blown up. It was big news at the time. Houses weren't supposed to explode. It was the kind of thing you heard about on TV, happening elsewhere, usually at construction sites, not in your own backyard. And again, it nearly was in her backyard. Just a few houses down.

Cassie parked the van. She could still see the old redbrick two-story home in her mind's eye. It had been a beautiful house, but run-down, mainly because it had been empty for decades. Or not empty, as Cassie had learned. Now all that remained were a few blackened trees with bare, twisted branches reaching for the sky.

Frosty air nipped Cassie's cheeks as she walked over the patchy grass and dried weeds to where the front wall of the house would have been. She wasn't sure why she wanted to see the spot up close. Maybe it was to reconcile the past with her life now. She remembered the moment it happened so clearly. Sadie had been at school, and Cassie had been giving the boys a bath after they'd done some face painting with chocolate pudding. When the explosion rocked their world, she'd jumped up and put her arms over the boys almost as if she had wings. But when the roof didn't come down on their heads, she scooped them up in towels and headed for the window. A stream of giant fireballs soared into the sky, but she had this strange instinct that everything would be okay.

Looking back now, she supposed it wasn't all that strange. Maybe she had some witchy predispositions after all.

So instead of running, she got the boys dressed and went outside. The neighborhood was full of people, fire trucks, police cars, and ambulances, but they weren't really needed. The flames had gone out almost by themselves. The firefighters still watered down the pile of what was left of the house, but beyond that there wasn't a whole lot to do. Nobody had been injured, and there wasn't a speck of damage beyond the lot's property lines. Again, it was strange, but people were mainly grateful that the explosion hadn't caused more damage.

Cassie kicked a chunk of old brick. The lot had been filled after all the debris had been cleared away, but there were spots where she could make out the foundation.

Standing where it all happened made her realize how powerful her aunt was. And yet Dorcas still hadn't been able to kill Del.

This wasn't helping. Besides, they had a plan now. Hopefully the final battle would be canceled due to assassination. She glanced at her phone. She had to get Eliza if they were going to make it back to Sea House before dusk. Just as she was about to leave, something caught her eye, leading her over to the back of the property. There was an odd depression in the ground, maybe two feet wide, but it was longish, coffin-sized. Cassie stiffened. That was also an unhelpful thought. She stood at the edge of the strange dip. Maybe it had been some sort of cold cellar, and they hadn't used enough fill. It was only an inch lower than the rest of the yard. It certainly wouldn't pose any danger to kids wanting to check out the abandoned lot.

Again, she needed to get going. The mystery of the suspicious dip could wait for another day. She smiled and stuck the toe of her boot out to give the shallow trench a poke.

And that's when the earth swallowed her whole.

CHAPTER 21

Cassie rocketed through the soil, too shocked to scream. One second, she had been in the autumn sunshine, the next she was grasping at dirt and rocks to slow her fall. She landed on her feet, but the force threw her back and she hit the earth with a thud.

For a second, she didn't feel anything. No pain. No fear. Nothing. Her brain was too busy trying to make sense of what had happened and figure out if she was okay.

She stared at the patch of blue sky above her. The hole had to be at least twenty feet deep.

This was bad. She was trapped. She had fallen into her own grave. She—

She couldn't panic. Cassie curled her fingers into fists. She was fine, very cold, but okay. She hadn't broken anything, and as far as she could tell, she hadn't even been hurt. She would call for help and everything would be fine. Although there was a strange smell down here. Mainly it was the scent of dirt, which wasn't so bad, but underneath it, there was something pungent fighting through, something vinegary, rancid. Meaty.

Cassie pressed the flashlight icon on her phone. For a second, she was worried she had landed in a vampire den and there would be human skulls everywhere, but nope, it was a tunnel. It started from where the house used to be, but then it branched out in three directions. While she was grateful it wasn't a den, she also knew these had to be vampire tunnels. That was probably how the butler had disappeared so quickly.

She had to get out. Now.

Cassie called Eliza four times before she picked up. "I'm sorry. Did you want to talk? Normally I'd love to, but I'm busy sewing part of Tommy's scalp back on."

"I need your help." Cassie explained as quickly as she could. When she was through, she thought Eliza would answer with *Oh my God, are you okay?* or *I'm on my way,* but instead she got, "My, my, my, how the tables have turned."

"What?"

"I find it ironic that after all the grief you gave me for following Tommy, you went off adventuring by yourself and fell into the earth."

"Eliza, this is not the time. Can you just come get me?"

"I don't know." She could practically see her sister examining her fingernails. "As I mentioned, I'm kind of busy. Maybe you should call the fire department."

Cassie's eyes widened. "I am not going to put any more people in danger."

"Fine. Ask me nicely."

"I am not playing right now," Cassie hissed. "I'm sorry if I hurt your feelings earlier, but . . . it smells like death down here!"

"That didn't sound like a *pretty please.*"

"I'm going to cut all your hair off while you sleep. How's that?"

"Hostile. But I do like my hair. Okay. Sit tight. I'm on my way."

"Eliza! Don't—"

The line went dead.

"Hang up."

☾

Like most people, Cassie had never spent much time underground. There were bugs, but maybe not as many as she had expected. She also couldn't see any rats or snakes, so that was good. Then again, she was standing completely still beneath the hole from which she had fallen. The sunlight didn't make it all the way down, but the sky was reassuring.

On closer examination, the walls of the tunnel were bricked. A section had crumbled, though, which had to be the cause of the sunken earth above. Regardless, someone had put a lot of work into building these underground passages. Into making a burrow. This must have been how her neighborhood got its name. She was guessing if she followed any one of the three tunnels, she'd stumble across a vampire or two. Not that she was going to do that. She was going to wait right here for her annoying sister. And on that topic, falling into a vampire tunnel was not the same thing as following a vampire to a remote location. She couldn't exactly say how it was different, but it most definitely was.

Cassie took a breath of cold, moldy air. She couldn't get herself all riled up. If she did and let it show, Eliza might leave her down here.

And where was her sister?

Cassie looked at her phone. Fifteen minutes had passed. That was more than enough time to make it over from the Grub. She opened the app that allowed her to track her sister's location. *Oh, come on.* Eliza was at the store! What was she still doing there?

THE LATE-NIGHT WITCHES

Actually, maybe she didn't want to know. Her sister always seemed to be doing gross stuff these days. But still, this was unacceptable. She called her again.

"I'm coming!"

"What's taking so long?"

"I had to find the keys for Carl's truck, which he told me not to borrow, by the way, and then get a rope and a ladder. I might have chipped some paint getting it all in. You're paying for that."

"Fine. Whatever. Just get here. And—" Cassie cut herself off. She'd heard something, a rustling, and it hadn't come from aboveground. "Eliza," she whispered, "I think someone's down here."

"Oh shit. Are you sure? Who do you think it is?"

"How should I know?! But I'm pretty sure it's a vampire." Oh God, she had woken up a vampire. Cassie heard the noise again. Louder this time.

"Okay, stay put. I'm coming. And remember you have training in this."

"It's barely been a week!"

"What potions do you have on you?"

Cassie clenched her teeth. "I forgot to bring any."

"You forgot to bring any?! What did Dorcas tell you?"

Hmm, after the graveyard test, Dorcas had mentioned something about never leaving the house without potions, but—

She heard the noise again! It was a rustle and a drag this time. And it was getting closer. "I have to move. It's coming."

"How am I going to find you?" Eliza shouted.

"Open the location app on your phone."

The line went silent. "Okay, I see you."

"Track me." Cassie stepped deeper into the tunnel, stopping when she reached the spot where it branched off in three directions. She listened carefully for the noise and jolted when it came again, but she couldn't tell from which direction!

"Eliza, pick a number between one and three."

A horn blared through the phone. "I know it's red! You saw me coming!" Eliza yelled. "What did you say?"

"Pick a number between one and three."

"I don't know . . . two."

Cassie headed down number one. Eliza was always finding trouble, so it seemed like a safer bet. Besides, tunnel one led in the direction of her house. Maybe. It was hard to tell down here. But right now, she wanted nothing more than to be home.

"What's happening?" Eliza asked.

"Nothing," Cassie whispered. "The noise stopped. Where am I?"

"I think you're under your neighbor's pool."

Oh, she did not like the sound of that. While the odds were probably low, drowning in a vampire tunnel seemed like a bad way to go. A crunch sounded beneath her foot. She tilted the flashlight on her phone to the dirt floor. Bones. Animal bones. Hopefully animal bones. The skin on Cassie's back rippled with disgust like there was a spider crawling up her spine. Oh God, now it felt like millions of spiders were crawling up her spine, and her legs, and her arms. "I'm going to keep going."

"Do it," Eliza shouted over the sound of more screaming horns. "It looks like you're almost at your house. I'll have to dig you out or something."

Cassie moaned. That wouldn't work. Eliza couldn't dig twenty feet. What were they going to do? *Wait.* It looked lighter up ahead. Maybe there was a way out. Yes. There had to be ways out. The vampires needed to feed!

"I found something." Cassie picked her steps up to a jog.

"There's a corner up ahead. I think there might be an exit tunnel." She ran the last few steps and whipped around the bend. What she saw there made her jolt so hard her feet slipped out from underneath her, and she dropped to the ground.

"What happened? Are you there?" Eliza's voice called out from the phone glowing in the dirt.

Cassie reached for it with trembling fingers, then brought it to her ear. "I found an exit."

"Okay, good."

"I also found a vampire. I think it's dead."

CHAPTER 22

"What are you talking about? A dead vampire? All vampires are dead."

Cassie shone the light onto the skeleton chained to the wall. It still had some patches of skin sprouting straggly hair on its head, but the face was gone; only a yellowed skull remained. A skull with fangs. Beyond the horror, though, just past the skeleton, there was light. The tunnel came to a dead end, but weak sunbeams filtered down through wood planks at its top. And the planks weren't even that far up. Maybe eight or ten feet instead of twenty. She must have been walking up at an angle this whole time. Cassie craned her neck to get a better view, not wanting to get too close to the skeleton. Wait a minute . . .

She caught a glimpse of a pink bicycle with streamers on the handles through the planks. Sadie's old bike. It was her shed! They hadn't used it in years because it was in such bad shape. "I'm in the shed! My shed!"

"I'm almost there."

Cassie eyed the fanged collection of bones. There was no way around it. "I may be able to get myself out. But I have to step over the vampire."

"Are you sure it's dead?"

"Almost a hundred percent. It must have starved down here. Maybe they don't disintegrate when they starve."

"How could you possibly know it starved?"

"It's chained to the wall." The butler had mentioned Del's punishments. "And I think it's been here awhile. It's wearing an *NSYNC T-shirt."

"Don't do anything until I get there. My hands are tingling."

Cassie looked at her own hands. Nothing. Eliza's tingling couldn't be coming from this skeleton, but that must mean there were other vampires nearby. Maybe right behind her! She spun around. *Nope.* But that didn't mean there wasn't one coming. Something had made that noise. She really didn't want to be down here anymore.

Cassie moved to the far wall by the vampire's bony feet and pressed herself up against the cold, damp brick. She had watched enough horror movies to know she was taking a risk, but she was also very close to losing her mind, so—

A whisper suddenly echoed over the brick walls.

Cassandra, show me your magic.

Cassie slapped a hand over her mouth to stop herself from screaming. That was Del. She knew it. Definitely time to go. She lifted her boot over the skeleton's legs. It didn't grab her ankle, but . . . its jawbone dropped. It must have been a trick of the light, or maybe she had disturbed the air currents enough that it fell. She stared at the skull, taking small breaths. It moved again. And then again! The jaw was going up and down now, and it was chittering like a cat watching a bird. How was that even possible? Suddenly its leg jumped. *Not cool.* She hopped over the skeleton, racing to stand under the shed's floorboards. "Eliza!"

No answer.

She tossed a look back over her shoulder. The vampire was clattering to its feet, but it was still chained to the wall. Then the wretched monster took a quaking step toward her, its hand slipping right out of the manacle.

No.No.No.

A metallic screech came from above. The old tin door! "I'm coming!" Eliza shouted. "Hang on!"

Cassie whipped around to face the skeleton staggering toward her. It moved slowly, but it was only feet away, and it was reaching its hand toward her, its long, yellowed claws headed for her face.

"I'm trying to find something to get the boards up," Eliza shouted. "Screw it!" A bang crashed over Cassie's head, sending dirt raining down on her.

Where is your magic, little witch?

God, she hated that voice. And the vampire who came with it.

Cassie closed her eyes, pushing away the sound of the skeleton's jaw clacking, trying to go as deep as she could into her consciousness. Where *was* her magic?! Maybe it was hiding in the subterranean depths of her mind, away from all the internal screaming she was doing these days. It *was* quiet down here. In fact, the only sign of life was the sound of her heartbeat rushing through her ears. She was completely alone with herself. *Holy crap!* That was the last place she wanted to be! That witch had no idea what she was doing! Cassie's eyes flew open just in time to see the vampire's skeleton claws inches from her nose. "He's going to bite me!"

"Don't let it!" Eliza screamed. "Even if he can't suck your blood, Dorcas told me vampire bites are poisonous to witches!"

Of course they were.

The vampire grabbed her throat with steely fingers and

pushed her against the wall. Cassie grabbed its forearm, trying to wrench it away, but it was too strong. How was it that strong? It had no muscle! Vampires made no sense.

The dark gaping pits of the skeleton's eyes leaned toward her. Cassie screamed as it closed in, but then a plank cracked above, and a beam of sunlight poured into the darkness, right onto the vampire's bony skull.

The cursed skeleton exploded into a cloud of grit and bone.

As the dust settled, Cassie coughed then blinked up at her sister, leaning precariously down into the hole, her hands gripping the planks on either side.

"Oh my God," Eliza said. "Are you okay?"

"I would like to get out now," Cassie replied in a small voice.

Eliza reached down for her. "Give me your hand. I'll pull and you push yourself up on the bricks with your feet."

Cassie lifted her hand, but then she heard the noise again. She looked over her shoulder into the dark.

No . . .

She was seeing things. Her eyes were adjusting to the sunlight. That was all. But the thrumming in her veins told her that wasn't the truth.

Two faint yellow patches glinted like the scales of a fish in the inky darkness. Eyes.

"Cassie?" Eliza called.

She blindly reached out for her sister, unable to look away from the tunnel. Her hand shook as she grabbed hold.

The last thing Cassie saw as Eliza pulled her up was the white burn of a fanged smile.

CHAPTER 23

The glittering Milky Way stretched across the sky over Sea House. Cassie walked along the shore as her boys raced over the beach clutching sparklers. The temperature had risen, so Dorcas suggested she give the twins a lesson in constellations. She promised that they'd be safe, that Del wouldn't dare attack on their home turf, but then again, she had also promised there would be no magic, and the boys' sparklers were taking an awfully long time to go out.

Sadie had opted not to join them. Cassie glanced up to the window on the second floor. Yellow light beamed around her daughter's silhouette. Still reading. Being a mom was weird. How many times had she told her children to go read a book? And now that Sadie had read at least a dozen, she wanted her to stop. Actually, no, it wasn't that she wanted her to stop. She wanted to know if she was okay. It seemed like a big ask, though, considering Cassie wasn't sure she could answer that question herself.

She had not had enough time to recover from her experience in the tunnels. There were still times when Cassie felt like she was covered with spiders, and when she blinked, she saw yellow eyes. She also couldn't get *NSYNC's song "Bye Bye Bye" out of her head. That was only moderately torturous though. But ready or not, the big meeting with Del was only one sleep away, and there were a lot of unknowns attached to that.

"That's what makes it so exciting, Polliwog!"

Cassie screamed. Again. She hadn't heard her aunt coming up behind her. "Would you please stop doing that?"

"Doing what?" Dorcas asked innocently.

Sneaking up on her. Reading her mind. Calling her Polliwog. *Polliwog* didn't exactly feel like a ferocious vampire killer's name. Cassie folded her arms back around her waist. "Aren't you supposed to be teaching the boys about dippers?"

Dorcas chuckled. "They'll need to run a few more laps around the beach before they settle, and I got the impression there was something you wanted to ask me."

"Got the impression or read my mind?" Cassie raised an eyebrow.

Dorcas's eyes twinkled. "You'll never know. Now fire away."

Her aunt was right. There was something Cassie wanted to ask her. Something that had been bothering her more with every passing day. "Well, it's just . . ." She might as well say it. "I know you're going to be the one to battle Del, but he's going to be coming after me. I mean, I'm meeting him for a drink tomorrow night." Hopefully she wouldn't be the one filling his cup. "Given that's the case, I've been wondering . . . if I really am the witch of her generation, don't you think I should have shown some magical ability by now? Like big, impressive magical ability? Maybe we got the details of the curse wrong or—"

"First, the Deliverer knows killing you tomorrow night won't break the curse, so you'll be completely safe. Second, you have shown magical ability. No human could have survived the number of times you've been thrown around a graveyard."

Cassie snorted grimly right before Dorcas hopped in front of her, making her jolt. "And I have a theory about why your magic hasn't fully come in. Ninety-nine percent of magic—and life, for that matter—is intention and belief. Now, you have remarkable intention in your sense of duty. The way you threw yourself again and again at that vampire when you had absolutely no chance of—" Dorcas smiled. "Never mind that. The point is it's the believing part that's giving you trouble. A witch's special gifts flow from love. I think you should think about that." Dorcas grabbed Cassie's hand and spun her around in a surprise pirouette. "Better?"

"Um, not really," Cassie said, batting her aunt's hand away. She was getting tired of all these vague instructions about believing and flowing. "You know, it is possible I don't have the gigantic reservoir of power you seem to think I do."

"Well, it's not only a reservoir of power. It's also the ability to channel it, but let's not quibble." Dorcas gathered her long skirt up to her shins, then walked to the water's edge. "And we can agree to disagree on your magic, but, as long as you disagree, your powers will disagree, and on that I think we can both agree."

Made perfect sense.

"Stop worrying, Polliwog. We'll have lots of time to figure out your magic once I kill Del tomorrow night."

"That right there," Cassie said with a point. "How do you do that? *Once I kill Del tomorrow night.* Like it's a done deal. Where do you get your confidence? Your *belief*?"

"Oh," Dorcas said looking up at the starry sky. "I simply made the choice to believe I could do anything. My life has been far too terrifying not to." She widened her eyes comically. "If I didn't believe I was the most powerful witch alive, I would have gone insane with fear a long time ago."

Fair enough.

The two walked on in silence another moment before Dorcas said, "Now, there was something I wanted to talk to you about." Cassie looked over at her. "Tomorrow night, the Deliverer will almost certainly try to get in your head when you meet. He will take advantage of all your weaknesses, and to do that there is no telling what lies he might invent."

Cassie's heart tightened. "I'm going to stop you right there," she said, digging her feet into the sand. "Dorcas, we have come a long way. I believe you care about all of us, and you and I are . . . good." That probably shouldn't have been so difficult to say. "But unless you can promise me we will continue to be good after you share whatever truth you're about to tell me, then I don't want to hear it."

Dorcas wilted with a sigh.

"Let's save the big, painful rehashing of the past along with the mystery of my magic for after the battle . . . or the assassination," Cassie said. "Besides, I have no intention of having any lengthy conversations with Del. I will do my part of the plan and that's it. In and out."

Dorcas smiled but looked uncharacteristically sad. "I should probably go back." She glanced over her shoulder. "I think the boys are waiting."

As she stepped away, Cassie said, "You know, Eddie and Sly really love spending time with you." It was the least she could give her.

True to form, the sparkle returned to Dorcas's eye. "I can't wait to show them the scorpion and the crab!" She curved her thumbs and forefingers together. "There may be some pinching involved." For a second it looked as though Dorcas would walk away, but then she added, "You know, Polliwog, if you really want to discover who you are, you could always try asking the sea." She winked, then left.

Ask the sea?

Suddenly Cassie couldn't ignore the feeling that there was a vast, unfathomable presence staring at her just over her shoulder. She turned slowly, her gaze traveling over the dark water all the way back to where it met the sky. There was a whole other world lying beneath that sparkling surface. One filled with roaring, brilliant, beautiful life. There were peaceful giants, fearsome predators, and awe-inspiring creatures that made their homes there. There were sunken ships and lost civilizations in its mysterious depths, and dazzling aquatic lands built around rock and coral that no land dweller could ever fully understand. The ocean was alive and ancient and held more secrets than there were stars in the sky, so . . .

It was worth a shot.

"Hey, sea," Cassie muttered. She didn't want her family overhearing because even with all the magnificence-of-life stuff, this still felt ridiculous. She picked up a stone from the sand, running her thumb over its smooth surface. "I was wondering if you could maybe help me out with something." She bounced on her feet. "You wouldn't happen to have an idea of . . . who I am?" She closed her eyes. "I know, I know, funny question, especially since it has been awhile since we've talked, but I've been having some trouble figuring that one out lately."

The sea continued its gentle lapping of the shore.

THE LATE-NIGHT WITCHES

Cassie had secretly been hoping a mermaid might pop up for a chat, but it was fine. She threw the rock. Instead of skipping over the soft waves, it dropped with a plunk. At the end of the day, Cassie knew exactly who she was.

She was the magicless witch going for a drink with a vampire.

CHAPTER 24

Cassie glanced up at the beat-up clock hanging on the wall behind the bar.

Eleven fifty. October thirteenth. Date night.

Salty's was packed. The box-shaped concrete building wasn't much to look at, which made it the perfect spot for locals to get away from tourists. It had a basic setup: a bar with stools, a few tables—nothing fancy—and normally it was very *normal*, but somehow it didn't feel that way tonight. The crowd was making Cassie uneasy. The music, the clinking bottles, the shouts at the hockey game playing out on the TV—together, they made it impossible to hear anything else. And there were bodies—live bodies—everywhere. The bar was a rocking sea of people who had no idea of the danger they were in. It was awful. There could be vampires everywhere and Cassie wouldn't know it. That was probably why Del had chosen it as a location. To put her on edge. That, along with the assumption that she wouldn't dare use her magic in front of all these people. *Ha!* Joke was on him.

Cassie knew she wouldn't die tonight. Though she had to keep reminding herself of it. The magical contract dictated he had to wait until Halloween. But what about Dorcas? And Eliza?

Her ridiculously stubborn sister insisted she come but promised to stay in the car, and Dorcas thought it might be useful to have a getaway driver should the need arise.

At least Cassie didn't have to worry about the kids too much. Ben offered to take Olive to his mother's house in Halifax so that he could come watch them at Sea House. He had some trouble getting there, but after a few missed turns, Cassie was able to wave him down at the drive. And even with his difficulty following the nonsensical directions, he had still managed to arrive early enough that Dorcas was able to give him a lesson in crossbows. He was much better at it than Cassie.

Eleven fifty-five.

Time to get this over with.

Cassie lifted her wineglass, taking surreptitious glances over its rim, but everyone seemed too drunk to notice her or what she might be doing. Her timing had to be perfect—five minutes before midnight for potency's sake. Hopefully Del wasn't early. Cassie reached into her pocket, palming the small vial she had tucked away. Vervain. Otherwise known as vampire kryptonite. It wouldn't kill Del, but it would hopefully weaken him. All Cassie had to do was tip the contents onto his exposed skin, and Dorcas would take care of the rest.

Ever so slowly, Cassie pushed the cork stopper off the vial with her thumb. It fell to the floor. She then brought her wineglass low to her waist and glanced over at the door, pretending to be looking for someone. Her heart thumped as she poured the liquid. *Frick!* She glanced down. Half of it had spilled onto her hand instead of into the wine. Hopefully half would be enough. She returned the empty vial to her pocket.

After a few minutes, Cassie glanced up at the clock again, then down at her phone.

Midnight.

No sign of Del.

The beginnings of panic thrummed in her veins. As much as she didn't want to face him, this had to happen. He had to show. This was their chance. She looked over at the door, and then in a bizarre hiccup of time, Cassie knew the vampire was seated on the other side of her.

She bit her lip and slowly turned. She was afraid she might faint when she looked Del in the eye for the first time, but seeing him up close wasn't terrifying. It wasn't anything. He was there, but somehow *not*. Cassie tried to focus on his face, but her gaze couldn't rest on any one feature. Every time she tried, her eyes slid away, almost as if they were bored. Everything about him—his height, his build, his coloring—was so average-white-guy that together his features created a sensation of invisibility. Except for his smile. His lips were slightly open, revealing a gleaming hint of fang.

"Cassandra, it is wonderful to meet you. As you can imagine, I've been looking forward to this for years—centuries, in fact."

The second her name left his lips the background cacophony of voices, music, and clinking glass faded away. Cassie's mouth went dry as she struggled to find words. She almost said *Nice to meet you too* but caught herself in time. Dorcas would be proud.

Prickles rose on the back of her neck as he leaned toward her cheek and sniffed the air. "Hmm." Cassie focused on the bottles lining the mirrored wall across from them. Hers was the only reflection in the glass. "I've been watching you. You're not at all what I expected." He brushed her hair over her shoulder, leaning in closer still. "You are . . . disappointing."

Wow, he was swinging right out of the gate. Cassie's cheeks burned. She had to say something. "You too." Not exactly the best comeback, but she might as well go with it. "You're disappointing."

"Do tell."

She had no follow-up planned. "In all the ways," she mumbled. "You're bland." *Nice.*

"What you call bland, I call camouflage." He dipped forward into her sight line. "Would you like me to drop the mask?" Suddenly the lines of his face deepened, pulling Cassie's gaze. His lips stretched and curved into a wide, inhuman grin as his hair darkened and grew, twisting like snakes until it reached his shoulders. But worst of all, his eyes turned completely black, losing any guise of humanity. They transformed into endless sucking pits that threatened to drown her in their hold. The change wasn't like it had been with the other vampires she had met. It was subtle, controlled, like being led into a trap.

Cassie swallowed to stop herself from whimpering.

With a smug smile, he glanced up at the game on the TV, his real face hidden once more. "Every time the quarter century passes, and I wake up, I spend a few days marveling at how the world has changed. Did you know I can hear when I'm imprisoned in my sleep? I catch snippets of conversations in my dreams. But the size and clarity of that glowing box—"

"Why am I here?" That had just come out too. Cassie flicked her gaze to her wineglass. Asking questions wasn't part of the plan. And yet, she couldn't seem to stop herself. She was curious about the monster who wanted her dead. She didn't know if that was weird or not.

He chuckled. The sound felt like a thousand blades being dragged across her skin. "I wondered when I saw you fight—if we can call it that—at the graveyard, but then I knew for sure in the tunnel. It pains me to say it, but you don't have any magic, do you?" He sighed. "After my rest, I was longing to fight the strongest of the witches, but instead, in a peculiar twist of fate, I got a worn-out mother of three."

Seriously, *wow*. He was worse than Mrs. MacDonald. "You still haven't told me why I'm here."

"I thought we should meet! The final battle is nigh. Witches versus vampires." He rolled his eyes upward. "I've always suspected it's a favorite of whoever is up there in the sky." His gaze dropped, pinning her again. "Tell me, what do you know about your grandmother from centuries ago?" He didn't wait for her to answer. "Now, she was a monumental force. The night she came for me, the waves raged and the clouds rolled at her back. The hurricane she summoned tore at me from all directions. I couldn't get off my knees. But she walked through it all as though it were nothing more than a summer's breeze and dumped that hexed potion on my head like I was a dog." His eyes shone with both anger and admiration. "I was asleep before I had the chance to watch her die. Luckily, my minions helped me to a more suitable resting place. Since that time, I have killed twelve Beckett witches, and with each generation, your bloodline has weakened. Each sorceress less powerful. Now here we are with you, a mouse, a shadow, a faint memory of a witch." He sighed. "The great war ends with a whimper."

"You didn't kill Dorcas."

"Dorcas was a coward!" The force behind his words snatched Cassie's breath away. "It was your mother who came to the fight, and she was a cheat."

Cassie pressed her hands on her thighs. Her mother fought him? Did that mean . . .

Dorcas hid?

"Oh, you didn't know?" He tsked and shook his head. "How

tragic." His anger was gone as though it had never existed. "Regardless, I suppose we must play the cards we're dealt." Del tapped the varnished wood of the bar. Sometime during his speech his fingers had grown long and skeletal, and his nails had curved into thick yellow claws. "I will rest no more." He licked his lips. "It is time for me to feed until all of humanity is either turned or part of my herd."

Chills ran up Cassie's arms. "That will never happen." Her children would never live in that world. Dorcas would make sure of it.

Del smiled. "Cassandra, you have a hint of fire after all. Let me guess. You're thinking of your little ones."

Cassie kept still, but fear gripped her heart.

"Mothers." Del smiled and shook his head. "There are many stories about my making, but did you know, after I was bitten, I survived for over three months on animal blood? The pain worsened as the days passed until it became excruciating. My mother couldn't stand to see me that way. She offered herself up. It was a remarkable experience. I could quite literally feel her love flowing into me as I fed. It was so beautiful, so pure, that even as her life drained away, I didn't want to stop." He patted her wrist with icy fingers. "That's mothers for you. They give, give, give."

Cassie jerked her arm away, rubbing the cold burn his touch had left behind.

"Now, let us go over some formalities. Look at me." Cassie obeyed, helpless to the sickening pull of his gaze.

"You will not cheat me. You will not hide. If you do manage to escape, you should know I have left orders with my faithful servants to kill your sons, your sister, your aunt, and then you while I sleep. They will not rest until it is done. Then when I wake it will be a new generation, and sweet Sadie will be all alone when it comes her turn to die."

Cassie gripped the bowl of her wineglass, its contents shining bloodred in the low light. "So," she said quietly, "you brought me here just to tell me not to hide?"

He gave the bar a jaunty slap. "No! I brought you here so that we could bang our swords against our shields, shout battle cries to the sky, stare into each other's eyes as we stand chest to chest."

Cassie steeled herself and tilted the glass. "I didn't come here to play games."

"No, you came to kill me." In a movement too fast for her to comprehend, Del knocked her hand back, spilling the poisoned wine over the back edge of the bar. "So disappointed."

Cassie felt like he had knocked her to the floor.

"Even if you didn't reek of vervain, did you not think I would anticipate your plans? Or your aunt's?" He contorted his features into mock sadness. "Dorcas wants to fight for you, doesn't she? You should know, she's not as smart or as strong as she'd have you believe." Del flicked his gaze to the front entrance.

Cassie looked over to the plate glass windows, spotting the swirl of Dorcas's cloak. But she should be hiding! Pushing herself up on her stool, Cassie strained to see over the many heads.

"Allow me."

The crowd parted from Cassie's line of sight without a single person seeming to notice.

"I took the liberty of inviting some friends to the dance." Suddenly all the noise in the bar crashed back into existence, but Cassie barely noticed. Dorcas was in the road, along with Tommy, Gary and . . . Eliza. Of course she hadn't stayed in the car. There was someone else too. A new vampire. Cassie recognized her instantly, but her mind fought against it.

Gary and Tommy weren't attacking. In fact, if anything, they looked confused. They stood facing the bar, but Dorcas and Eliza blocked their path. As a swaying couple exited the front door, the vampires tensed, instantly ready to pounce. Tommy took a step toward them, but Eliza shot her hand out for him to stop. Despite the clamor around her, Cassie could hear her sister shout *Stay*. Tommy's one foot stayed in the direction of the couple while his other pointed at Eliza. He looked like he would be torn in two. Meanwhile Dorcas blocked Gary, who was trying to deke around her, head bobbing. She shot her hand out, and a gust of wind knocked him to the ground. The other vampire, the woman, did nothing but wander in confused circles.

A whisper came to Cassie's ear. "My, what a terrifying coven you three have created."

Suddenly she felt the familiar—almost expected—burn of her coin against her thigh, compelling her to do something. To end this. The thought of using it still filled her with dread, but she didn't care anymore. She'd pay whatever price was attached to using its power if it meant she could stop Del.

Cassie jabbed her fingers into her pocket. The uneven bit of metal was hot to the touch. She pinched it between her thumb and forefinger, yanking it free.

But it was too late.

He was gone.

CHAPTER 25

Cassie had always tried to keep her emotions in check. She was the older sister, the mom, the one who had to be strong. But as she walked out of the bar, knowing she'd have to tell everyone depending on her how she had let them down, it was almost more than she could take.

And then there was the new vampire.

Whatever compulsion Del had put on Tommy and Gary was over. They stood calmly by Dorcas and Eliza, solemnly watching the recently initiated member to their rank wander the parking lot. The woman's shoulders were slumped, her jaw was slack, and there was blood caked on the work vest she wore every day. She was weakly digging through her purse, occasionally looking up, scanning the rows of cars.

"Patty?"

"Cassie." Her voice trembled, making her sound vulnerable, older. "I'm so glad you're here. I'm . . ." Patty's eyes, watery and bloodshot, trailed off again. Cassie could only imagine how difficult it would be to finish that statement. *I am*. Patty was a mother and grandmother, a hard worker, and a friend to everyone she met. And now?

"Are you all right?" It was a colossally stupid question, but Cassie didn't know what else to say.

Her coworker's frown deepened as she looked over the parking lot again. "I can't find my car. Isn't that funny? I don't remember driving here." On one foot she wore her usual black sneaker that fit her orthotics. The other was bare and dirty. Cassie tracked the bloody trail of a single footprint behind her.

Out of all the people he could have turned, why did he have to pick her? Patty, who brought over casseroles when she could tell Cassie was drowning in work, chores, and all that came with having three kids. Patty, who listened whenever the boys got in trouble at school or Sadie wouldn't talk to her. And Patty, who had hugged her in the break room when Cassie's fourteen-year-old cat, Whiskers, had died, and she had broken down in ugly, ugly tears. Patty had even wiped her nose.

"It's been the strangest night. I'm not sure what happened. I was working late. The Christmas inventory is coming in." Her smile trembled. Patty loved Christmas. "But when I was walking to my car, I think something happened? It was so fast. Maybe a bat? It couldn't have been a bug. Look at all this blood?" She chuckled, but it sounded nauseous. "Then there was this voice. It told me to come here for a drink. I'm very thirsty."

"I'm so sorry about all this." *Don't cry, Cassie. Not now.*

"Oh honey, you shouldn't apologize. It isn't your fault."

But it was. Del hadn't chosen her by chance. Cassie reached for Patty's hand. The skin was cold and dry. "There's a place I know where you can get a drink. It's cool and dark and just a bit damp." Patty smiled. "And Tommy and Gary over there, they can answer a lot of your questions."

"You can trust Cassie," Tommy called out.

"She's going to save us," Gary added. "She's our hero."

Cassie's vision suddenly darkened, and it felt like her feet were slipping away from the road.

Hero . . .

What a joke.

Dorcas was the hero. Cassie was just the one who had to stay alive. But now, after all that Del had told her, Cassie wondered if the powers that be had other plans.

No. She wasn't going there. Everything had to play out the way Dorcas said it would. If it didn't . . .

She couldn't do this.

If everybody only knew how scared she was all the time. How she wanted to curl up into a ball and hide in bed. How at any given moment there was a part of her that wanted to forget everything, take her kids and run away. She wasn't a hero. She was a coward through and through.

"That sounds lovely," Patty said. "I always knew you were a good egg."

Cassie smiled, fraud that she was. "Let's get you in the car."

☾

They drove back to the basement lair in what amounted to a clown car stuffed full of vampires—the circus act nobody wanted to be a part of. They had taken Eliza's car, even though the hood still had a crater in it, because the van had been making some interesting noises, but that had definitely been a mistake. Eliza drove and Dorcas had taken the passenger seat, so Cassie squished herself into the back, half seated on Patty's lap. Gary kept leaning over to sniff her neck. He'd apologize immediately, then do it again less than a minute later.

Overall, the vampires seemed to be doing better than the witches. While it must have been terrible to have had their free will ripped away when Del called them to feed, they were grateful they hadn't harmed anyone.

Once the vamps were settled, they headed back to Sea House. Cassie told her aunt and sister most of what Del had said in a detached way, like it had happened to someone else. And then there was the part she didn't share. The part about Dorcas and her mother. Last night, she had told her aunt she didn't want to know the truth, and Cassie knew she couldn't trust Del, but how *had* Dorcas survived all those years ago?

As they walked over the sand up to the house, Cassie spotted Ben through the window. He looked so natural sitting with his legs crossed by the fire, his book on his lap, tea on the end table by his side. Janet was curled up on the back of his chair. Cassie's heart ached, and she was too tired from discouragement to lie anymore. She had a crush on her neighbor. It wasn't a big deal. Matt was probably . . .

She was tired of thinking about what Matt was doing too.

When they stepped inside, Ben jumped up and pulled his glasses off. It only took a second for him to say, "We're not celebrating, are we?"

Cassie shook her head. "Are the kids okay?"

He tucked a hand in his pocket and nodded. "The boys beat me at backgammon, and even though Sadie didn't say much, she did bring us some amazing pumpkin bread."

The fire crackled in the silence that followed. Cassie suspected no one knew what to say. Or how to start. There was a lot to go over, but it all sucked. It was Ben who finally found the courage to go first. "I have to tell you guys something." He rocked on his feet. "I think your plan tonight was doomed from the start."

"Seriously? What now?" Eliza collapsed into her regular chair. Dorcas and Cassie followed suit.

"I didn't mention it earlier—I wanted to check it out first—but something has been bothering me for a while now," Ben said, sitting back down. "I was able to find a relative of yours living in Maine. She doesn't know anything about you all, but, incredibly, she has one of your grandmother's journals. Your first witch grandmother. She's under the impression that it's a work of fiction. I was able to get her to copy some passages and send them to me."

He was too good to them.

"I told you the fates seem somewhat obsessed with making sure the fight between you all and the Deliverer is fair." He frowned. "Hence there's another caveat."

"Hence," Eliza said with a tired smile. "Ben, you are adorable. And don't worry. I'm not hitting on you. I'm committed to an animated corpse."

Ben looked flustered as the cat by his ear rubbed her face against his cheek. "Uh, thank you, Eliza, Janet. Where was I?"

"Another caveat?" Dorcas looked confused, but Cassie already knew what Ben was about to say. It was the same thing she had been worried about after meeting with Del. Actually, if she were being completely honest, she had somehow known all along.

"Right. So, it turns out there was—is—another condition." He looked at Cassie so gently, it almost broke her heart.

"It's okay," she said. "I'll tell them."

Eliza and Dorcas looked at her questioningly.

"It's up to me. The witch of her generation is the only one who can kill Del."

CHAPTER 26

The fates wanted a battle, and they would make sure they got one. There was no way Cassie was getting out of this fight. The terms had been set before she had been born.

Dorcas paled. Ben saw it too and said, "So even though you staked him and then blew up the house, he would have regenerated. Cassie might also have to kill him on Halloween, but I'm not a hundred percent sure about that."

"My mother—your grandmother—never said . . ." Dorcas's eyes darted side to side. "I didn't know. That knowledge must have slipped away over the centuries, or it was lost in the fire. But it's no excuse. Why didn't I . . . ?" She put her hand on her throat and looked at Cassie. "If I had known you were the only one who could kill him, I never would have . . . I would have trained you. I wanted to give you a childhood, a life free of this, but . . ."

"You know what?" Eliza slapped her thighs. "It doesn't matter. We go back to what we were doing before. We train. We practice. And we fight. Cassie will just have to be the one to strike the final blow." Eliza looked over at her. "You've got this."

Cassie dropped her face into her hands. "Stop. You can't keep saying stuff like that, and we can't keep doing this."

"Doing what?"

"Pretending I can kill vampires. Pretending that I have magic. Pretending that I'm some kind of hero. I'm not the one who was meant to save humanity. That was probably you, Dorcas, and now you *can't* kill him. It's time to face facts. I can't do this. And Del has probably already thought of ways to stop you two from helping me."

Eliza was on the verge of arguing, but Cassie couldn't let her.

"We need to plan for me losing this fight. There are three vampires back in town who think I'm going to save them. There is an entire island that may be decimated if Del is set free. Who knows how far he'll go after that. And then there's you guys. The kids. I couldn't even spill a drink on Del tonight. Maybe once I'm dead and he's free, the curse will be over, and Dorcas will be able to kill him like any other vampire. Maybe—"

"No," Dorcas snapped. "You must trust me. We will find a way. I have made mistakes. So many mistakes. But believe me when I say my every decision was to protect you."

Cassie shrugged. "Well, great job."

She hadn't meant to say it. Not this way. But she was so done with everything.

"What the hell, Cass?" Eliza shouted. "What is the matter with you? This woman has done nothing but try to save your life for weeks now."

"But why?" Now that Cassie had started, she couldn't seem to stop. "Because she loves me? Or is it the guilt?"

Eliza's expression shifted from anger to confusion.

"Dorcas, do you want to tell us how you fought Del twenty-five years ago?" Cassie asked. "What potions you used? Weapons? Do you have any details to share?"

"Cassie," Dorcas said quietly. "I don't know what that monster told you, but—"

"He said you didn't show up. That it was our mother who went to battle. Is that a lie?"

Dorcas opened her mouth but said nothing.

Cassie nodded and looked down at the floor. "She never stood a chance going in your place. How did you get her to do it?"

"I would never—"

"You know, the day she died, she told me not to trust you." Cassie exhaled a shaky breath. "I don't remember much about living at Sea House, but those were her dying words. *You can't trust Dorcas.*"

Given the pain on her aunt's face, it would have hurt less if she had slapped her. Suddenly Cassie felt like everything that had happened was coming down on her, burying her, trapping her under a pile of boulders. She pushed herself up from the divan.

"Where are you going?" Eliza shouted. "You can't just drop another bomb and leave."

Cassie stepped back into the end table beside the divan, sending it crashing to the floor. "I need some air."

"What? No!" Eliza called after her. "We have to talk about this!"

"Eliza—I can't."

Cassie stumbled outside and walked over to the porch railing, gasping down the cold sea air. Over the years, there had been times she had fantasized about lashing out at Dorcas. Telling her what her mother had said before she died. But now that she had actually done it, she didn't feel satisfied or righteous. She felt like a monster.

But this life Dorcas had shown them! This strange, beautiful life! Forget Del, forget what was true and what wasn't. How could Dorcas take all this away from them?

Cassie squeezed her eyes shut. This was probably exactly what Del had hoped would happen, and she had walked right into it.

The front door creaked open behind her. *Great.* Cassie didn't want to fight anymore, but she wasn't sure she could control herself either. She turned, expecting to see her aunt or sister, but it was Ben.

Cassie looked down at the faded planks of the porch and slid her toe on a bit of sand. "I am so sorry and so embarrassed."

"Embarrassed is the last thing you should be." He grabbed the back of his neck. "You are all under incredible stress, you in particular."

"Oh God." She groaned. "Please don't tell me how strong I am."

"I might have thought of going that route, but not after . . ." He grimaced and jerked his chin over to the window.

Cassie stifled a laugh.

"I hope you know you can talk to me," he said. "I'm kind of a neutral party. Not a witch. Not a vampire. Just a terrified human who doesn't want to become livestock."

Cassie turned back to the water. "I think maybe I've done enough talking for one night. Just so you know, I'm not usually like that."

"It seems like you guys have a lot of history to unpack at the absolute worst time." He moved beside her, and they watched the water ripple silver under the thin crescent moon. She could feel the heat of his body, smell his unique, bookish, Earl Grey scent. "I wish . . ."

Cassie glanced up at him. "What?"

"Nah, it's stupid."

"What?"

He gripped the railing. "This is going to sound all wrong, but I wish I could be the witch of her generation for you. I'd probably be terrible at it, but . . ."

A lump swelled in Cassie's throat. Her nose prickled too. *Gah*. It would probably start running. That always happened when she was teary. "That is incredibly sweet of you to say."

He smiled down at her. An intense desire to bury her face in his shoulder came over Cassie, but she couldn't do it. These were complicated times, and she wasn't sure Ben wanted to be entangled with a semi-married mother of three who was embroiled in a fight to the death with a vampire.

He jerked his head toward the woods. "I should be going. I have to pick up Olive first thing."

She nodded. "I'll keep watch for any vampires until you're safely on your way." Dorcas was convinced Del wouldn't dare come to Sea House but had put some sort of vampire repellent spell on Ben's car anyway.

He walked to the stairs, dropping down a step. "Can I say one more thing?"

"Of course."

"Again, it may come out wrong." He winced and pushed up his glasses.

"Hey, it's that kind of night."

"I've been watching you since I moved to the Burrow." His eyes widened with horror. "That definitely came out wrong. Let me try again. I heard you when you said you can't do this." He scratched his temple. "But from where this lowly human is standing, I think you already are."

Cassie tilted her head. "I don't understand."

He gazed at the sea, the house, the vampire dummy—that held him up a beat. "Everything you're doing. The getting up every day. The trying. The failing. The facing literal demons. You're already doing it. This is *it*."

Out of all the things she had been expecting him to say, she hadn't anticipated that. She didn't quite understand what he meant, but it somehow felt *big*. "Thank you, Ben. For everything."

He held his hand up, then stuffed it back in his pocket. Cassie watched him walk away, memorizing his every footfall over the moon-bright sand.

☾

The next morning, Cassie woke with the dawn, and she instantly knew something was off.

Sea House felt different.

In the past, she might have tried to dismiss it, but not now. The house had a life of its own. When they were all together and happy, it was too. The wood beams glowed with more warmth, the stone floors felt more connected to the earth, and the fire crackled more joyously behind the grate. The house's ether transformed into a rich expression of home. When they were hurting, though, the house showed that too. Today it felt quiet, worn, older than its already substantial age.

Crap. She had even hurt the house's feelings.

The temperature dropped as Cassie walked down the stairs. There was no fire in the hearth, and the kitchen was quiet. Dorcas was normally up first, but not today. Cassie went into the kitchen and made herself a cup of tea, mulling how best to handle things. Once she realized she had no clue what *best* was, she picked up her mug and walked down the hallway that led to the side of the house. She needed to do something other than feel sorry for herself. Now that she was over the shock of the night's revelations, she realized that maybe Eliza was right. Maybe all was not lost.

When she reached the honeyed door with the elaborate vined flower carving, she noticed Janet at her feet. "Where did you come from?"

Janet tilted her head, regarding Cassie curiously, then looked at the blocked threshold.

"I know how you feel about closed doors, but you can't come in. Cats aren't allowed." She put up her hands. "Dorcas's rule, not mine."

Janet tilted her head the other way.

"You don't care, do you?"

She mewed. It was very cute.

Cassie grumbled in return but scooped her up. "Okay, you can come in, but no eating anything or knocking stuff off counters. We both know how much you love doing that."

Hot, humid air wafted over Cassie as she opened the door to the conservatory. Her aching muscles instantly relaxed, and the sweet, rich scent of flora deepened her breath. God, she loved the greenhouse. Long tables lined the walls, each overflowing with a stunning variety of potted plants, some with colorful flowers, others with hardy leaves that crowded each other and spilled over to the floor. A tall, wide cupboard stood at the far end of the room packed with wooden boxes and tiny burlap bags filled with dried herbs, crushed stones, and probably a lot of other things Cassie didn't want to know about. There were also jugs of sparkling liquids and an enormous vat of what looked to be seaweed stewing in dark green water. She had been meaning to ask Dorcas about that. Basically, the room contained everything a witch might need to make a potion.

Not that Cassie would do that. Mainly because Cassie couldn't do that.

Ben's information about potions having to be lit with a witch's magic was true. Dorcas had demonstrated the process for Cassie and Eliza a few times. Basically, she would mix ingredients from one of the *family recipes* in her giant potion book, then heat it—if the spell required—over the small firepit at the other end of the room from the cabinet, after which she would pour the liquid into glass bottles and place them on the worktable. At that point, as far as Cassie could tell, Dorcas would stare at them with the ever-baffling *belief* and *intention* until they ignited with swirling light. Cassie didn't have any luck making potions herself, but Eliza—she had lit a bottled sunshine concoction on her very first try. *Whatever.* After that, the potions would be left to marinate for a few hours to a few days at a time.

Potions were an important part of a witch's arsenal. While every sorceress had her own special gifts—*theoretically*—potions were a way of supplementing the powers that she didn't possess or couldn't hold for long periods of time, giving her the magical prowess of an endless number of witches. As a result, it was important to keep the spelled brews flowing. And just because Cassie couldn't ignite anything didn't mean she was completely useless in the craft. She could make bases. Dorcas didn't have all the recipes for the potions in the dining room. Many had been lost in the fire. But fortunately, they could be re-created if a single drop was added to a potion base. Kind of like a sourdough starter. Something Cassie had never tried because she never had sourdough time.

Cassie lowered Janet onto the old wooden worktable. "Now remember you're only here to watch." She reached for the giant book resting at the corner, then flipped the yellowed pages until she found the right one. The ingredients were fairly simple—willow bark, yarrow, some petals from a special variety of orchid that only grew on the island, ground shells, and seawater. She busied about the room collecting ingredients, then ground them up with the oversized mortar and pestle. Because the base didn't need to be heated, all she had to do after that was add seawater and give it a good stir with a long spoon.

There.

Cassie looked at her handiwork, wiping her palms on her jeans. Janet looked at it too. She didn't seem impressed. Next Cassie pulled out glass bottles of various shapes and sizes from a wooden crate underneath the table and set to divvying up the base. She managed to fill six in total. After putting them away on the shelves, she was about to close the cupboard door when a strange compulsion hit her. Granted, her last impulse had dropped her into a vampire tunnel, but this one seemed harmless given it probably wouldn't work.

She reached for the hexagon-shaped bottle she had just filled and brought it back to the worktable. Janet eyed Cassie suspiciously as she cleared all the other ingredients from the space. Dorcas had also taught them that witches could sometimes make unique potions by adding deeply personal ingredients and infusing them with the force of their most desperate desires. She had also said something about those potions being dangerous, but Cassie's life was all about danger these days.

Going back to the cupboard, she rifled around until she found the crushed moonstone. That was for the boys. They were born in June. Then she headed over to a potted plant with deep purple flowers to clip a few blossoms. Violets. Sadie's birth flower. She brought both ingredients back to the table and added them to the base. It was very pretty. It might make a nice centerpiece in the likely event she couldn't infuse it with magic. She stirred the potion again with the long skinny spoon, then regarded the swirling liquid with her arms crossed over her chest.

"Now for my deepest, most desperate desire."

Cassie could feel her cat looking at her, but she kept her focus on the bottle. A sudden beam of sunlight broke through the clouds, filling the room with golden light, and a strange sense of calm fell over her. What was her most desperate dream? Of course it was for Del to be dead, but if the legends were true, she couldn't just do that with a quick potion.

Maybe it was to be stronger. Or more courageous. Someone who could protect her family. Cassie closed her eyes. Yes, that was it.

She wanted to be a hero.

Suddenly an image of her sister popped to mind. She hadn't expected it, but truthfully, she did want to be a little more like Eliza.

A whirlpool of energy swirled through Cassie's being. It was an amazing feeling, like she was being lifted out of herself into something more. Suddenly she felt in harmony with the highest powers of the universe, and she was safe and happy and—

There was a rap on the door. Cassie yelped and her eyes flew open.

"Polliwog?" Dorcas stood on the threshold, joy blooming on her face. "You did it! You ignited a potion!"

Cassie's eyes slid back to the worktable. Janet's nose was touching the bottle, now swirling with golden light.

Holy frick.

CHAPTER 27

Light spun gently in the bottle, dappling the room with brilliant patches.

"Tell me everything! I've never seen anything like it." Dorcas's eyes suddenly narrowed. "Janet, you know you're not supposed to be in here." Her smile returned. "Don't tell the others." She focused back on Cassie. "What did you make, Polliwog?"

"Um, well . . ." Janet bumped her head against Cassie's arm. *Wait a minute.* "Is it at all possible Janet ignited the potion? She was touching the bottle with her nose."

"Let's hope not," Dorcas said, stepping toward the table. "While rare, when cat familiars ignite potions, they usually do so with the intent to enslave others, but she doesn't seem like the type." Janet dipped her chin into Dorcas's outstretched palm. "Come on now. Tell me what you made."

"No, I don't want to." Cassie's cheeks grew hot. "It's embarrassing."

Dorcas winced sympathetically. "Was it a love potion to ensnare the handsome professor?"

"No!" Cassie shouted. Too loudly. "I would never do that. That's wrong." Although she couldn't help but wonder what a spell like that might entail. "No, I . . ." She scratched her temple and squinted. "You know how you gave us that whole lesson on most desperate dreams and desires? I may have done one of those. Or Janet did."

Dorcas's smile dropped along with the sunlight, leaving a chill in the room. "What was your intention?"

Cassie shrugged. "I suppose my intention was to make a potion that would . . ." She mumbled the rest.

Her aunt's eyebrow arched. "I'm sorry. I couldn't hear you."

Cassie shook her head. "Nope. I still don't want to say it."

"Polliwog," Dorcas said, capturing her in a dark gaze, "this is very serious. And you know how much I dislike being serious. Tell me what your intention was."

"Fine." Cassie brushed some dust from the table, startling a daddy longlegs. "My intention was to make a potion that would turn me into someone different, someone better, like a hero."

Dorcas's eyes went wild. "Nobody touches that bottle."

Cassie gripped the table. "Why?"

"You can't just ask the powers to change your nature, to turn you into something you believe you're not. That's cheating! And cheaters are always punished. Oh no, no, no, the fates love that sort of thing. Who's to say their interpretation of a hero is the same as yours? That potion could turn you into a monster! A hero of vampires!"

Oh God. Or a Cassie-Eliza hybrid.

"Stand back, Janet," Dorcas ordered. The cat jumped to the floor. Dorcas swirled her fingers and mumbled a few words under her breath. Cassie always marveled at how she could just do that, infuse her intentions into magical powers. Suddenly Cassie heard a rustle to her side and she spotted vines crawling up the windows. They stretched up to the peak of the glass-paneled ceiling, then dropped down to the bottle, swirling around it in a tight grip before receding back to the highest point of the greenhouse. When it was secured, Dorcas collapsed against one of the tables and wiped her brow. "Polliwog, how have you survived this long unsupervised?"

"It was a onetime thing! I didn't drink it," Cassie stammered. "And the good news is I ignited a potion." *Maybe.* "You don't have to worry about this. It was just a whim."

"But I am worried." Dorcas's gaze turned sad. "Why would you want to be someone different from who you are?"

Cassie rolled her eyes. "I don't know. Maybe because I can't do cool things like that." She threw her hand up to the vines on the ceiling.

"It is true," Dorcas said with an unhappy sigh. "I am very cool."

"Listen, this isn't a big deal. I didn't know what the potion would do. I suppose I was just feeling bad about my witch fail last night, and . . ." Cassie picked at the table with her thumbnail before looking back to her aunt. "I shouldn't have spoken to you the way that I did. At least not without hearing your side. For that, I'm really—"

"No! Do not apologize." Dorcas grabbed her, folding her into a tight hug before whispering, "Although I did tell you we should talk about the past before you met the Deliverer." She then pushed Cassie back to look her in the eye. "We're family. That means I've already forgiven you. And in return perhaps you could forgive me for something, without knowing what it is." She smiled. "Yes?"

Cassie blinked, then studied her aunt. "I'm sorry, what?"

"No, you're not sorry. I'm sorry," Dorcas said, still gripping her arms. "Do you forgive me? For all the things? Known and unknown?"

"Um, I think I'm going to need a few more details."

"I knew you'd say that." Dorcas's hands dropped away. "But if I tell you, it's going to be painful, and I'm not fond of painful. And I'd rather not do what you're then going to want to do when you know what I know. So, what do you say?"

"What are you talking about? Do what?"

Her aunt frowned, pressing her lips into a tight line before mumbling, "Give you something back."

"Give me what back?"

Dorcas huffed and swirled away, walking toward the cupboard. "This is going to be terrible, painful, and sad. All things I don't like."

Suddenly the door opened again, allowing more cats to stream in. Eliza stood on the threshold, her gaze tracking the vines up to the ceiling. "Whoa. What are you two doing?"

"Well," Dorcas said, "Cassie is practicing horrifying magic, and I'm about to confess to past lapses in judgment that, while well intended, in hindsight were also very wrong." Instead of going to the cabinet, Dorcas bent to the floor and opened a chest hidden under the waxy fronds of a dark green plant. Inside was a small bronze box. She lifted it out and placed it on the table. It glowed dully in the low light. "That night on the beach, Cassie, I wanted to tell you the truth about the last time the Deliverer was awake. Admittedly, I wasn't necessarily going to share this part. But given our trust issues . . ." Dorcas peeked up at Cassie. "Before I open it, you should know I made what I thought was the best decision under very trying circumstances. I wanted to protect you—little you. Now you're big you, and big you is likely going to be very mad."

Eliza looked at Cassie and mouthed, *What the . . . ?*

She shrugged.

Dorcas waved her hand over the box and a panel drew back, revealing hundreds of tiny gears. "Now, let me think." She clicked her tongue, then twirled her finger above the many cogs and wheels, clockwise then counterclockwise. After a minute or so of swirling, there was a snap and the gears parted. Dorcas reached inside and pulled out a glittering silver chain. At the bottom of it hung a black vial.

"What is that?" Eliza asked.

Dorcas sighed. "My decision."

Cassie walked over, reaching for the bottle. When her fingertips touched the glass, she hissed and jerked them back. It was freezing. "What's inside?"

"Your memories."

CHAPTER 28

The library at Sea House was a bastion of comfort. The shelves overflowing with old books, the stone fireplace, and the tall lead glass windows with the heavy drapes created a quiet place of refuge. The only sign of the fire that had taken place all those years ago was on a side wall. The flames had scorched the wood, leaving a permanent reminder. The new shelving had been filled with antique paintings, half a ship's wheel, jewelry boxes, seashells, and photographs. In truth, it was nearly impossible not to feel relaxed in the library. *Nearly*. Cassie was presently pretty tense because the witch seated across from her had stolen her memories!

"It was only supposed to be for that day," Dorcas said. "I never wanted you to forget about our life at Sea House. That was never my intention."

Dorcas had insisted they move to the library for her confession, as she was beginning to sweat.

"First," Cassie said tightly, "that's still not okay. Second, what happened to the rest of my memories?"

Dorcas slumped dramatically into her green-velvet wing

chair, flopping her hands over the armrests. What with all the igniting of potions earlier, Cassie hadn't noticed that her aunt was wearing a long cotton nightgown, and her hair was resting over her shoulder in a loose braid. It was a very innocent look. One Cassie couldn't help but think was intentional.

"I do have a theory."

Janet jumped up onto Cassie's lap, but instead of curling herself into a ball like she normally did, she sat upright, which wasn't stable, but given she was staring at Dorcas, Cassie appreciated it as a gesture of support.

Dorcas noticed too. "Janet, I had no idea you were so judgmental."

"I know, right?" Eliza muttered.

"Your theory?"

"I didn't use a potion to take your memories," Dorcas said. "I used an incantation to call them forth so that I could keep them safe in that bottle." She glanced at the vial dangling beneath the chain clutched in Cassie's fist. It was radiating so much cold she couldn't keep it near her flesh. "I wanted to be as gentle as possible given how scared you already were, so I used my siren powers to draw the memory out."

Cassie's eyes widened. "Not the lullaby about the moon man fishing the sea?!"

Dorcas cringed.

"I sang that song to my kids!" Cassie shouted. The library muffled her voice in what felt like a disapproving manner. She could see whose side it was on.

"It's remarkable you remember the song at all," Dorcas said with a big smile. "But you were always so smart. And pretty! And very, very forgiving."

"Dorcas!"

Her aunt looked away and cleared her throat. "I think maybe the whole situation was so painful for you that while I was taking the memory, you felt such intense relief that you picked up where I left off and forgot *everything*."

Cassie's chin dropped to her chest. "Are you saying I wiped my own memories?"

Dorcas picked at a loose thread on her nightgown, refusing eye contact. "It's just a theory."

"Are those memories in here too?" Cassie asked, holding up the chain.

"I don't think so." Dorcas scrunched her brow. "It's very small."

"Then where are they?"

Her aunt shrugged. "I would guess still in your mind. Maybe with your magic?"

Maybe with her magic?! *Fantastic*. She'd had so much luck tracking that down. "Dorcas, don't you think this is information you should have shared with me before now?"

"Um, Cass?" Eliza interjected, crossing her legs and resting her elbow on her knee just like she had that first day at Sea House. "I'm not sure holding back information is really something you want to be righteous about."

Cassie slid her gaze over to her sister, giving her a filthy look, but she kept her mouth shut.

"In fairness," Dorcas said, "it's in a witch's nature to be secretive, tricky, and maybe a touch deceptive." Her features transformed into a picture of sadness. "But it's time—past time—for you to know the truth about what happened." She waved a hand up and down. "So, bottoms up."

"You want me to drink this?" Cassie stared at the swirling black liquid. Or was it a gas?

"Yes, then I'll tell the story of that day. The memories should come back as I'm speaking. Then you'll know I'm telling the truth."

Drinking mystery liquids from witchy old vials was not something Cassie would have done a month ago, but Dorcas was right. She needed to know the truth. Cassie pulled off the stopper, releasing an icy cloud that made Janet crouch down in her lap. "Is this going to turn me into a block of ice?"

"Of course not," Dorcas said with a scoff. "At least it shouldn't."

Cassie tilted the bottle against her lips. Biting cold burned down her throat. When she was through, Eliza leaned over and touched her arm. "You good?"

Cassie nodded but couldn't speak. She couldn't concentrate on anything but the icy sensation rushing through her body, reaching for her mind, her heart.

"How to start," Dorcas said tiredly. "I've told you both that, much like your grandmother discovered all those centuries ago, there is no way to kill the Deliverer outright. The powers that be don't approve of that sort of behavior, but there are ways around the fates." Once again, the room hushed all noise. "That kind of magic, though, used with dark intent, can change a witch. Make them do things they never thought they would do. Behave in ways they will always regret."

Strange pictures, sounds, and feelings cascaded through Cassie's mind.

"What are you talking about?" Eliza asked.

Dorcas exhaled heavily. "I'm talking about the night the Deliverer killed your mother."

"No," Eliza said, snapping her gaze to Cassie. "You told me she died from an infection."

"I thought that was true." Cassie breathed through the tightness in her chest as she fought to stay in the moment. "I wondered about the timing though." It had been so obvious after what Del had said. It should have been obvious before that. Actually, it might have been. But she hadn't wanted to think about it. She suspected her sister hadn't either. Eliza was so engrossed with her newfound life that, like the kids, she didn't want to question it in case it all disappeared.

Eliza turned back to Dorcas. "That makes no sense. You're the oldest. You were the witch of her generation."

"I was. It should have been me who faced him. I wanted it to be me. But your mother had other plans." She folded her hands together. "My mother—your grandmother—she was the second-born in her family, Del killed her older sister, so she was fiercely determined to teach us the skills we needed to fight vampires." A ghost of a smile touched her lips. "The techniques never came naturally to your mother." She closed her eyes. "When I think of her, I see her on the beach laughing. She was a fresh summer breeze, a sparkling wave, a strawberry moon. She wasn't a fighter. Not like me." Dorcas blinked and a tear rolled down her cheek. "After your grandmother died, your mother and I lived alone in Sea House. We were isolated but happy, and we depended on each other completely. As the years went by, she started pleading with me to hide from the Deliverer when the time came. We fought about it, again and again, but she wouldn't give up . . . until everything changed."

"How?" Eliza asked.

Dorcas gave them a beautiful smile. "She had a baby."

Cassie looked up, but she was caught in a riptide of sensation.

"Breathe, Polliwog," Dorcas said gently. "It will pass. Anyway, much like the Beckett witches who came before, your mother lived freely and loved passionately, but when she became a parent, everything changed. I certainly didn't want to pass the curse on to my precious niece, and as much as your mother loved me, she also knew protecting Cassie came first. So, there would be no hiding. I would fight!" Orange glints flashed in Dorcas's eyes. "I was happy. I didn't want to die, but I never thought I would. I was young and naïve. I thought it was fated that I would be the witch to finally kill the Deliverer. I never thought your mother would . . ."

A crackle came from the fireplace. The wood in the hearth had lit all on its own, dispelling the chill that had fallen over them.

"Despite growing up with this curse," Dorcas went on, "when the Deliverer first woke, we weren't prepared. We didn't know what it was like to be at war. What it meant to lose people. He's careful, you know. He turns and kills just enough to stay beneath the outside radar, but he always picks a select few who mean something to us."

Images of Tommy with his blood-soaked bandage, Gary with his crooked sweatband, and Patty with her missing shoe turned through Cassie's mind along with all the new images flooding in. A curtain floating in the breeze . . . paintings rattling on the walls . . . a gut-wrenching scream of pain . . .

"He turned my only childhood friend." Dorcas exhaled a shuddering breath. "I had to release her." The thin blanket on the back of her chair dropped over her shoulders. She closed her eyes and patted the wool. "Night after night I hunted him, but hiding is his greatest skill. I knew the time would come, though, when I'd have my chance to end his wretched existence. What

I didn't know was that your mother had plans to take the fight from me. She thought she knew a way to kill him. A way she believed couldn't fail."

A dark wave of memory threatened in the back of Cassie's mind.

"Do you remember the coin?" Dorcas flicked her gaze to her. "You found it in the garden when you were little. You knew right away it was special. I was practicing on the beach with my scythe, and you ran across the sand, covered in dirt, your hand high in the air. You held it out to me, but I was too preoccupied to see what you were trying to show me. You knew though." Dorcas clutched the blanket to her shoulders, got up, and walked to the shelf on the other side of the room. She pulled out a cloth-covered book with yellowed pages and blew the dust from the top. "Here."

Cassie accepted it with both hands. Janet scooted to the side as she laid it on her lap.

Dorcas waited as Cassie pinched the soft front cover and pulled it back. Suddenly the pages flipped with blazing speed. Janet's ears pressed flat against her head.

"Sorry," Dorcas muttered.

Eliza scooted in beside Cassie, and they studied the open page. Both sides of Cassie's coin—the sun and the moon—were before them, drawn in exquisite detail in faded brown ink. Beneath the renderings there was a long passage written in a language Cassie couldn't understand. "I can't read it."

"No," Dorcas said. "You couldn't then either. How you managed to find that book in the library I'll never know. But once you had, you did what any child would do."

"I took it to my mom." Cassie's breath caught. Suddenly she

could see her mother in a rocking chair, holding an infant, smiling. *What do you have there?*

"The coin was thousands of years old," Dorcas said. "An ancient coven had infused it with power, crafting it into a terrible weapon."

Was. Dorcas thought the coin was gone. A knot of guilt twisted in Cassie's chest, but she pushed it down, struggling to keep it from her thoughts in case her aunt tried to read them.

"What did it do?" Eliza asked.

"It turned fate at the flip of a coin. A little like what you do with your stories, but much more concrete, brutal. Your tales are a nudge, a gentle push of fate. If you cast a spell on another, they must believe at least a little that their fate is deserved. Then the universe takes its course. If they don't believe, it's just a story. It's unlikely it would ever work on someone who knows you well. But that is not the case for the coin. All that is required is that the witch who flips it must be able to look her target in the eye. I believe over the millennia the coin took on a life of its own, seeking out opportunities for its own amusement, not caring if it caused pain or joy." Dorcas sighed tiredly. "You see, all magic has its cost. In our case, well, the coin had two sides. Your mother could kill the Deliverer, but . . ."

"She would die," Cassie whispered.

"That's what your mother believed." Dorcas's jaw clenched. "I'm sure she went over all the scenarios that were possible that night. In the most obvious, the Deliverer would kill me. He had killed twelve already—why not me? But this time—given that I would be his thirteenth—if he succeeded, evil would be unleashed upon the island. In another scenario, I would hide, or escape, or live long enough that he had to return to sleep, but then Cassie would become the witch of her generation and, again, that was not something your mother could bear."

"What about the other scenario?" Eliza asked. "The one where you win? The one where you kill him?"

"I guess she didn't think that one was likely." A sad smile came to her lips. "The night of the battle, I was to meet the Deliverer in the Burrow. As the sun got low, I went to say goodbye to your mother and you two, but I couldn't find her. She was gone, and Cassie, you were looking at that very same page in front of you now. It didn't take long to figure out what she had done."

"Did you go after her?" Eliza asked.

"I wanted to, but she had left a note. *Please, Dorrie. Let me do this. Don't leave the children alone. I love you.*" Dorcas shook her head. "How could I leave a child with a newborn baby when there were vampires after us? I didn't think I would make it through the night. I had never experienced such dread or powerlessness. I hoped against hope that somehow your mother would survive. That maybe she had changed her mind and hid or found a way to kill the Deliverer with her powers. The second the sun came up, I told you, Cassie, to stay with your sister, and I was out the door. I ran for over an hour until I was able to steal a car. I didn't want to leave, but I had to find her. And you were so good with Eliza. Do you know what happened after that?"

Even if she wanted to, Cassie couldn't stop the memories now.

She remembered standing beside the bassinet watching Dorcas leave. She had been so afraid, but she had to take care of her sister. "She came home on her own." Cassie saw her mother stumbling across the beach and she had run down to meet her. They hugged, but then her mother groaned and sat on the floor. Cassie had asked her if she was having another baby. Her mother laughed, then said she was tired and asked for help upstairs. Cassie could still see her lying on her bed with her hand draped over the wooden bassinet. She was so pale.

Then a car door slammed in the distance.

Dorcas. Dorcas would make everything all right.

Cassie had jumped to her feet, but her mother grabbed her arm. *Sweetheart, I need you to listen to me very carefully. Take this coin. Dorcas cannot have it. You must hide it from her. What she wants to do, it's not right. The first chance you get you throw it in the sea. Do you understand me?* Her mother had pressed the coin into her palm. The metal warmed against her skin almost until it burned. *You go downstairs. Tell her I'm here. But she can't have the coin. Don't trust her. You can't trust a word she says. Throw it in the sea.*

When she got to the door, her mother called out again. She wanted Cassie to tell her aunt one more thing. But later. After.

Cassie didn't know what *after* meant, but she ran down the stairs as Dorcas charged through the door. Even with what her mother had said, she was so happy. Dorcas would make everything all right. She could do anything. But her aunt pushed by her and ran up the stairs.

"I knew exactly what she had done," Dorcas said. "And I knew she was dying."

Cassie remembered the shouting. She had sat in the corner near the bottom of the stairs, her hands over her ears.

"She was fading so quickly," Dorcas continued, "but she tried to tell me what happened. She had used the coin, but it didn't kill the Deliverer. As we now know, she couldn't kill him. She wasn't the witch of her generation. Not even the power of the coin could negate the curse. But it did hurt him. And her. She kept on fighting to keep him from leaving, from going after us.

Even though she didn't have the skills or the power, she had so much heart. She forced the battle until it was nearly dawn. Then he fed on her. He fled before he could finish, but he had drained so much blood, and the coin had already done its damage. I don't know how she made it home."

In the memory, Dorcas was screaming *Where is it?!* And then Cassie knew. "You were going to use it. You were going to use the coin to save her. You were going to sacrifice yourself."

Dorcas blinked. "Yes, of course I was. There was never any question in my mind. Your mother was my heart, and you two our everything. You deserved to grow up with her. Not me."

As the memories tumbled in, Cassie felt caught between two worlds. "But you couldn't find it."

"Because she gave it to you." Dorcas held her in her gaze. "She told me you had already thrown it in the sea."

Dorcas had run down the stairs, hitting the walls and missing steps. She had grabbed her by the shoulders. *You still have it. I know you still have it.*

Cassie had shaken her head, trying to control the trembling of her body. She knew if she didn't stop trembling, her aunt would see right through her.

You're lying. Give me the coin.

She couldn't speak. Dorcas would hear the lie.

Give it to me. Her aunt had transformed from the loving, joyful woman she had always known into someone else, a terrifying stranger. *I need it. Everything will be all right if you give me the coin.*

I threw it in the sea.

No, you didn't, Dorcas cried, stroking the hair back from Cassie's face. *You didn't throw it away. Please, baby.*

Cassie nodded.

Then she screamed. Dorcas screamed so loudly the veins in her neck bulged like snakes, the paintings rattled on the walls, and glasses exploded in the kitchen. Cassie had run back upstairs. She couldn't see her aunt like that. When she got back to her mother's room, the windows were closed, but the curtains were floating gently, beautifully, in an impossible breeze. Sea House was saying goodbye. Her mother had gone nearly white, but she managed to reach her hand out. It was cold when Cassie touched it. *I am so sorry. I thought I could protect you from something, but I was wrong. This won't make sense right now, but when the time comes and it's your turn, Cassie, things will be different. You are so special, and Dorcas will be there to help. I believe in you.* She smiled weakly. *Take care of your sister. And know I love you both with everything I am.* Then her eyelids fluttered shut, and she was gone.

How could Cassie have forgotten? Those were her final words.

"I know how badly I scared you," Dorcas said, pulling her back. "There's no excuse. And you were right to throw that coin into the sea. It belongs there. No one should have that kind of power. No one should be faced with making those choices. After, I wanted so badly to keep you both with me, but I was consumed with guilt. She was dead, and I lived. I was poison. It would have been selfish. I wasn't as strong as our ancestors. I couldn't live life to the fullest. I couldn't cherish every day. My sole purpose was to kill the Deliverer. To save you from a similar fate. I couldn't make you both live that life, and I knew I wouldn't be able to live any other. You deserved better than me."

It was all back now. Dorcas had taken them out of the house

that morning without saying a word. She gave Cassie the book of fairy tales and kissed them both when she dropped them off at that cold brick building where they would start their new lives.

"I was wrong," Cassie whispered. "What I told you about my mother saying not to trust you was true, but she was talking about the coin, and . . . she said to tell you something else."

Dorcas suddenly looked so vulnerable that Cassie feared if she breathed too hard, her aunt might blow away. "She said to tell you that she was sorry. That there was nothing you could have done to stop her. And that she hoped one day you could forgive her." Cassie blinked tears from her eyes. "I am so sorry. I didn't remember."

Dorcas gasped. It was a light, almost silly sound. "I . . ." She rose to her feet, then stared at Cassie quizzically. "Are you sure?"

"I'm certain."

"I see. Yes." She patted her chest with light taps. "I am going to go upstairs for a little while. I . . ." Dorcas spun on her heel then was out of the room.

Cassie closed her eyes as the door shut. She finally understood what happened, and Dorcas had told her the truth. But she couldn't say the same. Cassie hadn't been able to throw the coin in the sea, and even if she'd had the chance, she wasn't sure she would have. It was the last thing her mother had given her, and now that she knew what it could do . . .

It almost felt like fate.

"This changes everything," Eliza said, gripping her arm. "You have to know that. You had your doubts about Dorcas, but that's all over now. You can trust her, believe in her like our mother believed in you. Your magic will flow. We have to help fight Del. We—"

"Slow down," Cassie said laying her hand over her sister's. "I need a minute to think."

"No! No more thinking. Your thoughts always suck! It's time to train, to find your magic."

"I can't right now." It was true. Cassie's brain was too full... and her thoughts didn't always suck!

Eliza jumped to her feet, letting out a scream of frustration before she left the room, slamming the door behind her.

Cassie looked down at Janet. "What did I do?"

CHAPTER 29

Once Cassie had some time to think about it, she realized Eliza was right. *Again.* So in the week that followed, she pushed her body beyond what should have been possible. She kept up her morning run, but now she could do it for well over an hour. She pushed herself to do pull-ups and sit-ups until she collapsed, and planks until one of the boys jumped on her back, which always seemed to happen, no matter where she did them. And then she trained with weapons. While she still was useless with a stake, she was getting a lot better with a battle-ax.

The coin had freed her.

Her mother hadn't been able to trade her life for Del's, but that was because she hadn't been the witch of her generation. Cassie didn't have that problem. It wasn't as though she wanted to give up her life, but now that she had a way to protect her family and humanity—which still sounded weird—she was free to give her all. And for the first time in weeks, she felt good, almost joyful with relief, especially when she was looking at her children.

Cassie leaned on the doorframe of the boys' room, watching them sleep. Their breath was soft, and their eyelids twitched with hidden dreams. They had pushed their beds together and were once again surrounded by cats curled up in tight, furry balls. Normally their windows revealed sand dunes glowing in starlight, but thick clouds had blown in, leaving only the darkest of shadows and the faint wink of a distant lighthouse.

Eliza was staying the night again so they could take inventory of their potions, but Cassie wanted to use the opportunity to run an idea by both her and Dorcas. It was hard to say how they would react. It was something Cassie needed to do though.

"Ah, they sleep," Dorcas whispered, laying a hand on her shoulder.

After her confession, they had all settled back into their usual routines. Cassie knew she needed to talk to her aunt again so they could work through all their residual emotions, but for now they were focused on vampire slaying.

"They love this place," Cassie murmured.

"They *need* this place. Boys are rare in the Beckett family. It's hard to say what their powers might be, and their magic will come out one way or another. You must talk to them. They can't control what they don't understand."

"I know," Cassie said. "I'm trying to figure out how to tell them in a way they'll understand."

"And Sadie?"

Her daughter was a different story. Sadie would understand everything, and what it all meant. But Cassie had put that conversation off long enough too. "I'll talk to her."

Dorcas tilted her head down the hall, and they descended the creaking stairs to join Eliza by the fire. She sat on a mustard-yellow cushion surrounded by candles, oiling the crossbow they had purchased from Hank. They had spelled the grease to help the stake find its mark. Well, her aunt and Eliza had. Cassie watched intently though. She hadn't been able to ignite any more potions, but she thought she might have rattled a fork during lunch, so that was something.

"It is a beautiful piece," Dorcas mused. "Hank was always talented in the way of crossbows." Her gaze turned mischievous. "Among other things."

"He mentioned you," Eliza said slyly. "Something about you still being mad?"

Dorcas scoffed. "We used to date back in our prehistoric days."

Cassie smiled, lowering herself onto the divan. "Seriously?"

A gust of wind blew down the chimney, emboldening the flames. "Yes, seriously. I dated. I was quite good at dating. Not so good at relationships. But the Becketts have never been lucky in love. Although Cassie," she said with a knowing look, "I know you're conflicted, but I am completely astonished by your professor. All his research. He must really care about you."

"He is not *my* professor."

"I wouldn't be so sure," Dorcas said, moving her basket of yarn from her chair so she could sit.

Suddenly Cassie desperately wanted to know if her aunt had talent when it came to foresight, but she wasn't about to reveal any of her complicated feelings about Ben. Or Matt.

Eliza kept her focus on the crossbow, but said, "I feel the unlucky-in-love thing. Tommy is so sweet and kind and loyal, but the vampirism has become a real sticky point. Sticking! Oh God, I meant *sticking*. But he is also very sticky." Cassie didn't want to think about what that meant.

"I certainly haven't been living alone all these years by choice." Dorcas rose even though she had just sat down. She headed for the kitchen, probably to bring out some snacks. She could never relax until everyone had been properly fed. Actually, she could never relax, period. "My unending, bloodthirsty quest for revenge has been a contributing factor, but really there are few men who can handle a powerful, free-spirited woman such as myself."

"True. True," Eliza said, watching their aunt leave the room. "Or it could be the cats."

"What was that?" Dorcas called out.

"Nothing!"

Eliza smiled at Cassie, but it dropped quickly.

They really needed to hash things out. She suspected her sister was still mad about not being invited to the big Halloween bash, but Cassie wasn't changing her mind.

Dorcas returned with a tray of soft cheese, baked crackers, and some sort of jellied spread. Before anyone could speak, Cassie said, "I know we were supposed to be going over potions, but I wanted to run an idea past you guys." Dorcas exchanged a glance with Eliza.

"I want to retake the graveyard test."

And now Cassie could hear the grandfather clock ticking. It really knew how to punctuate awkward moments. Eliza and Dorcas exchanged another look—an intensely concerned look—but then an excited gleam came to her aunt's eye. "Have you done more magic since your incredibly ill-advised, horrifying potion? If so, there's no time to lose. We should go to the graveyard right now. We—"

Cassie waved her hands to derail her aunt. "Nope. No magic." Now didn't seem like the time to bring up the fork. "And I know the classic version of the test doesn't involve weapons, but given my magicless state, I think an exception can be made. I've been getting better with my training, and I think it would be good for me to practice throwing potions. I mean, Dorcas, you must have the most impressive collection in the world. I want to be able to make use of it."

Dorcas tittered at the flattery but then looked sick.

This was not exactly the robust response Cassie had been hoping for. "Thoughts?"

Eliza shook her head. "I don't know about this plan." She peered up from beneath her brow. "You got any others you want to tell us about?"

"What is the matter with you two?" Cassie slapped her thighs. "You're always telling me I can do this!"

"I'm confused." Eliza lowered the crossbow to the floor. "I thought you didn't want us to say stuff like that."

Cassie groaned. "That was then. It's different now." She turned back to Dorcas. "Look, I know you are going to be the one to fight Del—"

"And me," Eliza interjected.

Cassie chuckled and wagged her finger. "Nice try. But I'm the one who needs to strike the final blow. If I can't handle a regular—albeit gigantic—vampire, I have no chance against Del. And while I know we have to stay safe for . . . humanity, what are we doing letting the big guy run free? He could be biting someone right now."

"You make an interesting argument." Dorcas offered Cassie a piece of cheese on a cracker covered with red currant jelly, but Cassie did not want cheese. Not when she sensed a *but* coming. Hopefully there would be cheese left over when this conversation was through, but right now she did not want cheese. Her aunt put the cracker in her own mouth and chewed with contemplation before saying, "I'm concerned that if it doesn't go well, it will shake your confidence when you need it most."

Cassie knew that was a risk, but now that she had the idea in her head, she'd feel like a coward if she didn't do it, and she didn't need that going into Halloween. "I really think I can do it this time."

"Huh," Eliza said, grabbing a cracker of her own. "If she dies before Halloween, does that mean I become the witch of her generation?"

"That is an excellent question," Dorcas remarked, reaching for more cheese from the rapidly diminishing supply. "You know, I am not sure. Normally I think it can be passed on to a younger sister if the elder dies in that generation, but he's already awake, so the timing—"

"Guys! Still here. Still alive. And I'm not going to die! At the graveyard at least. Del told him not to kill me."

Dorcas emitted a hum of doubt. "Vampires are not known for their self-control."

"You weren't exactly concerned about that the first time I took the test."

"That was before I knew about your powers"—her aunt's voice dropped to a mumble—"and your inability to access them."

"That's on you. I tried to tell you." Cassie pressed her palms toward the floor and closed her eyes. "Look, by all means, if I'm about to die, feel free to save me. But I am doing this."

"Well, if you're sure."

"I'm sure."

Eliza reached again for the crackers, but Cassie grabbed the entire plate and put it on her lap.

Her sister frowned at her power move. "Okay, then. But I'm coming this time. Think of it as an educational experience. Can Ben babysit?"

Cassie stuffed two pieces of cheese in her mouth. It *was* really good. "He did say anytime," she mumbled. "He wants another look at the library."

"I think you should leave Sadie in charge," Dorcas said. "We'll give her instructions. And if you tell her not to let anyone in, she won't. Under those circumstances, Sea House is the safest place they can be."

Cassie stopped chewing. "I don't know."

Dorcas captured her gaze, staring right into her. "The children need to see that you believe in them."

Cassie nodded, filling in *Before it's too late*.

CHAPTER 30

The tombstones floated on a sea of dreary fog as Cassie crunched over the gravel path with her aunt and sister. The gloomy atmosphere reminded her of the dream she'd had of being lost in the mist, but she wasn't scared in the same way she had been in that nightmare. This was not a panicked fear. It was the dread and dismay that came from a place seeping with loneliness. A place trapped in limbo. This was the emptiness that came with death. A nothingness that—

Dorcas swatted her on the shoulder. God, that was annoying, but the privacy creep was right. Now was not the time for self-defeating thoughts. Or for wondering obsessively about what her kids were doing every other minute. She had a vampire to kill.

When they reached the bottom of the slope that led up to the dead house, Cassie did a few jumping jacks and twists, ignoring Eliza's eye-rolling. She was strong. She had skills. And she was wearing a turtleneck.

She could do this.

"You two stay here," Cassie said, stepping away from Dorcas and Eliza. "Don't help me unless I ask you to."

Her aunt and sister nodded without much conviction.

Cassie strode up the path, faking the confidence she didn't feel. She didn't stop until she was a couple of steps away from the door. Her eyes popped up to the roof—*fool her once*—but it was free of vampires. She slipped her hand into her back jean pocket for a potion. She had only brought three, not wanting to overcomplicate things. And really, three should be enough if she did things right. She gripped the glowing yellow bottle in her right hand and rapped on the heavy door with her left. A shuffle came from inside and a critter screeched. Icy fear flooded Cassie's mind, spurring horrible thoughts like *I can't do this. I'm the worst witch who ever witched. I'm going to die.* But she shut those thoughts down as quickly as they came. She *was* the witch of her generation. And this was good. It was what she wanted. Someone to be home . . . eating rats.

Heavy thuds approached the door. The earth-trembling steps were unmistakable. She backed up two, maybe three feet, then folded her hands in front of her, hiding the light beaming from the bottle wrapped in her palm.

The door banged open, and the vampire stepped out, ducking to clear the low beam. He straightened to his full enormous height, then looked her over. "Why are you back?"

"We are going to fight." Cassie had planned to throw the potion right away, but she seemed to be temporarily frozen.

"I'm busy," he thundered and reached back for the door.

Busy? Cassie leaned to peer into the dark enclosure. Wild, terrified eyes shone in the darkness. A young woman with glasses was cowering inside. When she saw Cassie, she mouthed the words *Help me*.

"Oh my God!" Cassie shouted. "Did you kidnap that woman? What is wrong with you?"

He cocked his head quizzically.

"We are so going to fight now." Cassie heard footsteps coming up the hill, but she put her hand back to stop any reinforcements.

"The Deliverer said no blood." He snorted, bouncing his massive chest. "No blood. No interest."

"You don't have a choice." *Nice.* And she didn't say it like a question either.

"Witch, what are you doing?" He suddenly sounded much more human. A tired, exasperated human. "Wasn't last time enough?"

"More than enough." *Dammit.* And she had been doing so well. Time to quit while she was ahead. Cassie closed her eyes and threw the potion. A burst of blinding light erupted. Even with her eyes closed she could see the glaring sunshine.

The vampire roared. When she peeked her eyes open, he had his back turned with his hands over his face. Cassie frantically waved at the young woman. "Go. Run." She pushed her away as the vampire turned back around. His face was very red. In fact, with his bald head, he looked like a plump tomato . . . a steaming, plump tomato. In a flash, he grabbed Cassie by the collar of her coat and tossed her like a Frisbee, but she was ready this time. She rolled down the hill like a log, and when she stopped, she popped back up, reaching for her next potion and the stake holstered to her thigh. She'd wanted to bring a battle-ax, but she was worried about cutting herself in half should she be thrown down the hill. Turned out to be a good call.

The giant bloodsucker lumbered toward her. As his shadow stretched over the grass, Cassie couldn't help but think that this felt all too familiar.

"Hey, Cass, you know what you're doing, right?" Eliza called out.

Of course she knew what she was doing. Mostly. She was

going to throw a freezing potion and then stake the fang-faced giant right . . . now!

Cassie threw the potion, but the vampire ducked, and the bottle fell harmlessly to the grass.

Huh. She hadn't anticipated ducking.

Cassie lunged at him with the stake, but he easily batted it from her hand, then punched her in the chest. She fell back to the grass and her last potion shattered in her pocket.

"Polliwog?" Dorcas called. "You look like you could use a hand."

"Not yet," she grunted. For once, her coin wasn't burning in her pocket. She had been hiding it underneath the floorboards in her room at Sea House when she thought she might be tempted to use it—which was a lot of the time. She needed it as backup for Halloween, and there was no way she was trading her life for some cemetery rat. *Stupid coin.* She didn't need that kind of manipulative magic in her life. She had her own magic. *Probably.* She hadn't told Eliza and Dorcas, but she'd planned on using this second chance to try once again to draw her magic out. She *was* pretty scared. Maybe now her powers would be in the mood to help. She just needed more time and space to focus.

Cassie held up a finger to the vampire. "Hang on one sec." She popped up to her feet and ran.

"What are you doing?" Eliza yelled.

Once she had made it about a couple hundred meters, she stopped and turned to face the enormous bloodsucker. "Okay, you can start walking again. But not too fast."

She snapped her eyes shut, not waiting for an answer. *Okay, Cassie, dig deep.* All she could see was darkness. Once again she was back in the abyss. *Come to me, magic. I am ready to receive you.* Nothing. And that sounded weird. *I would be honored if you came out to play.* Still nothing. *I know you're in there.* But did she? Did she really? Now wasn't the time for doubts, but should it really be this hard? Eliza and Dorcas made it sound so easy, but this felt like an awkward first date . . . *and* the once-distant vampire grunts were closing in. *Come on, magic, erupt!*

But instead of magical eruptions, dark laughter ricocheted through her mind. *Where's your magic, Cassandra?*

Del . . .

It was Del's voice, and she wasn't even imagining it. Somehow, he was actually talking in her head. Like it wasn't bad enough he had come into her life? And her dreams? But now he was in her waking mind! How was she supposed to focus on drawing out her magic when . . . wait, that's probably why he was doing it. "Oh my God, I freaking hate you!"

"It's mutual."

Cassie's eyes snapped open. *Oh crap.* Well, nose ring had made it over quicker than she had anticipated. Cassie took small backward steps. Okay, forget magic. It was time to come up with a new plan. *Fire. Staking. Decapitation.* That was how you killed a vampire. Seeing as fire was out of the question, she needed a weapon. *There are weapons everywhere.* Cassie's eyes darted frantically around the graveyard. Her stake was too far away now.

The vampire lumbered toward her. His face was still purplish red, but the bones had sharpened to peaks. It was time to call in the cavalry. But just as Cassie opened her mouth to call for help, her back hit something—a post, like the kind used for parking signs on streets. It was made of thick steel, but it had wobbled when she hit it. At the top was a sheet metal sign in the shape of an arrow . . . that looked an awful lot like an ax head.

Cassie jumped to the side, wrapped her hands around the pole, and yanked.

It wobbled again but didn't come free. She looked down. The weak spot was at the base. It was nearly rusted through.

"Hurry!" Eliza sounded scared. That couldn't be good. Cassie pounded the post with the sole of her boot. It bent an inch but didn't break free.

"He's coming!" her sister yelled this time. That was helpful.

"Forget the Deliverer," the vampire growled. "You're mine."

He was going to kill her.

"Polliwog?" Dorcas called out.

Cassie jumped and hit the pole again. Her muscles screamed with the effort. *Come on!*

Finally, a low, thick crack came from the base. The pole snapped free and dropped to the grass. Cassie dove in a somersault, grabbing it as she rolled up to her feet, and in a single fluid motion, she swung the makeshift ax, driving the pointed sheet metal toward the vampire's neck. The force of the swing spun her all the way around.

Frick!

She missed. She must have missed. The sign felt like it had cut through air. She glanced back over her shoulder. The vampire glared at her, his fangs still bared . . . but then his head tipped over and fell to the ground.

Cassie let out a surprised huff as the pole dropped from her hands.

The monster's body thudded to the earth right beside his head still rolling on the grass.

She . . . had done it. Cassie looked over at her aunt and sister to be sure. The shock on their faces was all she needed.

Cassie's fists shot up into the air. Then she ripped off her coat and her turtleneck, and she ran like she had just won the Vampire Cup. She sprinted through the tombstones screaming in triumph. When she had looped the cemetery, she ran back to the vampire. His face was tilted up at the black sky. He hissed at her, and she dropped her boot down on his nose ring. His head exploded into dust.

Then she ran again.

As she sped past Dorcas and Eliza, she heard her aunt say, "This is another way witches get bad reputations. I should know."

When she made it to the other end of the cemetery for the second time, a person stepped out in front of her. Cassie screamed.

It was her. The young woman with the glasses who'd been in the dead house. Cassie draped an arm over her chest, suddenly acutely aware that she was in her bra.

"I wanted to say thank you," the woman said, holding her hands up. "You saved my life." She then scurried away.

Cassie's arm dropped to her side. *You saved my life.* She had saved a life.

An even purer rush of elation swept her all the way through. Every cell in Cassie's being sparked with joy and hope and life... but before she even had a moment to bask in the glow, it was snatched away.

Lucky, lucky, little witch. But where is your magic?

Cassie whirled around in a circle, but the voice was still in her mind.

You will never defeat me without magic. You will be my thirteenth.

"What's wrong?" Dorcas asked, rushing to her side. "What happened?"

Del's voice faded away.

"Nothing." Cassie forced a smile. "Just the vampire in my head."

CHAPTER 31

Dorcas didn't stop chattering the entire way back to Sea House—she was ridiculously proud—but Cassie couldn't share in her enthusiasm. Stupid Del had gone and wrecked her first vampire kill. He was such a jerk. And to make matters worse, Eliza didn't say anything on the ride back at all. No *Nice job, slayer!* or *Way to go, witch!* Nothing. She was still sulking about not being included on Halloween. At least that's what Cassie thought she was sulking about. Who knew anymore.

When they finally arrived back at the house, all was still. Hopefully the kids had gone to bed sometime before midnight. Dorcas wanted to celebrate, but Cassie was in no mood. After dragging herself up the stairs, she peeked in on the kids then headed straight for bed.

She tried really hard to sleep. She counted sheep. She threw the covers off, thinking she might be too hot, then pulled them on again when she got too cold. She stared at the ceiling without blinking, hoping her eyes would get tired, but they just burned. Eventually, Cassie gave up and surrendered to all the thoughts she had been holding back. The night hadn't been a disaster—far from it—but it hadn't exactly gone the way she'd hoped either.

She couldn't shake the sound of Del's voice. Or the certainty in it.

Everything was still fine. The plan had always been for Dorcas to face Del, regardless of who finally killed him. It was the only option that made sense, but that didn't make Cassie any less scared . . . or feel any less guilty. She had to be the first witch of her generation to just hand over all the fighting to a proxy. Obviously that wasn't her fault, but still, if something happened to her aunt . . .

As the hours passed, Cassie's thoughts slipped and tumbled into horrible not-quite-awake, not-quite-asleep imaginings of all the things that could happen on Halloween. It wasn't until she heard—or maybe just sensed—something from down the hall that her thoughts snapped into focus.

When the kids were babies, Cassie used to joke that they could do anything at night, even blink, and she'd wake up. That was especially true for Sadie. They'd had an interconnected existence in those early years. And while she could be imagining it, Cassie felt that connection now. She tiptoed down the hall and put her ear against the door. *Oh no.* She knocked gently and turned the knob. Sadie sat in her pajamas at the top of the bed, propped up against pillows, her eyes and lips swollen from crying.

"Baby, what happened?" Cassie rushed in, forgetting all the unspoken rules they had come up with in the last year. "Was it the boys? What did they do? I'll kill them."

Sadie pressed her face into her knees and rolled her head side to side. Now clearly wasn't the time for jokes. Cassie sat on the edge of the mattress and put a hand on her daughter's foot. "You don't have to say anything if you don't want to, but I'm here to help if I can."

"What's going on?" she mumbled. "Why did we come to Sea House?"

Cassie exhaled in a heavy gush. "It's complicated."

Sadie peeked up with fresh tears. "Just say it. It's because of me."

"Because of you?" Cassie searched her daughter's face for answers.

"You don't have to lie. We're here because you all are trying to figure out what to do with me."

"I'm not following. This has nothing to do with you. It affects you, but you're not the reason why we're here."

"Stop lying!" Sadie jumped off the bed, making the springs bounce, and paced the floor in front of the window. "Are you seriously telling me you don't know?"

Cassie gripped the side of the bed. "Baby, know what?"

"Just—" Sadie moaned with frustration.

This had to be one of the hardest parts of parenting. Those times when you knew something was hurting your child, but you didn't know what it was, and they couldn't find a way to tell you.

"I can't say it. I have to show you." Sadie crossed a patch of moonlight stretched across the floor to stand in front of Cassie. She shook her hands out, then held them by her waist, palms up. Orange flames tinged with pink sprouted from each of her fingertips, then blazed trails down to her palms. There the flames came together and grew to the size of pumpkins, lighting up the room.

Whoa.

Her daughter clenched her hands and the flames disappeared.

Cassie must have looked shocked, because Sadie said, "I know. It started happening after Dad left. At first it was only when I was upset, but now I can do it anytime." She covered her face. "Are you going to take me to a doctor? I can't handle that. I know you have to look after the boys, take them back to school, so I'll stay here with Dorcas if she'll let me. She has lots of books on weird stuff, so I don't think she'll mind. No one will ever know."

Cassie jumped to her feet and wrapped her daughter up in her arms. "Oh no. No. You don't have to worry about doctors," she murmured into her hair. "You don't need a doctor."

"Mom," she groaned into her chest, "I have flames shooting from my freaking fingertips!"

Cassie stroked her daughter's hair. "Sweetheart, we all do."

"What do you mean?" Sadie stiffened in her arms. "What are you talking about? You can make fireballs?"

Cassie wished. "Okay, not me. But Eliza can." She had caught her sister lighting up a vampire dummy the other day. With blue flames no less. She was just mastering all the powers. Cassie pushed her daughter back to look in her eyes. "This is what you wanted to tell me that night when I went to find your aunt, isn't it?" She nodded and Cassie's heart broke. Out of all the black marks on her mom record, this had to be the worst. "I am so sorry. I should have talked to you sooner, but I had trouble believing it myself." *Just say it.* "Sadie, we're witches."

Her daughter didn't react. The guilt clutching Cassie's chest made it almost impossible to breathe. "I can only imagine how confusing this has been. But there is nothing wrong with you. You are incredible."

"Dorcas too?" Sadie stepped back.

"Dorcas most of all. She's been at it for a while. She can teach you so much."

Sadie shook her head. "No, there's more. I know there's more. What aren't you telling me?" And here Cassie had thought the whole witch reveal might be enough for one night. "If we're all witches, and everything is fine, why do you guys always look so worried? And why are you always sneaking around? And what is going on in the dining room?"

And who would have thought a chained room would spark curiosity? "So," Cassie said, drawing out the word, "the witch thing is great. We'll figure that all out. But there is something else going on. I don't want you to worry, though, because we, the adult witches, have everything under control."

"You're lying again."

Cassie squinted. "Do you know that because of what you've pulled together? Or can you see into my head?"

Sadie's eyes widened.

Sweet relief tingled up Cassie's spine. Having Dorcas read her thoughts was one thing. Having her children do it was unspeakable. She would never survive that kind of shift in the balance of power.

"Mom?"

"Okay, okay." She just had to say this too. Get it all out there. "Um, the island *may*—no—the island *has*, definitely has . . . the island has a vampire problem."

Her daughter went still.

"And this vampire has a grudge against our family, but I want you to know that keeping you and the boys safe is our number one priority."

"Who is this vampire? How bad is he?"

Cassie let out a considering whine. "You know, I've only met him once or twice."

"Mom!"

"He's a total dick. Really bad. Hate the guy."

Sadie's brow raised, but a smile touched the corner of her mouth.

Cassie led her to sit back on the bed. They might as well get comfortable. She had a lot of explaining to do. "I'm going to tell you everything, but I need you to know how sorry I am that you didn't feel like you could come to me with this sooner."

Sadie shrugged. "You already had so much on your plate with Dad leaving."

Leaving. Not away. Not on tour. He had left them. Cassie pressed her daughter's forehead to her chest, feeling the tears soak through her shirt. "He loves you. Know that. He loves you and the boys so much. And we're going to figure this out, together." Cassie gently pushed Sadie back. "Or if you're ready, maybe we could have this conversation with Dorcas and Eliza."

"Do you think they'll be happy?" she asked, wiping her nose with her pajama sleeve.

Cassie laughed hard for a good ten, twenty seconds before letting it fade into a sigh. "Yes."

Sadie gave her a small smile, which almost immediately dropped to horror. "Wait. You said we're all witches. Does that include the boys? Do the boys have powers?"

"I think so. Or they will one day. Yes." Cassie paused before adding, "Terrifying, isn't it?"

Sadie looked out the window. "Scarier than vampires."

☾

Eliza and Dorcas had been thrilled, of course, and they spent the next few days initiating Sadie into the world of witches. Dorcas taught her potion making and fireball throwing while Eliza introduced her to levitation. The teenage witch was floating books in no time. If the boys noticed anything was different, they didn't show it. Cassie was grateful things had happened this way. Sadie was so distracted by her new world that she couldn't focus on being afraid of vampires—especially not after seeing the things her aunts could do.

It was hard to believe how much had changed since October first. Cassie had spent so much of her life on autopilot, but now it felt like every moment was precious.

And there was barely a week left until Halloween.

The sense of urgency got Cassie up at dawn. She wanted to make the most of every minute she had left, so she headed to the beach. She climbed slopes of rust-colored cliffs and ran her fingers over the ancient faces of sandstone formations. She collected shells at the water's edge and then walked to the tide pool to see if she could spot any starfish. After that she spread a blanket on the sand to watch the water.

The moon glowed pale in the lightening sky as sandpipers ran along the shoreline. With every wave, Cassie's worries faded. Even Del seemed small in the face of the sea.

But there *was* one tiny thing still bothering her.

Cassie turned her coin between her thumb and forefinger as the sun pulled up the last of the golden strip of light resting on the horizon. She never thought she could both love and hate a bit of metal so much, but she was grateful she had it. Now she just had to figure out how best to use it. She wanted to stay positive. It seemed to come naturally to Eliza and Dorcas. But she couldn't shake the feeling that defeating Del wasn't going to be as easy as anyone thought.

She flipped her phone up. Three bars. A miracle. Or maybe a sign.

Ben answered on the first ring. "Cassie, are you all right?"

He sounded so far away and yet his voice still warmed her. "I'm fine. Sorry, I didn't mean to worry you."

"No, I'm sorry." He chuckled. "Tense times, I guess. What's going on?"

A cold but gentle breeze blew strands of hair across Cassie's face. She dragged them back with her fingertips, tucking them behind her ear. "Remember how you said I could talk to you? That you were a neutral party?"

"Yes." He said it without hesitation.

"If you're not busy, do you think I could pick your brain on something? But maybe without going into any details about why I'm asking?" She grimaced, which was funny, given Ben couldn't see her, and the seagulls didn't seem to care.

"Okay." He sounded confused but not quite suspicious. "How can I help?"

Cassie knew this wasn't a fair thing to ask of him, but she didn't know what else to do. This wasn't exactly a conversation she could have with her family. "So, given that you're a history guy, I was hoping maybe you'd have some ideas on what it means"—God, this was going to sound stupid—"to be a hero."

"Oh." Ben clearly hadn't seen that coming. "Right. I get why that's on your mind. Let me think. Well, throughout history there have been many interpretations of what it means to be heroic. Some Greek philosophers felt that it was heroic to be in charge of oneself. But that doesn't really apply here."

Oh, but it did. Cassie was constantly having trouble keeping hysterical Cassie in check, but Ben didn't need to know about all that.

"In myth, though, being a hero was usually connected in some way to being a god. Take Hercules. His heroism came from being incredibly strong thanks to his father Zeus, but his story is also one of resilience. He had twelve labors to get through as punishment for killing his family, so—"

"He killed his family?"

"It wasn't his fault," Ben said quickly. "But that's another story."

"Got it." Cassie squinted at the sun. "Well, being god-strong is cool but hard for the average person to achieve. There have to be other factors that play into it, like..." She paused, pretending she was pondering many possibilities. "What about sacrifice?"

"Sacrifice? Like martyrdom? Wait. Cassie, what are you—"

"I'm sorry." *Frick.* She knew he'd figure things out. Not that she'd been subtle. "You don't need this." And he didn't. It was selfish for her to bring her problems to him, but somehow Ben had become her go-to guy.

"No." He actually sounded worried that she might hang up. "I want to help if I can. You shouldn't have to do this alone. And you probably don't have many people to talk about... *history* with right now."

Cassie smiled.

"So, sacrifice." He exhaled heavily. "I mean, there are lots of stories of people sacrificing themselves to save others. The engineers on the *Titanic*, for example, or the Chernobyl divers. There are countless examples of soldiers taking fire to save others in their units. So yes, sacrifice is certainly an element of heroism, but..." The line went quiet.

"I don't want you to think I'm giving up," Cassie said, digging the toe of her boot into the sand. "I'm still hoping Dorcas can weaken Del enough for me to kill him. If things go wrong, though, I have a weapon that can help. It has a cost to it, but that's not the problem." She squeezed her eyes shut. "I guess I'm wondering how a hero knows when it's time to do what needs to be done."

Ben exhaled softly. "I'm not sure what history has to say on that, but I could try to give you my take, for what it's worth."

"I would love that."

"If it were solely up to me," he said carefully, "I'd tell you to never give up."

The cold wind striped a tear from Cassie's eye.

"But that's not fair. Life isn't always fair. And now that I have Olive, I guess if I were in your situation, and I knew I could save her by sacrificing myself, I'd probably want to do it sooner than later just in case."

Cassie held her breath as waves gently lapped the shore.

"I also think there won't likely be a single clear-cut moment when you know it's time. But there's a famous quote that might apply in this situation. 'A hero is no braver than an ordinary man, but he is braver five minutes longer.' That might also hold true for the witch of her generation. So, maybe if you get to the point where you think it might be time, for all our sakes, ask yourself if you've got a little bit more. If you don't, there's peace in that. But if you do, sometimes the good guys *do* win."

A cascade of shivers rushed over her arms. "Thank you, Ben. That was perfect."

"I hope it helps in some way. But again, if it were solely up to me . . ."

"I know. And thank you for that too." Cassie ached to say more, but it felt like too much to handle right now. Suddenly a strange, garbled noise crackled in her ear.

"Sorry," Ben called out. "That's Olive chewing on my phone. She's got quick hands."

"Hi, Olive!" A loud squeal pealed through in response. "Give her a squeeze for me."

"Will do," Ben said. "Talk later?"

"Yeah."

"Thanks for calling."

Cassie rested her phone on the blanket. *Thanks for calling.* That never got old. She looked back at her coin, feeling its grooves with the pad of her thumb. The sun and moon. Witches and vampires. Somehow it looked different. Maybe because she was seeing it with fresh eyes. What if it had found its way to her on purpose? Maybe the universe wanted her to have it, so she could make sure Del would never go free.

"I knew it!" a voice shouted behind her. "I knew you still had the coin."

CHAPTER 32

Cassie should have been cowering at the tone in her sister's voice, but a wave of love washed over her instead. Eliza looked so beautiful and fierce in the morning sun.

"I remembered it from when we were kids. Were you going to tell me?"

Cassie patted the spot on the blanket beside her.

"No, answer the question," Eliza said, raking her windblown hair back from her face.

"Honestly, at first I wasn't sure." Cassie turned back to the horizon. "I was trying to figure out if it was crueler to tell you something that might not happen, or to let you deal with the pain if it did. But yes, I was going to tell you. You can't change my mind about having it with me on Halloween though."

"So, you're giving up before Dorcas even fights?"

"I did not say that. Look, I know this is hard." Cassie reached up to touch her sister's hand, but Eliza batted it away. "I need you to be realistic. This might not go our way." She held up the coin. "This here. It's a guaranteed win. And there's nothing I have to do. Just flip it, and it will kill him."

"It will kill you!"

Cassie squinted up at her. "Would you sit down? My neck muscles are sore."

Eliza folded her arms over her chest.

This wasn't turning out to be the heart-to-heart Cassie had envisioned. "Look, I'm still hoping Dorcas can bring Del to his knees. And I promise, using it won't be my first move. But if it comes down to it, it will be my last."

"You know what?" Eliza pointed at her viciously. Cassie almost ducked. There was no telling what she could do with that finger anymore. "That's the problem right there. You're spending more time preparing for the worst-case scenario than fighting for the best!"

"Again, I am not giving up." Cassie needed to stay calm. This was the hardest thing her sister had ever faced. Patience was the key. "I'm trying to figure out the best way forward in an impossible situation. That's all. I'm hoping you will try to understand that. If not now, then—"

"That's total crap! Even before this, you were always giving up. You're a total freaking pushover. Look at your relationship with Matt. Matt wanted to pursue his dream, so you gave up yours. Then when it was your turn, of course he wanted more training, so you stayed home to take care of the kids, alone, even though you had just had twins."

Cassie rubbed the spot between her eyebrows. "That's ancient history."

"And what's your plan for when he comes home? And he will come home when he's finally bored of what he's doing or . . . *who*."

What? Cassie had never told anyone her suspicions. But Eliza clearly knew *something*. How long had Cassie been the only one not to know?

"He's an endless pit of need. Nobody can admire him enough to keep him satisfied. But you'll take him back. You'll do it for the kids. That's easiest."

Cassie chewed her lip. *Patience.*

"Just admit it, you're afraid," Eliza went on. "You're too afraid to live, to put yourself out there, and you use your family as an excuse not to."

Calm. Breathe. Remember, you love your freaking sister. "Eliza, you have no idea what you're talking about."

"I know exactly what I'm talking about. You know it too. At first, I thought your magic couldn't flow because you couldn't trust Dorcas. But it's you! You don't trust yourself!"

Cassie pushed herself to her feet. "I'm done." She walked a few steps then spun around. "Actually, I'm not done. You know what, Eliza? You're right. I am a pushover and maybe I don't trust myself. You want to know why that is? It's because I don't know what I'm doing. Never did. I didn't know how to raise you. I sure as hell don't know how to get Matt to love me. I'm still trying to figure out how to parent the kids when it's clear my life is a mess. And beyond all of that, I don't know how to keep any of you safe without this." She looked down at the coin in her fingers. "But here's the really messed-up thing. Even though I have no idea what I'm doing, I'm still responsible for all of you. And the entire island. And maybe the world! So, you'll have to excuse me for thinking about what to do in the worst-case scenario."

"You are not alone! Dorcas will use every bit of power she has to weaken Del. And if you let me help—"

"No! Even if you could help, you're not going to. I won't risk it. Not when I have a way to keep you safe."

Eliza jumped forward. "Give me that!" She made a swipe for the coin.

Cassie snatched her hand back. "Are you freaking serious right now?!" She shoved the coin into her pocket. "We're done." She turned and took a few quick steps. Not too quick. She wasn't running. She wasn't afraid of Eliza. And she wasn't about to look over her shoulder to see what her sister was do—

Something cold and wet slapped against her shoulder blade.

Cassie twisted her head, arching to look down her back. Mud. Her sister had thrown a fistful of mud. And it had hit her! *Mud!* She rolled her gaze up to Eliza. "You did not just do that."

Another punch of sea sludge hit the back of her knee.

Cassie whipped around. "That's enough."

Her sister planted one fist on her hip, the other dangled by her side, thick drops of mud slipping between her clenched fingers. "Make me."

"Eliza," Cassie said in her calmest voice, which she knew made her sister insane. "We are not doing this." Before she had even finished speaking, mud splattered against her neck, up the side of her cheek, and into her ear.

"Not going to fight back?" Eliza shouted. "Just going to take it? I'm shocked. But it's your choice. I can do this all day."

"I swear to God this is your last warning."

She shrugged. "Is this the example you want to set for the kids? Give up before you've even fought?"

"I never said I was giving up!" Cassie shouted. And she wasn't! She had just been talking to Ben about this very thing! Why couldn't her sister have eavesdropped on that part of the conversation? "Eliza, what would you know about it? You have never had to take care of anyone but yourself!"

Her sister's eyes shone with angry glee. "Yes, there she is. I see you, Cassie." She bent, reaching for more ammunition.

"Stop."

Eliza stood back up and cocked her head. "Make me. Coward."

Oh ho ho. "You want to go?" Cassie pushed up her sleeves. "Let's go!"

CHAPTER 33

There had been times in Cassie's life when she'd realized too late that she had made a mistake. The worst had been when she'd told the nurse at Sadie's birth that she didn't want an epidural. That had been a very bad call. But when Cassie dipped her shoulder and hit her sister in the gut, driving her back into the ocean, she knew instantly that this mistake might be just as bad as that one, if not worse.

Time stopped as they hit the frigid water. Cassie's flesh screamed, her muscles froze, and her lungs flapped like dying fish. This was ridiculous. They were going to die of hypothermia. They were going to—

Her sister's hand smashed into her cheek, squishing cold mud across her face and into her mouth. *Into her mouth!*

Cassie let out a battle cry worthy of the gods, then lifted her sister by the waist and threw her. She laughed as Eliza disappeared under the waves. After lugging twins around for years, Cassie had the upper-body strength of . . . well, she had more upper-body strength than her sister. Suddenly rapid-fire wads of mud hit every square inch of Cassie's torso. She dropped under the waves to escape the onslaught but immediately pumped her feet against the rocky sand to charge her sister again. Eliza planted the heel of her palm on her forehead to hold her back, so Cassie went deeper, wrapped her arms around her sister's calves, and tossed her over her shoulder.

A manic smile came to her face. This felt good. Better than good. There had been far too much simmering beneath the surface. It was time to get it all out.

But Cassie's smile faded when her sister didn't re-emerge from the water.

It was a trap.

She knew it was a trap.

The age-old childhood dilemma that siblings had faced since the beginning of time. The *Is she really dead?* ruse. Cassie could fall for the trap and allow her sister to humiliate her, or she could risk Eliza's life and keep her pride. It was an impossible call.

Seconds ticked past. Eliza was fine. Cassie was sure she was fine. Her sister was simply lying in wait like some evil mermaid brat.

Air bubbles rose to the surface. Cassie narrowed her eyes with wicked satisfaction. She would have to come up now.

Except she didn't. *Uh-oh.*

What if her sister had smacked her head on a rock when she threw her? What if she'd hit the ground so hard, she'd fractured her spine? What if the cold somehow froze all her muscles, and she was drowning, wondering with her last thought why her sister hadn't come to save her?

Cassie pushed her legs through the water, her upper body twisting with the effort. What if—

Suddenly hands grabbed her ankles, launching her into the air at an impossible speed. Cassie screamed as the hands released her, and she fell to the water. Before her back slapped the surface, she saw Eliza towering above her . . . standing on a wave?! Her arms stretched out to her sides, and her eyes glinted through strips of black hair that hung over her face like seaweed.

Holy crap. What a freak.

Cassie went under, hitting the rocky bottom. She got her feet beneath her and pushed herself up at the very same moment Eliza dropped down.

"How did you . . . ?"

"You'd be surprised at what I can do now." She flicked her wet hair back. "Magic feels good. You should try it sometime."

Why you little . . .

Cassie dove underwater and shot between her sister's legs, grabbing her feet and tossing her again. She then spun around as Eliza emerged from the water. They were both gulping air, holding fistfuls of mud.

"You've gotten stronger," Eliza said.

"And you've gotten scarier." Cassie's chest heaved. "So, are we done now? Did you get everything out of your system?"

"That depends. Will you let me fight? Will you let yourself fight?"

"Eliza, it's not that simple and you know it."

Her sister let the mud slip from her hand, then pushed through the water, headed for the shore.

"Come on. Don't go. Not like this," Cassie shouted after her. "Can't you even try to see where I'm coming from? I want to protect you!"

Eliza stopped without turning at the shoreline. "You know, instead of always protecting me, it might be nice if just once you believed in me." She shook her head. "And yourself."

Cassie closed her eyes like she had taken another hit. "You can't tell Dorcas about this!" she called out. "It's my choice!"

Eliza didn't answer.

In the last days before Halloween, instead of focusing on her training, Dorcas suggested Cassie just *be* with the kids. It was incredible, but the time passed far too quickly. Before Cassie could blink, October twenty-ninth had come, right on schedule, and it was looking like the thirtieth and thirty-first would follow.

Cassie and the kids spent that morning collecting sea glass on the beach before having a picnic on the porch. After that they watched the clouds, finding hidden sea monsters in their shapes before napping in the sun. Sadie even curled up in the crook of Cassie's shoulder. Something she hadn't done since she was small.

When the afternoon drew long, the wind picked up and Sadie took the boys to fly a kite. Cassie had used the word *beautiful* countless times in her life. But her children laughing and running was beautiful in the way the ocean was beautiful, the sky was beautiful, the universe and all of time was beautiful.

Eventually the sun dropped low, casting shadows on the small ridges of sand over the beach, and Cassie caught sight of Dorcas walking down from the house, her arms wrapped around her waist, keeping her sweater closed against the wind. Her aunt's footsteps hummed and squeaked over the island's famous singing sands.

Dorcas sat beside Cassie on her blanket. "Good day?" she asked, the wind lifting her corkscrew curls.

"The best." Cassie smiled. "Is it time to get to work?"

"No, not right now."

"Shouldn't we go over weapons? I also want to organize the potions and—"

"There's time for all that." Dorcas patted her hand.

Her aunt was awfully relaxed. A disturbing thought occurred

to Cassie. "You're not going to wake me up at two in the morning with a bucket of ice water to simulate a surprise vampire attack, are you?"

Dorcas's face lit up. "What an exhilarating idea. I do love your sense of fun, but no. We're ready."

Again, she said it with such certainty. Faith. "Dorcas, can I ask you something?"

"Always, Polliwog."

"I want you to be honest with me."

Her aunt's eyes widened. "When have I not been honest with you?" Cassie raised an eyebrow, and she laughed. "Okay, I promise to tell the truth. Just this once."

"Are you scared?"

Dorcas smiled, her eyes twinkling in the fading sunlight. "Well, bravery cannot exist without fear, and I am very brave. But I take comfort in knowing what needs to be done. I've waited a long time for this."

"I wish I could help you more," Cassie said. "I wish I could figure out this magic thing."

"I've been thinking more about your problem, so pay attention. I'm about to be very wise." She gave Cassie a playfully stern look before turning back to the sea. "It's a hard thing to reveal who we truly are to ourselves, let alone the world. Everything could change—our closest relationships, our understanding of life—and even if the change is for the better, that doesn't make it any less frightening." Dorcas took her hand. "I know you have your doubts, but I can feel your power, Polliwog. It's yours, and it's vast, and it's beautiful, but it won't shine through unless you allow it to."

Cassie didn't know if any of that was true, but as she studied her aunt's profile lit up in the dying sun, she did know with complete certainty that she loved every angle, line, and crease of her face. "Thank you, Dorcas. I mean, obviously for fighting the master vampire who wants to kill me, but for everything else too. And I'm sorry that you have to be the one to face Del."

"I wouldn't have it any other way." Dorcas's eyes turned steely. "I want this fight. I have wanted this fight half my life. I want the Deliverer more than undead. I want him dead-dead, and I want to be the one to make that happen. I am practically salivating to tear his black heart from his chest and—"

"Okay, you can stop." Cassie patted her knee. "This here is a nice moment. Let's not ruin it."

Dorcas wrapped her arm around her, and Cassie leaned her head into the crook of her neck. There had been a few times—maybe more than a few—over the past month that Cassie had asked *Why me?* But right now, how could she possibly ask for more? She was here, in this beautiful corner of the world with her family, reunited with her aunt in a home she loved. It was a perfect moment. A gift.

So help me . . .

Cassie pushed herself to her feet. "Boys! Get off that rock! How many times do I have to tell you! It's bad for the sandstone!"

The boys jumped to the ground. Cassie sweetened her voice. "Love you!"

Dorcas laughed and got to her feet. "It's time to come in anyway. Eliza and I have something planned."

Cassie blocked the sun with her hand and frowned.

"Stop looking so scared! It's a good surprise. We're celebrating!"

"Celebrating? Like a party?"

"Not just any party. A witch party."

☾

Dorcas led them up a set of stairs hidden behind a wall panel after having given them each a candle. The thin stack of cobwebbed steps led them up, at a perilous angle, to the attic, then in a box turn up to the roof. The boys tried to get off at the first stop. It was hard for them to resist the dusty boxes, wardrobes, and draped furniture, but Dorcas prodded them along with the promise that they could explore to their heart's content another day.

As they neared the top, Dorcas looked over her shoulder down the line. "Now, I know it must appear like I have done nothing with the house over these past decades, but . . ." She pushed open a wood flap above her head and led them out.

They all gathered in a loose circle, turning slowly to take it all in.

"It was once a widow's walk," Dorcas said, beaming. "But I renovated."

It was so much more than a widow's walk. *Rooftop patio* didn't seem to do it justice either. A giant steel bowl firepit crackled, but there were also lanterns tucked away in every corner and hanging from the wood pergola. Gauze drapes floated in the sea breeze by low outdoor couches and giant velvet poufs, and there was a table with a blue glass punch bowl and more food than they'd be able to eat in a single night. Finally, an altar stood solemnly near the back, carved with an intricate design of shells and sea creatures.

Cassie walked over to run her fingers over its grooves. On its top lay an ancient-looking handbell, a crescent-shaped boline knife and athame, and yet another thick leather-bound book.

"Now, I have a lot planned for this evening, so—"

THE LATE-NIGHT WITCHES

"Um. Before we get started," Cassie said, pointing to the boys, "could we have a minute?"

Cassie was nearing the end of the talks she had been putting off. While they had all been difficult, in some ways, she worried this one might be the worst. The boys were so young and so fearless. She didn't want to scare them, but she had left things too long with Sadie, and she didn't want to lie anymore either.

She guided the twins to a corner and squatted low so that she could look them in the eye. "I know you both must have a lot of questions about why we came to Sea House."

They stared at her from underneath their sun-streaked curls.

"No? No questions?" Cassie scratched the back of her head. So much for them getting her started. "Let's try this another way. You know how proud I am of both of you, right?"

They frowned.

"I realize I give you a hard time about some of your choices, but you remind me every day what it means to have fun and go on adventures."

"Like Dad?" Sylvester asked.

Cassie's heart twisted. "Yes, like Dad. You two got the absolute best of your father. Come here." She dropped to her knees and pulled them in for a hug. "I love you so, so, so much." She leaned back, just enough to look at them. "Now, tonight. You may hear or see things that are strange. I need to explain, but first, I want you to know that you are safe, and this party, well, it's—"

Sylvester shot a fist in the air. "A witch party!" He zoomed past her to run circles around the patio.

"Die, vampire! Die!" Eddie shouted, chasing after him.

Huh. That had been easier than she'd thought.

CHAPTER 34

"Being a Beckett witch is a tremendous gift, a gift that is meant to be shared. The power we are granted is preordained to foster and protect life so that beauty can unfold."

Dorcas stood at the altar with her hood pulled up over her head. The candle resting on the slab before her cast strange shadows over her face while stars twinkled in the rich peacock sky at her back. The kids were seated on pillows on the floor, taking in every word.

"There is a legend that the first vampire was in fact a witch. Instead of sharing his power, he hoarded it, keeping it only for himself, until it rotted within. That darkness he held created an insatiable hunger to feed. The vampires we are meant to kill are cursed beings. We send them on to the merciful universe so that they may be granted the chance to purify the light that was once their soul."

"By cutting their heads off?" Sylvester asked. It was amazing how much they had picked up when Cassie thought they weren't paying attention.

"That's right!" Dorcas's eyes sparkled with delight before she turned to Eddie. "And?"

"Burning them alive!"

"Well, they are technically *undead*, but yes!" She pointed a finger in the air. "And we can't forget staking."

Cassie wanted to forget staking. Staking sucked.

Dorcas gripped the altar and captured all three of the kids in her gaze. "Children, you should know your mother is ready," she said, voice rising. "She has found the courage to battle the bringers of death. And she will end this curse!" Dorcas shook her fist in the air. "For she is the witch of her generation!"

Cassie scratched her elbow. It was a nice callout, but maybe an exaggeration.

"Do we have to call her that?" Eddie asked. "The witch of her generation?" He half-heartedly shook his own fist.

Sadie elbowed him in the ribs. "No, weirdo. Her name is Mom." She grinned at Cassie while Sylvester hugged his knees to his chest.

"But how do you know, Aunt Dorcas?"

She came around the altar. "How do I know what?"

"How you know for sure Mom is ready to face the vampire?" Sylvester peeked over his shoulder at Cassie.

"Oh, that's easy." Dorcas straightened to her full height and reached back to the altar. In a lightning-fast movement, she flung the boline knife at Cassie's head. Cassie barely caught sight of the blade flashing in the firelight before she hit the ground. The knife struck the wooden pole of the pergola above her head, vibrating wildly.

"Well," Dorcas said. "I thought she might catch it but look at how she ducked!"

The boys cheered.

Cassie pushed herself to her feet, smiling weakly.

"Now," Dorcas boomed, "enough talking." She plunked a foot

down on a wooden crate by her feet. "Eliza, go get our other guests. As for the rest of you, I have a question." She cocked an eyebrow to a dangerous degree. "Who wants to blow stuff up?"

☾

Cassie never imagined her aunt would allow vampires into Sea House, even half-vampires, but Eliza led all three basement dwellers up to the roof. Upon arrival, Dorcas offered them bloodred drinks in special glasses, which they gulped down greedily. Cassie made a mental note to keep track of whose glass was whose. Dorcas had also invited Ben, but he thought Olive might be too young for vampire parties.

Then came the explosions.

The crate was crammed full of potion-filled balloons, and in another box, there were pebbles and broken shells. Dorcas taught the kids how to throw the *bombs* off the roof and then hit them with rocks midair. The first one erupted in a spectacular blue fireball and the kids were hooked. But not all the balloons erupted in flames. Some exploded like fireworks while others bloomed in colorful clouds that rained down to the beach, making the sand sparkle like gemstones.

Every now and then they would take breaks and head over to the food. Warm apple cider, harvest bread, Malpeque oysters, baked pears, raspberry cream-cheese pie, and potato fudge. Dorcas continually refilled the vampires' cups, and with each glass, they seemed more *lively*.

When the balloons were all gone, Dorcas pulled out her fiddle, and they danced made-up jigs.

As the hours passed, the music shifted from rousing foot-stompers to sweet, melancholic ballads with lyrics about doomed

THE LATE-NIGHT WITCHES

lovers and ships lost at sea. When Dorcas finally tired, Gary and Patty left to walk on the beach—they were antsy in the late-night hours—while the rest of them found spots to contemplate the stars. Cassie watched Dorcas's eyelids flutter shut as she snuggled a dozing boy under each arm. So, she did sleep. It had occurred to Cassie that her aunt had reasons—other than vampire revenge—for keeping so busy over the years. She wondered if Dorcas had been running not just from literal demons but from the ones that haunted her past, but she looked peaceful now. Sadie slept in a wicker chair, blanket around her shoulders, knees tucked to her chest, while Eliza stood by the far cresting of the roof, looking out over the water. Cassie settled into a love seat by the fire and glanced at her watch. Just after midnight. October thirtieth. Conflicting thoughts came to mind but evaporated in a puff of smoke when someone came up behind her. "Hey."

Cassie yelped, smacking her hand over her heart. "Tommy! I didn't see you there." He really did need a bell.

"Sorry." He ambled around to the front. "Can I sit?"

Cassie gestured to the space beside her. She'd been wanting to get to know him better. "You're looking good tonight, if you don't mind me saying." In fact, now that she was seeing him up close, with skin that wasn't the color of chalk, she remembered how good-looking he was when he was human. He had a certain boyish charm that was endearing.

"It's the wine Dorcas gave us," he said, wrinkling his nose. "She mixed in a few drops of her own blood."

What? Ew.

Tommy mirrored her grossed-out expression. "I know. It's weird, but I'm not lying when I say you haven't tasted blood until you've tasted witch blood."

Cassie did her best to smile. "But how are you feeling overall? Dorcas mentioned you might be having a tough time not drinking from *humans*."

His eyes widened with horror. "Yeah, it's like this endless voice in my head saying *Kill, kill, kill.* I think about smashing my skull against the walls in the basement all the time to make it stop." He smiled suddenly. "Crazy, huh?"

Well, this conversation was going beautifully. Cassie pulled a throw over her lap. "How do you stop yourself from giving in?"

His eyes softened. "Your sister. Thinking about her makes everything better." He glanced over at Eliza, doe-eyed. "She's incredible even without the witch powers. She's funny and smart. She doesn't put up with anybody's—" He cleared his throat. "She told me you don't like swearing."

Cassie smirked. "Maybe just not around the kids." She stretched her feet out to the flames crackling in the steel bowl. Tommy's eyes widened with fear, so she pulled them back in. He must be a little paranoid about fire these days. "Eliza is special."

"Strong too," he said, picking at some loose skin around his thumbnail, which, even with Dorcas's special wine, seemed reckless. "The way her powers have exploded." His eyes bulged. "I bet she could take on a vampire army all by herself."

Wait a minute . . .

Cassie squinted. "Tommy, is this about Eliza fighting alongside Dorcas? Did she send you over here?"

"No." He shook his head violently, making both ears wobble. Cassie would give him her own blood just to make that stop. "She'd kill me if she knew I was talking to you about this."

"Good," Cassie replied. "Because I'm not changing my mind."

"Wouldn't want you to." Tommy looked up at the stars. "I'd take Eliza to Vegas in a heartbeat if I could, but she'd never leave

THE LATE-NIGHT WITCHES

you and the kids." He nodded. "But, you know, if she ever were to fight, I wouldn't leave her side. I'd give whatever life I have left for her."

Right. Cassie could feel Tommy peeking over, but she stared into the flames. "Are you sure you're not trying to convince me to let Eliza fight?"

"No way. But I did have this crazy question pop into my head this evening when I woke up." They finally looked at each other. "I asked myself if I was protecting her for her own good or . . . my own."

"Tommy!" Cassie's jaw dropped. What a thing to say? And on All Hallows' Eve Eve? Wait, was there another *Eve*? Didn't matter. It was one of the nights before her maybe-impending death!

He cringed. "She really wants to fight for you guys. And is it fair for us to hold her back from something she really wants to do? Maybe we should support her."

Cassie shot up in the love seat. "I'm not going to support her to death!"

"But then you're taking the choice away from her."

Cassie gasped. "Oh my God, why do you keep saying these horrible things?" Eliza looked back at them.

Tommy waved with a goofy smile before dropping his voice. "It's like I told you—"

"I know what you told me," Cassie grumbled. This was it. She was done with all these heart-to-heart discussions. Fighting was starting to look a whole lot more attractive.

"You don't hate me, do you?" Tommy asked with his zombie puppy dog eyes. "Because your approval is really important to Eliza. I'm not sure I stand a chance if you hate me."

"I don't hate you." But she totally wished she had never had this conversation with him. First, there was Eliza with her whole *I wish you'd believe in me* thing, and now this.

"So, what do we do?" Tommy asked.

"We—" A buzz sounded from Cassie's pocket. Eliza had been keeping everyone's phone charged. Cassie slid it out and looked at the screen. "Ben." She swiped to answer. "Hey, is everything—"

"Cassie. Thank God."

The panic in his voice gripped her heart. "What's going on?"

"Listen to me. You may not have much time. You have to go."

"Ben, what are you talking about?"

"You need to leave Sea House now!"

CHAPTER 35

The peaceful cocoon they had conjured over the rooftop with their music and laughter vanished.

"Cassie? Can you hear me? Is Hank there?"

"Hank?" She rose to her feet. "You mean crossbow Hank? No. Why would he be here?" Dorcas sat up and the boys rubbed their eyes.

"Just check. Please."

Eliza jogged over. "My hands are burning."

"Hang on." Cassie ran to the cresting at the back of the house. The sand was perfect, serene, still glowing with magic . . . except there were footprints that hadn't been there before. She traced them back to the clearing in the woods. "I see his truck."

"Get out!" Ben shouted. "Or get him out! He's going to invite them in!"

Dorcas was already lifting the boys to their feet. Tommy jumped over in two steps. "Who wants to ride the vampire?" He dropped to his knees and the boys clambered on his back. He reached around, securing them at his waist.

"Mom?" Sadie's eyes were round with fear.

"Downstairs. Fast! Get to the van." Dorcas grabbed Sadie's arm and pulled her to the hatch.

In less than a minute, they were out the front door. All except Dorcas, who had stopped dead inside.

"Come on! Let's go!" Cassie grabbed her aunt's arm, but she wasn't budging. *Frick!* Cassie ran back to the porch. Tommy had already made it halfway over the beach. Her sister and Sadie weren't far behind. "Eliza," she shouted. "Get the kids in the van! We're coming!" The keys were in the cup holder. Cassie never thought to bring them inside. It was safe. Sea House was safe. Until it wasn't.

Sadie stopped, but Eliza yanked her forward, shouting for Gary and Patty. Cassie ran back inside and pulled her aunt by the elbow again. "We have to go now."

Dorcas didn't budge. She was focused solely on a man standing by the fireplace in the parlor, wearing only an undershirt with his pants and rubber boots. "What's going on, Hank?"

"I'm sorry, Dorrie." He squinted through some unseen light.

"You know better than to let him in your mind."

"It happened so fast. You should go."

"I will not leave Sea House." Dorcas's eyes flashed with fury. "He will not take my home from me."

"No," Cassie said, tugging her. "You can't—"

"If you don't go, Cassie, I'll be forced to make you. Take care of the children." Dorcas pushed her toward the door. "Go! Hide! All of you!" Cats materialized from the shadows and raced into the night.

Cassie gave her aunt one last look but then sprinted over the beach. Her lungs and legs burned at the sudden demand, but she pushed over the dunes to the van faster than she thought possible.

"Where's Dorcas?" Eliza shouted.

Cassie jumped in the passenger seat. "She's not coming. Go!"

Eliza hit the gas and spun the van in reverse, nearly smashing into a tree before slamming it into drive. Everyone braced themselves as they banged over the dirt trail. Once they made it to the main road, a timid voice came from the far back seat. "Mom?" Sylvester was pressed against Patty's arm.

"It's okay. We're okay." Cassie looked beyond him through the rear window. There was nothing but road in the taillights.

"Is it the vampires?"

"Yes, sweetheart. But they're not following us."

"Here," Sadie said, tossing him her phone. Her tone had its normal bored-teenager ring, but a quaver ran beneath. "Have at it." She always kept a few games for her brothers.

Once they were settled, Eliza whispered, "I was kind of expecting hordes of vampires to be following us."

Cassie nodded, glancing at the sideview mirror, still thinking she'd see Del, transformed into some galloping monster chasing them. "Me too."

"Somehow this feels worse."

Somehow it did.

CHAPTER 36

The last of the night dragged its way to dawn, and every second felt like a trial of worry and waiting. After dropping the vampires off at the Grub, Eliza wanted to take the rest of them home and go right back to Dorcas. Cassie did too, but how could they leave the kids? If Del had found a way to breach the safety of Sea House, they weren't safe anywhere, and Eliza was the only one with magic.

At the first ray of light, they were off. Cassie had planned for the kids to stay home, but they wanted to come. She couldn't say no. They were part of this whether she liked it or not, and Dorcas was family now.

Relief almost dropped Cassie to the sand when she saw the house still standing, but she couldn't ignore that it looked different in the dreary morning light. The lines sagged and the gray wood shingles looked tired. After she sent the kids to the beach, she and Eliza jogged up the steps of the porch. Cats swarmed them from every side, picking their way around shards of glass from the broken windows. Janet bumped her head against Cassie's leg. She picked her up, pressing her lips into her fur as she walked toward the front screen door, swinging limply in the breeze. Its top hinges were broken, and the mesh was torn.

"Wait," Eliza said, trotting over to the far end of the porch.

Blue-green smoke rose from a mound of charred wood and faintly glowing embers. Stakes. Their stockpile was gone.

Cassie pulled back the screen and pushed open the door. "Dorcas?"

Sharp footsteps slapped against the stone tiles before her aunt appeared, wearing overalls and a kerchief tied around her hair. "Thank the stars you're here. I am close to exploding with fury, and the house has already been through enough."

Cassie's heart clenched. She gave quick thanks to all the powers in the universe as she and Eliza rushed toward her.

Dorcas shot her hands out. "Stop! I love you both dearly"—she threw angry kisses in the air—"but I also have a sore rib, which is not helping with my scorching fury."

"But you're okay?" Eliza asked in a quiet voice.

"Of course I'm okay." Dorcas gave her a saucy wink. "But I am most certainly not okay! Take a look for yourself!" She flapped a hand over to the dining room.

The sliding doors had been hacked to shreds, and the air was full of conflicting scents: smoke, flowers, sulfur, and many more. The long cabinets had been overturned, and spilled potions coated every inch of the floor. The battle-axes and Dorcas's scythe had been snapped in half, their blades warped, and the garments in the corner had been torn to shreds.

"Centuries of work destroyed," Dorcas said, right before a groan floated in from the parlor.

Cassie's eyes widened. "Is that . . . ?"

"*That* is the reason everything was demolished." Dorcas

jutted her finger in the air but then grabbed her rib with her other hand. "If I hadn't had to save his traitorous life, I would have killed them all before they destroyed everything!"

Cassie and Eliza crept past the stairs to see Hank on the parlor floor with his back resting against the wall by the fireplace, his legs splayed out in front of him. A stake jutted out of his chest at the junction of his shoulder and collarbone, and his undershirt was soaked with blood.

"Um, Dorcas?" Eliza said lightly. "You said you saved his life, but I'm not sure you finished the job."

"Oh he's fine," she snapped. "I performed an incantation of healing. He won't die."

"She's been skimpy on the pain relief spells though," Hank muttered.

Dorcas's irises suddenly swirled with orange fire.

Cassie blinked. She did not know her aunt could do that. Hank didn't seem too surprised though. "I wanted to warn you girls." He wheezed, spittle catching on his lips. "But he told me I couldn't. I was able to call that professor though. I heard you all were tight, and he'd been around my place asking questions." He coughed, and his chest convulsed around the stake.

"I don't understand," Cassie said looking to Dorcas. "You said you spelled the dining room doors against vampires."

"But I did not spell them against Hanks! He hacked them apart before we even realized he was here." Dorcas inhaled sharply. "This is terrible. I pride myself on not normally being enraged. You should all be terrified. I need a cat." She flapped her hands out. "Someone give me a cat. Quickly!"

Eliza stooped to pick up a gray tabby. Dorcas snatched it from her and brought the cat's face up to her own. The feline tentatively licked the tip of her nose. She closed her eyes. "That's better."

Cassie looked back to Hank. "How did you get staked?"

"I was in here with your aunt when they came through the windows and doors. They couldn't have seen me, but somehow they set off a crossbow, and the stake came right through the wall." He pointed to a hole between the wood beams.

"They must have used our crossbow! The spell worked! It fires true!" Eliza cried joyously before crossing her arms, pinning her hands to her ribs. "Sorry, that was insensitive. It was one of my first potions."

"No kidding," Hank remarked. "Do you think you could send some of that my way? I have buyers who would be interested in that sort of thing." He shot a nervous glance at Dorcas. "We can talk about that later. Anyway, after the stake, others crashed through that window there and dragged me off." Shattered glass from the once-beautiful mullioned windows covered the floor.

Dorcas inhaled stiffly, but before she could say anything, Eliza passed her another cat.

"But what happened after they destroyed everything?" Cassie asked. "Did they just leave?"

"No, no," Hank croaked. "A few got away, but the rest are still here."

Eliza's eyes bulged. "What do you mean they're still here?"

Hank dropped his gaze. Cassie hadn't noticed it when they first came in, but there were at least two to three inches of dust covering the floor. She flicked her gaze up to her aunt, but she was nuzzling the cats in her arms. "How many vampires were there?"

"At least twenty. Maybe even thirty." Hank winced, pain creasing the crow's-feet at his eyes. "There's one other thing you girls should know."

"Hank!" Dorcas snapped, making the cats squirm.

"They have a right to hear it." The two glared at each other, but Dorcas relented first. "Before the big bad vamp sent me here, he told me to give you all a message. One witch. One vampire. No cheating."

Heat blazed up Cassie's neck to her scalp.

"Do not make that face, Polliwog!" Dorcas snapped. The nickname suddenly felt a lot less affectionate. "We don't have to listen to him. I will cheat if I want to cheat." She looked down at the cats. "He can't tell me not to cheat because he will cheat too, won't he? Because he eats people. And people-eaters can't be trusted."

"But how can you face Del now?" Cassie gestured around the wreckage. "After this?"

"This changes nothing."

"But your scythe . . ." Eliza looked over to the shattered pole with the warped blade lying just outside the dining room door.

Dorcas sighed with annoyance. "I will just have to use the poleax in my bed."

"You have a poleax in your bed?" Cassie asked.

"Well, it doesn't bring me the same joy as a good scythe, but it still gives me comfort."

Hank coughed. "I hate to interrupt, but I don't suppose one of you could give me a lift to the hospital?"

Dorcas glared at him, suddenly remembering she was infuriated. "Oh yes, girls. Please take Hank to the hospital. I would have taken him already, but both my Jeep and his truck have had their guts torn out." She closed her eyes. "I may need another cat."

Eliza lifted a fluffy white one this time. "I'm headed that way," she said, passing it to Dorcas. "I need to check on Tommy and the others." She went over to help Hank get to his feet. "But how are we going to explain this to the doctor?"

Hank grunted as he slid up the wall. "Bah. They know me there. This ain't my first staking." His bushy eyebrows raised as he looked over to Dorcas. "I guess this means you're going to stay mad another ten years?"

"At least." She spun away with her cats and tromped off to the kitchen.

Eliza and Hank shuffled toward Cassie. When they reached her, Hank mumbled, "You girls keep an eye on your aunt. She'll never admit it, but I think one of those vamps got her good."

☾

A sparkling path of moonlight reached across the still, black water. Cassie sat on the porch in a rocking chair, holding a quilt around her shoulders.

Only one more sleep.

After she helped Eliza get Hank in her car, she brought the kids inside, and Dorcas's mood instantly lifted; if she was injured, she wasn't showing any sign of it. She cleaned the dining room with Cassie's help, then set to fixing her Jeep.

Now that night had fallen, everyone was inside preparing for what the following day would bring, but Cassie had some other business she needed to take care of before she snuck in some last-minute decapitation training. She lifted her phone and pressed the contact on the screen before she could give it more thought. A crackling buzz trilled in her ear.

"Hello?"

A woman's voice. A woman had answered her husband's phone. "Um, hi? I'm looking for Matt?"

"Who's calling?"

"It's his *wife.*"

"Oh." There was something in the woman's voice that told Cassie all she needed to know. "He's busy right now."

"Miranda," Cassie said sharply, "why don't you hang up, and I'll call back and leave a message." Part of her was still hoping that the woman on the other end was anyone but Miranda, but she knew.

"Sure. We are expecting a call though."

We are expecting a call?

When the line went dead, Cassie jabbed the screen, and the same crackling ring filled her ear. This time it ended with her husband's voice. *It's Matt. Leave a message.*

"Hey, it's me." There were so many things Cassie wanted to say. She wanted to scream, yell, or at the very least be snide or cutting, but for the first time in her married life, she had bigger problems than Matt. "You need to come home. Get the first flight out. It's an emergency and the kids need you." In no way was this a lie. She might live through tomorrow night, but there was no guarantee. Her kids—*their* kids—would need their father for emotional support . . . and possibly the resulting vampire invasion. *Oh God.* "This isn't something I can explain over the phone, not that I can ever get you on the phone." *Oops.* So much for not being snide. "Just trust me and do it. Don't bother trying to—"

Beep. *Son of a . . .*

Cassie called back.

"Hello?"

What was wrong with this woman?!

"Me again," Cassie said with a strained chuckle. "My message was too long and—"

"Matt's still busy, and again, we are expecting an urgent call."

That was it. Cassie was going to find her powers, learn all the spells, and then fly on a freaking broomstick across the ocean and—

"I'll be quick. Don't pick up." Cassie redialed. "I got cut off there. Anyway, come home. Now. I can't explain except to say... I guess I've found my own life's purpose." Cassie ended the call, then threw her phone onto the porch just as it binged, indicating a new message. She lunged out of her chair and picked it up. The screen was cracked, but that didn't matter. Certainly not in the grand scheme of things.

> I hope you're doing okay. I'm thinking about you.

Ben.

Cassie shook her head, not sure if she should laugh or cry. How had everything become so complicated? A month ago, things had been ... suddenly she didn't know what they had been, but strangely, she couldn't say *better*. At least not in every way. The vampire thing was still bad though. Cassie pushed herself up. She didn't have time for boy trouble. It was time for decapitation practice. The boys had stumbled across a rusty machete in the shed and had come running—machete in hand—to show her. *Still going for mom of the year.* Meanwhile Dorcas had pulled out some decent-sized gourds from the garden. The plan was that once Cassie finished splitting them all, Dorcas would roast the seeds in butter. So that was exciting.

Cassie reached for the door when she noticed blue-green light stretching across the sand to the side of the house. She hopped down the porch steps and walked over.

Through the leaves pressing up against the glass, Cassie could see a figure inside carrying a lantern with colored glass. *Dorcas.* Cassie crept up the sand as two more figures with lanterns came into view. Sadie and Eliza. The boys tumbled in next.

Huh. Nobody had told her about this witchy gathering.

They crowded in around the crackling firepit, its flames licking the cauldron hanging above from an iron spit.

Dorcas's voice traveled through an open window. "Thankfully, those ridiculous vampires—may the powers that be grant them peace—didn't have time to look in here before I swiftly brought them to their merciful end."

"How did you kill all the vampires, Aunt Dorcas?" Eddie asked.

"Well, I started with streams of fire. Don't worry, after the library was burned, the house was coated with a potion ensuring it would never happen again. It took three generations of work. Anyway, once I burned the first five or so fiends, the rest panicked. I don't blame them. The smell alone was—"

"Um, Dorcas?" Eliza interjected.

"Ah, this is perhaps a story for when you are older. Now, go sit over there." Dejected, the boys looked over at the empty wooden table. It was at least ten feet back from the fire. "Off you go. There's no telling what could happen with the potion your sister has in mind. Speaking of which, are you sure this is the one you want to make, Sadie? You must be able to visualize exactly what it is you want."

"I'm sure," she said, rolling her shoulders back.

"Well, it's an excellent choice!" A mischievous twinkle came to Dorcas's eye. "I can't wait to see Del's face when your mother uses it."

Sadie picked up a bottle. "Don't tell her, okay? I want it to be a surprise."

"Our lips are sealed."

Cassie smiled and backed away. She didn't want to ruin the surprise either.

☾

After chopping a few gourds and leaving a bowl filled with seeds in the kitchen, Cassie headed for bed. All day, she had been worried about being able to sleep, but she was out the moment her head touched the pillow.

CHAPTER 37

Vampire!

Cassie shot up in bed, looking frantically around the room. She then groaned and flopped back down.

The big day was finally here.

A cat mewed from the bedside table. "Happy Halloween to you too, Janet."

Although Cassie had fallen asleep easily, her dreams had been heavily fang-focused. But as she lay there staring at the ceiling, the nightmares faded from her consciousness and were replaced by the scent of something *good*. Maple coffee, bacon, freshly baked bread—which Cassie just *knew* Dorcas was turning into French toast—and the homemade crispy hash browns that she loved more than—well, maybe not more than her family, but potato-love was certainly less complicated.

Cassie threw her quilt off. She had to make it downstairs before the kids got to the food. This was going to be awesome. It was the perfect . . . *last meal*.

After some jostling on the stairs, everyone made it to the table at the same time. Breakfast was everything Cassie could have hoped for. The food was amazing, and for hours they talked and laughed as though it were any other day, maybe because they all desperately wished it was. Well, not the boys. They weren't thinking past the bacon.

The adults spent the afternoon continuing their cleanup efforts, searching for any untouched weapons, and the kids once again headed for the beach. They didn't say anything, but it was clear that no one could predict with any certainty when they'd be back.

As the afternoon drew to a close, Cassie and the kids headed back to the Burrow. It was a stressful trip. Cassie had Dorcas's poleax leaning against the passenger seat. Every time she turned, she feared she might be decapitated. Why she hadn't thought to put the ax-head on the floor was anyone's guess. But she didn't want to stop. She might never get going again. At least it was Halloween, so none of the other drivers on the road called the authorities. One motorist did, however, smile and slice his finger across his throat . . . which was just *swell*.

The sky had taken on an odd yellowish hue as they pulled onto their street. The neighborhood had become a ghost town. Delivery boxes were piling up at front doors. A garbage can rolled dully in the street. Every house looked deserted. Apparently her neighborhood's collective memory had returned. At least, Cassie really hoped everyone had packed up and left, and there wasn't a more sinister explanation.

There was something else too. Pumpkins. Every home had one. Which wouldn't have been strange except that each had been carved to look exactly like the jack-o'-lantern that had been left on her porch. Every house had fangs.

Cassie parked on the street. Ben's sedan was already in her driveway. Eliza didn't know it yet, but he was going to be the one to take the kids. He would take them as far away as he could on the island; then, if things went badly, they'd go to Halifax, maybe beyond. Ben also wanted to give the boys a chance to do some trick-or-treating. It seemed like a good idea to keep them distracted. Overall, the twins were still handling the situation well. Extremely well. And thankfully, Dorcas had been able to throw together some wolf costumes last-minute. After all her storytelling, the boys decided to go as Romulus and Remus, the founders of Rome. Cassie recalled one of the wolf brothers killing the other in that fable, but as always, she had bigger problems.

As they got out of the van, they were greeted by a strange sound. It was a papery, rustling noise, loud but low, and it wasn't coming from fallen leaves. Cassie walked to the middle of the street, the kids following behind. Starlings—hundreds, maybe thousands of them—twisted and waved in a dark cloud overhead.

"What are they doing?" Eddie asked, wrapping his arms around hers like he was clinging to a rope.

Leaving, Cassie thought. But she said, "It's a murmuration. They do that sometimes."

They watched the birds dance and spin until the cloud drifted away, leaving an eerie silence in its wake.

"You guys ready to go?" Ben called from the porch. "Do you have your treat bags? Costumes?"

Cassie smiled as he trotted down the steps. She had asked Ben to leave with the kids as quickly as possible. If they hung around even for a little while, she was worried she might not be able to let them go. "Everything is still in the van. Go get it, guys." She almost asked Sadie to help the boys with their stuff, but they weren't babies anymore.

Cassie walked over to the porch.

"I guess the big night is finally here," Ben said, rocking on his feet.

"Guess so."

"I want you to know you have my promise that I will not let your kids out of my sight." And there was that warm, empathic look again. The one that made Cassie want to put her forehead into his chest and will the world away. She didn't, though, because tonight she had to be a stone-cold killer. Killers didn't need hugs.

"Thank you. Really, thank you." Did killers cry? Because her eyes were prickling. "I wish I could somehow let you in my head so that you'd know how grateful I am."

"Don't worry about that." He fiddled with his glasses then raked his hair back. "I wish I could do more."

"I know you do." And she did. There was something growing between them, no point pretending there wasn't. "But hey, you've already killed one vampire. You've done your part. And I need to know the kids are safe." Cassie dug her hand into her jean pocket, and her knuckles brushed against her coin. She passed Ben a folded bit of paper. "This is Matt's number," she said. "I left him a message earlier. He doesn't know much, but he should be on his way home." Matt had left her a few messages of his own. She only listened to the first one. He was upset, and now wasn't a good time to come home, but there was another doctor who could cover for him if it was *really* necessary. Cassie didn't call him back. She had said what she needed to, and she suspected her silence would be more convincing than anything else she could say.

"If things don't go the way we're hoping, the kids will need him. Eliza will be a mess and—"

"I'll take care of it."

She couldn't take it anymore. Cassie stepped forward and wrapped her arms around him.

"I've been thinking a lot about our last conversation," he said quietly. The heat of his breath sent chills down her neck. "I'm not sure if the advice I gave was . . ." He sighed with frustration.

"It's okay. I know, and if it comes down to it, you're one of the reasons I'll see if I can keep going." For so long she had wanted to know what it was like to be in his arms. It was cruel how wonderful it felt. She didn't want to let go, but it was time.

Once the boys had their things, Ben led them to his sedan. There were hugs and kisses, but again the twins didn't seem upset. Given their age, Cassie supposed that was a natural reaction, and she was grateful for it, but then there was Sadie.

Cassie put her hand on her daughter's shoulder and guided her to stand under one of the towering red maples on the front lawn.

"I don't want to go," Sadie said.

Cassie brushed her daughter's hair back over her shoulder.

"But you're going to make me."

She nodded.

"You guys don't have to do this," Sadie pleaded. "You could hide. You can train me, and—"

"Not a chance." Cassie caught her daughter's eye. "This isn't your choice. Know that. It's what I want, and it's what Dorcas really, really wants. Del should be the one hiding."

Sadie tried to smile, but the tiny muscles of her face twitched with the struggle of keeping her emotions in check. It tore Cassie's heart to shreds.

"I made you something." Her daughter pulled out a bottle from her jacket pocket. "Throw it on Del if you get in trouble. It won't kill him. But it should help."

Cassie took the vial. A sparkling pink liquid shone in the last rays of sunlight. It reminded her of the days when everything

Sadie owned was pink and sparkly. Her room had been littered with princesses and unicorns. "Thank you."

Sadie shrugged half-heartedly.

Cassie pressed her daughter to her chest and closed her eyes. There was so much more she wanted to say, a lifetime's worth, but they were out of time, so she said the thing that mattered most. "I love you."

"I love you too."

"Now get going." Cassie gave her one last squeeze. "You've got candy to steal from your brothers, and I've got a job to do."

Sadie walked to the driveway, turning one last time to wave goodbye. A single tear rolled down her cheek... and Cassie died a little.

☾

Cassie and Dorcas stood in the street watching the fiery-red sun drop off the edge of the earth. Her aunt had arrived after the kids left—she had managed to get her Jeep working again—and Cassie had come out of the house to see if she needed help bringing in their *battle dress*. Luckily, Dorcas had kept it in her sewing room, so it hadn't been destroyed by the vampires.

Standing there, Cassie couldn't help but think that sunsets were a lot like dying. When that fiery ball dips below the horizon, that last moment is the death of the day. There is so much lead-up to it, but then it's over in a second. Dying—

Dorcas whapped her on the shoulder. "We are not dying."

Cassie smiled. "Stay out of my head, witch."

"I try. I really do. But your thoughts are pointy."

If only she could stake Del with them.

Dorcas chuckled. "Good one."

"How is your rib feeling?" Cassie asked.

"It's—" Dorcas cut herself off, pointing down the street. "There they are."

Eliza pulled into the driveway. When the car stopped, the three passengers inside dragged the sheets off their heads.

"Thank you for coming." Cassie did her best to ignore the rotten stench wafting from the car as they climbed out.

"Wouldn't miss it," Tommy said, giving her a thumbs-up. Cassie was relieved to see that he did in fact still have a thumb. Patty waved before reaching back into the car for her purse while Gary broke into a fighting stance, making his jowls wobble disconcertingly. It didn't go unnoticed by Dorcas either. She dipped her hands into one of her boxes and pulled out three small bottles.

Gary licked his lips. "Is that more of your blood?"

"That was a one-night affair only. Cherish the memories." Dorcas winked. "No, these were, fortunately, still marinating in the conservatory when Sea House was attacked. While they are not made with my blood, they should help with your degeneration, maybe even give you an extra kick."

"That is so sweet of you," Patty said, accepting a bottle. "I would really like to kill something tonight."

Dorcas tilted her chin to an angle of obvious appreciation. "That, my fanged one, is an excellent attitude."

Tommy accepted his with a toothy smile. His gums had greatly receded. "You rock, Dorcas."

She tittered and batted a hand.

Gary took his bottle next. He thanked Dorcas and she put her fists up. They sparred with air punches in a tight circle. Unfortunately, in all the excitement Gary dropped his vial, and it smashed on the pavement. His eyebrows went up, making his cheeks wobble again.

"Don't worry. I made a large batch." Dorcas threw her hands

in the air and clapped in rapid bursts. "Vampires, entertain yourselves. We have time to kill. I doubt the Deliverer will arrive before midnight when he is at his most powerful, and we need that time to dress."

They needed six hours to dress?

Dorcas must have seen the horror on Cassie's face because she said, "Don't worry, Polliwog. I will make you both beautiful and terrifying." She turned to the vampires. "I'll call you when it's time to discuss the battle plan."

Tommy cleared his throat. "We may have some friends like us coming. So don't kill them, okay?"

"The more the merrier! And I'll do my best." Dorcas swirled her fingers then flicked some sweat from her brow.

Cassie frowned. The night was cool. It was probably nothing, but—

"So, where are the kids? We should probably get going," Eliza said sullenly, pulling her attention away.

Ugh. Cassie really didn't want to do this, but it was too late to change her mind. "The kids are with Ben."

Eliza's eyes darted over her face. "Wait . . ." Excitement lit up her entire being. And that right there was the problem! There was nothing to be excited about. Were warriors excited before they went into battle? Cassie felt her brow furrow. She didn't really know the answer to that question. Maybe they were. Maybe she was battling wrong.

"You're staying in the house with me though."

"Sure," Eliza said with a big nod. "No problem."

Cassie narrowed her eyes. "When you say it that quickly, I don't believe you."

"Thank you." Eliza threw her arms around her neck. "I need to be here."

Cassie was going to say something about living to regret this before remembering what her sister had said on the beach. "I'm glad you're here."

Eliza laughed. "No, you're not."

"No, I'm not. But we're doing this anyway."

☾

Five and a half hours later, Cassie was seated at her kitchen table with her aunt and her sister, feeling ridiculous. Dorcas had braided her hair close to her scalp and dressed her in the outfit she had brought from Sea House. The seaweed—not leather—bodysuit shone under the kitchen's chandelier with blue-green hues. Dorcas apparently made her own marine-based fabric in the vat in the greenhouse. The collar went all the way up to Cassie's chin—which admittedly was better than a turtleneck—and if she got thrown across the pavement, she was almost certain she'd slide right down the street. It was a far cry from her mom-sweats and oversized T-shirts, but it made her feel even more like a fraud, especially sitting at her kitchen table with the dried patch of tomato sauce still cemented to the top.

On the bright side, it had pockets. They were designed for potions, which was nice, even though she only had the one Sadie made, but Cassie had found another use for them.

Her coin. She had tucked it away in a pocket at her ribs when no one was looking. Eliza had to know Cassie brought it, but she didn't bring it up.

Speaking of outfits, Eliza's suit was almost identical to Cassie's but pure midnight black. It went well with her hair, and she didn't look like an impostor at all. Dorcas opted to wear her cloak, but it still matched the vibe.

And now, it was time for the pre-battle meeting.

Tommy wasn't the only vampire at the window anymore. Their postal carrier Keith had shown up, along with Megan, a local vet tech, and Bruce the Zamboni driver at the rink. There were many more too. Some she recognized, others she didn't, but they were all good people who had yet to succumb to Del's curse. Funnily enough, even though Tommy was no longer the only one there, he still took up the most space given that he was dressed in full hockey gear. Helmet and stick included.

It was heartening to have so many half-humans on their side. Of course, Cassie knew fighting was their best chance to regain their humanity, but it still felt nice to have backup. She forced herself to stay seated though and not offer everyone snacks.

"Welcome, all, living and dead," Dorcas boomed, rising to her feet. "By joining our cause, you have proven yourselves to be worthy mortal beings. It is my hope that before the night is through, you will be restored to your living states. As I'm sure you have heard, the Deliverer is intent on ending our dear Cassie's life. In doing so, he will break the curse that has held him at bay for hundreds of years. We can't let that happen."

"So, wait, how is it going to work?" A middle-aged half-vampire in a golf shirt pushed his way forward. "How are we all going to fight one guy? Won't we get in each other's way?"

"I'm sorry. You said your name was Ron?" He nodded. "Well, Ron, *we* are not fighting one *guy*," Dorcas said. "I will fight the vampire. The rest of you will guard the house. We must protect Cassie. If she dies, we are done for. You will never regain your humanity, and your families will likely die."

Ron scoffed. "But if she's inside, this Deliverer guy can't get to her anyway. She's safe."

Dorcas blinked slowly. "Cassie will come out at the very end of the battle to kill the Deliverer, but until that time we must make sure she is protected. And we must be prepared for anything. We have no idea what the fiend has planned."

"Yeah, but—"

"That's enough questions."

"But—"

"Stop talking, Ron, or my goal of killing one vampire tonight will become a goal of killing one and a half." Dorcas sighed. "This is what happens when you can't make your own vampire soldiers." She clapped her hands again. "Now break yourselves up into groups so that every side of the house is protected. You'll want to—"

"I'd like to be included in this posse."

Hank elbowed his way through the vampires, not giving them the friendliest of looks. His face was pale, and bandages peeked out of the collar of his shirt, but he looked determined, and he had swapped out his John Deere hat for one that read *TRY ME*.

"It appears we have a traitor in our midst." Dorcas leaned over the table, resting on her fingertips. Beads of sweat glistened on her forehead under the light of the chandelier.

"I brought stakes." Hank pushed up to the screen. "More than you can use. And a real nice crossbow for Ms. Trigger-Happy." He nodded at Eliza.

"Yay! That's me! I love crossbows! You're in." She tossed a fearful look back at Dorcas, then over to Cassie. "I mean, if Dorcas agrees, and I'll only shoot from inside the house. Promise."

"There might also be a scythe," Hank continued. "Made it myself awhile back. Had someone special in mind when I did."

Dorcas held her stern frown a second longer, then smiled. "Hank, you old charmer. Scythes do bring me joy. I suppose..." Suddenly her eyes went distant, and a cold, bitter wind swept through the kitchen.

Cassie stiffened. "What's wrong? What happened?"

Eliza reached her hands out over the table. "They're tingling."

Cassie glanced at her non-tingling hands, then folded them in her lap.

"He's close," Dorcas said darkly. "It is time. I must prepare for my entrance. Hank, get the crossbow for Eliza and the scythe. Cassie, you have the poleax. The rest of you know what it is you must do. Tommy, make sure everyone holds the line." She did the two-finger *I'm watching you* point from her eyes to Ron's. "Together we will defeat the Deliverer." Dorcas's irises blazed with swirling fire. "Tonight, we become legends."

The half-vampires cheered.

"Oh!" Dorcas gasped. "And afterward let's take a group photo!"

CHAPTER 38

A line of half-vampires marched around either side of Cassie's house, meeting at the porch steps by the front door. Tommy stood dead center in his hockey gear, Gary and Patty at his sides—except now Patty was wearing Tommy's helmet. It wobbled on her head given its size, but it did look protective. Cassie was starting to see what her sister liked so much about her undead boyfriend.

Eliza and Cassie turned off the kitchen lights and stood side by side at the sink.

The Burrow was still, but the jack-o'-lanterns running up and down the street had been lit and moved to the end of the driveways. Low mist swirled as they stared out blankly, waiting for the battle to begin.

"Where's Dorcas?" Eliza whispered.

Cassie thought the more important question might be *Where's Del?*

They waited, caught in an agonizing pocket of time, before Eliza gripped the sink and pointed into the darkness. "Look!"

At first, Cassie couldn't see anything because the roof of the porch blocked most of the view, but then boots appeared dangling in the air. Dorcas's boots. Their aunt floated down to the street, her cloak rippling. She must have been up on the roof. "Did you know she could do that?" Cassie asked.

Eliza blinked at her. That must be a *no*.

The second Dorcas's feet touched the ground, Del appeared, also in black, on the opposite side of the street. In the gloom, he was nothing more than a shadow, but his voice reached inside the house in a jagged ripple of ice. "Dorcas, we finally meet," he said. "And only twenty-five years too late."

Cassie couldn't see her aunt's expression, only the silhouette of her dark cloak and the outline of her scythe. Del moved in slow steps toward her. "I suspect you've been yearning for this fight as much as I have. It's sad given you have no chance of winning. You're not the witch of her generation anymore."

"Say what you wish, vampire," Dorcas replied in a voice that made Cassie shiver. "I have had this conversation a thousand times in my mind. Your death screams are the only things I'm interested in hearing now."

Eliza grabbed Cassie's wrist and shook it.

"Such fire, such confidence." Del laughed. "And in my Burrow no less."

With all the flickering jack-o'-lanterns up and down the street, in front of all the abandoned homes, he was right, the Burrow didn't look like Cassie's neighborhood anymore—it was his.

"Did you know I made my den here when I was first turned?" he asked lightly. "The soil must still be rich with my victims' blood."

Dorcas slammed the butt of the scythe against the concrete, setting off a miniature explosion of magical sparks. "No more talk. Fight me, Deliverer."

"Oh, I don't think so. You see, despite all my warnings, you have cheated. This fight is between me and Cassandra, and yet here you are with an army to guard the castle. Albeit a sad and decaying one." The half-vampires surrounding the house jostled against one another at the mention. "Don't feel bad though. I may have also bent the rules."

Suddenly the Burrow came alive. The street, the houses, the trees slithered to life. Every shadow writhed and shifted. Vampire after vampire slunk down from the trees, crawled up from the ditches, and crept over and around the houses and cars.

"Oh shit," Eliza whispered.

Del faded back into the fog as his army of killer vampires charged.

Dorcas struck her free hand out. Bright orange flames engulfed the first fanged soldiers leading the charge. She then raised her palm to the sky, lifting the next line of vampires into the air. When she flipped it back down, they crashed into the pavement. The next wave of vampires closed in, but Dorcas swung her scythe, cutting through them as though they were nothing more than stalks of wheat.

"She's incredible," Cassie whispered. "I knew she was powerful, but . . ." Her attention snapped over to the vampires dropping in the street with arrows protruding from their chests. Cassie tracked the wooden bolts back to the garage. She craned her neck to look out the side of the window and saw Hank on the roof firing at will.

"Hold the line!" Tommy yelled.

The half-vampires were pushing against each other, growling. They wanted in on the fight.

"I will see you dead, Deliverer!" Dorcas shouted. "Show yourself to me!"

Del's army had stalled its assault, unable or unwilling to choose a point of attack, but only silence answered Dorcas's call.

"As you wish." Her draped arm rose to her sight line. She reached her fingers out and then curled them back in. Del appeared from the shadow of a tree, an unseen force dragging him across the pavement. He screamed in rage, his head thrashing, but he couldn't break free from the magical bonds.

"She's going to do it," Cassie whispered. Dorcas had told them a thousand times she could, but Cassie hadn't dared to hope. But her aunt *was* going to bring Del to his knees, so she could kill him once and for all. Cassie's eyes prickled with happy tears. Then in the space of a heartbeat, her joy fell to horror as her aunt's body suddenly rolled in a violent jerk.

Eliza gripped Cassie's elbow, her fingers pressing with enough force to bruise. "What's happening?"

Dorcas's body rolled in spasmatic waves, her arm shaking furiously in the air. She was losing control of the magic surging through her. Then with another jerk, her arm dropped . . . and both the witch and the vampire collapsed to the street.

CHAPTER 39

The Burrow fell silent. Del hadn't moved from where he lay on the pavement, but neither had Dorcas. Mist descended over both vampire armies, cloaking them in a damp shroud. Now that the leaders had fallen, the soldiers were lost.

Cassie clenched a dishrag in her fist, not able to speak or move, but thankfully, that wasn't the case for Eliza. "Tommy!" she screamed, slapping the window frame.

The half-vampire in the hockey gear didn't need an explanation. He leaped across the lawn, smashing his stick into any vampire blocking his path. When he reached Dorcas, he dropped his makeshift weapon and scooped her up. Before Cassie could process what was happening, he was at the door, Dorcas hanging limply in his arms.

Eliza pushed back the kitchen table as battle cries erupted from outside. "Bring her in."

"I can't," Tommy moaned.

"What do you mean—"

"Get in here," Cassie shouted, flipping on the stove light. "You're invited."

Tommy crossed the threshold and gently set Dorcas down on

the linoleum. Her head lolled to her shoulder, and her limbs splayed loosely to her sides. Cassie had expected her aunt to be wearing a seaweed corset of some kind or another under her cloak, but she had on a loose-fitting black T-shirt. Eliza rolled up the hem, revealing thick black veins snaking over her abdomen, all stemming from a dark bandage. Eliza pulled lightly at the gauze, uncovering an ugly wound oozing red and black blood. It looked like a chunk had been torn out of Dorcas's side. No, *bitten*.

"Is that . . . ?"

"A vampire bite," Cassie whispered.

A second later, the door banged open. Hank jabbed a foot inside, but Tommy blocked his path.

"Get out of my way, Fangs," Hank growled. "Don't think I won't stake you."

Eliza snapped her gaze over. "Tommy, let him in, but so help me, Hank, if you threaten my boyfriend again, I'll turn my pretty new crossbow on you." Tommy looked momentarily stunned, but then he smiled down at the floor.

"Just like your aunt," Hank grumbled, struggling to get down to his knees by Dorcas's other side. "I knew that vamp got her. Dammit!"

Dorcas's eyes fluttered open. "Where did you all come from? Did I kill the Deliverer already?"

"Not quite," Cassie said gently. "But you did turn half of his army to dust."

"Drat." Dorcas flinched with pain as she planted her hands on the floor. "Back into the fray I go!"

"You're not going anywhere, Dorrie." Hank laid a hand on her shoulder. His eyes dropped to the wound on her abdomen. "You should have told me you were bit."

She smiled tiredly. "What for? There's nothing you could

have done about it. Besides, I'm fine. If someone could lift me to my feet, walk me outside, point me in the direction of the Deliverer, and raise my hand, I'll do the rest, and . . . strawberry ice cream! Don't mind if I do." Dorcas's eyes rolled up into her head as she slumped back against the floor.

"Is that true?" Eliza looked up to Hank. "Will she be fine?"

He scratched his beard. "Maybe. Not many witches survive a vamp bite, but there's nobody like Dorcas. It might help if she had the blood of the vamp who bit her." He scratched his brow next, looking confused about what to do with his hands. "But she must have killed him before she realized what happened. The Deliverer, though, he likely sired that vamp, or the one who sired him, so his blood might help too if—" Hank stiffened as an eerie voice floated through the window.

Little witch. Little witch. Let me come in . . .

Dorcas's eyes snapped open, her irises glowing hot. "Where is he?" Her gaze darted about like bats trapped in a cave. "There! Behind that wall!" She raised her hands to the ceiling, but before she could unleash, Hank cupped her fingers together. "Now, don't you go setting Cassie's house on fire."

Dorcas's face abruptly softened, the fire fading from her eyes. She looked so pale in the dim light. "Hank, do you remember the last time we held hands?"

He chuckled then fiddled with the bandage sticking up through his collar.

"It was during that full moon on the beach." She smiled coquettishly. "We went skinny-dipping, then . . ." Dorcas lost consciousness again.

Cassie stood and walked over to the fridge.

"What are you doing?" Eliza asked.

Part of Cassie knew exactly what she was doing, but the other part was slipping down into a spiral. Dorcas couldn't fight anymore. There was no way she could fight. Cassie grabbed the first aid kit in the high cabinet above the fridge and brought it back over. What were they going to do? She took out a wad of gauze and laid it gently over the wound on her aunt's side, then pulled out the tape. *Scissors.* She needed scissors. Cassie dumped the contents of the kit onto the floor. No scissors. She got up again and opened the junk drawer. Notepad. Elastic bands. At least fifty pens, of which probably only two worked. But no scissors. How many times had she begged the kids to put them back after they were done? She shifted the contents around. Dorcas had been their best hope. Their only hope, really. Cassie's hand froze over a pile of loose change. Unless she used the coin.

"Hey," Eliza said quietly. "You okay?"

Cassie placed her palms on the counter and inhaled slowly, trying to stay afloat in the rising ocean of panic. "I can't find my scissors."

Eliza got up and looked in the drawer. "Don't worry about it. We'll just—" She cut herself off when she glanced over at Cassie's face. "Oh no. Absolutely not. Stop it."

Cassie couldn't concentrate on what her sister was saying. She was suddenly mesmerized by her coffee maker standing stoically on the counter. She had put it through a lot over the years, but it had never let her down. It's funny, the things you think about when—

Eliza shook her arm. "Stop!"

"Stop what?"

"Thinking!" Eliza snapped. "Listen, you are not the same woman you were a month ago. We are not going backward."

"Here." Hank pushed up to a kneeling position and reached into his back pocket. "I've got my knife. I'll cut the—"

Eliza glared down at him. "This is not about the scissors, Hank."

He put his hands up and lowered back down.

"I don't understand what's going on," Tommy said from where he was standing by the door. "What is Cassie thinking?"

Eliza slid her gaze over to him. "You want to know what she's thinking?"

Tommy crossed his arms over his chest in a self-hug. "Maybe?" He took a small step back toward the door.

"She's thinking nobody ever listens to her," Eliza snapped, "that she's a bad mom, and if she can't get her family to put a pair of scissors back in a drawer, what chance does she have of defeating Del?" Eliza whirled back to Cassie. "Go ahead, tell me I'm wrong."

Cassie opened her mouth to argue, but she may have been thinking a few of those things.

"You're giving up!" Eliza zeroed in on the pocket at her side. "*That* is not your only way out."

Cassie resisted the urge to cover the spot with her hand. How had her sister even known the coin was in that pocket? "Eliza, we're not arguing about this again. I need to do the right thing. We're out of options."

"No, we are not!"

By the way her sister's eyes were flashing, Cassie suddenly wondered if she should move the crossbow resting on the counter. There was no sense in her death going to waste.

"Come on, Cass. Where is the woman who decapitated a giant vampire then ran topless through a graveyard?"

"Just like her aunt," Hank muttered.

"That was different." Cassie roughly rubbed both hands over her face. "I got lucky. It was instinct."

"And what is your instinct telling you now?" Eliza asked. "What do you want?"

Cassie's hands dropped away. *What?* She was having a lot of trouble keeping up with this conversation. Or lecture. Or whatever this was. She looked over to Tommy for clues, but he had shrunk down into his shoulder pads.

"Come on. It's not a hard question. What do you want?"

Cassie almost said *scissors* but caught herself in time. She suspected that might push her sister right over the edge. "I don't know what it is you want me to say right now."

Eliza shook her fingers roughly through her hair. "This is just like your birthday. *What do you want for your birthday, Cass?*" She then put her fingertips on her chest and said in a mock voice, "*Oh, I don't need anything. Don't worry about me.*" Cassie was guessing that was supposed to be her. "But I didn't ask you what you needed," Eliza snapped. "I asked you what you wanted."

"But you never have any money," Cassie muttered. "That's why—"

"That's why it's a *me* problem!" Before Eliza could go on, Del's voice floated in through the window. *Cassandra, come out, come out, wherever you are.* Eliza screamed in frustration and ran over to the screen. "She's busy! Not everything is about you!" She leaned her back against the counter and put her hand over her eyes. "I hate that guy so much." She then flung the hand away. "Okay, look, I get it. All this has been unfair, and shocking and scary, and you haven't been given enough time to wrap your head around it, let alone prepare."

Cassie's shoulders dropped. *Exactly.* She needed a lifetime to prepare for this, at least.

"And," Eliza continued, "you have three—sometimes four—kids to worry about, which makes it hard to be a dedicated, full-time vampire-killer."

True. Very true.

"And really," Eliza said, "when you think about it, nobody deserves to have a vampire—let alone one with a title for a name—hunting them down."

Cassie tilted her head. Where exactly was this going? Did she sense a *but* coming? No, couldn't be. They were finally getting somewhere.

Eliza inhaled deeply. "Now I say this with love, but . . ."

There was a but!

"Cass, it is time for you to witch up."

That was the but?! Witch up? Seriously?

"Now tell me what you want." Eliza folded her arms over her chest. "And don't tell me what's best for everybody else. Don't tell me about being out of options. What do you, Cassandra Beckett, want?"

Cassie didn't know whether to laugh, cry, or scream, but . . .

What *did* she want?

Her knee-jerk reaction was to say she only wanted to protect everyone, but she realized that wasn't entirely true. She wanted a lot of things. She wanted to take Sadie prom dress shopping. She wanted to see Sly and Eddie graduate high school. She wanted to take the kids to Sea House next summer, swim in the ocean, and toast marshmallows around a fire while Dorcas played songs on her fiddle. She also wanted to feel what it was like to be loved by someone again. Someone who wasn't a relative. And she wanted the chance to take everything that had happened this past month, everything she had learned, and maybe try to live life differently, better. But for any of that to happen, she had to want something else. And she did want that thing so very badly.

"I want to kill Del. I want to kill him with my bare hands."

"Great!" Eliza shouted. "Let's do that! Happy birthday!"

"Eliza..."

"Now ask me what I want." Her sister was trembling. Actually, the whole kitchen was trembling. Cassie hadn't noticed, but the spice bottles, the cutlery, the toaster were all quivering. Even the cupboards were banging a little. The entire room was shaking with her sister. "If you even care about what I want. You've never bothered to ask."

"That's because I already know what you want," Cassie said helplessly. "You want me to let my magic flow, to *believe* in myself, but—"

"Nope. Wrong. That's not it. That's not what I want most of all." All the rattling died away, leaving heavy silence in its wake. "Actually, it's more of what I don't want." Eliza tilted her head back and blinked. Tommy stepped toward her, but she lifted her fingertips to hold him back.

"What is it?" Cassie took her hand. "Tell me."

"How do you not know?" Eliza's voice cracked, and suddenly she was a little girl again. "I don't want you to leave me, Cass. What made you think you could just leave? Without even putting up a fight?"

Oh no. No. No. No.

Cassie grabbed Eliza's shoulders and pulled her into her arms. "That's not... I never..." She pressed her sister's damp cheek against her own. "I am so sorry. I never wanted you to think that I wouldn't fight to stay with you." She squeezed her eyes shut, cursing herself. "I am so sorry. I've done this all wrong."

Eliza let go of a trembling sigh. "It's just . . . do you have any idea what it's like to watch someone you love not embrace their full potential?"

Cassie leaned back and cocked her head.

"Okay, maybe don't answer that." She wiped her nose. "Look, I know you want to protect us. But guess what? We want to protect you too."

"I love you guys so much." Cassie closed her eyes, willing herself to stay strong. "I don't want to leave you. But you're asking me to put my needs ahead of . . . all of humanity's."

"For like five minutes!"

Cassie opened her eyes.

"If it doesn't work, then flip the coin. But at least try!" Eliza stamped her foot. Literally stamped her foot. It was adorable. "Look. We get to choose how we face this. I don't know about you, but I want to fight."

"No way," Cassie said. "You are staying in this house and—"

Eliza gripped her hand. "You can't tell me what to do anymore. Whether you like it or not, I am going out that door, and I am going to face Del." She squeezed Cassie's hand tighter. "Come with me. Fight with me. Please . . . for just one moment believe we can do this."

She made it sound so easy.

But she also had a point. Cassie had been telling herself she'd done everything she could this past month to become the witch of her generation, but she had never allowed herself to believe she could fight Del and win. Maybe it wasn't impossible. She wasn't alone. They had the half-vampires on their side. Eliza had her magic. And she *had* been doing a lot of squats. "It's a huge risk. If he kills me before I get the chance to use the coin . . ."

"You are worth the risk," Eliza said, searching her face. "And don't forget. The fates love an underdog."

A shout suddenly came from the floor. "Bring my scythe! I will fight the dog!"

Despite everything, Cassie smiled and mouthed the words *I've got this* to her sister.

"I'm not done. I have more in me," Dorcas said as she knelt. Her aunt's eyes were lucid, but Cassie could see the struggle. "I know you do." She took Dorcas's hand. Her fingers were so cold. "Here's the thing. You have been fighting this battle alone for twenty-five years. Nobody should have to do that. It's time to let someone else fight for you."

Dorcas's lips quivered. "I'm not feeling very well, Polliwog."

"I know. It's okay. You rest now." Cassie stroked her forehead. "I love you. We all love you."

Her aunt exhaled a soft, surprised *oh* before she drifted away again.

Hank brushed a silver tendril from Dorcas's face. "Don't worry. I'll take care of her."

"Does that mean you're going to fight with me?" Eliza asked.

Cassie got back up to her feet. "Well, it's not like I'm going to let you go out there alone." A smile stretched across her sister's face. "But you have to promise me something. If things go wrong, and it looks like Del is going to kill me before I have a chance to kill him, you promise me you will go back into the house." Conflicting emotions warred over Eliza's face. "I mean it. Do not try to save me. This is bigger than us now. You'll have to regroup somehow. Find another way to kill Del. The future of the planet will be depending on you." Cassie smiled inwardly as her sister's eyes pooled with horror. *Yeah, that's right. Not so fun when the shoe is on the other foot, is it?* "Do I have your promise?"

Her sister didn't look happy, but she nodded.

"Good." Cassie planted her hands on her hips. "So, if my plan is being moved to the back burner, what's yours?"

"I say we keep it simple." Eliza grabbed the poleax leaning against the counter and handed it to Cassie. "I'll tell him a story. You finish him off."

CHAPTER 40

It was here.
After the longest, most terrifying month of Cassie's life, the death match was finally here. As she stepped out onto the porch, she couldn't help but think that even with her poleax, Dorcas's entrance had been much cooler.

Del stood on her lawn, calm and still, despite the battles raging around him.

"Trick or treat." His lips curved into his too-wide, inhuman smile. "How is your aunt feeling, Cassandra?" He sniffed the air. "I smell rotten witch."

Cassie's heart pounded in her throat. "You got lucky."

"Luck?" He chuckled. "Come now, you don't believe that. How many times must I say it? You and I were born for this fight. All the gears of the universe have been turning to bring us here."

Cassie didn't answer. She was not having this conversation with him again.

"Cat got your tongue?" His brow raised. "I suppose I do get a bit chatty after my sleep. It's lonely in the dark."

She shrugged. "We're not friends."

"Well, in that case, instead of talking, perhaps you'd like to come down the steps." He bowed, waving his hand out in a courtly gesture. "I'm sure I can keep you entertained."

Gulp.

Cassie peered into the chaos. Where was Eliza? She was supposed to be sneaking up on Del. "I . . . no?" Suddenly a chill washed over Cassie like she had been swallowed by an iceberg.

"I'm afraid your preferences won't be taken into consideration."

Cassie's eyes widened as she looked back to see the sallow, ghastly face of Del's butler looming over her. She lunged to the side, but it was too late. He swung his umbrella, batting her square on the shoulder, knocking her ax from her hand, and sending her tumbling down onto the grass.

Before she could blink, Del sprang with rocket speed. While part of her registered the impossible blur, another part saw him coming in slow motion. His hands, hooked in claws, reached for her as his feet left the ground. Cassie reacted without thought; she grabbed the potion Sadie had given her and flung it at him. The glass smashed against the vampire's cheek, and Cassie rolled to the side. When she looked back, Del was shielding his face, steam twisting around his fingers.

Cassie backpedaled as his hands dropped to his sides.

So much for princesses and unicorns.

The right side of Del's face was gone, leaving the glowing bone and shadows of his skull. It looked almost ridiculous, like something out of a comic book. Much worse than a steamed tomato. And if potions were fueled by intention, her daughter's was . . . *disturbing*. Then again, Sadie had gone through that anime phase.

Del glowered at her with his remaining eye. "Now you die, little witch."

Cassie did what she thought any self-respecting, magicless witch would do in her situation. She ran. She ran away and dove right into the raging vampire battles because *that* was the better option.

Fangs and claws flew around her as she pushed her way through the many bodies, but it wasn't long before she was knocked to the ground. She rolled onto her hands and knees, maneuvering through the chaotic dance of legs. She had to find Eliza and a weapon. Thankfully, Dorcas had been right, there were weapons everywhere. Cassie's palm landed on a discarded stake. She gripped it and rocked back on her heels just as a vamp slammed into her. The point of the stake went right into the back of his thigh, and with a scream he fell to the street. "Oh my God." Cassie's fingertips flew to her lips. "I am so sorry."

"Watch out!"

Cassie skittered back as a scimitar sliced down through the vampire's neck, clanging against the pavement. Hank had really brought the good stuff. The half-vampire responsible for the killing blow smiled and loped away, shouting, "Thanks!"

"No problem," she mumbled. Staking vampires in the leg was kind of her go-to move.

Cassie crawled on. She had lost all sense of where she was, but then she saw blue fire flaring in between the tangle of bodies. *Eliza!* Cassie popped up like a prairie dog. It took a second, but she spotted her sister shooting her crossbow near Mrs. MacDonald's house. *Thunk!* The stake hit one vampire in the heart only to go right through and hit another. Eliza dropped the weapon and more blue flames erupted from her hands, swallowing another fanged attacker. As he went down, she planted a foot on his back and launched into the air, spinning, and kicking yet another one of Del's undead soldiers with the side of her boot.

Perhaps Cassie *had* underestimated her sister. She ducked back down.

"Witch!" Del roared, not too far behind her. "Do not hide from me. You will be my thirteenth!"

That didn't exactly feel like an incentive to show herself.

Thighs burning, she scuttled in a bear crawl around more legs, ducking below swinging axes, swords, and claws. She was almost there. Cassie spotted a clear path along the sidewalk to get to the scrum surrounding her sister. *Thank God.*

Suddenly, a half-vampire dropped in front of her, forcing her to rear back. Hey, it was the kid from the grocery store! He bagged her produce.

"Help me!" he screamed, pointing to the street.

Cassie's first-grade teacher, Mrs. Warwick, sprang toward him like a flying monkey. She had always been awful. Once, she had made Cassie stand in the corner of the classroom for chewing gum *with* the piece of gum stuck to her nose. She had to be at least eighty but was looking spry now. Cassie picked up a jack-o'-lantern sitting at the end of the driveway and threw it. It smashed into the vampire, engulfing her in flames. She should've given Del a lesson about bringing fire to a vampire battle. Cassie clamped her lips shut. Now was not the time for hysterical laughter.

"Thanks. You saved me," grocery guy said. "Wait. Oh my God, you're her. You're the Thirteenth Witch."

Cassie made a face. "I prefer witch of her generation."

"Guys!" he shouted. "Look! It's the Thirteenth Witch! She saved—"

"Don't!" Cassie lunged at him to slap her hand over his mouth. "He'll—"

A boot slammed down between her shoulder blades, crushing her to the pavement.

Find me.

Even if Cassie had another potion to throw, she didn't have time to react. Faster than she could think, Del kicked her in the side. White-hot pain bloomed in her ribs as she tumbled over the asphalt, her head smacking against the pavement when she finally stopped.

Get up...

She had to get up. Cassie struggled to push herself to her knees, blinking her eyes open. Where was he? *Wait*... there were two of him! That wasn't fair! Her vision swam back into focus. Oh, it was just her. She rocked back onto her hands, attempting to crabwalk away, but her movements were thick and slow. Del, with half of his tongue missing, laughed in a wet, slippery hiss. He knew he had her now.

This couldn't be it. It was too soon.

There were battles raging everywhere, but Cassie had lost sight of who was who in the chaos. There had to be something she could do. She was not ready to use the coin. But... she couldn't even feel the coin. That was strange. It always burned when she was in trouble. She slipped her hand over the thick seaweed covering her abdomen. Her fingertips dipped into the pocket. She wasn't going to use it. Not yet. But she had to be ready.

Cassie pulled the small disk out, but as she gazed down at its face, the world slipped away.

It wasn't her coin at all. It was a heart-shaped piece of candy with two words printed on the front.

BE MINE

CHAPTER 41

"Looking for this?"

Cassie rolled her gaze up as Del flipped his hand in the air. Her coin was pinched between his index and middle finger.

"How did you . . . ?" Cassie spit out blood.

"I have some talent in illusion." He looked down to her hand. For a second, Cassie saw her coin lying in her palm, but then it was the candy again. This was bad. So very bad. Her backup plan was gone. How could she have let this happen? How had he even stolen it? She always had her coin with her . . . except she didn't. Not lately. Forget being tempted to use it. The bigger concern had been that Eliza might steal it. Cassie had thought the coin would be safer hidden away, but then Sea House was attacked.

"You'd be surprised how easily vampires can sniff out dark magic. You might call it our special gift."

Cassie collapsed back onto the street, barely holding herself up with her hands. That was why they had set upon the house that night. It had never been about the stockpile. Not really. Del hadn't forgotten about the coin. Cassie shook her head in defeat. She knew she should be paralyzed with fear, but her brain had stalled. She literally couldn't think about what this meant. The enormity of it. All she knew was that she was tired, hurt, and really kind of annoyed that people—and *vampires*—kept taking her stuff. "Why would you even bring that here, you big . . . dummy."

Del barked with laughter, then looked at her like she was a bug he was about to crush. "I've been asking myself the same question. I wonder if perhaps the coin wanted to come. Charmed objects with this kind of power have a way of turning up where they're meant to be. That, and I was hoping to see the look on your face when you realized your last hope of defeating me was gone." He turned the coin in the light of the streetlamp. "You look just like your mother when you despair."

Suddenly a stake whizzed through the night, piercing through Del's palm and sending the coin skittering down the street.

Cassie blinked. Had she just seen that?

Del looked ridiculously shocked with his half-fleshed jaw dropped. His hand was still in the air with a big hole right in the middle of it. Cassie could see the full moon on the other side.

With blinding speed, he lunged to the right as another stake skimmed his face. Then another zipped through the air, hitting him in the shoulder. He pulled it free, growling, then leaped into a tree as more wood spears chased him down. A second later, he dropped onto the hood of a car, then flipped back, another stake sliding past his belly.

Eliza stalked through the fanged masses, her long black hair rippling in the breeze, her irises swirling fluorescent blue. Tommy was loping behind her, throwing off any would-be attackers. She reached over her shoulder, pulling out a stake from the bag strapped to her back, but instead of using a crossbow, she threw it, firing with inhuman speed before reaching back for another. A big smile came to Cassie's split lips.

Show-off.

Her sister kept on firing stakes, but Del was fast, and before Eliza could incapacitate him, the sack was empty. She slipped the straps off her shoulders, and the bag fell to the ground. In her hand was one last stake. She wasn't going to miss this time. She knew it. And Del knew it. This was Cassie's chance. The second he was down she'd have to kill him.

And she might have done just that . . .

If it were not for the shadows swimming in the dark. They sensed the moment too, and a swarm of vampires fell on Eliza.

Cassie jumped to her feet, oblivious to any pain. She had to get to her sister. But before she could even think of a way, a fist smashed into the side of her head. She staggered back, hands searching for anything that would keep her up. There was nothing. She swayed on her feet as the street tipped, sending her crashing to the pavement. Everything went black.

No . . .

Please . . .

Those were the only words Cassie could manage as she sank deep into the darkness. But words couldn't help her. Not anymore. She was going to die. Del was going to kill her, and . . .

Suddenly Cassie was floating in the abyss.

It felt so good to be back! She'd missed the abyss since that night Dorcas had killed the vampire at her door. Although she'd been back a few other times, hadn't she? At the graveyard, maybe? It didn't matter. Nothing mattered. Her head didn't hurt in the abyss, nothing did, and she couldn't hear Del's voice slithering all over her. Even her thoughts were floating away. All the terrible, terrible thoughts. No, this was better. She was warm and welcome here. It was where she had always belonged. And it wasn't really an abyss—not really—because she wasn't alone.

There was a presence with her, making her feel all these nice things. Or maybe it wasn't with her so much as it was surrounding her, cradling her, like a baby.

And she could hear something.

It was the same sound she had heard in the vampire tunnel. Back then, she had thought it was blood rushing in her ears, but that wasn't it. It was water, lots and lots of water. An unfathomable amount of water. Wait . . .

Surprise opened Cassie's eyes. She could see tree branches, the moon and stars, and Del's acid-eaten face coming toward her, the empty socket of his eye peering into her soul.

He crouched beside her, gently brushing back the hair that had come free from her braids. She struggled to lift her hands, to push him back, scratch at his face, but her arms were useless.

"Oh Cassandra, have we reached the end so soon? Is this all you have?" He sighed, the air hissing through the exposed side of his jaw. "I had been hoping I was wrong, but you really are as pathetic as I feared." His one eye searched both of hers. "I know you didn't have much time to prepare, but what *have* you been doing all month?" He shook his head. "How have you been filling your days? Did you even try?"

An explosion went off in Cassie's head.

What had she been doing all month? How had she been filling her days?

Cassie knew exactly what she had been doing. She had been surviving. And she had been trying—*really hard*—to fulfill a prophecy she had known nothing about. And in order to do that, she'd faced all her childhood stuff and resolved super deep-seated abandonment issues in less time than it probably took most people to call a therapist. She had run on the beach until she dropped to the sand wanting to vomit, and she had staked a vampire dummy thousands of times, everywhere but in the heart, which was really freaking annoying! She had survived Joanne, the delivery guy, the vampire tunnels, and the graveyard test twice! And yes, surviving those things had mostly been due to luck—except the second graveyard test, which was all her. But even though each and every one of those instances made her want to curl up in a ball, she had always gotten up the next morning to face some new horror.

Eliza was right—she wasn't the same person she had been a month ago . . . and now she knew where her magic was. It had been there all along.

A colossal presence—a mammoth, living entity with ancient wisdom that was too vast to understand—was with her, and just by being there, it was making her more than she was. Her puny life was a speck compared to its existence, but for some reason it was speaking to her in its secret language, and it wanted to help.

The sea.

Thunder rumbled in the distance.

Del sneered down at her. "It must have been hard for you knowing all along that you were never going to be strong enough to save the people you love. But don't worry. It's almost over now. I have you, I have the Burrow, and soon I will have the entire island." He leaned in and sliced a claw through her seaweed collar. Cold breath rippled over her neck. "So, are you ready to die, little witch?"

Cassie had asked herself that very question countless times this past month, but when he said it, somehow it felt different. She met Del's gaze, a smile on her bloody lips. "You know, I think I have a little bit more."

She snapped her head, smashing her forehead against what remained of his brow. He staggered back, and Cassie rolled away,

THE LATE-NIGHT WITCHES

clutching her own forehead. Oh God, that had really hurt. She struggled to her feet, fighting to regain her equilibrium, when she realized something.

Her hands were tingling.

Cassie closed her eyes, allowing the sea's presence to envelop her. *Let's play.*

A tremendous surge of magic rushed through Cassie's being, and when she opened her eyes, she saw through a sea-green haze. Her eyes were glowing just like Dorcas's! And Eliza's! This was incredible. She had done it. She *was* the witch of her generation! She believed!

And she still had a vampire to kill.

She stared down at Del, his face green from her gaze. "This is my home, vampire. You are not welcome here."

Storm clouds roiled overhead as countless bolts of lightning cracked the night sky into jagged pieces, heralding the arrival of a coming force. Del cringed at the roar of what sounded like a freight train barreling toward them before the first rush of hurricane-force winds tore over the street. This was no regular storm. Del's vampires howled, clinging to trees, mailboxes, and stop signs, but none could resist the force for long. The wind ripped them loose, sending them tumbling down the street like paper cutouts. And yet, no cars flipped, no trees were uprooted, and the half-vampires, while confused, were fine. Even the remaining jack-o'-lanterns that had survived the battle thus far were still. So, this was intention. Cassie's hair lifted around her, but the wind felt like nothing more than a refreshing breeze. All the power of the sea was suddenly at her command. It was exhilarating, almost maddening. She was giddy, drunk with the monstrousness of the magic. She felt like Poseidon, Neptune, and Aquaman rolled into one.

No, she felt like a sea witch.

Del, the only full vampire remaining, fought against the wind, fangs bared, claws reaching for her. "You are not your grandmother, witch! And I am not the dog she brought to heel."

Cassie should have been terrified, but it was so hard. Del was nothing in the face of . . . *life*. That's what the sea was showing her. The magnificence of life. Existence. Not just hers, but all of it. And in that space, each second of being alive was its own miracle. She was too lucky to be afraid.

The experience was glorious, and she wanted it to last forever, but even as she had the thought, she was quivering with the effort of channeling the power. As exhilarating as it had felt rushing in, it was quickly becoming too much. She would have to release it soon or be torn apart.

Del forced a step toward her. He was gaining ground, and it was all Cassie could do to hold him back, to slow him down. But with his every step, more of her strength slipped away. She couldn't keep this up. She had to think of something else. She—

Cassie felt her control break. All the power she had been holding rushed out of her body, and the wind vanished as though it had never been.

Del lunged, hitting her with the force of a truck.

"I will sleep no more!" He ground Cassie's shoulders into the asphalt. "We are at the end. The battle is over. And I have won!" Cassie held him back with the last of her strength, twisting her head side to side. He was so strong. Too strong. But . . .

A surprising noise escaped her. It took a second to figure out what it was, but then it happened again, and this time it didn't stop.

She was laughing.

Del lifted her shoulders and slammed her back against the

concrete, but she didn't stop. He twisted his head, following her gaze down the street. Her coin burned bright on the pavement just a few feet away. "You still think a bit of metal can kill me? You would make the same mistake as your mother?" Liquid dripped from the exposed cavity of his face onto her cheek, but she didn't care as long as he faced that direction.

It turned out Cassie didn't need the coin to win, or even her own magic. What she needed—the thing the Deliverer could not see with his one good eye on the coin—was her sister on their other side.

"Eliza! Now!"

CHAPTER 42

Eliza rose from the asphalt like a sea creature emerging from the deep. Claw marks were raked down her every limb, and blood and dirt stained her face, but the horde was gone, blown away in the wind, or brought to dust by the last stake in her hand.

Del turned just in time to see Eliza fling the wooden spike like a javelin. Its path cut through the sky, headed straight for him, but he was still too fast. He slammed his body down onto Cassie. The spike would have sailed right over, but she was fast now too. She grabbed the stake midair and drove it into Del's back... right beneath his ribs. His body jerked, arching his chest off her, but it only took half a second for a wicked half-smile to spread across what remained of his face. "You missed."

"Would you like to hear a story?" Del snapped his gaze up to Eliza, looming over him. She didn't wait for him to answer. "Once upon a time, my big sister killed you. The End."

Sensing the danger, Del tossed his head back, his fangs pointed at Cassie's throat, but this time he was much too slow. Cassie drove the stake up through his torso until the wooden tip hit a rubbery edge of muscle.

"No!" Del screamed. "The Thirteenth Witch will die!"

Cassie tilted her head up and put her lips to his ear. "There is no Thirteenth Witch, Del. Never will be." She twisted the stake all the way through his heart.

Del rolled off her, writhing in agony, his hands curled in the air. Dark satisfaction swelled in Cassie's chest as she rose to her feet.

But something was wrong.

Oh God! She forgot. She forgot Dorcas. Her aunt needed Del's blood!

Here Cassie had nearly died trying to kill Del, and now she had to find a way to save him before he exploded into dust! But how was she supposed to do that? How . . .

Cassie's thoughts evaporated as a presence approached her from behind. She peeked over her shoulder. A hooded figure, hovering inches above the ground, floated in beside her, its hand reaching out from underneath the draped folds of its cloak. Hank trailed behind with his arms outstretched.

The Deliverer's eye rolled in its socket before landing on Dorcas beaming pure hate. "Die with me, witch."

Explosions suddenly roared up and down both sides of the street. Every one of the fanged jack-o'-lanterns erupted in a tower of flame just before a stream of fire shot from Dorcas's outstretched palm, dousing Del's undead flesh.

Unholy howls filled the Burrow, but finally, inevitably, the Deliverer exploded, not into dust, but into a shower of blood.

Wide-eyed, Cassie turned to her aunt. Dorcas's hood was down, and her face was painted red. She smiled at Cassie and gave her a thumbs-up before crumpling into Hank's arms.

CHAPTER 43

Every cell in Cassie's body quivered, vibrating with life.
It was over. He was dead.

A crowd of half-vampires—no humans—had gathered round, all focused on the mess pooled on the concrete. One by one they looked up at her. She wasn't sure what she had been expecting. Shouts of joy, maybe? Cries of elation? But they were silent, and they looked *horrified*. Eliza pushed her way through. When she saw Cassie, she jolted on the spot. "Whoa."

"What?" Cassie asked, but then she heard the telltale *pat, pat, pat*. She looked down to the pavement. *Oh*. Dorcas wasn't the only one who got vampire on her. Wait, Dorcas!

Hank was already helping their aunt up to a seated position. Her eyes fluttered open as Eliza and Cassie dropped in front of her. "Did I dream that? Is he dead?"

"Oh, he's dead," Eliza said. "He's dead all over you. Why didn't he turn to dust?"

Dorcas blinked. "Sometimes when you boil the blood—wait, are you sure he's dead?"

Cassie looked back at the street. "Yup."

A hum swelled all around them. A hum rising in volume and

pitch that Cassie hadn't heard since the farmer's market, but it sounded louder this time. "Everyone plug your ears!" Cassie jabbed her fingers into her own right before Dorcas screamed a scream that shook the trees and shattered streetlamps.

When she stopped, Eliza said, "That was a happy scream, right?"

"Happy? Happy!" Dorcas shouted, throwing her hands up. "I'm so happy I could—"

"Wait!" Cassie pressed a hand down on her aunt's shoulder. "Before you do anything. Are you okay?"

Dorcas lifted her shirt up, revealing perfectly sculpted abs completely free of any sign of vampire poisoning. "I am perfection. No, we are perfection. Or gods! We are witch gods! *And* . . . we have an audience." Dorcas smiled sweetly at the crowd that had moved from what was left of Del to gather around them. "I, of course, don't really believe we're gods. That might be frightening to you all. And nobody likes it when the humans are frightened. I merely meant—" She dropped the smile. "Who cares? You'll probably forget all this in a few days."

Cassie stood, wiping her hands on her thighs. The crowd wasn't looking at her with horror now, so that was good. She searched the many faces. Gary was there. Patty too. And Tommy! Thank God he was okay. Cassie had lost sight of him at the end there. And the others—Keith, Megan, Bruce, *Ron*—they were there too. Tears welled in Cassie's eyes as she looked at her friends and neighbors. They'd made it. They'd all made it. Granted, some of her other neighbors had to be dead, along with her first-grade teacher, but these guys had made it!

Suddenly the fresh humans charged her, shouting with their fists in the air. Cassie staggered back. What was happening? Had the transition made them insane? Were they zombies now? She couldn't go back to worrying about zombies. But then she was being lifted into the air. And they weren't shouting. They were cheering.

The next thing Cassie knew she was soaring into the night sky. They were throwing her up and down. It was incredible! It hurt really badly! But mostly it was incredible!

It went on for some time before Cassie grew concerned that she might throw up and asked to be set down.

"Me next!" Dorcas shouted, racing toward them.

When Cassie was back on her feet, Patty hugged her. "I knew you could do it." Cassie smiled. Patty definitely didn't smell like cookies yet, but she had every faith her coworker would get there.

Gary came up next. He hugged her too.

"Thank you for believing in me," Cassie said.

"You believed I could run when nobody else did, so . . ." A human blush came to his cheeks. They high-fived, and Cassie turned to see Eliza and Tommy embracing. Her sister was running her fingers over his face, seemingly enjoying his human flesh. He did look a lot less sticky.

"Mom!" Suddenly Cassie was hit from all sides.

What? Kids! Cassie clutched at the twins, looking around for possible dangers. "What are you guys doing here? You're supposed to be halfway to Halifax."

"I'm so sorry," Ben said, coming in behind them. He looked miserable. Incredibly relieved. But also miserable.

"Sadie escaped!" Sly shouted up at her. "We thought she ditched us when we stopped for burgers!"

Cassie scanned the street. "So where is she?"

"Let me tell it," Eddie said, elbowing his brother. Cassie tried not to grimace. Eddie had some trouble getting to the point quickly. "We knew she would come here, so we looked up and down the street."

"We didn't get near the fight," Ben said. "We drove side streets and ducked into a few yards. That's all."

"But we couldn't find her!" Eddie went on. "So—"

"She was in the car the whole time! She was tricking Ben into driving us back!" Sly shouted. He punched the air by his side and Sadie rippled into view.

"That hurt, you little jerk," she said, punching him back. Eddie then punched Sly's other arm for ruining the story. Sly smirked, rubbing both spots.

"Invisibility? That's incredible," Dorcas gushed, looking a little unsteady after being tossed in the air. "Just think of all the forbidden places you'll go!" She caught the look on Cassie's face. "Not that I would encourage such a thing."

"You did it!" Eddie suddenly shouted. "You won!"

Sylvester screamed in mock rage and mimicked driving a stake into the heart of an invisible vampire, and Eddie threw his hands out, shooting invisible flames. "I will burn this street to the ground."

"Okay then," Cassie murmured.

Sadie pushed past her brothers and collapsed into her arms. She buried her forehead in her chest. "Mom."

"I know, baby." She stroked Sadie's hair. "It's okay. I'm okay."

"Are you mad?"

"No. No." And she wasn't. Life was too short to be mad in a moment like this. "I'm so glad you're here. I'm so glad I'm here." They would have to have a discussion later though. This invisibility thing added a whole new layer to parenting. "Oh! And your potion came in super handy."

Sadie leaned back. "Really?"

"Melted half his face right off."

"Stop." An excited gleam came to her daughter's eye.

"I could see right into his skull. And there was nothing there! I don't even know how that works!"

Sadie squealed and then jumped away to give Dorcas a hug. That left Ben.

Cassie tried to rub the blood from her face, but she doubted it made much of a difference. It didn't matter anyway. Ben was distracted by his own worries. He looked so cute with his expression trying to figure out whether to land on relief or guilt.

"You okay?" she asked.

"I should be asking you that, but... seeing you standing here, alive, it's amazing. You're amazing. I'm so happy." He was nodding in that adorably manic way of his. "And I am so sorry. I promised you I wouldn't take my eyes off them. I didn't factor in invisibility. Teenagers are not the same as babies. You don't have car seats to lock them in." He froze. "That was a weird thought."

"Aw, Ben," she said, hugging him. "It's okay. You're a parent now. Your thought process will never be normal again. And really, you didn't stand a chance against Sadie. I'm not sure anybody stands a chance against her now." Cassie reveled in the warmth of his arms, but she let go quicker than she would have liked. She needed to have a lot of conversations with a lot of people before she could even think about longer hugs. "And I want to thank you. Again. I'm not sure I would have made it if it weren't for your advice and—"

"Finally!" a voice boomed, echoing through the street. All the celebrating came to an abrupt stop. The yell had come from Mrs. MacDonald's property. The butler stood on her lawn with his fists raised in victory.

Cassie reached for the boys, tucking them under her arms. "Sadie, get behind me." Ben moved to her side as Dorcas, Eliza, and Tommy gathered in.

"Finally, my time has come. For centuries I have served that sleepy bastard, but now I rule." Del's butler shook his fists in the air. "My reign of terror begins! I will bring humanity to its knees! You all will serve me!"

Cassie pulled free from the boys, pushing them back to Dorcas and Eliza. So help her, she was going to kill that toad-eating freak if it was the last thing she did.

A motor roared to life.

The ghoul turned as Mrs. MacDonald drove the blade of her hedge trimmer into his neck. Blood splattered as she pushed its whirring teeth all the way through. His head dropped and rolled toward the street while his body crumpled to the grass, his limbs landing in weird right angles. Mrs. MacDonald whipped her plastic visor off. Her silk pajamas were covered in blood.

"You all should be ashamed of yourselves."

No one moved.

"Did I not spread the word that you needed to stay indoors after dark, and that under no circumstances were you to invite anyone in? Hmm? Did I not tell you to avoid all eye contact with strangers?"

The freshly turned humans suddenly looked like a flock of sheep.

"You are lucky you had the Becketts here to save you."

Holy crap. Had Mrs. MacDonald just complimented them?

"And Cassandra."

Cassie tried to raise her brow in acknowledgment, but it was sticky with blood.

"Your side of the fence." Mrs. MacDonald pointed to Cassie's lawn. "My side of the fence." She pointed to her lawn. The one with the decapitated ghoul. Then, for just a second, maybe half a second, her lips twitched with a smile.

Mrs. MacDonald tossed the hedge trimmer to the side and turned in her fuzzy slippers. "Out of all the houses on the island, a Beckett had to move into the one next to mine." She slammed her front door, and the ghoul exploded into dust.

"Oh, I like her," Dorcas said, dropping her hands from the twins' faces.

"Aunt Dorcas?" Sadie asked.

"Hmm?"

"We won."

"Yes, we did."

"So does that mean . . . ?"

Dorcas's eyes sparkled. "We must celebrate! It's time for a—"

"No! No witch party," Cassie said. "We are going to bed. All of us."

"Mom," Sly whined.

"Guys, it has been a long day and night. And tomorrow is going to be busy." They had to clean up the street and look for stray vampires hidden in burrows. Speaking of which, they should probably call the city about the underground tunnels. They definitely had to hose the pavement off. Maybe bleach it. Start therapy. Or not. Again, finding the right counselor could be tricky. She really needed to find her coin. Like immediately. It couldn't be out there just waiting for someone to flip it. Oh God! And Matt was coming. Well, at least that would make the kids happy. What else was she forgetting? She should start a list. Where was her calendar?

Cassie looked around the street as though it might appear, and her eyes landed on the puddle of muck Del had left behind.

She had made that puddle. That was her. She was the witch of her generation, and she had killed the Deliverer of Fear, Pain . . . Scabies and Rats? That wasn't right. Didn't matter. He was dead.

Screw it.

"You know what? Forget everything I just said." She smiled. "Who wants to blow stuff up?"

Cheers erupted. The kids raced over the street and lawns while the adult humans flocked in different directions doing God knows what. Cassie fought her way through the happy crowd, searching for her sister. She spotted Tommy first. *Perfect.* He'd know where Eliza was, except he was busy talking to her boys. Cassie crept in closer to listen to what he was saying. "Damn, bros, are those your mom's scissors?" The twins nodded with big eyes. "We need to put those back. Like right now." Cassie smiled and turned the other way.

Eliza.

A cool, dry breeze rushed down the street, taking all the fog with it. Cassie walked toward her sister, stopping when she got within a few feet of her. "You didn't go in the house like you promised."

Eliza furrowed her brow and nodded. "I did not."

"You saved my life."

Cassie jumped forward, grabbed her sister around the waist, and spun her in a circle that almost took them both to the ground. When they stopped, Eliza smiled then shrugged, tears spilling down her face. "We did it, Cass."

Cassie gently pulled her sister's forehead to her own and closed her eyes. "We did it."

CHAPTER 44

Olive toddled toward the Christmas tree with her hands outstretched, ready to grab whatever she could from the branches. Ben followed behind with his hands outstretched, ready to grab Olive from her inevitable fall to the stone floor. To say that Sea House was not babyproofed was an understatement, but Cassie was glad he had agreed to come for their solstice dinner anyway.

Nearly two months had passed since they had killed the Deliverer. In some ways Cassie's life hadn't changed at all. In others it felt like it had changed completely. She did mark up her calendar. There was no way around that. And for a while, the boys and Sadie were drowning in catch-up homework, which meant Cassie was drowning too. Then there were the holiday events and school recitals to prepare for, the Christmas shopping and the wrapping of presents, and of course there was the daily search for mittens in the seconds before the boys had to leave for school. That one was a beast. But on the flip side, Cassie and Eliza were spending a lot of time at Sea House. Cassie was really enjoying her magical training now that she could actually do magic. She was naturally inclined to the battle arts, but now that Del was dead, there wasn't much use for that, so Dorcas was teaching them more subtle enchantments like glamour, invisibility, and pumpkin bread making. On top of all that, the three were coming up with ways to grow Dorcas's farmer's market business. It looked promising.

Tonight wasn't about work though. Tonight, they were celebrating Yule, the end of the descent into darkness and the beginning of the return to light. The house was filled with scents of candles, pine, roasting turkey, and warm apple pie. The rooms were filled with fresh wreaths and garlands, and the tree was decorated with handcrafted ornaments from centuries past. Beyond all that, Dorcas had added a little magic to the air itself. Tiny golden sparks of light floated about like dust motes. Every now and then a cat would jump at one, but they always swirled out of reach.

While all those elements were lovely, it was the joy emanating from Sea House itself that made the evening magical. Its deep yearning for family had finally been satisfied, and its warm, fulfilled presence cocooned them against the bitter cold.

Janet circled Cassie as she knelt to join Ben by the tree. Olive had a glass ornament in her grip that he was ever so carefully prying away. Olive's angry squeals communicated her displeasure. "Do you need a break?"

"A break from what?" Ben asked wryly.

When Olive saw her, she released the decoration and toddled into her arms. She smelled so good and not the least bit like spaghetti. "And how are you?" Cassie asked, lifting her up. "Do you like Christmas?" Olive answered by putting a damp bit of gingerbread cookie into Cassie's mouth. "Oh, wow," she mumbled. "Thank you. Where did you have that hidden?"

Ben grimaced sweetly. "Sorry."

"No worries." It was still pretty good and was probably giving her immune system a workout.

"There she is," Dorcas said, swooping over and scooping Olive out of her arms. "The delicious baby. I must have her."

"Why?" Ben asked.

Dorcas's eyes widened with offense. "I need her for a spell." She whirled away.

Ben darted his gaze back and forth between her and Cassie. "I'm going to . . ." He jerked a thumb toward the kitchen.

"Go," she said, shooing him. As he walked away, for a second Cassie felt like she was floating in the air with the sparkles, but then her boys dropped her right back down to earth. She caught them hopping onto the divan, gearing up to jump off the back. She grabbed them by their sweaters and pulled them down to the cushions. She then sat between them and put both in a headlock. "I'm sorry. Do we jump on other people's furniture?"

"Aunt Dorcas said jumping on furniture is one of life's greatest pleasures," Sly recounted dutifully.

She would say that. "The correct answer is no."

They mumbled apologies.

"But now that I've got you here. I want to talk to you both about something."

"Mom," Sly whined, twisting under her arm. "We gotta go. Tommy is going to take us tobogganing."

"Tommy is getting the sleds and warming up the truck. You have a few minutes." Cassie released her grip. "You know, we never really talked about what happened on Halloween, and I thought given that we're back at Sea House and it's a holiday, you might have questions, or maybe you wanted to talk about how you felt that night. It must have been scary."

"No," Eddie said.

"You weren't scared?" Cassie asked, studying his sweet face. His lips were chapped. She needed to get her balm out before he left.

Sly threw his head back on the couch and answered for his brother. "Not really."

Hmm. Not exactly the response she had been expecting. "Okay, I know you guys really want to go sledding, but you know you don't have to hide being afraid."

"But we weren't afraid," Eddie said, rolling his eyes.

This was starting to feel personal. "Not even a little bit?"

They shook their heads.

Well, that was good. It wasn't like she wanted her boys to be afraid. Sure, it might be touching if they had some concern for their mother's well-being, but—

"We knew you were going to win," Sly said, cutting into her thoughts.

"Aw." She smiled. "That's so sweet. Thank you for believing in me."

"We didn't believe in you," Eddie said. "We saw you win."

Cassie's smile turned to a frown. "What do you mean you saw me win? You guys didn't come until after it was all over."

Sly flopped over the arm of the chaise in a backbend. "We saw the battle in our heads," he said to the beamed ceiling.

"You saw the . . ."

Eddie jumped up in front of her, making her jolt. *"Eliza! Now!"* He then drove a phantom stake up in the air.

Sly rolled off the couch to join his brother. *"There is no Thirteenth Witch. Never will be,"* he said in a voice that sounded eerily like hers. He then shot his hands out and made a whooshing noise like he was blasting fire.

For a second, Cassie's soul left her body. "Wait. So, you guys knew? You knew before the battle that I was going to win?"

"Yes," Sly said, drawing out the word in annoyance.

"Can we go now?" Eddie asked.

They didn't wait for an answer, just tore away.

"You could have told me!" Cassie shouted after them before slumping into the divan.

"What was that about?" Eliza asked, dropping down beside her. "Actually, hang on. Sadie? Can you go explain to Ben that Dorcas's spells are safe?"

Sadie lifted her head out of the book she had been reading by the fire. "But Dorcas's spells aren't safe."

Eliza pointed at her niece. "That right there is probably why he trusts you. And you're right. New plan. Go make Dorcas give his baby back. She wants a lock of her hair, but it's a very cute lock."

"Aunt Dorcas," Sadie called out on her way to the kitchen, "you can't steal babies. You told me that's how witches get bad reputations."

Cassie's heart clenched watching her daughter walk away. She had grown so much in the past few months. She was loving her witch lessons, and she was going out more with her friends. She had also come to like Ben, and she absolutely adored Olive. That being said, she was still working through some things. Cassie had found her a counselor, and to her surprise, Sadie had agreed to talk to her about non-witchy matters. Unfortunately, she still wasn't talking all that much to Cassie, but she wasn't being snarky anymore either. So much had happened. Cassie had nearly died. It would take time for everyone to process. Except for the boys, who apparently could see into the future.

Eliza rolled her head against the back of the chaise to look at her. "At last, we're alone."

Cassie smiled. "I would have grabbed you sooner, but you and Tommy were looking pretty cozy."

"I know. The boy can't keep his hands off me." She turned her gaze to the fire. "It's weird. It's like he believes—really, *really* believes—that I'm great."

"Why is that surprising? You are great."

"I know that. And you know that. But I wasn't expecting to find a guy who knew that." She frowned. "I hope I make him feel the same way."

Cassie's heart clenched again, or maybe it was swelling like the Grinch's. Either way, she had never heard her sister say something like that about anyone she had dated.

"He's just so *good*. I mean, he's taking my nephews tobogganing. How hot is that?"

"You can stop there." Cassie patted her leg. "I don't want to hear about your freaky vampire love."

"And that's another thing," Eliza said, her eyes widening at whatever was going on in her head. "He's back to his original hotness now that he's human again, but he still has that dark edge, you know?"

Cassie smiled, but she did not know. She did not see Tommy that way. Not even when he was a half-vampire. It was probably the lost pinky situation.

"Moving on. Shall we reflect, as is the yuletide tradition?" Eliza asked raising her brow. "Are you happy these days?"

"I am." She really was. Matt had come home a week after Halloween. He had trouble getting a flight. It nearly killed Cassie, but she had to lie and say she had made up the emergency to get him to come home. Even the kids agreed they needed time before they told him anything. She and Matt had talked a lot after that, and together they decided that separating was the best course of action. Matt wasn't ready to give up his life's purpose for the family, and Cassie wasn't ready to accept that anymore.

They didn't talk about the other people in their lives. It had been sad. Cassie was still sad, but also proud that she was taking care of her own needs for a change. "I feel like I'm becoming the Cassie I was always meant to be."

"That makes me happy." Eliza exhaled heavily and looked around the candlelit parlor. "Sometimes I still can't believe we found our way back here. Do you feel like you're finally home?"

It was an interesting question. Cassie's childhood memories had been slowly returning. She knew now that all her dreams had been real, and she loved remembering the life she had shared with her mother and Dorcas, but at the same time, she was overwhelmed with gratitude for the life she was living now. "I love Sea House and I love the Burrow." She grabbed her sister's head and gave it a kiss. "But you have always been my home."

"Stop," Eliza said with a smile. "You're embarrassing yourself." But she leaned her head on Cassie's shoulder and peeked up at her. "So does that mean I can move in when the Grub opens back up for summer?"

"Let's talk later. About rent." She patted Eliza's leg again. "Go get Dorcas. We're going outside."

"Outside?" she whined. "It's cold outside. Inside is nice and toasty."

"We won't be long. I have to do something, and I want you both there when I do it. Bring Sadie too."

☾

The frozen beach sparkled under the frosty moon as they crunched their way down to the shoreline. Aside from their footsteps, the night was quiet, muffled by the deep cold.

"What are we doing out here?" Eliza moaned as snow dust

swirled around her. She grabbed Sadie—who let out a startled yelp—and clutched her to her side. "I'm freezing."

Of course she was freezing. She was still wearing her faux leather moto jacket. Cassie had decided against buying her a winter coat. Eliza needed to take responsibility for herself. Cassie just hoped she wouldn't die before that happened.

"I am doing something I should have done a long time ago." Cassie pulled off her mitten and took her coin from her pocket. She hadn't been able to find it that night on the street, but funnily enough it turned up on her dresser the following morning. Del had been right about it having a mind of its own. "I'm throwing this in the sea."

Dorcas gasped. "A yuletide surprise! I love to be surprised at yuletide. But are you sure?" Cassie had told Dorcas about the coin after everything had happened, but she got the sense her aunt might have already known.

"No one should have the power to control fate." She smiled at her daughter, but Sadie's expression was unreadable. Cassie had told her about the coin too. She had made a promise not to keep any more secrets, and Sadie had wanted to know everything about that night.

"I don't know." Eliza tilted her head to the side. "How do you feel about nudging fate? Because I'm not throwing my stories in the sea."

"I'm not asking you to give up your stories. This is about my choices. As a wise witch once taught me, with the coin as a backup plan, I may not have the necessary fear to live life to the fullest." She winked at Dorcas, who smiled and batted a hand. "Also, it was burning up in my pocket all the time. I think it wants me dead."

"Okay," Eliza said, arms still wrapped tight around her niece. "Go for it."

Cassie tossed the coin as high and as far as she could, which was pretty high and far with her new abilities. The metal glinted like a shooting star as it soared through the sky, but before long it disappeared into the inky darkness.

Dorcas squeezed her shoulders. "Your mother would be proud."

Before Cassie could answer, Eliza piped up. "Awesome. Let's go."

"Wait, my little barnacle," Dorcas said.

Cassie snickered. Her aunt was trying out nicknames for Eliza.

"Before we go inside, there is something more we need to discuss." Dorcas's breath clouded the air, obscuring her face in a mysterious veil.

"What now?" Eliza asked, jumping on the spot.

Cassie almost reminded her she had the ability to use a spell to keep herself warm, but this felt like a learning opportunity.

"We need to talk about the island's latest problem."

"What latest problem?"

"The werewolves."

Cassie blinked, melting the ice that had formed on her eyelashes. "I'm sorry. I must have misheard you. Did you say *werewolves*?"

Eliza squealed. "No way! When I was younger, I always wanted a werewolf boyfriend. Not that I'd leave Tommy, but—" She cut herself off, looking Sadie in the eye. "Forget everything I just said. Bad boys are bad news."

Cassie pressed her mittened hand against her sister's mouth. "No. Seriously, Dorcas. You're joking, right?"

Her aunt threw her head back and laughed. "Your face."

Cassie's shoulders dropped from her ears—right as a howl

tore through the peace of the night. A second later, three or four more howls joined in.

"There they are now." Dorcas pointed a gloved finger in the air. "And so close!" Her irises swirled with fire and her lips curved into a wicked grin. "The good news is they aren't always senseless killers. Who wants to go say hello?"

"Hell yeah!" Eliza shouted, running back for the house in big crunchy steps. "I'll get the weapons."

Dorcas smiled. "I better follow her. She doesn't know where I keep the silver."

As soon as they were gone, Sadie asked, "Are you going?"

"I think I should. I don't like the idea of werewolves being within howling distance of my kids." Cassie wrapped Sadie's scarf in another loop around her neck. "Plus, I need to supervise. Those two can't be trusted to make good decisions."

"You can't do it, can you?"

"Do what?"

"Admit that you want to go. That you like being a witch."

Cassie stared into her daughter's eyes. She couldn't tell if she was mad or not. Having a mom putting herself in danger couldn't be easy. "Maybe that's somewhat true," she said carefully. "But I want you to know that nothing is more important to me than you guys. So, if you don't want me to go . . ."

"I didn't say that."

"Okay, in that case, I will be careful. I won't take any unnecessary chances or do anything stupid. I swear I won't be a hero."

"Too late, Mom." A smile twisted Sadie's lips. "You kind of already are."

Suddenly, everything disappeared except for their tiny bit of frozen sand. "Sadie . . ."

Her daughter rolled her eyes. "Let's not get all emotional."

"I'm not getting emotional." Cassie dabbed her eyes with her mittens. "Come here." She pulled her daughter under her arm, and they stood together watching the black sea under the star-pricked sky.

A minute or so later, Sadie peeked up at her from underneath her woolen hat, the tip of her nose red from the cold, just like it had always been when she was little. "So, I was thinking. Now that I have powers, maybe I could—"

"Nope."

"You didn't even let me finish."

"No."

"But I want a werewolf boyfriend too."

Cassie's irises swirled with green fire.

"I was kidding!" Sadie laughed. "You're such a mom, Mom."

"Thank you, daughter, but I prefer witch of her generation or hero-mom."

"Yeah," Sadie said quietly. "Me too."

KEEP READING FOR A PREVIEW OF
AURALEE WALLACE'S
COZY AUTUMNAL MYSTERY

IN THE COMPANY OF WITCHES

AVAILABLE NOW!

"I'm going to kill her."

The corner of my mouth twitched, but I kept my gaze on my book. I was very cozy curled up in the green velvet sofa by the fire. I did not want to encourage the tear my aunt was working herself up to.

"I never should have agreed to this," she went on, completely ignoring the fact that I was ignoring her. She was also ignoring the annoyed cat on the chaise lounge behind her, thumping his tail. He was trying to sleep. "You know I can't tolerate the vast majority of people for longer than a day or two—"

I would have said a couple of hours tops, but who was I to quibble?

"—but to let that woman stay for five days? Madness."

I reached for my mug of Honeybush orange tea. It was very soothing. I probably should have made a pot to share. And I don't know if I would call it madness. The woman in question was paying for her stay while her historic home was undergoing some much-needed renovations, and when you run a B&B, you have to expect that on occasion you are going to have demanding guests. Although some guests really were more demanding than others.

Case in point, Constance Graves.

Constance had been staying with us at Ivywood Hollow the past week, and it hadn't taken long for us to discover it was not going to be an easy stay. Evenfall, Connecticut, was a small town, so we knew Constance could be demanding, but we really hadn't been concerned. After all, we had always been able to win over hard-to-please guests in the past—we were *very* good at what we did—but Constance turned out to be a special case.

To begin, she insisted there be no other guests staying at the B&B while she was there. It was a completely reasonable request given she was willing to pay for all the rooms, and it seemed like it would make our lives a whole lot easier. Less people, less work, right? Not so. Not. So.

Personally, I knew we were in for trouble when I showed her where she'd be staying. The Rosewater Room. It's gorgeous. Four-poster bed. Floor-to-ceiling windows. A silk upholstered divan that was perfect for reclining when life became too much. What Constance saw, however, was the white Egyptian cotton sheets peeking out from under the damask comforter on her bed. They were too white. She was afraid of the glare they might give off in the morning sun. When I changed them to a lovely taupe, she found the shade a bit too muddy. I was able to get away with a blush-colored set, but I'm pretty sure that was only because she couldn't think of an objection to throw at them quickly enough.

And it didn't end there.

The meals were always too hot. Or too cold. Too spicy. Or too bland. And all these complaints usually came before she had even lifted her fork, if she lifted it at all. Oh! And her room temperature. We could never get that right. Seventy-four degrees at Ivywood Hollow Bed-and-Breakfast did not feel like the seventy-four degrees she was used to in her house. My absolute favorite, though, was when she told me she found the antique blue inlay of the fireplace to be a little garish. I asked her if she'd like to change rooms, given she was paying for them all, but she told me with a drawn-out sigh that she'd suffer through.

I couldn't help but feel for her though. She was obviously unhappy, and someone that unhappy deserved a little leeway.

"I could push her off the balconette."

Or not.

I smiled at my aunt Nora. She couldn't help herself. She was fiery by nature. Constance had just asked for the flower arrangement in her room to be replaced because the fresh-cut hydrangeas were a little *much*, and it was a miracle Nora hadn't finished her off then and there. Most people had the good sense not to trifle with my aunt and her plants.

Nora, along with her sister Izzy and I, ran the B&B together, but she was the one who took care of the gardens and general *ambiance* of the bed-and-breakfast. It was amazing how she could take the simplest of places and transform it into something warm and welcoming, especially given the fact that *warm* and *welcoming* were probably two words that had never been used to describe her. When she walked down the street, usually dressed in black with her red hair flowing, you'd find at least two or three kids following behind. It was a game of bravery for them. Nora was a lot like a tiger in a rickety cage, beautiful to look at and dangerous. Those kids knew at any moment she might turn and lunge at them, giving them the thrill of a lifetime. Not that she ever really lunged. The turn was enough to send them off in peals of terrified laughter.

"I don't think pushing anyone off of anything will be necessary, Nora," a voice came from the top of the stairs. "I believe I finally have Constance settled for the night. She just needed a little help with the bath water."

My aunt Izzy came down the stairs, tucking some wayward strawberry blonde curls back up into the loose bun on her head. Izzy did the cooking and baking at Ivywood Hollow, and she was fabulous at it. She knew it too. Izzy could get anyone to do just about anything with her culinary creations. Thankfully, she was also just about the sweetest woman to have ever lived, given it wasn't uncommon for guests to promise their firstborns for another bite of dessert. Izzy sat herself down beside me on the sofa and patted my leg companionably.

"Oh, you think you have her settled, do you? I'll believe that when I hear it," Nora drawled. "And by the way, I will never forgive you for giving that woman a bell."

My smile widened. That's right. Izzy had given Constance a bell. Our esteemed guest had found all the stairs of the house difficult to manage, and she felt she required a way to get ahold of us should she need anything. I didn't really think the stairs were that much of an issue for her, but Constance needed a lot of things, so if she had to go up and down the stairs every time she needed one of those things, well, that would be a lot. For an Olympic athlete it would be a lot.

"Did you hear it ringing last night at three a.m.?" Nora asked me. "No, of course you didn't. Tucked away in your little nest."

I lived in the loft above the old carriage house, now garage, of the B&B, unlike my aunts whose rooms were in the house. The small loft certainly wasn't as beautiful or as impressive as any of the spaces inside Ivywood Hollow, but it was cozy, and I had come to believe a little bit of privacy was good for the soul.

"She needed me to fluff her pillow. At three in the morning.

Oh! I just realized I could have smothered her with it, and this would all be over."

"Evanora," Izzy chided with a laugh. As the older sister, she was the only one permitted to use Nora's full name. It wasn't a harsh reprimand though. We both knew Nora was just being Nora. "What a terrible thing to say. And, really, she's a lovely woman. She just knows what she likes."

"Don't be ridiculous," Nora replied. "She's a horrible woman, and you know it. Brynn and I were just discussing how much we'd both like to strangle her."

"What?" I asked in the high-pitched voice of the falsely accused. I straightened up on the sofa, which wasn't easy because it was ridiculously plush. "We'd *both* like to strangle her?" I was pretty sure Nora had had that particular conversation all by herself.

"She finally speaks." Nora collapsed dramatically back against the chaise longue and draped her arm over her forehead. The cat resting above her peeked one eye open, probably trying to determine if my aunt was actually settling down or just resting momentarily before she worked herself up again. "And yes, you might not have said the words, but I could tell you were thinking them."

"I didn't realize mind reading was one of your many talents." I took another sip of my tea.

"What else can I do? You've become so quiet. You're practically a—"

Nora caught herself before she said the word out loud, but it was too late.

Ghost.

A softness came to her face as she met my eye. "Brynn, I'm sorry. That was insensitive."

"It's okay. I know." I gave her a weak smile. How could I be upset? Maybe she shouldn't have said it, but she wasn't exactly wrong. I had changed a lot. My life had fallen apart over a year ago now, and I wasn't the person I used to be.

"Let's just enjoy what's left of the evening, shall we?" Izzy said, giving my knee a squeeze. "It's the perfect fall night to be snug inside by the fire."

I smiled, grateful to let the subject drop. My aunts had been expressing more and more concern about my well-being lately, and I didn't feel up to yet another discussion about how I was doing. Besides, this was very cozy, the three of us listening to the wind whistle outside while the firelight danced over the dark honeyed walls of the parlor. It was a nice moment.

"When was the last time you tried a little mascara?"

And the moment was over.

I slid my gaze over to Nora.

"What? You have such beautiful eyes. Do you think everybody has that shade of green? And what about your hair?" She swirled a finger in the direction of the black braid that hung over my shoulder. "Is this style permanent now?"

"Evanora, leave the girl alone," Izzy said. "Now's not the time. We've all had a long day."

I shot her a thankful smile.

"Nonsense!"

My smile dropped.

"Since the subject has been raised, we should discuss it. You know as well as I do, Sister, that this situation isn't healthy. And we're all pretending it isn't happening. She doesn't want to *help*. She doesn't want to do that other job she used to go on about. All she wants to do is hide herself away here in the house doing chores. And, again, just look at her."

I frowned.

Excerpt from IN THE COMPANY OF WITCHES

"What? You look terrible."

I didn't look that terrible. Nora's expectations for everyday fashion were child-beauty-pageant high.

"Soon enough she'll be up in the attic with Gideon. Is that what you want?"

The cat behind Nora finally gave up on getting rest anywhere near my aunt. He dropped to the floor with a thud and padded over to the foot of the stairs.

"Oh, see now," Izzy scolded. "You've upset Faustus."

Faustus, the B&B's resident Maine coon cat, was a lovely large beast. He was covered in black fur except for a faint frosting of gray across his face, which gave him quite the dignified look. We did lose some business from visitors with allergies, but that was the price of beauty I suppose.

"I'm sure his highness will survive," Nora said before shooting up to a seated position. "You have got to be kidding me!"

A half second later a bell tinkled upstairs.

"That woman is insufferable!"

A loud crack sounded from the fireplace as flames surged up the chimney.

"Calm down. Calm down," Izzy said, getting to her feet. "I forgot I said I'd bring her up some chamomile tea. I'll go get it. You get the door. It's almost nine o'clock. I wonder who it could be?"

Before the words had left Izzy's mouth, the doorbell rang.

Nora swept to her feet as Izzy headed for the kitchen.

"I've finally got it," Nora said, pointing a finger in the air while reaching with the other hand for the door. "I could shove that bell down Constance's throat. Wouldn't that be poetic? Oh, it's you."

"That's a fine way to open the door. Who are you trying to kill now?"

I stifled a laugh as a cold little wind rushed through the door along with Williams, our neighbor from across the street.

Now, I really liked Williams. I found her to be super stylish, not unlike Nora, supremely intelligent, and incredibly interesting. She had moved in ten years ago when she started teaching music history at the university—although Nora still referred to her as the *new* neighbor—and since that time she had become a valued member of Evenfall's town council. I knew Izzy felt the same way about our neighbor as I did, but the rapport between Nora and Williams was a touch more contentious. Like most neighbor relationships, we did have the occasional issue to work out, and Nora, unfortunately, was willing to fight to the death over each and every one of them. Once, a branch from one of the B&B's many trees was blocking light to Williams's azaleas, and she requested we prune it back. Nora was horrified. They had argued about it in the street for nearly three straight hours before Izzy was able to negotiate a peace treaty. In all honesty, though, I think both women liked sparring.

That being said, Williams's latest complaint was proving a touch more difficult to resolve.

"I'm sorry," Nora said, moving to shut the door, "but we're very busy discussing how to murder one of our guests right now, so if you've come to complain about Dog, we'll have to discuss your murder at a later date."

"Nora!" Izzy said, sweeping in from the dining room with a silver tea platter. "I can't leave you alone for a second. Is that any way to greet a guest? Come in, Williams, please. The nights are getting chilly, aren't they?"

Williams raised a finely sculpted eyebrow at Nora before stepping past her.

Excerpt from IN THE COMPANY OF WITCHES

"What brings you by?" Izzy asked. "Not that it isn't always a pleasure to see you."

"Don't lie, Izzy," Nora said before Williams could answer. "It's bad for the complexion."

Izzy ignored her. "I was just bringing up some tea for Constance Graves, but I could always pour you a cup if you'd like."

Williams cringed a little at Constance's name. Evenfall really was a small town. "That explains somebody's bad mood."

"What mood?" Nora asked, shooting up to her full height again. "I can hardly be blamed for—what in the world is going on up there?"

Just then the bell from upstairs started ringing again and then a door slammed.

Faustus let out a low meow. I eyed the cat as he adjusted his feet on the bottom step of the staircase. He didn't often deign to speak to us, so I could only imagine Constance's behavior was getting to him too.

Nora rolled her eyes back to Williams. "If you'll excuse me, I have to go take care of something. Or rather someone."

Izzy's eyes widened. "Oh, don't you think I should be the one to check on Constance?"

"Oh no, no," Nora said, waving both hands in the air. "I'll take good care of our guest. Williams, please feel free to share your stories of doggy woe with my sister. After all, she has the more sympathetic ear."

I couldn't help but think Nora *taking care* of Constance was probably not the best plan. I snapped my book shut and pushed myself up, but the moment I got to my feet, Nora pointed at me and said, "Sit."

I plopped back down.

Izzy took a step to head off her sister's path. "Are you at least going to take the—"

Nora swept by her and up the stairs, Faustus leading the way.

"—tea?" Izzy finished, her shoulders slumping. True to form, though, my aunt recovered quickly. "So sorry about that," she said, hurrying over to Williams. "How are things at the university? I used to love the beginning of the fall semester. The smell of new books. The start of sweater season. The crisp fall air so ripe with possibility!"

Izzy tended to ramble when she got nervous.

"Well said," Williams agreed. "And it will be at least a few more weeks before all the students are beaten down and sleep-deprived. Now, could we discuss the reason for my visit?"

"I know. It's Dog. He's still—goodness!"

We all looked up. Something had hit the floor with enough force to rattle the chandelier.

I was much more successful getting myself up off the sofa on my second attempt. "Why don't you go see what's going on up there?" I suggested to Izzy. "I'd be more than happy to entertain Williams."

"Oh, well, if you don't mind," Izzy said, looking to our neighbor. Ever the hostess, my aunt could hardly imagine being so rude as to leave a guest mid-conversation.

"Not at all," Williams said, looking just the teensiest bit annoyed at having to begin her complaint a third time.

I waited until my aunt had made it all the way to the top of the stairs before I turned back to Williams. "Let me guess. Dog's been after Oscar again?"

"I don't know what to do, Brynn. That crow of your uncle's just won't leave him alone," she said, worry creasing her otherwise unlined forehead. Williams could be aloof at times, definitely professorial, but she really loved her dog.

I nodded sympathetically. Dog, the crow, just to be clear, did have a habit of plucking at our neighbor's English bulldog's tail. But in fairness, Oscar did also have a habit of losing his mind barking every time he saw Dog, and if Dog dared land anywhere near his yard, he'd go tearing after him. Well, tearing after him as fast as an older, heavier English bulldog can. "I get it, but I'm not sure you could say Uncle Gideon owns Dog. He just feeds him occasionally."

"And that's another thing. I'm finding peanut shells everywhere. In the garden. On the walk. Over the—"

"Brynn!"

I shot a quick look over to the stairs. Nora's voice sounded panicked. I looked back to Williams and took a step toward the door. "We may have to finish this later."

"Certainly, but could you at least talk to him?"

Another crash came from upstairs. This time it sounded like the tea service.

"Absolutely," I said, opening the door so that she could step out. "I'll have a word with Gideon tonight."

"Brynn! We need you!"

"Bye!" I clicked the door shut probably a little too close to my neighbor's face and hurried up the stairs. "Coming!" I raced for Constance's room. The door was open, as was the one to the adjoining bathroom. I jumped over the teapot and tray toppled on the floor, then rushed past Faustus standing guard at the threshold of the en suite. "Sorry. I just had to see Williams out."

I stopped dead in my tracks.

Constance Graves lay motionless on the floor, her eyes open and lifeless, blood seeping from her head.

"Oh my, is she . . . ?"

"She's dead," Izzy said, twisting her fingers together. "Dead. Dead. Dead. Oh dear. She's very dead."

I looked to Nora.

"What are you looking at me for?!"

"I don't know! No reason!"

"If you're looking for confirmation, she's really dead. We checked."

The three of us stared down at poor Constance.

It seemed like ages before any of us even breathed.

It was Nora who finally broke the silence.

"You know, in hindsight, Brynn, I think *our* previous conversation may have been in poor taste."

© Auralee Wallace

After spending her formative years reading *Grimms' Fairy Tales* and stirring up potions in the creek behind her house, **Auralee Wallace** knew she would grow up to be a witch. When that didn't work out, she decided becoming a writer was the next best thing. Now Auralee is the author of multiple novels, including the Otter Lake mystery series and the Evenfall Witches B&B mysteries. She lives in Ottawa with her husband, three kids, two cats, and one dog.

VISIT AURALEE WALLACE ONLINE

AuraleeWallace.com
 AuraleeWallace.Author

Ready to find
your next great read?

Let us help.

Visit prh.com/nextread

Penguin
Random
House